MAN, MYTH, AND MAGIC

MAN, MYTH, AND MAGIC

Apocalyptic Visions: End of Life, the Afterlife, and the End of the World

Cavendish Square
New York

MAN, MYTH, AND MAGIC

Published in 2015 by Cavendish Square Publishing, LLC
243 5th Avenue, Suite 136, New York, NY 10016

First Edition

CPSIA Compliance Information: Batch #WS14CSQ

Library of Congress Cataloging-in-Publication Data
Gauld, Alan.
Apocalyptic visions: end of life, the afterlife, and the end of the world / ALAN GAULD, Et. Al.
pages cm. — (Man, myth, and magic)
ISBN 978-1-62712-681-6 (hardcover) ISBN 978-1-62712-683-0 (ebook)
1. Eschatology—Dictionaries. 2. Parapsychology—Dictionaries. 3. Occultism—Dictionaries. I. Title.

BF1999.G325 2014
202'.303—dc23

2014001524

Editorial Director: Dean Miller
Editor: Amy Hayes
Art Director: Jeffrey Talbot
Designer: Jessica Moon
Photo Researcher: J8 Media
Production Manager: Jennifer Ryder-Talbot
Production Editor: David McNamara

Photo credits: Cover: Universal Images Group/Superstock, File:BD Weighing of the Heart.jpg/The British Museum/*, Workshop of Lucas Cranach/File:Whore-babylon-luther-bible-1534-saturated.jpg/*; File:Dance-of-death-german-18th.jpg/*, 1; Chinook Burial Grounds, c.1870 (oil on canvas), Stanley, John Mix (1814-72)/Detroit Institute of Arts, USA/The Bridgeman Art Library, 2–3; Wrathful Deities of the Bar-do (opaque w/c & gold on cotton), Tibetan School, (18th century)/Museum of Fine Arts, Boston, Massachusetts, USA/Gift of George and Verena Rybicki, in memory of/William Stanley and Janet Morgan/The Bridgeman Art Library, 5t; Gawain and the Green Knight/British Library, London, UK/© British Library Board. All Rights Reserved/The Bridgeman Art Library, 5c; Cyrus McCrimmon/Denver Post/Getty Images, 5b; Marie-Lan Nguyen/File:Consultation with a witch MAN Napoli Inv9987.jpg/*, 7; 1450 Fra Angelico Last Judgement anagoria/Fra Angelico, photographer anagoria/*, 8; Godong/Universal Images Group/Getty Images, 9; lgGE7j6ULOiYfg/File:Jaume Huguet - Saint Michael Vanquishes the Antichrist - Google Art Project.jpg/*, 10; Mary Evans Picture Library 11; Wallace Kirkland/The Life Pictures/Getty Images, 12; Robert Swain Gifford/File:WLA brooklynmuseum Robert Swain Gifford.jpg/*, 14; Wrathful Deities of the Bar-do (opaque w/c & gold on cotton), Tibetan School, (18th century)/Museum of Fine Arts, Boston, Massachusetts, USA/Gift of George and Verena Rybicki, in memory of/William Stanley and Janet Morgan/The Bridgeman Art Library, 16; Sotirios Christidis/File:Funeral procession of George I of Greece.jpg/*, 17; Abraham Lambertz van den Tempel/File:Portrait of a woman Abraham Lambertsz van den Tempel.jpg/*, 19; Albert Edwin Roberts/File:Hearse-r.jpg/*, 20; Universal Images Group/Superstock, 21; Chinook Burial Grounds, c.1870 (oil on canvas), Stanley, John Mix (1814-72)/Detroit Institute of Arts, USA/The Bridgeman Art Library, 22; The Funeral Pile of Patroclus (engraving), English School, (19th century)/Private Collection/© Look and Learn/The Bridgeman Art Library, 25; Dennis Jarvis/File:Manikarnika Cremation Ghat, Varanasi.jpg/*, 26; A1C Rebecca Niemener/File:KC-135R Another Nightmare.jpeg/*, 30; Yan Li/File:Peking Man Skull (replica) presented at Paleozoological Museum of China.JPG/*, 31; LIU JIN/AFP/Getty Images, 32; Arturo Nikolai/File:Dolmen de Axeitos.jpg/*, 33; Rolfmueller/File:Xiaotang shrine gate 2009 03 09.jpg/*, 34; Veronique DURRUTY/Gamma-Rapho/Getty Images, 35; AFP/Getty Images, 36; File:The Coming of the Ashanti Golden Stool - NARA – 558798.jpg/*, 37; File:Dance-of-death-german-18th.jpg/*, 40; Samuel Daniell/File:Sameul Daniell - Kora-Khokhoi preparing to move – 1805.jpg/*, 41; The British Library/Robana/Hulton Fine Art Collection/Getty Images, 43; Independent Picture Service/Universal Images Group/Getty Images, 44; John S Lander/LightRocket/Getty Images, 46; File:Bodacolectivasectamoon.jpg/*, 49; Giuseppe Mazzuoli/File:Giuseppe-Mazzuoli-The-Death-of-Adonis-hermitag.jpg/*, 51; Andrew Bossi/File:Hermitage Egyptian statuettes.jpg/*, 52; Marie-Lan Nguyen/File:Attis Altieri Chiaramonti Inv1656.jpg/*, 53; shakko/File:Dionysos fresco pushkin.jpg/*, 54; Joan de Joanes/File:Última Cena - Juan de Juanes.jpg/*, 55; Lambert Sustris/File:Lille Pdba sustris noli me tangere.JPG/*, 56; Claire Greenway/Getty Images, 57; Hulton Archive/Getty Images, 59; © johnrochaphoto/England/Alamy, 60; Shiva (red earthenware), Indian School/The Israel Museum, Jerusalem, Israel/Bequest of Wolf Ladejinsky, Washington, DC./The Bridgeman Art Library, 62; Valhalla and the Midgard Serpent, 1680, Icelandic School, (17th century)/Arni Magnusson Institute, Reykjavik, Iceland/The Bridgeman Art Library, 63; Albert Durer/ File:Four Horsemen of the Apocalypse by Dürer.png/*, 64; Nancy Wong/File:Jones3.jpg/*, 65; Bruno Comby/ File:James Lovelock in 2005.jpg/*, 66; Matthias Gerung /File:Ottheinrich Folio295r Rev12.jpg/*, 68; Workshop of Lucas Cranach/File:Whore-babylon-luther-bible-1534-saturated.jpg/*, 69; Gawain and the Green Knight/British Library, London, UK/© British Library Board. All Rights Reserved/The Bridgeman Art Library 71; Pvasiliadis/File:KLONTZAS GEORGIOS End of 16th cent The Second Coming detail The Hell.png/*, 72; William Blake/File:Illustrations to Dante's Divine Comedy object 4 Butlin 812-4 The Inscription over Hell-Gate.jpg/*, 74; Times are hard your Majesty - you leave us nothing to do (colour litho), American School, (20th century)/Private Collection/© Galerie Bilderwelt/The Bridgeman Art Library, 75; ogGa9nhkV_-oNQ/File:Unknow - Descent into Hell with Deesis and Selected Saints. Pskov - Google Art Project.jpg/*, 76; Anishshah19/File:Seven Jain Hells/*, 77; Hedwig Storch/File:Kom Ombo 0333.JPG/*, 79; Mosaic depicting School of Athens, from Pompei, Italy/De Agostini Picture Library/A. Dagli Orti/The Bridgeman Art Library, 80; File:BD Weighing of the Heart.jpg/The British Museum/*, 82; Facsimile made by E. A. Wallis Budge/File:BD Funeral.jpg/*, 84–85; File:MHS Sad Ostateczny XVII w Lipie p.jpg/Przykuta/*, 85; Michelangelo Buonarroti/File:Last Judgment (Michelangelo).jpg/*, 87; Painting depicting the profet Mohammed sitting between other profets in the ancient temple of Kubbet Al Sahara, from Bahram Mirza mirajname/De Agostini Picture Library/G. Dagli Orti/The Bridgeman Art Library, 88; Hieronymus Bosch/File:Hieronymus Bosch 013.jpg/*, 89; Stéphane Magnenat/File:Sassetta - The blessed Ranieri frees the poors from a jail Florence - Louvre - frameless/*, 90–91; COLUMBIA PICTURES/Ronald Grant Archive/Mary Evans, 93; Science & Society Picture Library/Getty Images, 95; Edward Kelly (b.1555) a magician, and his partner the mathematician and astrologer, John Dee (1527-1608) raising a ghost (hand-coloured engraving), English School, (19th century)/Private Collection/The Bridgeman Art Library, 96; Scenes of divination, including haruspication, pyromancy and necromancy (engraving) (b/w photo), Burgkmair, Hans (c.1473-1531)/Bibliotheque Nationale, Paris, France/Archives Charmet/The Bridgeman Art Library, 97; ClassicStock.com/Superstock, 98; Cyrus McCrimmon/Denver Post/Getty Images, 99; Orlando/Hulton Archive/Getty Images, 100; QgF5Hmcsm3xzww/File:Lucas Cranach the Elder - Adam und Eva im Paradies (Sündenfall) - Google Art Project.jpg/*, 102; St. Brendan and a siren, from the German translation of 'Navigatio Sancti Brendani Abbatis', c.1476 (vellum), German School, (15th century)/Universitatsbibliothek, Heidelberg, Germany/The Bridgeman Art Library, 103; Zhongguo gu dai shu hua jian ding zu/File:Anonymous-Baoen Sutra Paradise.png/*, 105; OR 2265 Ascent of the Prophet Muhammad to Heaven, Mirak, Aqa (fl.c.1520-76)/British Library, London, UK/© British Library Board. All Rights Reserved/The Bridgeman Art Library, 106; Nina Leen/The LIFE Picture Collection/Getty Images, 108; Time Life Pictures/The LIFE Picture Collection/Getty Images, 112; Of predestynacion, illustration from Alexander Barclay's English translation of 'The Ship of Fools', from an edition published in 1874 (engraving), German School, (15th century) (after)/Private Collection/The Bridgeman Art Library, 115; Mbzt/File:P1070867 Louvre Mosaïque Pelagius Ma2995 rwk.JPG/*, 116; Saint Augustine of Hippo (354-430) 1590, Greco, El (Domenico Theotocopuli) (1541-1614)/Museo de Santa Cruz, Toledo, Spain/The Bridgeman Art Library, 117; GFreihalter/File:Hockenheim Evangelische Kirche Glasfenster125.JPG/*, 119; Domenico di Michelino/File:Dante Domenico di Michelino Duomo Florence.jpg/*, 120; Janezdrilc/Slika:Gospa Sveta, oltar svetega Križa1.jpg/*, 121; Statue of Strabo in Amasia/Erturac/*, 124; 3a06258u/Lithograph after a daguerreotype by Appleby. Published by N. Currier, New York./Library of Congress/*, 126; Science & Society Picture Library/Getty Images, 127; Spirit unmasked at a London seance. Top: Forming circle by joining hands. Centre: Medium's assistant being placed behind curtain (left). Spirit manifestations (right). Bottom: A very substantial 'spirit' apprehended while trying to slip away. There were/Universal History Archive/UIG/The Bridgeman Art Library, 128; A table levitating during a seance with Eusapia Palladino (1854-1918) 12th November 1898 (b/w photo), French Photographer, (19th century)/Bibliotheque Nationale, Paris, France/Archives Charmet/The Bridgeman Art Library, 131; Buste AK/FFFFFF6/Own work/*, 132; AF archive/Alamy, 134–135; Following the Red Asphalt Road/Jason Lybeck/Own work/*, 136. * Wikimedia Commons.

Cavendish Square would like to acknowledge the outstanding work, research, writing, and professionalism of Man, Myth, and Magic's original Editor-in-Chief Richard Cavendish, Executive Editor Brian Innes, Editorial Advisory Board Members and Consultants C.A. Burland, Glyn Daniel, E.R Dodds, Mircea Eliade, William Sargent, John Symonds, RJ. Zwi Werblowsky, and R.C. Zaechner, as well as the numerous authors, consultants, and contributors that shaped the original Man, Myth, and Magic that served as the basis and model for these new books.

Printed in the United States of America

Contents

Introduction	6
Angels	9
Antichrist	10
Automatic art	11
Book of the Dead (Tibetan)u	15
Burial	17
Burning	24
Cremation	24
Cross Correspondences	27
Cult of the Dead	29
Dance of Death	39
Death	41
Divine Principles	47
Drummer of Tedworth	50
Dying God	50
Dystopian Literature	57
Ectoplasm	59
End of the World	60
End of the World Cults	65
Environmental Apocalypse	66
Eschatology	67
Eyeless in the Next World	67
Glass Mountain	68
The Great Beast	68
Harrowing of Hell	70
Headless Spirits	70
Heaven	72
Hell	72
Immortality	78
Judgment of the Dead	83
Near-Death Experience	90
Necromancy	94
Nuclear Holocaust	99
Ouija Boards	99
Paradise	102
Poltergeists	108
Predestination	116
Purgatory	120
Raudive Voices	123
Refrigerium	123
Revenant	124
Sin Eater	124
Specter	125
Spiritualism	125
Table Turning	134
Wraith	134
Zombie Apocalypse	134
Glossary	138
Index	139
Author List	144

A Reader's Guide to *Man, Myth, and Magic: Apocalyptic Visions: End of Life, the Afterlife, and the End of the World*

Where we go when we die and the ultimate fate of the planet are questions that have preoccupied people since the dawn of civilization. In search for purpose and higher meaning in their lives, people look to what comes after their death, and most faiths throughout the world have complex mythologies built around the afterlife, ascribing rich rewards for the virtuous and painful eternal punishments for the wicked.

Man, Myth, and Magic: Apocalyptic Visions: End of Life, the Afterlife, and the End of the World is a volume devoted to the mythology, rites, and symbols that describe how various cultures approach death, as well as to various interpretations of heaven, hell, and the last days of planet Earth.

> *. . . primitive man conceived of the cosmic process not as something stable, but as a great and continuous battle between the forces of creation and destruction, order and chaos.*

Objectives of *Man, Myth, and Magic*

For the *Man, Myth and Magic* series, educating readers takes precedence over advocating any singular viewpoint. In *Apocalyptic Visions: End of Life, the Afterlife, and the End of the World,* discussions of how various Eastern and Western religions preach their views of the afterlife will help readers understand the topic and develop their own position on the practice. The comprehensive coverage of the Cult of the Dead, as well as its major deities and sacred texts, for example, can aid students researching the faiths of the world and how they approach crucial aspects of everyday life. A wide variety of theories and hypotheses of how the world will end, from man-made disasters through plagues of zombies, are presented, too.

The Text

Each article is written by an expert subject-matter contributor, and the depth of coverage varies from short entries defining a singular subject through multipage contributions providing far-ranging discussion of complex issues. From Angels to the Zombie Apocalypse, key rites, myths, beliefs, and concepts are presented, with articles focusing on how different civilizations throughout history have viewed these matters of life and death, as well as beyond.

The work is highly illustrated, with striking imagery of angels, devils, and burial rites and ceremonies. Subjects of major interest are provided with individual bibliographies of further reading on the subject at the end of each article, making *Man, Myth, and Magic* an important resource for any avid researcher.

For the past few decades, there's been an explosion in the popularity of mythology and history in the realms of both popular culture and scholarly study. In recent years, there has been an explosion of books, films, and websites devoted to the afterlife and the end of the world. The revival of scholarly interest has created the modern study of comparative religion, and shaped modern anthropology with its investigation of indigenous or first peoples and their beliefs and rituals (which have been found far more complex that originally believed). At the same time there has been a flourishing revival of popular interest in ancient civilizations, mythology, magic, and alternative paths to truth. This interest has shown no sign of diminishing this century; on the contrary, it has grown stronger and has explored new pathways. Scholarly investigation of these subjects has continued and has thrown much new light on some of our topics. The present edition of *Man, Myth, and Magic: Apocalyptic Visions: End of Life, the Afterlife, and the End of the World* takes account of both these developments. Articles have been updated to cover fresh discoveries and new theories since they first appeared.

With all this, *Man, Myth, and Magic: Apocalyptic Visions: End of Life, the Afterlife, and the End of the World* is not intended to convert you, to or from any belief or set of beliefs and attitudes. The purpose of the articles is not to persuade or justify, but to describe what people have believed and trace the consequences of those beliefs in action. The editorial

Roman mosaic *A Consultation with the Witch*, showing a seance from around the second century AD

attitude is one of sympathetic neutrality. It is for the reader to decide where truth and value may lie. We hope that there is as much interest, pleasure and satisfaction in reading these pages as all those involved took in creating them.

Illustrations

Since much of what we know about myth, folklore, and religion has been passed down over the centuries by word of mouth, and recorded only comparatively recently, visual images are often the most powerful and vivid links we have with the past. The wealth of illustration in *Man, Myth, and Magic: Apocalyptic Visions: End of Life, the Afterlife, and the End of the World* is invaluable, not only because of the diversity of sources, but also because of the superb quality of color reproduction.

Index

The A-Z index provides immediate access to any specific item sought by the reader. The reference distinguishes the nature of the entry in terms of a main entry, supplementary subject entries, and illustrations.

Skill Development for Students

The books of the *Man, Myth, and Magic* series can be consulted as the basic text for a subject or as a source of enrichment for students. It can act as a reference for a simple reading or writing assignment, or as the inspiration for a major research or term paper. The additional reading at the end of many entries is an invaluable resource for students looking to further their studies on a specific topic. *Man, Myth, and Magic* offers an opportunity for students that is extremely valuable; twenty volumes that are both multi-disciplinary and inter-disciplinary; a wealth of fine illustrations; a research source well-suited to a variety of age levels that will provoke interest and encourage speculation in both teachers and students.

Scope

As well as being a major asset to social studies teaching, the book provides students from a wide range of disciplines with a stimulating, accessible and beautifully illustrated reference work.

Fra Angelico's *The Last Judgement*, a triptych envisioning the Christian apocalypse c. 1450

The *Man, Myth, and Magic* series lends itself very easily to a multi-disciplinary approach to study. In *End of Life, the Afterlife, and the End of the World,* literature students will be interested in myths and legends, as well as classics including Dante's *Divine Comedy* and Joyce's *A Portrait of the Artist as a Young Man.* Science students will be fascinated to read about the possibility of an environmental apocalypse or nuclear holocaust, while students of art, sculpture, carving, pottery, photography, and other crafts will find the marvelous illustrations and special articles on the subjects particularly helpful. Readers interested in history will gravitate to the discussion of the Spiritualism movement. As well as its relevance to study areas already mentioned, the book will provide strong background reference in history, anthropology, philosophy, and comparative religion.

Conceptual Themes

As students become involved in the work, they will gradually become sensitive to the major concepts emerging from research. Students can begin to understand the role of the different belief systems and how religious traditions and societies were built around the concept of death. In many ways, the way a culture views death dictates the norms and expectations of society. Burial was the first step humans took towards civilization. *Man, Myth, and Magic: Apocalyptic Visions: End of Life, the Afterlife, and the End of the World* examines the way in which civilizations have developed beyond that step, looking at how humanity confronts the universal truth that all life, even the planet itself, will end.

Man, Myth, and Magic offers a unique opportunity for students to tackle this often-horrifying concept. It is a volume that is both multi-disciplinary and inter-disciplinary; a wealth of fine illustrations; a research source well suited to a variety of age levels that will provoke interest and encourage speculation in both teachers and students.

Angels

Angels, whose name comes from the Latin *angelus* meaning 'envoy,' are supernatural creatures able to discern good and evil, and who act as messengers from an unseen deity. In Judaeo-Christianity they are believed, as recorded in both Old and New Testaments, to make announcements of impending good fortune, prosperity—and doom. They are also able to guard ordinary mortals on Earth from evil, and to execute God's wrath on sinners. Similarly, in Islam, angels are divine messengers without free will, able only to perform the acts they have as ordered by God, while Zoroastrians believe in a variety of angel figures, including guardian angels or *Fravashis* imbued with God's energy.

The role of God-created angels in human life is believed to encompass every moment between of life until, at our last, the angel of death appears. Having guided and protected a human through their life, the guardian angel or Angel of Peace is charged, in the words of the Jesuit theologian Jean Daniélou (1905–May 1974) with 'receiving the soul as it leaves the body and leading it to Paradise.'

Angels take charge of time, the fourth dimension of our universe, and are typified by the Zoroastrian angels, the *Yazatas*, who represent the years, months, days, hours, and minutes of our existence. They are believed to live in a 'created eternity' of sacred time. And just as angels presided over Christ's Resurrection, symbolizing the unification of heaven and Earth, and guard him on his eternal throne, it is believed by Christians that they will be present at the apocalypse, the second coming, and at the end of all time.

When this happens, so Christians believe, an angel sent from God will reveal their fate to them. A vision of such an ending is vividly described in the Book of Revelation (chapter 15): 'Then I saw in heaven another great and astonishing sign: seven angels with seven plagues, the last plagues of all, for, with them the wrath of God was completed.' The destructive deeds of each angel, wiping out humans, Earth, and sun are recorded. Every angel pours out a bowl of God's wrath, ending with the seventh angel who 'poured our his bowl on the air; and out of the sanctuary came a loud voice from the throne, which said: 'It is over!'

Seeing Angels

Experiences of angels are legion, but none more evocative in the context of death and eternity than this account recorded in his 1879 work *Wild Life in a Southern County* by the English writer Richard Jefferies (1848–87):

> *'Now and then the Western clouds after the sunset assume a shape resembling that of a vast extended wing, as of a gigantic bird in full flight—the extreme tip nearly reaching the zenith, the body of the bird just below the horizon. The resemblance is sometimes so perfect that the layers of feathers are traceable by an imaginative eye. This, the old folk say, is the wing of the Archangel Michael, and it bodes no good to the evil ones among the nations, for he is on his way to execute a dread command.'*

Stained glass in St. George Anglican Cathedral, Jerusalem, Israel, showing a winged angel

In the 1914–18 conflict, 'the war to end all wars,' many British soldiers claimed to have seen visions in the sky of St. George, England's patron saint, surrounded by angels, horsemen, and cavalry. Best documented of these sightings were the 'Angels of Mons' believed to have come, with St. George, to the aid of Allied troops in the Battle of Mons on August 22–23, 1914. As recounted subsequently by journalist Arthur Machen (1863–1947), one soldier is said to have experienced 'before him beyond the trench, a long line of shapes, with a shining about them. They were like men who drew the bow, and with another shout their cloud of arrows flew singing and tingling through the air toward the German hosts.' The report may well be fictional, but the fact remains that belief in angels is known to have boosted the morale of troops facing their deaths in their thousands throughout the conflict.

Angels also feature in some accounts of near-death experience. In 2012 the US neurosurgeon Dr. Eben Alexander (1953–), a confessed Christian, described in his book *Proof of Heaven* seeing 'flocks of transparent, shimmering beings arced across the sky, leaving long, streamerlike lines behind them. Bird? Angels?' he queries, 'These words registered later, when I was writing down my recollections.' He answers, continuing 'But neither of these words do justice to the beings themselves, which were quite simply different from anything I have known on this planet. They were more advanced. Higher forms.' Alexander goes on to describe '. . . a sound, a huge and booming glorious chant' made by these beings that was 'palpable and almost material.'

RUTH BINNEY

FURTHER READING: P. L. Wilson. Angels. *(London, UK: Thames and Hudson, 1980); G. Davidson.* A Dictionary of Angels, Including the Fallen Angels. *(New York, NY: Free Press, 1994).*

***Saint Michael Vanquishes the Antichrist* by Jaume Huguet (1412–1492)**

Antichrist

The fear of a messiah of evil, who would come with war, plague, famine, and destruction to enslave the world, haunted men for hundreds of years in Europe, though with a consolation, the belief that Antichrist would eventually be overthrown by God. As Christ's opposite, Antichrist would claim to be God and would work miracles, raising the dead, walking on water, healing the sick, turning stones into bread, but his miracles would be shams. The Jews also expected the coming of the evil power and it was said that he would be bald, with one eye bigger than the other, his left arm longer than his right, and deaf in his right ear; right being traditionally the side of good.

The early Christians adopted the Jewish belief in a coming titanic battle between God and an evil adversary. The first human model for the adversary was the Syrian king, Antiochus IV Epiphanes, who captured Jerusalem in the second century BC and used the temple for the worship of pagan gods.

The New Testament (2 Thessalonians, chapter 2) predicts the coming of 'the man of lawlessness, the son of perdition,' who will claim to be God. Revelation (chapter 13) predicts the appearance of the Great Beast 666, supported by a second beast, who was later identified as Antichrist. The first and second letters of John describe rebels inside the Christian flock itself as 'antichrists,' which set a precedent for the later employment of the word as a term of abuse, used by Christians for other Christians who failed to agree with them.

Opponents of Popes Boniface VIII (c. 1235–1303) and John XXII (1244–1334) labeled each of them as Antichrist and many Protestants later regarded all Popes as Antichrist, an idea that lingers on among a few extreme Protestants. In the past century Hitler (1889–1945) was described as Antichrist.

Automatic art

The term 'automatic' applied to writing, speaking, painting, drawing, and music means the production of work not consciously directed by the person whose hand executed it. It belongs to, and cannot be sharply separated from, a whole range of phenomena commonly regarded by psychologists as manifestations of layers of the personality that are subconscious or dissociated, cut off from the conscious mind. This includes habitual tics, loss of memory, sleep-walking, multiple personality, 'speaking in tongues,' prophecy, and mediumship in trance.

It is quite impossible to generalize about the automatist's state of mind during the production of automatic writing and drawings. Some go into a deep trance and are quite oblivious of their surroundings; some are drowsy but partially aware of what is going on; some are awake but abstracted; and some are fully conscious and may read or talk normally. Some automatists are aware of the movements of the hand and of what it is writing or drawing; some are conscious but quite insensible of what is written or drawn and some are unaware even that their hands are moving.

In their early stages automatic writing and drawing are generally very crude and monotonous; they may begin with incessant repetition of the same figure or letter, and they often proceed no further than the production of a few empty phrases or irregular shapes. However, in a few cases the automatist comes in time to exhibit skill or knowledge beyond his ordinary capacities. Automatic writing has been known to report events forgotten or unnoticed by the waking self, to produce fragments of languages not consciously known to the writer, and to exhibit what look like flashes of telepathy. The writing not infrequently develops a 'character' of its own, professing beliefs and opinions differing from those of the automatist and sometimes it will display a much greater fluency in composition.

Inspiration from the Dead

Automatic writing may not merely possess a character of its own, it is liable to claim an origin from some source other than the automatist—perhaps a supernatural being, a dead person, or even a person still living. This fact, in combination with the heightened faculties often exhibited, has made automatic writing (together with some of the related phenomena mentioned earlier) an important influence in the development of certain religious movements, particularly modern Spiritualism.

The majority of published automatic scripts fall into one or two classes. The first class consists of moral and religious precepts and accounts of the nature of the next world and of life in it, purportedly coming from deceased persons.

A girl, blindfolded, uses the planchette with a pencil fixed in it, hoping to receive by 'automatic writing' a message from the spirits in the beyond.

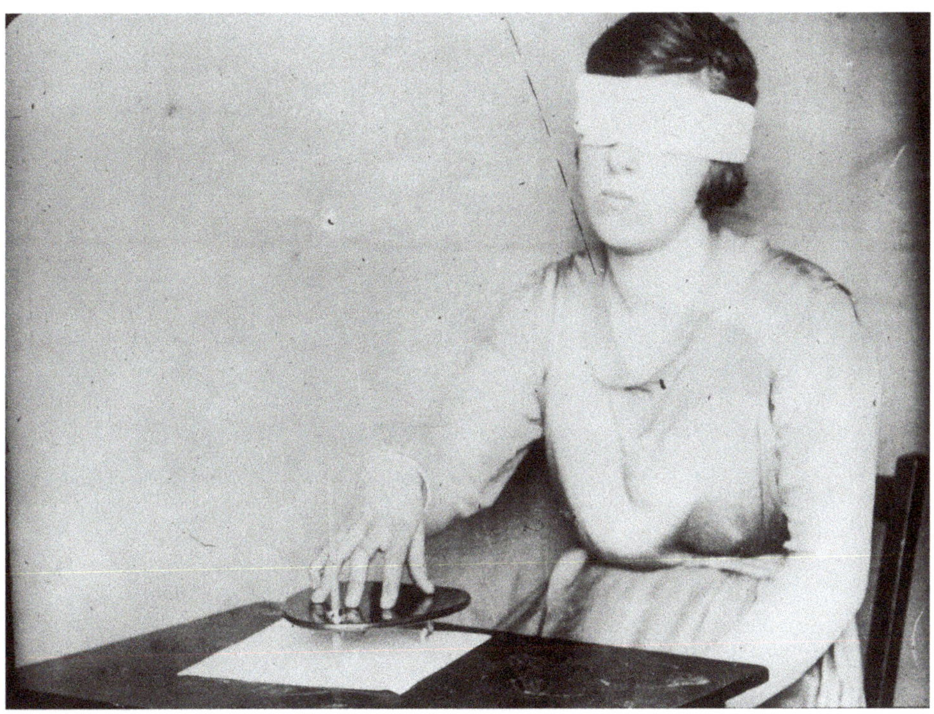

The religious teachings and the accounts of the next world vary in detail from one automatist to another, but on the whole, the general resemblances outweigh the individual differences, and the similarities of tone are often striking. As the US philosopher William James (1842–1910) remarked, automatic scripts and utterances abound 'in a curiously vague optimistic philosophy-and-water, in which phrases about spirit, harmony, beauty, law, development, keep recurring. It seems exactly as if one author composed more than half of the trance messages.'

Some notable productions of this type are *Spirit Teachings* (1873) by W. Stainton Moses, the 'Bible' of British Spiritualism; W. T. Stead's *After Death* (1897); Miss K. Wingfield's *Guidance from Beyond* (1923); and two books by Geraldine Cummins: *The Road to Immortality* (1932) and *Beyond Human Personality* (1935).

A contemporary variant of these philosophico-religious writings is the phenomenon of 'channeling' that has been such a feature of New Age movements. In channeling, some departed sage, now on a higher plane of being, speaks through a medium who acts as the 'channel' for the transmission of his (generally unremarkable) wisdom.

It is characteristic of these sages that, as Robert A. Baker (1921–2005) has put it, their identities are 'buried forever in timeless mud and sand, safely beyond the possibility of any historical resuscitation and denial.' In this they contrast somewhat unfavourably with some of the spirits who communicated through the automatists just mentioned.

The second major category of automatic writings consists of poetry, plays, and (especially) historical romances, commonly related from the standpoint of some deceased person possessing firsthand information or enhanced knowledge of the events and periods concerned. There is no doubt that such writings sometimes display knowledge, dramatic flair or literary gifts in excess of those that the automatist ordinarily possesses. Among the more interesting examples are works by Hélène Smith (in T. Flournoy, *From India to the Planet Mars*, 1900); by Geraldine Cummins (*The Scripts of Cleophas*, 1928; *When Nero was Dictator*, 1939), and by Mrs. J. H. Curran (*The Sorrv Tale*, 1917; *Hope Trueblood*, 1918; *Telka*, 1928).

The Story of Patience Worth

The writings of Mrs. Curran achieved in their day considerable celebrity, and they have been the subject of a number of serious studies (e.g. W. F. Prince, *The Case of Patience Worth*, 1927; I. Litvag, *Singer in the Shadows: the Strange Story of Patience Worth*, 1972). Mrs. Curran, a housewife from St. Louis, Missouri, began experimenting with a ouija board in 1913. She started to receive communications from a deceased English girl, Patience Worth, who had supposedly lived in the seventeenth century. Patience produced, sometimes at extraordinary speed, a series of historical novels, very varied in style and setting, and considerable quantities of poetry. She also showed a remarkable ability to extemporise poems on topics suggested by persons present.

While operating the ouija board, Mrs. Curran remained fully conscious of her surroundings, though not of the impending words. However, after some years she came little by little to speak, first letters and then words as they came into her mind; the communications became more adumbrated, and accompanied by spontaneous pictures that seem to have reached an almost hallucinatory tendency.

Painting in the Dark

Like automatic writings, automatic drawings may be superior to anything that the automatist can accomplish in

People using a Ouija board to channel spirits

a normal state. The development of automatic drawing is often preceded and accompanied by the development of automatic writing. For instance, the complicated symbolic drawings described in two famous early British works, W. M. Wilkinson's *Spirit Drawings* (1858) and Mrs. de Morgan's *From Matter to Spirit* (1863) were preceded and subsequently interpreted by automatic writing. Automatic drawing sometimes develops into automatic painting, but automatic painting has also, and perhaps more often, been known to develop independently. A curious feature of certain instances of automatic painting has been not merely that the paintings were executed with unusual speed, but that they were allegedly produced in the dark, as in the cases of David Duguid of Glasgow in the 1870–80s and of Marjan Gruzewski, a Pole, during the 1920–30s.

A distinction can be made between cases of automatic drawing and painting, and cases of 'psychic art' in which a clairvoyant or sensitive gifted in the use of crayon or brush has sketched some spirit or otherworldly scene allegedly revealed to him by his supernormal faculties. Many of William Blake's (1757–1827) pictures belong in this class. However, it is probable that no sharp line can be drawn between automatic drawing and painting and the 'psychic' drawing or painting of clairvoyants, for many 'psychic artists' would claim not merely to discern the subjects of their sketches by some form of nonsensory perception, but to be inspired or 'overshadowed' by departed spirits (often those of famous artists).

Madge Gill (1882–1961), an uneducated London housewife whose drawings attracted some notice, worked in a state of semitrance, and said that she 'felt impelled to execute drawings on a large scale . . . I am undoubtedly guided by an unseen force.' The contemporary British psychic Matthew Manning has produced a large collection of paintings and drawings in a variety of styles inspired by his concentration on the creative force of dead artists such as Picasso, Arthur Rackham, aul Klee, Albrecht Dürer, Aubrey Beardsley, and Leonardo da Vinci.

. . . made it conceivable that intelligent activities can occur of which a person is unaware; and such activities may exhibit knowledge and dramatic gifts that the person does not ordinarily possess.

In addition to cases of automatic speaking, writing, drawing, and painting, there have also been cases of the automatic playing and composing of music. The best-known recent case has been that of Rosemary Brown, a lady of some (but not extensive) musical education, whose book, *Unfinished Symphonies*, appeared in 1971. Mrs. Brown believed that from the age of seven onward she had been in touch with the deceased composer Franz Liszt, whom she could both see and hear. She believed that at times Liszt guided her hands as she played or wrote music; but more often he dictated compositions to her, as did other composers (Brahms, Debussy, Beethoven, Chopin, and Stravinsky) whom he brought with him. Expert opinions as to the merits of the music vary considerably.

As the nineteenth century wore on, observations of hysterical and brain-damaged patients, and experiments on various hypnotic phenomena, made it conceivable that intelligent activities can occur of which a person is unaware; and such activities may exhibit knowledge and dramatic gifts that the person does not ordinarily possess.

These findings made the Spiritualist interpretation of automatic writing, drawing, and painting seem less compelling. They led to a demand that automatic writings should be 'evidential,' which means that the deceased persons who purportedly inspired them should establish their identities conclusively by giving correct information about themselves, which could not possibly have been known to the automatist, consciously or unconsciously.

Suicide in Baker Street

One of the first automatists to produce what at first appeared to be evidence of this kind was W. Stainton Moses (1839–92). The spirits who purported to 'control' Moses's hand during his automatic writing, or to 'communicate' through him as a medium by means of table-tilting and raps, were sometimes persons apparently unknown to him; and yet occasionally they gave information about themselves that it was subsequently possible to verify. For example, on the evening of February 21, 1874, Moses, at a party of friends in London, suddenly felt impelled to sit down and write. His hand drew a rough sketch of an object that resembled a horse fastened to a kind of truck, and then wrote some disjointed sentences that purported to come from a man who had committed suicide that morning. The man said that he had killed himself under a steam roller in Baker Street. Subsequent inquiry revealed that a man had committed suicide there that morning by throwing himself under a steam roller. On the front of the steam roller was the brass figure of a horse.

The Thompson-Gifford Case

There have been similar cases in connection with other automatists, but the difficulty with these 'drop-in communicators' is that one can hardly

An oil painting by Robert Swain Gifford (1840–1905): *The Coast of New England, 1890*

ever be completely certain that the information they give about themselves could not have come within the automatist's ken and have been subconsciously stored away. The famous US clairvoyant and trance medium, Eileen Garrett 1893–1970), has said that outbursts of automatic drawing or writing have occurred to her, but she has not seen them as spirit messages. She believes that they, and her controls as well, are properties or personalities from her own unconscious mind—or, in her own words, they are 'working symbols of the subconscious.'

Drawing and writing has figured in a number of 'evidential' cases, and painting was central to the famous 'Thompson-Gifford' case. In 1905 a goldsmith named Frederic L. Thompson became overwhelmed with the urge to paint pictures. He began to suffer from hallucinations of trees and landscapes, hallucinations that served as a basis for some of his pictures. The following year he visited an exhibition of paintings by Robert Swain Gifford who had died some while previously. He there heard a hallucinatory voice that said to him: 'You see what I have done. Can you not take up and finish my work?' Thereafter Thompson's impulse to paint became stronger, and certain scenes impressed themselves on him especially. After some months it was discovered that his paintings closely resembled scenes that had been well known to the deceased Robert Swain Gifford in life. The resemblances between photographs of these scenes and Thompson's paintings is so striking that a casual observer could suppose that the pictures were based on the actual scenes, or else on the photographs. Thus Thompson had perceived in the form of hallucinations, and had felt impelled to paint, scenes resembling places well known to Gifford, but which Thompson had apparently never visited or seen in photographs.

The Telepathy Theory

The argument that automatists in fact derive their seemingly enhanced knowledge from their own subconscious memories cannot be convincingly applied to cases such as that of the celebrated US medium, Leonora Piper (1859–1950). Mrs. Piper was studied and supervised by prominent psychical researchers from about 1885 to 1915. They were in the habit of regularly bringing to sit with her persons quite unknown to her who were introduced to her under pseudonyms. Despite these precautions, Mrs. Piper was time and again able, by automatic painting or speaking, to give correct information about the deceased friends and relatives of these sitters.

It can hardly be supposed that, even if Mrs. Piper had somehow managed to penetrate the anonymity of all these sitters, she could previously have gleaned by ordinary means, and consciously or subconsciously retained, the information necessary to ensure success in such a large number of cases. Of course if we admit the possibility of telepathy, then another explanation of Mrs. Piper's successes becomes feasible;

namely that she obtained the necessary information telepathically from the sitters themselves. However, in some instances Mrs. Piper seems definitely to have given, as if from a deceased person, information not conceivably known to the sitters present.

Perhaps the most curious of all automatic writings are the series of interlinked scripts produced in the early years of this century by a number of automatists connected with the Society for Psychical Research. With one exception—Mrs. Piper—they were not professional mediums, principal automatists being Mrs. Verrall, Mrs. Coombe-Tennant ('Mrs. Willett'), Miss Helen Verrall (Mrs. W. H. Salter), Mrs. Fleming ('Mrs. Holland'), and Mrs. Stuart Wilson. The scripts that they produced, or at least the portions of them we are here concerned with, purported to be inspired by a group of deceased friends, two of whom, F. W. H. Myers (1843–1901) and Edmund Gurney (1847–88), had taken a prominent part in the early history of the Society for Psychical Research.

In order to provide evidence of human survival of bodily death, this group of deceased persons allegedly hit upon an ingenious scheme. They sent to their friends still on Earth, using different mediums, various parts of one communication (or else a series of related communications) so that the significance of the whole could only be perceived when the separate communications were compared. In a number of cases—the so-called 'cross-correspondences'—the ostensible communicators might be thought to have succeeded.

These cases are often extremely complex and many involve recondite allusions to classical literature. An interesting example of these 'concordant automatisms,' as they are called, is the following. On April 16, 1907, Mrs. Fleming (in India) wrote an automatic script that contained the words 'Maurice. Morris. Mors. And with that the shadow of death fell upon him.' *Mors* is the Latin for 'death.' The following day Mrs. Piper, emerging from trance, spoke the words 'Sanatos' and then 'Tanatos.' On April 23, again when emerging from trance, she spoke the word 'Thanatos,' which is the Greek for 'death'.

Pale death stamps impartially upon the hovels of the poor and the towers of the rich.

On April 29, Mrs. Verrall's hand wrote a slightly garbled quotation from Walter Savage Landor: 'Warmed both hands before the Fire of Life, it fails and I am ready to depart.' She then drew the Greek letter delta, which had always been a symbol of death to her. Next she wrote *Manibus date lilia plenis* ('give lilies with full hands'), a quotation from a passage in Virgil's *Aeneid* foretelling the early death of Marcellus, nephew of Emperor Augustus. Shortly after this she wrote 'Come away, Come away,' (the first four words of Shakespeare's 'Come away, come away death') followed immediately by '*Pallida mors aequo pede pauperum, Tabernas regumque turres,* Put in *pulsat,*' ('Pale death stamps impartially upon the hovels of the poor and the towers of the rich.'), a quotation from Horace (65–8 BC). Finally she wrote, 'You have got the word plainly written all along in your writing. Look back.' None of the three ladies knew anything of what the others had written or said. Mrs. Piper knew no Greek. The word 'death' occurred in Mrs. Holland's scripts on only three occasions; in Mrs. Verrall's scripts it occurred only once.

Many of the cross-correspondences are far more ingenious and remarkable. So it seems that the alternatives to a Spiritualist interpretation of automatic writing are not any easier to accept; for deliberate fraud is possible in only a small number of cases. But what makes the Spiritualist interpretation unacceptable to many researchers is the fact that the best cases are commonly found entangled with the worst. The most convincing of an automatist's 'communicators' will guarantee the credentials of the most implausible ones—a fact that opens up problems so complex it is difficult to see any way to approach them.

ALAN GAULD

FURTHER READING: F. W. H. Myers. Human Personality and its Survival of Bodily Death. *(New York, NY: Arno Press, 1975); Anita Mühl.* Automatic Writing. *(New York, NY: Helix Press, 1963); Rosalind Heywood.* Beyond the Reach of Sense. *(New York, NY: Dutton, 1961); Alan Gauld.* Mediumship and Survival. *(Portsmouth, NH: Heinemann, 1982).*

Book of the Dead (Tibetan)

The *Bardo Thodol,* as it is known in Tibetan, is a description of what happens after death. It represents only a small part of the Tibetan material on dying, and could better be called 'a' Tibetan book of the dead than 'the' one. The classic version in English was translated by a Tibetan lama, Kazi Dawa-Samdup (1868–1923), and edited by W. Y. Evans-Wentz (1878–1965), who was an enthusiastic theosophist and admirer of Madame

Blavatsky (1831–91), and studied with Buddhist lamas in Tibet. The ideas and the complex symbolism involved are unfamiliar to most Westerners and, inevitably, neither of the two available modern versions is easy for the uninstructed to grasp.

The text treats death not as the end but as a recurrent stage in the cycle of lives, deaths, and rebirths that in Buddhist belief we all experience many times over, and from which only the enlightened can escape into *Nirvana*.

Traditionally in Tibet the text was recited at a person's deathbed by a lama. It describes the extraordinary and frightening experiences that occur in the forty-nine days (the number is explained as symbolic rather than literal) in the interval between dying and being reborn. Its purpose is to teach the art of rightly dying and to banish fear of death and unwillingness to die, which produce 'unfavourable results.'

At the outset the dying person is told that the moment has come to leave the earthly plane and experience the Clear Light of the Void. Those who are exceptionally spiritually advanced will attain liberation; the great majority will be outside the body, but aware of the deathbed scene, hearing the weeping of friends and relatives, and wondering uneasily whether death has come or not. It will be some time before the truth dawns: now there follow awesome sounds and lights, but it is essential to understand that these are illusions, projections of the deceased's own consciousness.

Wrathful Deities of the Bar-do from the Tibetan School (eighteenth century)

Presently there are coloured lights and various deities appear. The blinding white light of wisdom will dazzle the dead person, who will shrink away, but must cleave to it rather than to the duller, smoky light that beckons the unwary to the hell-realms of misery. There are numerous visions of deities, terrifying sounds of thunder and voices crying 'Kill! Kill!' but these again are illusions.

The Wrathful Deities

Addional testing comes with the appearance of Wrathful Deities—flame-wrapped beings with many heads, arms, and legs, who brandish weapons in their numerous hands and drink blood from skulls: '. . . from the east, the Dark Brown Lion-Headed One, the hands crossed on the breast, and in the mouth holding a corpse, and shaking the mane; from the south, the Red Tiger-Headed One, the hands crossed downward, grinning and showing the fangs and looking on with protruding eyes; from the West, the Black Fox-Headed One, the right hand holding a shaving knife, the left holding an intestine, and she eating and licking the blood there from; from the north, the Dark Blue Wolf-Headed One, the two hands tearing open a corpse . . . '

These gruesome figures, too, can be vanquished by recognizing them for what they are and not giving way to panic. Lonely and afraid as the impulse toward rebirth gathers strength, the dead wander in a realm of illusions, confronted by thick darkness, beasts of prey, phantoms, snow and tempest, earthquakes, hallucinations of being pursued by a raging mob and hiding in crevices in rocks. In a judgment before the Lord of the Dead, each person's good deeds and bad deeds are counted out in the form of white and black pebbles, and the deceased is agonizingly torn to pieces over and over again. But all this is still illusion.

C. G. Jung (1875–1961) regarded the nightmare figures of the Tibetan text as images from the collective unconscious. The Buddhist tradition teaches that recognizing them for what they truly are is the path to enlightenment.

FURTHER READING: W. Y. Evans-Wentz, ed. The Tibetan Book of the Dead. *(New York, NY: Oxford University Press, 1960); F. Fremantle and Chogyam Trungpa.* The Tibetan Book of the Dead, *trans. (Boston, MA: Shambhala, 1975).*

Burial

Very few people want to die. Very few admit that they will, and almost everyone everywhere has hoped that survival can somehow be contrived if enough trouble is taken. The trouble can be taken by the hoper himself, behaving well enough in life to earn immortality; or even, if he is lucky in his religion, by repentance on his deathbed. Or his survivors may propitiate someone or something on his behalf.

Life after death can also be thought of in two ways. The spirit may survive, bodiless, or reborn in a new human, a tree, an animal, or an ancestor figure. Or the body itself may be resurrected in the flesh for the spirit to inhabit. Most funeral customs are the result

Lithograph depicting the funeral of the assassinated King George I of Greece in Athens on March, 20, 1913

of one of these two ways of thinking, and the most elaborate rites have come from the conviction that the reborn spirit will need in its future life all that it had on Earth, so that if it is to settle comfortably it must be as rich as possible, often at great cost to the living.

At the funeral of a king in Scythia, for instance, slaves and horses were killed and buried with him, while the Egyptians of the Middle Kingdom were content to bury the great with wooden and clay models of their slaves, houses, animals, and boats. In China, all the possessions, including whole armies, navies, and air forces, were traditionally fashioned out of paper and burned at the funeral. Through the centuries the importance accorded to death has declined, a sensible shift from human sacrifice through wood to paper.

Not all customs have been elaborate, but all successful religions have included in their rituals the means for ensuring some form of life beyond death. On the other hand, no religion has managed to demonstrate what *does* happen after death, and so there are also rituals to protect the living if anything goes wrong, preventing the furious ghost, unable to find a new body or paradise or whatever, from haunting his careless kin. Terror of the unsettled spirits of the dead dies very hard; food may be put out for them, or their names made taboo so that they are not inadvertently summoned. Graveyards are still shunned at night, fingers are crossed, and very few people are prepared to deny the existence of ghosts with complete confidence.

The Trappings of Fear

Over thousands of years, the world's customs have become such a tangle of facts, faiths, superstitions, and rationalizations that it is hard to be sure of the real meaning of any particular custom. However, the customs themselves, all rooted in the ancient and continuing hopes and fears, follow a consistent pattern. We have a common daydream of sudden wealth: 'What would you do if you won the Lotto?' We would be reborn, of course, a trip round the world, everything new, a new life. Usually, as losers, we make do with an occasional new suitcase, but our clothes are clean and we have a new face-flannel for a holiday. Similarly with the dead, the body is washed, straightened, and wrapped in new cloth for its new state, and it probably goes in a new box, in a new hole, six feet deep.

With all this there will be prayers to help the spirit leave the body and to comfort it in the afterlife; some religions, including Christianity, pass the responsibility on to God, and neither tell the dead what to do nor give him ghostly possessions. However, the love-hate ambivalence of all family relationships persists in death; gold, blood, hair, memorial plaques, flowers, ashes in an urn on the mantel—whichever we use, our motives are obscure and dark, coloured by superstition in the most rational of us, twitched back from the edge of common sense by a little nudge of fear. Hygiene and honour may seem to compel us, but the washing, anointing, parcelling-up, shutting in a box, burying deep, and pinning down with a heavy stone may also be seen to come from fright.

. . . relatives and close friends traditionally came to see the corpse and at night one of the family would sit up with it, with candles at head and feet . . .

The Business of Burial

A state funeral in England or the United States still has much pageantry; troops slow-marching with reversed rifles to bands playing the Dead March in *Saul*, black crepe muffling the drums, the coffin on a horse-drawn gun carriage, and the mournful notes of the 'Last Post;' but state funerals are rare.

When the average person dies at home, the funeral is organized by an undertaker, who is called in as soon as possible. Some people still keep the body in the house, and then one of the family, or a nurse, may lay it out before he comes. The corpse is stripped, straightened, washed, and dressed in clean or new nightdress or pyjamas, the eyes and mouth are closed, the hands folded on the breast, the hair brushed and combed, and a clean sheet is put over the body, turned down to show the face. If the undertaker's assistant comes to do the laying-out, he will also pin on a square like a nappy after the washing, shave a noticeable beard, and arrange the corpse, using bandages for arms and legs, to look as if it is asleep with the head a little on one side. He has been taught to step back at intervals to see that the effect is 'natural.' (If there is a delay before the funeral in hot weather, the corpse may be embalmed. It is not eviscerated; the blood is simply drawn off through a vein in the armpit and replaced with a formalin-based embalming fluid.) The corpse is then put into the coffin and covered with a shroud to match the pillow and lining, if the family prefers this to ordinary clothes.

In some parts of Britain, relatives and close friends traditionally came to see the corpse and at night one of the family would sit up with it, with candles at head and feet, but this is now rare, and viewing is becoming rare, too. More and more people prefer not to keep the body in the house, but have the undertaker's men lay it out and take it back to the shop, where there are rooms for visiting if required.

The coffin is made of wood. Most undertakers now sell caskets as well as coffins, an American fashion for a rectangular box instead of the traditional tapered shape.

Notices of the funeral are sent out privately and to the newspapers, and as soon as the arrangements can be made and the family gathered, the corpse is buried. The hearse is a black car such as an station-wagon, and either it is driven to the house with the coffin already in it, or it arrives empty and the undertaker's bearers carry the coffin out, on their shoulders in the south, down at arm's length by the handles in the north. All over the coffin and on the roof of the hearse (and sometimes in a special car as well) are the flowers, often made up into wreaths and crosses as in the nineteenth century, but mostly now in sheaves, large flat arrangements tied with bows and bagged in cellophane. The hearse drives very slowly to the church or the cemetery chapel, followed by the matching cars of the undertaker's fleet, containing the mourners.

When they arrive at the church, the coffin is carried in and set on draped trestles before the altar for the burial service. Then it is taken to the grave, already dug, and lowered in. The words of committal are read by the priest, and the mourners may throw a little earth onto the coffin before they leave. Later the grave is filled by the cemetery staff, and the flowers are put on top of it.

Some months later, there may be a memorial service that strangers can attend if the family feels the dead to have been very loved or distinguished, and when the grave has settled, a memorial stone, slab ('mousetrap' in the trade), or curb may be put up with name, dates of birth and death, and a remembering or loving message. In the last century, these stones were often large and fanciful; now the authorities in charge have clamped down on size and style, and also encourage lawn cemeteries, plain fields with little bronze plaques let flat into the ground so that the grass can easily be cut with a motor-mower. Graves may be visited, and flowers placed or planted, but not many people visit their family graves regularly.

No 'grave goods' are supplied, but the undertaker does everything he can to foster the belief that the incomplete embalming, the metal casket, and the concrete vault that may be bought to enclose it, will prevent decomposition.

Dutch artist Abraham van den Tempel's *Portrait of the Widow of Admiral van Balen* shows the subject posing in the black clothing associated with a period of mourning.

Cosmetics for the Corpse

During the nineteenth century, funerals were much more complicated than this, and hung over the family for at least a year, during which it was almost compulsory to wear black. The periods of mourning for different degrees of blood relationship were exactly laid down and exactly followed; a widow might wear black for the rest of her life. Now, some people wear dark clothes for the funeral, and men may wear a black tie or an armband for a little while, but that is all. The English see less and less necessity for 'a good funeral' and for the outward rites of grief and mourning.

In the United States of America, however, where funerals were once deliberately simple, the funeral directors with more conviction than they do in England, have steadily increased the possibilities of big spending on funerals, both as status symbols and as 'grief-therapy,' and though mourning clothes are as unfashionable as they are in England, everything else is more elaborate. The undertaker plays a more prominent part throughout. The corpse is almost always embalmed, the face and hands are carefully painted, hair tinted and waved, and spectacles set in place. A complete new outfit (dress or suit, underclothing, hose, shoes) is put on, though nothing shows below the waist, and an artistic arrangement made in a rich wooden or metal casket, lined with ruched and tucked velvet. It is set up in a bower of flowers in a reposing room at the funeral home, where friends can visit the corpse before the funeral.

The emphasis, exactly as in ancient Egypt, is on eternal preservation.

Black Crepe and Plumes

The Roman Catholic countries of Europe and South America have neither simplified their burial customs, as in England, nor changed their slant as in the United States, but rather continue the old black-and-baroque fashions of the eighteenth and nineteenth centuries. Mourning is still extensively worn, and there are sometimes horse-drawn hearses with black plumes and velvet caparisons. The motor-hearses have richly carved and gilded decorations, and there are longer processions and more flowers. Graves are still regularly visited.

Roman Catholics also preserve the custom of having a portrait of the dead person at the tomb, an ancient and widespread practice that produced superb portraits and ancestor figures. Some of the most interesting were carried on royal coffins in medieval England and France. The corpse was formerly carried exposed on top of the coffin so that all might see that the king was dead, but later it was put inside and was replaced by a portrait statue, robed, and crowned. The few that survive may be seen in Westminster Abbey. The modern pictures for the average man are a very dim reminder, photographs set in the tombstone.

There is less room for fear in our shrunken, bright, and crowded world. Millions of us are hardly conscious of night at all, the unknown is receding into space, and our funeral customs, already diluted from primitive rituals, are going the way of all religious ceremony, becoming more and more alike, less and less urgent.

BARBARA JONES

A horse-hearse from the early nineteenth century

The Origins of Burial

The deliberate burial of the dead is the first marker for determining human civilization. It was first associated with the culture of Neanderthal man, toward the close of the Middle Stone Age. In the later Stone Age when present-day man made his appearance, some 40,000 years ago, there was a great outburst of magical, artistic activity, evidence of which can be found in the cave art of southern France. At the same time, there was a greater elabouration both of graves and grave goods; objects were placed beside the corpse and the bones of the dead were sometimes coloured with red ochre. In living cultures, where it is possible to establish the meanings of such customs, the red of the ochre is often associated with blood, a basic element in life itself. In these same societies the burial of the grave goods implies their continued use by the dead though in a different form from life on Earth. It therefore seems probable that by the time of the Upper Paleolithic Age, the period of cave art, man had some idea of continuity after death, of another world, a land of the dead, of which the Christian heaven and hell is but a dualistic expression.

The basic logical requirement of such a conception is the development of a dualistic view of man's nature, which is seen as split into flesh and spirit, mind and matter, body, and soul. Of these two elements, one dies with the body, one lives on after death. So that life and death are not two completely opposed states: the spirit interpenetrates death and peoples the otherworld with the living dead.

The significance of the appearance of elaborate burial customs and artistic achievements in the Upper Paleolithic Age is greater than at first appears. For their existence suggests that by this time man had developed a means of elabourating concepts and ideas, a language such as we know today. The development of language from a more elementary sign system, such as animals possess, was undoubtedly the greatest technological advance in the history of man. It is the feature that most clearly separates contemporary man from the apes.

Thinking is not confined to the users of language, but there can be no doubt that the development of thought and its use as a major instrument of human growth is dependent upon the invention of a communication system of this kind. One of the first signs of this advance in the technology of communications is the appearance of burial customs that suggest that

The Symbolism of Funeral Rites

Men have lost their reason in nothing so much as their religion, wherein stones and clouts make martyrs; and, since the religion of one seems madness unto another, to afford an account or rationale of old Rites requires no rigid Reader. That they kindled the pyre aversely, or turning their face from it, was an handsome Symbol of unwilling ministration; that they washed their bones with wine and milk, that the mother wrapped them in linen and dried them in her bosom, the first fostering part, and place of their nourishment; that they opened their eyes toward heaven, before they kindled the fire, as the place of their hopes or original, were no improper Ceremonies . . . that in strewing their tombs the *Romans* affected the Rose, the Greeks *Amaranthus* and myrtle; that the Funeral pyre consisted of sweet fuel Cypress, Fir, Larix, Yew, and Trees perpetually verdant, lay silent expressions of their surviving hopes. Wherein Christians who deck their Coffins with Bays, have found a more elegant Emblem. For that he seeming dead will restore itself from the root, and its dry and exuccous leaves resume their verdure again; which, if we mistake not, we have also observed in furze. Whether the planting of yew in Churchyards hold not its original from ancient Funeral rites, or as an Emblem of Resurrection, from its perpetual verdure, may also admit conjecture . . .

That they buried their dead on their backs, or in a supine position, seems agreeable unto profound sleep, and common posture of dying; contrary to the most natural way of birth; Nor unlike our pendulous posture, in the doubtful state of the womb . . .

That they carried them out of the world with their feet forward, not inconsonant unto reason: as contrary unto the native posture of man, and his production first into it. And also agreeable unto their opinions, while they bid adieu unto the world, not to look again upon it; whereas *Mahometans* who think to return to a delightful life again, are carried forth with their heads forward . . .

Sir Thomas Browne
Urn Burial (1658)

man had developed a set of ideas that divided his nature into body and soul, and his universe into Earth and heaven, or this world and the next. The belief in immortality, as the anthropologist Malinowski (1884–1942) pointed out, is one of the principal sources of religious inspiration.

A Cemetery in the Belly

The burial customs we know from direct observation and written record, rather than from digging into the past, display a number of striking similarities, as well as a wide range of variation in other respects. The variations are in specific customs such as methods of disposal. Burial in the earth (inhumation) is only one such method. Other forms include burial in caves and in mounds or tumuli, obvious forerunners of the Egyptian pyramids and the mausoleums of Europe, by which the important dead are singled out for exceptional treatment. Water burial is practiced by seafaring peoples not only out of necessity but also as a way of honouring the great. In Scandinavian legend, the corpse of the slain Balder, with his wife and horse, and the gift of Odin's ring Draupnir, was laid in his ship upon a funeral pyre and launched blazing out to sea. Elsewhere, as among the LoDagaa of northern Ghana, burial in a river or its bank is a method of cleansing the community of someone who has died a 'bad death.'

The placing of the dead in trees or on scaffolds is found in many parts of the world and is especially associated with the Zoroastrian religion, practiced by the Parsi community of Bombay. Their holy book, the *Zend-Avesta*, proclaims a punishment of a thousand stripes for a person who shall bury in the earth the corpse of dog or man, and not disinter it before the end of the second year. For only such a treatment can secure the proper ascent of the dead to the other world.

The Sioux and other Plains Native Americans also buried their dead on platforms, and sat for days beneath them to keep the dead company. This may have been partly to protect the body against wild animals; for the same purpose other nomadic tribes used cremation. Eastern Native Americans often practiced a secondary burial—disinterring a corpse, scraping the bones clean, tying them into a skin and burying the bundle—sometimes in a pot, to be kept near the family. Plains Native Americans would often employ a symbolic second burial, cutting a lock of hair from the deceased, wrapping it in skins, and keeping it as a sacred possession.

Cannibalism, in those relatively rare parts of the world where it was practiced, was sometimes a recognized means of disposing of the dead and was an obligation on the surviving relatives. The meat of the funeral feast is 'nothing less than the corpse of the

Sea Burial of a Knight of the Round Table **by the Master of Charles of Maine (1440–1460)**

departed kinsman.' Of inhabitants of the eastern highlands of New Guinea it has been remarked that 'their cemeteries are their bellies.' Certainly this mode of disposal of the dead, the consumption of one generation by the next, is a striking way of conquering death.

Methods of disposing of the dead vary from people to people. But they may also vary within a particular group. We have already seen how important leaders may be accorded special treatment; 'sinners' or despised categories of persons may be differentiated in the same way, especially those who have died a 'bad death;' for example, suicides, witches, and those killed by drowning or by lightning, young children who have not yet been fully incorporated into the society and, in Africa, women who have died in childbirth. In each of these cases, whether intentionally or unintentionally, something is wrong.

In Europe, until recent times, certain Christian sects refused to bury unbaptized children and suicides in 'holy ground,' while the blood-guilty were interred at a crossroads with a stake in the heart. The last crossroads burial in England took place outside Lord's cricket ground in 1823. And in 1811, in the neighbourhood of Shoreditch, London, a corpse was arrested for debt, a survival of the procedure whereby the body of a debtor could be legally deprived of a proper burial until his creditors had been repaid.

Love and Fear

The dead are treated in different ways not only for reasons of status, but also as a sanction upon those who remain behind. The earthly system of reward and punishments is often projected onto the dead, and their destination after death may depend on the way in which they are buried. Only a full burial will ensure proper despatch to the other world; a partial performance may mean that the dead man becomes not a sanctified ancestor but an unsanctified ghost hanging around his Earthly dwelling, haunting those who survive in an attempt to get his grievances put right.

The attempt to put oneself at a distance from the ghost is a constant theme of funeral customs everywhere. It is the task of the living to set the dead on the path to the other world, the last journey from which there is no return. For this purpose, the dead may be provided (as in rural Greece) with a coin for the ferryman who rows them across the river of death, with food to sustain them on the way, and with property to use when they get there. This may include slaves (slaughtered on the tomb), or wives (burned on the funeral pyre), or the more humble possessions of the deceased: clothes, weapons, or drinking vessels.

The Northwestern Coast Tribe, the Chinook, are depicted in *Chinook Burial Grounds* by John Mix Stanley (1814–1872)

The general trend toward actions of this kind, which are implicit in the body-soul division, is illustrated by a report from Lincolnshire at the turn of the century. A widow had placed her husband's mug and jug on his grave, having first broken them both. Explaining her actions to the rector, she said, 'I was that moidered with crying that I clean forgot to put 'em in t'coffin . . . So I goes and does t'next best. I deads 'em both over his grave, and says I to mysen, my old man, he set a vast of store, he did, by yon mug and jug, and when their ghoastes gets over on yon side he'll holler out, 'Yon's mine, hand 'em over to me,' and I'd like to see them as would stop him a-having of them an' all.'

In hunting societies such as those of North America, where the social investment in property was small, a man's possessions were usually destroyed after his death. As the accumulation of capital goods becomes a more prominent feature of society, so grave goods become more nominal, tokens and toys being substituted for the real thing. Eventually expenditure on the dead is seen as neglect of the living, and efforts are made to cut down on such 'unnecessary' expenses.

The destruction of a man's property provides a clear instance of the double attitude that lies behind many aspects of funeral ceremonies. Sidney Hartland (1848–1927) commented (in his article on 'Death and Disposal of the Dead' in *Hasting's Encyclopedia of Religion and Ethics*): 'Throughout the rites and observances attendant on death, two motives two principles are found struggling for the mastery. On the one hand, there is the fear of death and of the dead, which produces the horror of the corpse, the fear of defilement, and the overlapping desire to ban the ghost. On the other hand, there is the affection, real or simulated, for the deceased, which bewails his departure and is unwilling to let him go.' The corpse is thus both loved and feared.

To take a cue from S. Freud (1856–1939), the double-edged attitude toward the dead, seen in so many funeral customs, is a projection of the love and hate that mark the relations we have with our nearest and dearest. Significantly it is often the closest kin, the dead man's heirs and widow, who are seen as being in the greatest danger from the ghost; it is they who have to be provided with the strongest protection from his revenging spirit. So it is they too who often have to undergo the severest ordeals during the course of these ceremonies, since they are the ones who have most to gain (and most to lose) from his death.

The funeral ceremony is not only a matter of disposing of the dead and dispatching them to the other world, but also of filling their place in the land of the living and redistributing their rights and duties over people and property.

The transition from life to death is the rite of passage through which all must go, and the change in status from living to dead cannot be performed just with a nod of the head. The process has to be a gradual one and the burial service is customarily followed, at a suitably discreet interval, by a second funeral, an obituary service, in which the close kin are released from mourning, the dead are dispatched to their final abode, and their life on Earth is summed up in what is the equivalent of a funeral oration.

Reaction to death mellows in the course of the funeral and one of the functions of such ceremonies is to relieve the bereaved, as well as to reconcile the community to the loss of one of their number, for death constitutes a threat to those who remain behind. However, such a threat can never be totally set aside. The idea of continuity after death is itself an aspect of the refusal to accept the reality of death. So too perhaps is the idea that death, except for the old, is 'unnatural.' In most preindustrial societies a specific supernatural cause was assigned for every event. Hence the frequent ordeals that occurred during the funerals, in an attempt to find out who killed the dead man. In one form or another, accusations of witchcraft or of sins against the supernatural powers were a constant accompaniment to funerals.

The Bishop Orders His Tomb

And so, about this tomb of mine. I fought
With tooth and nail to save my niche,
ye know:
— Old Gandolf cozened me, despite
my care;
Shrewd was the snatch from out the
corner South
He graced his carrion with, God curse
the same!
Yet still my niche is not so cramped
but thence
One sees the pulpit o' the epistle side,
And somewhat of the choir, those
silent seats,
And up into the aery dome where live
The angels, and a sunbeam's sure
to lurk:
And I shall fill my slab of basalt there,
And 'neath my tabernacle take my rest,
With those nine columns round me,
two and two,
The odd one at my feet. . .
Peach-blossom marble all, the rare,
the ripe
As fresh-poured red wine of a
mighty pulse
—Old Gandolf with his paltry onion-stone,
Put me where I may look at him! . . .
And then how I shall lie through
centuries,
And hear the blessed mutter of
the mass,
And see God made and eaten all
day long,
And feel the steady candle-flame,
and taste
Good strong thick stupefying
incense-smoke! . . .

Robert Browning
The Bishop Orders His Tomb in St. Praxed's Church

The Loss of Eternal Life

One striking illustration of this attempt to reject its inevitability is to be found in the tales of the origin of death. The biblical story of Adam, Eve, and the apple has its parallels in other stories that attribute the coming of death to man's disobedience. However, often what is remarkable is the triviality of the offense man has committed. Another set of stories, found in all parts of the world, contrasts the mortality of man and the waxing and waning of the moon. In one version God sends messengers to convey the news of immortality to man, and of death to the moon; the message to man gets delayed or reversed, with the result that he loses the gift of eternal life. But the manner in which this was lost is almost accidental, rather than a matter of deliberate planning. It is as if the chance introduction of death left open the possibility that the present state of affairs could be reversed.

It is doubtful if, in any society, men have placed much hope in such an outcome or much weight on tales of this kind. If an explanation of death was required, to meet the enquiries of children or the fears of the old, then these stories were ready to hand. In their actions, as distinct from their formal 'beliefs,' most people display a more practical attitude toward death. It is the elaborate funeral ceremonies that enable small face-to-face communities to meet the shock that the loss of a member inevitably brings. In our more impersonal society, the impact of death (unless of a national figure) is very localized; even close kin are shielded from immediate contact by specialist undertakers. However, in other societies, funerals are often the most elaborate ceremonies in the whole ritual calendar, the occasions on which a community gets together to dispose of the dead, redistribute his roles and property, and at the same time set its fears at rest by demonstrating the solidarity of the living in the face of loss and bereavement.

JACK GOODY

FURTHER READING: E. Bendann. Death Customs. *(Humanities, 1970); Jack Goody.* Death, Property and the Ancestors. *(Redwood City, CA: Stanford University Press, 1962); Barbara Jones.* Design for Death. *(Indianapolis, IN: Bobbs-Merrill, 1967).*

In Britain, meanwhile, the trend toward cremation has gone so far that more people are cremated than are buried . . .

Burning

Cremation marks second, in antiquity and popularity, only to earth burial as a way of disposing of the dead: burning an animal was a way of offering it to a god, the rising smell and smoke being thought to carry the essence of the beast up to the god: the belief that burning a substance releases its 'soul' or 'essence' is found in alchemy: in Europe, heretics and witches were burned to death.

Cremation

As a way of disposing of the remains of the dead, cremation gradually became more acceptable in North America in the twentieth century, despite strong resistance from high-pressure funeral salesmanship. In Britain, meanwhile, the trend toward cremation has gone so far that more people are cremated than are buried (this is also true in Germany, Denmark, and Japan). Yet it is barely over 100 years since cremation became legal in many countries. A long and heated battle was fought in England in the nineteenth century until the practice gained official sanction, when the Cremation Act was passed in 1902.

The earliest way of disposing of the dead was by burial. Cremation remained very rare until the invention of agriculture and the appearance of communities of peasant farmers in the period after 8000 BC. These communities spread throughout Europe and, while they continued mainly to dispose of their dead by burial, cremation occurred as a variant rite.

During the second millennium BC in Europe, cremation grew more and more common until it became the principal method of disposing of the dead. In Britain cremation had completely displaced burial by the Middle Bronze Age; throughout Europe, by the Late Bronze Age, the dead were interred after cremation in 'urnfields,' or cremation cemeteries. Previously, cremated remains in bags or urns had been interred in burial mounds, or barrows.

The prehistoric Iron Age saw mixed rites of burial and cremation. What changes of beliefs and ideas accompanied these alterations in funeral practice, there is no way of knowing, but it seems clear that the move from burial to cremation in the second millennium was one which occurred within society and was not the result of an incursion of a new people.

The Burning Ghats

The Greeks cremated their dead warriors: the *Iliad* describes the huge funeral pyre that Achilles constructed for his dearly loved friend Patroclus, and the impressive ceremonies with that the body of Achilles himself was burned after the hero's own death. When the flames of the pyre had been extinguished, the bones were washed in oil and wine, and were put in an urn with the bones of Patroclus.

Burning on the funeral pyre was also the custom in Rome from the end of the Republic to the end of the fourth century AD. Cremation has always been widely practiced in Hindu India and the burning *ghats*, usually near a river bank, are a feature of many Indian cities today. Here the bodies of the dead, not in coffins but in full view, are burned on funeral pyres in public. It is believed that as long as the physical body continues in existence, the dead person's spirit hovers near it and cannot break free to be reborn in another body. The corpse is dressed in new clothes, and the big toes may be tied together to prevent the ghost walking back into the world of the living. Sometimes the dead man's eldest son cracks the skull of the corpse with a blow from a hammer.

In the past it was the accepted custom for a widow to throw herself on to her husband's funeral pyre to be burned alive, her body consumed by the same flames that burned him. This custom was made illegal by the British administration in the nineteenth century, but there are occasional reports to this day of suicides by widows on the funeral pyre.

Engraving showing the funeral pile of Patroclus from *The Illustrated History of the World* (Ward Lock, c. 1880)

The Resurrection of the Body

In some societies there have been objections to cremation because it was thought that burning a dead body polluted the sacred principle of fire. This was not the objection of Christianity. The Christian religion rejected burning the dead because it seemed to violate and invalidate the doctrine of the resurrection of the body.

For centuries in Christian countries the concept of the Day of Judgment entailed the dead rising from their graves, their bones reclothed in flesh. How could this happen, people protested, if the bones had been reduced to a few fragments of ash? Cremation was consequently forbidden in the Christian world, though by the nineteenth century even some clergymen had begun to advocate it.

Calls for Reform

The main impetus toward cremation in nineteenth-century Europe came from people who were horrified by the insanitary conditions in towns created by the custom of burial. The problems caused by drainage from churchyards and cemeteries, and the waste of land involved in burying the dead, were set out in a book by the great social reformer Edwin Chadwick (1800–90), *A Special Inquiry into the Practice of Interment in Towns*, published in 1843. In the second half of the century many physicians and scientists, particularly in Italy and Switzerland, recommended the adoption of cremation.

In 1874 a congress at Milan petitioned for cremation to be allowed. In that same year the Cremation Society of England was founded to promote the practice. 'We disapprove of the present custom of burying the dead,' it declared, 'and desire to substitute some mode which shall rapidly resolve the body into its component elements by a process which cannot offend the living, and shall render the remains absolutely innocuous. Until some better method is devised, we desire to adopt that usually known as cremation.'

The founder of the Society was Sir Henry Thompson (1820–1904), surgeon to Queen Victoria (1819–1901). He had been bringing the question of cremation to the attention of the English public for years. Sir Henry used to say that the problem was a simple one: 'Given a dead body, to resolve it into carbonic acid, water, and ammonia, rapidly, safely, and not unpleasantly.' He himself experimented with a furnace in which a body weighing 144 pounds was reduced in 50 minutes to about 4 pounds of lime dust.

Action quickly followed in the United States, where the first crematorium was built in 1876 and the New York Cremation Society was founded soon afterward, in 1881. The Cremation Association of America dates from 1913, but the movement toward widespread cremation did not progress nearly as quickly as in Britain.

The Cremation Society of England encountered formidable opposition, even so. It was unable to purchase a freehold until 1878, when it obtained an acre of land at Woking in Surrey, close to a cemetery recently established there to deal with burials that could no longer be accommodated in London.

In 1882 the home secretary refused to give the Society permission to cremate two deceased persons who had left explicit instructions that their bodies were to be burned. The bodies were preserved and were eventually cremated in a specially-erected crematorium on a private estate in Dorset owned by a member of the Society. A year later this member himself died and was also cremated there.

These cremations were supervised by an official of the Cremation Society. No comment was made or action taken by the home office, which seemed nonplussed.

A Welsh Eccentric

In 1884 however, the home office took action when Welsh doctor William Price (1800–1903) announced that he intended to cremate the body of his deceased infant son, and proceeded to do so. Dr. Price, who now rates a peculiar statue in Llantrisant, is justly described in *The Dictionary of Welsh Biography* as 'eccentric.'

A practicing doctor, he claimed to be an arch-druid, practiced free love, and opposed vivisection and vaccination. He carried out his rites dressed in a white tunic with a huge fox skin on his head, and constantly advocated cremation. The dead child, who was born to him when he was aged 83, had been christened Jesus Christ.

At first the police did not know what to do, but Price was eventually arrested. His trial took place in Cardiff, where the judge, Mr. Justice Stephen, ruled that no offence had occurred and that cremation was legal, provided that it was carried out without nuisance to others. A year later, in 1885, the first publicly organized and controlled cremation in Britain took place at Woking. Price himself was cremated when he died in 1893.

There was still much opposition and prejudice in the early days and police protection was required at some cremations. Laws were passed in other European countries making cremation legal, but the Roman Catholic Church continued to set its face sternly against

The Manikarnika Cremation Ghat, in Varanasi, India

the practice. The Church suspected the motives of the movement's proponents, which it believed were largely materialistic and anti-Catholic, and in 1886 the Vatican condemned the campaign for cremation as un-Christian and Masonic in inspiration. As late as 1926 enthusiasts for cremation were officially denounced by Rome as 'enemies of Christianity.' Forty years later, however, the Church had withdrawn its ban.

Scattered on the Wind

The ashes from cremated bodies may be disposed of in a wide variety of ways. The remains of a Hindu funeral pyre are put into the river beside which the pyre was erected. In Europe and the United States the ashes may be stored in small boxes or in urns, buried in the ground, or in a grave inside a church, or sometimes thrown to the winds or scattered in a garden of remembrance. Cremation has dealt with the sanitary problem that worried the nineteenth-century reformers, and the scattering of ashes does away with difficulties over storage and grave-space. On the other hand, many mourners still find themselves uneasy with the mechanics of cremation and its adoption brings to an end the tombs and monuments for the dead which were a feature of European Christian civilization for so many centuries.

GLYN DANIEL

Cross Correspondences

The automatist Mrs. Verrall (1859–1916) invented the term 'cross correspondences' early in the present century to describe any concordance between the automatic scripts or trance utterances of two or more automatists operating independently.

The idea that such concordances might occur or might be experimentally induced was not entirely new but favourable conditions for testing it arose only after the death of F. W. H. Myers (1843–1901) of the Society for Psychical Research and the posthumous publication of his famous book, *Human Personality and its Survival of Bodily Death*. At that time a number of people who had been impressed by Myers began to produce automatic scripts purporting to come from Myers himself or from his friends and collabourators Edmund Gurney (1847–88) and Professor Henry Sidgwick (1838–1900), and comparison of their scripts soon began to reveal apparent concordances. The most important of these automatists were Mrs. Verrall, a lecturer in classics at Newnham; her daughter Helen Verrall (1883–1959), afterward Mrs. W. H. Salter; Mrs. Holland, pseudonym of Mrs. Fleming (1868–1948), a sister of Rudyard Kipling; and from 1908 onward Mrs. Willett, pseudonym of Mrs. Coombe-Tennant (1874–1956), who was a prominent public figure and a British delegate to the Assembly of the League of Nations.

All these were amateurs of the highest standing. The only professional medium concerned was the famous Mrs. Piper (1857–1950), who played a leading part in some of the earlier cross-correspondences. Later on, other amateur automatists were drawn into the group, which continued to function down to about 1930. By that date it is said to have produced more than 2,000 scripts—by far the largest body of automatic material now in existence anywhere. These scripts were carefully transcribed, compared, and annotated by a number of experienced investigators, of whom the most active were Alice Johnson, an official of the Society for Psychical Research, J. G. Piddington (1869–1952), president of the Society (1924–5), and Gerald Balfour (1853–1945). Many scripts showing cross-correspondences have been published and discussed in the *Proceedings* of the Society.

Mrs. Verrall was seized by an impulse to write automatically and produced a brief script in a mixture of Greek and Latin . . .

Spheres of Influence

Cross-correspondences can be classified in various ways. Most of them occurred spontaneously, without any prompting by the investigators; but there are one or two experimental cases in which the 'script-intelligence' of one automatist was asked to introduce a specified topic into the script of another and more-or-less successfully complied. The following is a curious instance.

On January 28, 1902, Mrs. Piper's script-intelligence, which called itself 'Rector,' was asked to show itself to Helen Verrall with a spear in its hand. 'Why a sphere?' asked Rector. The mishearing was corrected, but the confusion apparently persisted, for on February 4, Rector claimed to have shown himself to Helen Verrall with a 'sphear' (so spelt). The claim was unsubstantiated so far as Miss Verrall was concerned; but on January 31, Mrs. Verrall was seized by an impulse to write automatically and produced a brief script in a mixture of Greek and Latin that was only in part intelligible but contained both the word 'sphere' (in its original Greek form *sphaira*) and a Latin phrase descriptive of a spear (*volatile ferrum pro telo impinget*). This looks pretty much like a successful experiment in telepathy between the living, save that the telepathic 'message' was picked up by the mother instead of the daughter. That it emerged in a mixture of Greek and Latin is not particularly surprising: Mrs. Verrall was conversant with both languages, and her earlier scripts were mostly written in dog-Latin and Greek.

The very ambiguity and vagueness of even the best cross-correspondences is the surest proof of the automatist's honesty.

Another distinction is that between 'simple' and 'complementary' cross-correspon-dences. The most obvious kind of simple correspondence is one in which the same thought is independently expressed, preferably in the same words and at about the same date, in the scripts of two or more automatists. Examples of this have occurred occasionally. A good instance is the 'Thanatos' correspondence, where within a fortnight the key idea 'death' was independently expressed in three different languages by three different automatists—Mrs. Holland, Mrs. Piper, and Mrs. Verrall. The weakness of this case is that in a series of communications purporting to come from the dead the theme of death is, to say the least, a pretty obvious one. It does raise an interesting question: how did Mrs. Piper, who knew no Greek, get hold of *thanatos*, the Greek word for death, which seems to have conveyed nothing to her conscious mind?

Psychic Jigsaw

More frequent and more important, is the complementary type; indeed, some writers recognize only this type as constituting a true cross-correspondence. The ideal complementary case would be one in which a coherent and significant message was split into several fragments, each meaningless by itself, with each being successively communicated through as many different automatists; the sense of the whole appearing only when their contributions were put together, forming a kind of jigsaw puzzle. It must be admitted that no actual cross-correspondence fully conforms to this ideal model. The 'complementary' fragments are usually found interspersed with irrelevant matter; the interval of time between one such fragment and the next is often rather long; and the 'message' when finally deciphered is not always so meaningful as could be wished. There are, however, a large number of cases that approximate in varying degrees to the ideal type. Most of them are highly complicated, turning as a rule on obscure literary allusions. For that reason they can be appreciated only by intensive study and are virtually impossible to summarize. All that can be done here is to quote briefly a single, relatively straightforward, example.

On January 16, 1907, Piddington asked Mrs. Piper's 'Myers' intelligence to mark attempts at cross-correspondences in some way, say by drawing a circle with a triangle inside it.

On January 28, Mrs. Verrall's script opened with the word *aster* (Greek for 'star'), followed by a number of what seem to be free associations with the word. Then came the following passage (the words italicized are partly quotations from, partly garbled reminiscences of, Browning's poem *Abt Vogler*): 'the hope *that leaves the earth for the sky*—Abt Vogler *for Earth too hard* that found itself or *lost itself—in the sky*. That is what I want. *On Earth the broken sounds—threads—In the sky, the perfect arc. The C major of this life.* But your recollection is at fault.'

After this came two drawings of a triangle inside a circle, with another reference to 'the part that unseen completes the arc.'

On February 3, Miss Verrall's script included drawings of a star and a crescent moon, with the words 'the crescent moon, remember that, and the star.'

On February 11, 'Myers,' writing through Mrs. Piper, claimed to have referred through Mrs. Verrall to 'Hope and Browning' and also 'Star.'

On February 17, Miss Verrall's script contained another drawing of a star and the words 'the mystic three (?) and a star above it all.' (This has been taken as an allusion to the line in *Abt Vogler,* 'That out of three sounds he frame, not a fourth sound, but a star,' which is an apt analogy to a complementary cross-correspondence.) Finally, on April 8, 'Myers,' writing through Mrs. Piper, stated that through one of the other automatists he had drawn a star and a crescent.

Voices from the Grave

The question of how such complementary correspondences are to be explained is one of the most difficult and disputed questions in the whole field of psychical research. Four different explanations are theoretically possible: fraud, chance, telepathy from (or possession by) the dead, and telepathy between the living. The first of these, however, can be discarded with confidence. That a large number of persons of high intelligence and high moral standing should without apparent motive have conspired together to deceive the world and should have kept up the deception for some thirty years is psychologically incredible. The very ambiguity and vagueness of even the best cross-correspondences is the surest proof of the automatist's honesty.

The hypothesis of sheer chance has a different status. No exact limit can ever be set to the possibility of chance coincidence, and the sceptic can argue a number of considerations that suggest that chance may have played a greater part in the production of correspondences than the investigators have been willing to admit. However, the fact remains that very few who have made a careful study of the complete evidence have found it possible to regard the correspondences as *purely* accidental.

There remains the alternative choice either of postulating a rather unusual kind of telepathy between the living or of accepting in some form the actual agency of the dead. Most of the original investigators came to prefer the second view for three main reasons. There was, first, the testimony of the scripts themselves: if the true agents were the subconscious minds of the automatists, why did they persist in calling themselves 'Myers,' 'Gurney,' and so on? Would not this have been a joint 'conspiracy to deceive' such as we have already rejected? Second, and more important, there was the argument from design. 'Simple' correspondences might indeed be explained by telepathy between the automatists, but how could this apply to 'complementary' cases, where the overall design was not understood by any of the automatists until their scripts were put together and compared? If none of them knew the design, none of them could have invented it. And thirdly, if one of the automatists was nevertheless the designer, how did she collect the materials for her design, some of which were outside her normal knowledge? Are we to picture her subconscious mind rummaging in the minds of her colleagues, until she came on precisely the items required for the correspondence? Such *selective* telepathy, it was urged, was unexampled and hard to conceive.

Unsolved Problem

To these arguments tentative answers have been offered by a number of critics. (1) To the argument from the consensus of the scripts their reply is that such dramatization is characteristic of all subconscious products, including ordinary dreams, and that at this level no real distinction can be drawn between believing and make-believing. Since it was Myers's death that set the whole movement going, 'Myers' naturally becomes the hero of the drama; and a dissociated fragment of Mrs. Verrall's mind groping after an identity, may declare I am Myers 'with a confidence as innocent (and perhaps as temporary) as that of the small child who states I am a steam engine.'(2) The argument from design has been countered by pointing out that 'complementariness' does not in itself prove intention. Ordinary telepathic impressions often emerge undesignedly in just the same fragmentary and enigmatic way: the famous Gilbert Murray experiments furnish good examples. (3) If, however, we concede that some correspondences do involve deliberate planning, the critic may urge that it is still unnecessary to attribute the planning to the dead. We do not know how telepathy works, in this case or in any other, but we need not imagine it in terms of picking out bits of the jigsaw from someone else's mind; we are equally free to think of an automatist subconsciously constructing the puzzle out of material already available to her, some of it familiar to her conscious self, some of it once familiar but now dropped out of conscious memory, and some which has drifted in on the accidental winds of telepathy. And if we ask 'What automatist?' a case can be made for replying 'Mrs. Verrall.' She had known Myers well; she was the first of the group in the field and the first to hint at correspondences in her script; she possessed most of the classical learning needed for the construction of certain recondite puzzles; she had reported cases of spontaneous telepathy from her husband and her daughter long before she took to automatic writing; and, finally, after her death in 1916 there was a marked falling off both in the quantity and the quality of alleged correspondences.

There for the present the discussion rests, and there it is perhaps likely to remain until the complete body of script material is made available for study and analysis.

E. R. DODDS

FURTHER READING: Proceedings of the Society for Psychical Research. *(London, UK: 1906); H. F. Saltmarsh.* Evidence of Personal Survival from Cross Correspondences. *(New York, NY: Arno, 1975); E. D. Mitchell.* Psychic Exploration. *(Wiltshire, UK: Paragon, 1979).*

Cult of the Dead

In the Guattari cave on Monte Circeo, on the Italian coast north of Naples, there was found in 1939 a solitary skull, lying on a platform of earth and stones. Round the skull was a circle of stones, and strewn about the floor were the bones of deer, buffalo, and horses, and also the lower jaw of another human being. The skull belonged to a man aged forty or fifty, who had been killed by a blow on the right temple with a sharp weapon. There were indications that the brain had been extracted, perhaps to be eaten. The skull may originally have been set up on a stake, the ring of stones suggests a magic circle and the animal bones may be the remains of offerings to the skull or of meals eaten in its presence.

Since prehistoric men left no written explanation of themselves, much of what can be said of them is highly speculative but it looks as if this skull was worshipped in some fashion,

Art depicting a Grim Reaper titled *Another Nightmare,* found on an Royal Air Force plane

though it is not certain that its owner was murdered: he may have been killed in battle or by accident. What is certain is that one of the most striking differences between men and other animals is that animals ignore their dead and men do not. Men treat their dead with love, hatred, awe, sorrow, or even with appetite, but rarely with casual disregard.

Lying behind this is an even more important distinction. Unlike the other animals, a man is aware that he himself will eventually die. The effects of this realization on human behaviour have been incalculably great. It is the root of the hope for a life beyond death and it is probably one of the roots of belief in supernatural beings that do not die, which create and maintain the order of Nature, on which each man depends for his brief Earthly existence.

The Dear Departed

The men or manlike creatures who lived in the Choukoutien caves near Peking about 500,000 years ago already used fire and made rough tools. They may also have been cannibals who ate the brains and the marrow of the bones of their dead. Perhaps they did this (if they did it at all) merely because they liked the taste, but if they believed that in eating the dead they acquired their strength and skill, or that the dead lived on in the bodies of their eaters, this is the earliest trace of a cult of the dead, in the sense of a belief that something survives death and that what survives has power and requires special treatment.

Later, though still very early, burials suggest concern for the dead and possibly fear of their power. In the Teshik-Tash cave in Uzbekistan, in central Asia, a child had been buried in the middle of a circle of ibex skulls. In a cave on Mount Carmel in Palestine the bodies of five men, two women, and three children had been trussed up with their knees drawn up to their bodies. This may have been done to save space and so make grave-digging less taxing. Or it may have been a magical attempt to help the dead to be reborn, by arranging them in the position of a foetus in the womb. Or it may have been meant to stop the dead from getting out of their graves and attacking the living. Or death may have been seen as a kind of sleep and the bodies arranged in a sleeping position, in which case our euphemism 'laid to rest' is an extraordinarily old one.

Later still, though before true man had emerged, Neanderthal burials in Europe show care and respect for the dead, possibly tinged with fear. Of six skeletons discovered near La Ferrassie in central France, all except one had been buried facing west. The west is the direction of the dying sun in the evening, and it was later widely believed that the far west was the home of the dead. The single exception was a body that faced east and had been trussed before burial with the legs drawn up. Perhaps this elderly woman had been feared in life and was still feared in death.

But Neanderthal burials generally suggest an affection for the dead. They were buried under the floors of the caves in which the people lived, sometimes near the hearth, presumably to give the cold corpse warmth and perhaps with the feeling that the departed was still one of the family and should keep his accustomed place by the fire. The fact that tools and joints of meat were buried with the dead suggests that they were thought to be still alive somehow, somewhere, and that it was the duty of the survivors to help them.

The Place of Skulls

In the Upper Paleolithic period (c. 30,000 to 10,000 BC) *homo sapiens* himself, with a brain markedly larger than that of the average modern man, spread from Asia into central and Western Europe, and across northern Africa into Spain. He again buried his dead with care, close to the living, and often sprinkled red ochre on them, apparently to give them the blood-red colour of renewed vitality. The dead were dressed in their best, hung with valuable ornaments, and generously equipped with food and weapons, which means that the living made real sacrifices, in the literal sense of the term, for their dead.

Dating from the Mesolithic period in Europe (c. 10000 to 3500 BC) are the thirty-three human skulls found in the Great Ofnet cave near Ndrdlingen in Bavaria. All of them faced west and were covered with red ochre. At least five, and possibly twenty-one of these people had been killed by hatchet blows. This collection of relics may have belonged to headhunters, who thought that by taking their victims' heads they acquired an extra supply of human energy. Or the heads may have been buried with ceremony to pacify the angry ghosts of the murdered.

These heads, like the Monte Circeo skull and the human skulls found at Catal Huyiik in Turkey, resting on what was apparently an altar of the great mother goddess, suggest that the head was already regarded with particular awe, as it certainly was later. The head is the part of the body with which a man breathes, sees, hears, eats, talks, and thinks. It is the part that you think of as preeminently *you*, the home of your personality, and it was perhaps already believed to contain the essence of a person's life-energy and character.

The earliest surviving realistic portraits of human beings were found at Jericho in Palestine, dating from not later than 6250 BC. They are human skulls covered with plaster, in which the features were modeled, with eyes made of shells. They probably come from a family portrait gallery and represent ancestors who were venerated by their descendants. The practice was apparently fairly common at Jericho, because quite a number of decapitated skeletons were found buried under the floors of houses.

Replica of a man's skull found in the Choukoutien caves, Peking, China. Presented at the Paleozoological Museum of China

The Panoply of Death

The Neolithic period (from c. 3500 BC) saw the spread of the techniques of breeding cattle, as distinct from hunting them, and growing crops instead of merely gathering them. Presumably these changes would have strengthened the feeling that a man's land and herds were his because his forbears had owned them, that they were the gifts of his ancestors and belonged to his family—past, present, and future—a feeling that lies at the root of ancestor worship. This period has left plentiful evidence of human attention to the dead, especially to those who had been powerful in this life.

At Alaca Huyiik in Turkey the stone-lined graves of chieftains who ruled from c. 2400 to 2200 BC contained astonishing quantities of gold, silver, and copper objects—daggers, maces, battle-axes, cups, and jugs, ornate pins, and mirrors. At the same period in Mesopotamia the royal graves at Ur were magnificently equipped, and there courtiers, soldiers and servants had been killed with their masters, no doubt to continue serving them in the afterworld. At Maikop in southern Russia a man was buried under a canopy that was partly supported by golden figures of bulls, and he wore a robe on which were eighty-seven gold plaques representing bulls and lions.

For the living to spend so much on the dead suggests a mixture of affection for them, an obligation to equip them fittingly for the life to come, and a healthy respect for the help and protection that they could give to those who survived them. The earliest written records in human history are concerned with securing a happy immortality for the kings of Egypt. In the forteenth century BC in China, the rulers of the Shang dynasty were interred with what has been described as 'extravagant pomp.' The king was buried in a wooden room at the bottom of a pit 45 feet deep and 65 feet square.

Other human beings might be killed and buried with him and in some cases he was given chariots and horses as well.

In the fifth century BC the great traveler Herodotus wrote a famous account of the burial of a Scythian king (in his *Histories*, book four). The Scythians lived to the north of the Black Sea. When a king died, they slit open the corpse's belly and filled it with pleasant-smelling substances, sewed it up again and buried the body, lying comfortably on a mattress, in a great square pit. They strangled one of the king's concubines and several other members of his household and buried them with the king. They also buried horses, golden cups, and a selection of his other treasures with him. Then they piled up a mound of earth over the grave and waited for a year.

After a year, they strangled fifty of the king's remaining servants, whose bodies were gutted and filled with straw, and similarly fifty of his finest horses. Then the men and the horses were impaled on spikes and placed round the tomb, each horse with its rider, and left there.

Herodotus also remarked that when an ordinary Scythian died, the body was taken by his family on a round of visits to friends. The friends provided meals, serving the corpse with food just like the rest.

Archaeology assistants clean a grave chamber (from Shan and Zhou dynasties (1600–3000 BC) at the excavation site in Chengdu, in southwest China's Sichuan province

The Megaliths

Meanwhile in the eastern Mediterranean area, burying the dead underground had begun to be accompanied by the building of structures above ground. These structures were sometimes far more imposing than the homes the dead had inhabited in life, like the colossal pyramids built to tower over the mummified corpses of Egyptian pharaohs. Before 2000 BC in Crete, for example, the dead were being buried in caves, or in underground chambers resembling the rooms of houses, or in chambers above ground.

This fashion in burials spread westward to Malta, Spain, Portugal, and southern France. Large stones (megaliths) began to be used for the walls and roofs of the tombs, an architectural style that spread to the rest of France and into northern Europe. Some of the tombs and the stones used were of huge size. Near Seville in Spain there is a tomb close to 70 feet long with a block of granite at the front of it that is 11 feet high, weighs 21 tons, and had been fetched from a quarry more than 20 miles away. At New Grange in Ireland, a burial chamber, with a passage 62 feet long leading to its entrance, was covered with a circular mound of earth 265 feet across and about 45 feet high.

Not all megalithic tombs were anything like as big as this but even the smaller ones required human sweat and toil far in excess of what would have been needed to tuck the dead neatly away out of sight. The monuments imply a powerful sense of awe and respect for the dead, and possibly an urge to keep them tethered to their graves, close to their kinsmen and descendants for the help they could give.

Many of these tombs seem to have been the burying places of a family, or a larger group of people, used over a long period of time. When a man died, apparently, his corpse was left

Dolmen de Axeitos, a prehistoric megalithic dolmen in the Province of A Coruña, Galicia, northern Spain

in the tomb with food, weapons, and other equipment, and the door of the burial chamber was walled up, to keep him inside. When the next corpse was to be buried, the door was broken down again and offerings were burned to honour the spirit of the first occupant. This would go on until too many bodies had accumulated, and to make room for newcomers the skeletons already inside were pushed out of the way and piled up in disorderly heaps at the sides of the burial chamber. The apparent disregard of these elderly bones suggests that, not unnaturally, when a person had been long forgotten his remains were no longer treated with great respect.

In Brittany, there is often a menhir (a single upright stone) at the head of a grave and the entrance of the burial chamber inside points toward the menhir. It has been suggested that the people who built these graves believed that the souls of the dead liked to come out to take the air, and that the menhir was both a perch on which the soul could rest and also a marker that would help it find its way back.

The Dead and the Goddess

It is possible that the use of large stones and mounds of earth to wall in and roof over the dead was a development from the older tradition of cave burial, and was connected with the belief that burial under a weight of earth was the right way to put the dead where they belonged, in the domain of the earth goddess. Some megalithic tombs in Europe contain paintings and idols of a goddess, pottery decorated with a face or eyes, and geometrical patterns that may be symbols or stylized pictures of the goddess. These representations are almost certainly derived from figures of goddesses in Asia Minor and the eastern Mediterranean.

Both in Europe and elsewhere, many of the representations of a prehistoric mother and Earth goddess have been found in burying places. Her connection with the dead was a natural one, for the dead were buried in the earth and it was the earth from which the crops sprouted. Perhaps to be committed to the womb of the earth carried with it the hope of a new life, just as the plants which die drop their seeds into the earth and are reborn again in due season.

RICHARD CAVENDISH

Ancestor Worship

The basis of ancestor worship lies in the commemoration of the dead. There are obvious reasons why the dead live on in the memory of the

In the Belly of the Earth

Then Fa and the old woman laid Mal gently on his side. They pushed the great gaunt bones of his knees against his chest, tucked in his feet, lifted his head off the earth and put his two hands under it . . . Mal's fingers were moving aimlessly and his mouth was opening and closing. Fa and the old woman lifted the upper part of his body and held his head. The old woman spoke softly in his ear.

'Oa is warm. Sleep.'

The movements of his body became spasmodic. His head rolled sideways on the old woman's breast and stayed there.

Nil began to keen. The sound filled the overhang, pushed out across the water toward the island. The old woman lowered Mal on his side and folded his knees to his chest. She and Fa lifted him and lowered him into the hole. The old woman put his hands under his face and saw that his limbs lay low. She stood up and they saw no expression in her face. She went to a shelf of rock and chose one of the haunches of meat. She knelt and put it in the hole by his face.

'Eat, Mal, when you are hungry.'

. . . The old woman took handfuls of water and the others dipped their hands too. She came back and poured the water over Mai's face.

'Drink when you are thirsty.'

. . . At a sign from the old woman, Lok began to sweep the pyramid of earth into the hole. It fell with a soft swishing sound and soon Mal was blurred out of shape. Lok pressed the earth down with his hands and feet. . .

The old woman squatted down by the freshly stamped Earth and waited till they were all looking at her.

She spoke:

'Oa has taken Mal into her belly.'

William Golding
The Inheritors

The Xiaotang Mountain Han Shrine, south of the village of Xiaolipu, in Shandong Province, China, is a funerary stone shrine from the early Eastern Han Dynasty (25-220 AD)

living. The greater part of man's behaviour, as well as the material surroundings within which he works, is transmitted to him from his forbears. This body of customs and artefacts that we call culture includes his language, his buildings, his art, and his social organization. None of these stand still; each generation makes its own contribution; but each does so in a cumulative way on the basis of the achievements of earlier generations.

This is especially true of rural societies. There a man is often exploiting the same productive resources as his immediate predecessors. In Australia the territory of a band of hunters is usually one that has been passed down from earlier generations. In agricultural societies, men are yet more dependent upon their forbears. Among the Ashanti of West Africa, for example, land was regarded as belonging to the earth, a female principle, but it also belonged to the ancestors. When a farmer began to cultivate his land, he sacrificed a fowl upon some mashed yam and said: 'Grandfather, you once came and hoed here and then you left it to me.' It was because his ancestor had hoed the land before him that he himself had the right to farm there.

An Influence After Death

It is useful to distinguish ancestor worship proper from the cult of the dead and from forms of memorialization. The interment of Yuri Gagarin does not imply any idea of personal continuity after death, and yet it is difficult to disentangle personal continuity from social continuity, that is, from the influence a man continues to have after his death. The cult of the dead implies a belief in an afterlife of some sort; the worship of ancestors recognizes their participation in everyday affairs; by appeasing the dead, or more often by failing to do so, we bring about their intervention in the world of the living.

However, ancestors are not just any dead; they are a man's specific forbears, his lineal kin, those who have socially and physically brought him into being. Hence there is a close association between the kind of kinship groups that a society possesses and the custodianship of the ancestral shrines. In Chinese society, where men belonged to their father's clan, custodianship followed the paternal line; it was the sons that looked after their father's shrine. Indeed, here, as among the Hindus and the ancient Romans and Greeks, a childless man might adopt a son to ensure that he had worshippers at his shrine (and an heir).
Even a widow might adopt a son in her husband's name and so preserve, as the Chinese say, the continuity of the incense smoke, which is burned at the ancestral tablets.

Incense is burned daily; other offerings, such as fruit, preserves, sweets, rice sprouts, fragrant wood, lotus flowers, and cooked food are made on festive occasions. At the same time the richer families employ a priest to read from the scriptures and perform rituals before the shrines. His function is to report the names of the dead (he has a complete family genealogy) to superior deities and to uplift them by reading the scriptures so that they are able to proceed to the Western heaven of happiness as soon as possible.

The Hell Named Kalasutra

In India the ancient Hindu Law of Manu recognized the obligation of a man's sons, by birth or adoption, to provide food for the dead. 'The ancestors of men are satisfied a whole month with sesame, rice, barley, black lentils or vetches, water, roots, and fruit, given with prescribed ceremony; two months with fish, three months with venison, four with mutton, five with the flesh of such birds as the twice-born may eat . . .' Such offerings are made at the *Sraddha* or mind-rite of the orthodox Hindu, when offerings to the ancestors can be made indirectly through the priests. 'Whatever mouthfuls . . . are eaten by the Brahmins are eaten by the ancestors,' writes another lawgiver. The food may be given to a cow, a kid or burned but 'that fool . . . that gives the residue . . . to a man of servile class, falls headlong down to the hell named Kalasutra.'

In societies such as Ashanti in West Africa, where a man belonged to the kin group of his mother and her brother, then the matrilineal descendants, the sister's sons, looked after the shrines. This did not mean that a man could not sacrifice to his father, but he had to do so through a member of his father's clan.

Offerings for a ceremony for dead people near the holy water in Nasik, India

The Watchful Dead

Worship of the dead (of which ancestor worship is one form) varies between simply warding off the dead with gifts lest they should intervene, and asking for their positive blessing in the way the Ashanti did. In Eurasia, ancestor worship often seems to be of the placatory kind. 'Death and life,' wrote Sir Edward Tylor (1832–1917), 'dwell but ill together, and from savagery onward there is recorded many a device by which the survivors have sought to rid themselves of household ghosts.' Funeral ceremonies are full of examples of customs whereby the ghosts are set apart from the living, particularly from their nearest and dearest, the widows and the orphans, who are seen to be in the greatest danger from their loved ones. In more generalized form, such sentiments seem to be associated with many offerings to the tombs of the dead. In China, India, and in the classical world, the dead appear actively to intervene if they do not receive their due. When they are treated properly, they are benevolent. If the Hindu dead do not receive their due, then they wander around as ghosts; if neglected, the Chinese ancestors apparently turn into demons and bring trouble upon the world.

There seems to be a division in Europe and Asia between good, appeased ancestors and bad, rejected ghosts or demons. In Africa such ghosts exist, persons who have not yet reached the Land of the Dead. However, the ancestors, as ancestors, seem to play a more positive role, both good and bad, in the affairs of men; translation of their immaterial forms into masks, figures, shrines, is more developed. These differences are partly related to the wider distribution of literate, universal religions in Eurasia. Islam, for example, forbids the representation of the human image; and the worship of the One God allows little room for the propitiation of ancestors. Nevertheless, just as Christianity took over some local shrines and turned ancestors into saints, capable of acting as intermediaries between man and God, so too the Muslims of North Africa turned the graves of ancestors into the tombs of saints.

In addition to these religious influences, there were also some differences in the organization of kin groups and in systems of inheritance that may have affected the worship of ancestors. It is clear that attitudes toward parental figures must affect the attitude toward the ancestors, the dead parents. In China it has been suggested that because a man often took over his share of the patrimonial property during his father's lifetime, his relationship with his parents was less hostile as a result; his advancement no longer depended upon their death. In Africa it is generally those ancestors from whom one inherits that one has most to fear; 'guilt' feelings apart, it is to them that one has a particular debt that needs to be repaid in offerings.

A Cambodian-Chinese woman and her child pray by their ancestors' graves during the Chinese ceremony Cheng Meng in Kampoang Cham province, China, on April 3, 2011.

The Shrines of Ancestors

At death the dead make their journey to the other world. But communication with them has to continue from this world. Even the memorialization of the dead inevitably tends to take on material forms; the appropriate behaviour is directed toward and focused upon a grave, or an object associated with the dead man or an effigy, such as a statue or painting. In this context, great stress is placed upon the actual burial, the actual dwelling-place, the actual representation of the dead. It has been argued that drama began with the acts and scenes of burial ceremonies, which incorporated drama and mime. However this may be, many forms of representative art are rooted in ancestor worship and memorialization of the dead. For the living individual, the portrait on the walls of the ancestral home ensures one's survival after death: and the greater the artist, the greater the hope of immortality. For the survivors, the creation of an image provides a point of contact, a living and enduring memorial.

Such memorials and shrines range from the abstract to the representational, these different forms often being found side by side in the same region, though it is true that the simpler the society the more abstract the style. In West Africa, the poorer agriculturalists have shrines of mud mounds or earthenware pots, or even of selected stones. Among the Ashanti, with their elaborate state system and

An artwork depicting The Coming of the Ashanti Golden Stool

richer resources, the ancestor shrine is a carved stool, which is blackened on a man's death.

The Ashanti stool is an example of the complexity of such ancestral shrines. It is a sign of an individual's status. A child will be presented with a small stool when, after seven days, he goes through the 'out-dooring' ceremony and acquires a real human personality. Different chiefships and different clans have their own stools, carved in a traditional way and often illustrating some appropriate proverb.

On such a stool only the office-holder himself may sit; when he rises it is placed on its side. For someone else to sit there would be a direct challenge, not only to a man's office but to his very existence. For so closely is the stool identified with the individual, impregnated as it is with the 'dirt' of his body, that his life itself is threatened by such an act.

The stool is at once chair and throne, the symbol of authority. The Ashanti believe that at the birth of their nation a golden stool descended from the heavens and became the most valued part of their regalia, the symbol of their new-found unity, the 'soul of the nation.' In 1900 when the British Governor of the Gold Coast, Sir Frederick Hodgson (1851–1925), tried to take possession of it in the name of Queen Victoria (1819–1901), the result was insurrection.

The stool represents not only the spirit of the nation, but also the spirit of the individual. At death a man's stool is seized and the white wood blackened with soot. It is then placed in the 'stool-house' of the lineage to which the dead man belonged, normally just a room in the elder's compound. Here it rests among the shrines of earlier dead, receiving offerings of food and flesh from the living members of the lineage.

Shrines and memorials may be collective or individual, the former tending to be abstract, the latter representational. Among the Ashanti only the stools of important members of the lineage are placed in the shrine-room. To the north, in Ghana, each individual Tallensi has a shrine, but only when he has been survived by two generations of descendants and therefore established his own 'house.' Among the nearby LoDagaa every man who leaves behind him a son (or whose widow produces a son to his name by marrying his brother) has an ancestor shrine carved for him during the long course of the various funeral ceremonies.

Few systems of ancestor worship are as elaborate or as specific as these, nor yet so closely linked with organizing the relationships between living men; for to sacrifice together to common ancestors is clearly a unifying bond of the greatest importance. In most societies, it is the more immediate dead that are man's primary concern. But here too the tombs, relics, and shrines, both abstract and representational, provide a thread of continuity between the living and the dead; not only do they represent a continuation of the same personality but they provide a focus for communication between a man and his descendants.

Lopsided into Paradise

A Chinese girl goes to the grave of her mother:

. . . I would return to this place, this being the eighth year of her tenancy, and draw her forth. With a Taoist priest of Macau I would come, which would pay tribute to my mother, and a labourer. I would expose the coffin and lift the lid. One by one I would take out her bones, first hiding the skull under my coat away from eyes. Then I would polish the bones with sand, the little bones of her feet I would polish first and place them at the bottom of the Canton urn. Next the leg bones I would take, and these I would perfume, and lay them next in the urn, then the rib cage, the arms, the tiny bones of the fingers—all these I would place most carefully in the urn lest I bring her lopsided into Paradise. On these, amid the incantations of the priest, I would lay the skull and cover the mouth of the urn away from flies.

Alexander Cordell
The Bright Cantonese

Food for the Dead

Ancestor worship is simply a form of communication between the living and the dead. The forms of the communication vary, though all fall within the range of normal human intercourse. There are verbal forms—prayer, oaths, written formulae. There are visual forms—gesture (usually gestures of obeisance), painting, sculpture, the temple itself, then dance and more extensive types of movement such as the procession and the pilgrimage. Finally there are the offerings of flesh and food that form so important a part of ancestor worship. The worshippers pay homage to a 'divinity' that was once a man, a 'god' who was once a producer and consumer, and in many cases owner of the very means by which the living continue to produce—the land, the oxen or the ploughshare. So the dead continue to be offered the basic food and drink of the country, the bread and the wine, the yam and palm sap, the porridge and the beer.

But service to the dead cannot be the simple duplication of service to the living; the things of this world have a different meaning for those who can no longer enjoy them in the same way. With food the ancestors receive only a part of the whole; with livestock, the whole is offered in sacrifice, but the biggest portion is in fact consumed by those who remain behind. As far as the ancestors are concerned, a major element in the transaction would seem to be not so much giving as repaying; one is in perpetual debt to the forefathers, just as one is to parents who have raised one from infancy; one can repay this debt only by continual piety in the shape of sacrifice.

Human Sacrifice

Sacrifice is of two general kinds. The regular offerings to the dead are made on festivals such as the three day period (the period of moon's rebirth, the period of Christ's resurrection) of Hallowe'en, All Saints, and All Souls. Then there are the occasional sacrifices made at times of affliction, when one's child is ill and a diviner has pointed to an ancestor as the cause. For the dead, while beneficent to their descendants, can also punish. Indeed recent ghosts and others who have not been properly settled in the land of the true dead, are often plain vindictive, sometimes so that the living will be forced to undertake the correct rituals on their behalf, or to right a wrong that has been done them. Whereas the regular transactions approximate to the payment of debt, to the fulfillment of an obligation, the latter smack more of a gift that tries to repair some damage done. But often the damage has itself been caused by failing to give the ancestors their due, thereby incurring their wrath.

Sacrifice is not confined to the ancestors: it is a way of communicating with supernatural agencies of all kinds. But there is one kind of offering of living beings that is often directed toward the dead—human sacrifice. The ritual immolation of human beings was widely practiced; it was found among practically all the Indo-European peoples; in early Israel, Samuel 'hewed Agag in pieces before the Lord;' it occurred in India and Japan, among the Aztecs of Central America, and in the forest states of West Africa.

Human beings (often criminals, slaves, or war captives) were also sacrificed to accompany the dead on their journey to the other world. They were used, as in the West African kingdom of Dahomey, to convey messages from the living to the dead, especially to dead kings. As the nineteenth century explorer Richard Burton (1821–1890) wrote, 'They periodically supply the departed monarch with fresh attendants in the shadowy world. For unhappily these murderous scenes are an expression, lamentably mistaken but perfectly sincere, of the liveliest filial piety . . . Whatever action, however trivial, is performed by the king, it must dutifully be reported to his sire in the shadowy realm. A victim, almost always a war-captive, is chosen; the message is delivered to him, an intoxicating draught of rum follows it and he is despatched to Hades in the best of humours.'

In the United States, Plains Native Americans went to war after a death so they would not 'grieve alone.' The Natchez of the lower Mississippi, practiced sacrifice at the funeral of a sun, or leader, killing wives, relatives, friends, all to accompany the dead—and others not connected with the dead man often volunteered for the same honour, while parents killed their children as extra sacrifices and thereby gained great status.

Human sacrifice, or 'ceremonial murder,' is akin to ceremonial suicide. Again the act is often associated with the cult of the dead. In earlier times Hindu widows were expected to sacrifice themselves upon their husband's funeral pyre. So too the

Japanese *hara-kiri*, when committed at a funeral, is in the nature of an offering to the soul of the dead.

Human sacrifice also lies close to cannibalism. For just as animal sacrifices are consumed by both god and man, so too man may be expected to consume part at least of the fellow humans he has offered. This practice was not very common, except as a ritual gesture. Indeed many societies, especially those following the major world religions, disapproved of the sacrifice of animals, let alone humans.

Royal Ancestor Worship

While the ancestors of ordinary men continue to communicate with their descendants, guarding over them and receiving their due, so the royal ancestors continue to be involved in the affairs of the state.

Indeed one of the strengths of dynasties such as that of Egypt or of Ashanti, one of the sources of their legitimacy and a discouragement to their overthrow, was their role as intermediaries between their subjects and their ancestors, the earlier kings.

In Ashanti one can see royal ancestor worship as a simple extension of what occurred among the commoners. But in the Middle East and Eurasia, ancestor worship in the full sense seems largely confined to the royal dynasty. At death in Egypt every dead man became the god Osiris, who was the king of the dead, associated with the idea of resurrection and the annual life and death of the cereal crops. There was no specific worship directed toward the individual, though the relatives of the dead often commemorated them. The worship of individual ancestors was largely confined to the burning of incense for the royal dead who were installed in their monumental stone pyramids in the valley of the Nile.

Crime and Punishment

A belief in the continued influence of the ancestors on human life is often an important factor in maintaining the laws and customs on which social life rests. In Rome, the man who sold his wife was given over to the ancestors for punishment; so too was a child who struck his father, and the violator of graves. It is over the most serious offenses against one's fellow men, such as fratricide and incest, that the ancestors are often the main instruments of social control, more important than the judges who administer the earthly punishments.

. . . the ancestors are often the main instruments of social control, more important than the judges who administer the earthly punishments.

The ancestors are never completely cut off from this world. Often they are seen as returning to the world in the shape of their own descendants, either by the process of reincarnation or by other kinds of spiritual identification. Among the Murngin, a hunting tribe of northern Australia, the soul of a dying man goes back to the 'totemic well' on the territory of his clan; it is from here too that the spirits of the unborn emerge to find a home in the womb of a wife of a clan member. When a man dies, it is his father's father or other grandparent that escorts him back again. Thus there is a continuous chain of being.

JACK GOODY

FURTHER READING: G. Clark and S. Piggott. Prehistoric Societies. *(New York, NY: Knopf, 1965); J. Maringer.* The Gods of Prehistoric Man. *(New York, NY: Knopf, 1960); Glyn Daniel.* The Megalith Builders of Western Europe. *(New York, NY: Penguin, 1963); E. O. James.* The Ancient Gods. *(New York, NY: Putnam, 1964); E. Ahern.* Cult of the Dead in a Chinese Village. *(Stanford University. Press, 1973); Jack Goody.* Death, Property and the Ancestors. *(Redwood City, CA: Stanford University. Press, 1962); John Middleton.* Lughara Religion. *(New York, NY: Oxford University Press, 1960); M. Fortes and G. Dieterlen.* African Systems of Thought. *(New York, NY: Oxford University Press, 1960); Francis Hsu.* Under the Ancestors' Shadow. *(London, UK: Routledge, 1948); R. J. Smith.* Ancestor Worship in Contemporary Japan. *(Redwood City, CA: Stanford University Press, 1974).*

Dance of Death

In dances of death, people reflect their attitude toward this final, catastrophic crisis in human life. Some people have regarded death with horror and they have feared the ghosts of the dead. Some express their grief in mournful ceremonies. Others try to cheer each other and the departed spirit by dance and song. Others again consider death a transfiguration, a door to another, better life. Similarly, the celebrations take many forms: impersonations of the image of death, imageless homage to the deceased, or joyous dancing.

Death was often personified as a grotesque skeleton, as in the medieval European Dance of Death. This is best known through frescoes and woodcuts, but it had a foundation in actual miming dances. Death in the form of a skeleton capered in turn with sinners of all classes and ages, cardinal, labourer, child. This dance was an expression of the medieval horror of death, despite the Church's promises of a better afterlife. Clown-skeletons, still cavort

A German painting of the *Danse Macabre*. Nine women of different social rank, from empress to fool, dance with the dead. The entire economy of salvation is depicted

in ecclesiastical celebrations descended from the Middle Ages. In Catalonia, Spain, skeleton figures dance during religious holidays, notably Carnival and Holy Week, sometimes at Corpus Christi. In the *danza macabra* or *bal de la mort* of the Ampurdan area of Spain, a quadrille of skeletons carries a scythe, clock, and banner. In Mexican *carnavales* Death is a horrid clown, armed with a pitchfork, descended from the Spanish impersonations.

The burial wake is another common manifestation. A motif of cheer and consolation pervades Spanish wakes. The mourners dance a lively *iota* or *eanario*. Catholicism has introduced the word 'angelitos' (little angels) for the spirits of recently deceased children. Mourners celebrate wakes with a *baraban* or *lucia* in Sicily and Tuscany, and with a jig in Ireland. African American wakes in South Carolina work up to a frenzied pitch of dance and song. Food and liquor contribute to the festivity of these wakes.

Banishing the Dead

Another form that the celebration may take is the release or exorcism of the spirits, motivated by fear of their evil potentialities as well as by affection. Native Americans of many tribes perform a series of funerary and anniversary rites. The California Luiseño banished the spirit from his familiar haunts with the *tuvish* and *chuchamish* (wake), and in memorials for all the dead of the past year or several years. They imitated the character of the dead persons in the *yunish matackish*. They burned images in the *tauchanish*. Similarly, until recently, the Yuma tribe in the Mohave desert burned rush images in a circular dance and a cremation ritual termed *keruk*. The Tarahumara of Chihuahua, Mexico, perform a *rutuburi* circle dance and a special death dance around their belongings, during a three-week fiesta. After a year they perform other dances—the *yumari* and *pascol*. The Yaqui tribe of Sonora, Mexico holds a fiesta and dance at the wake of a child, similar to a Catalan wake. They hold a special *matachina* dance or a *chapayekas* dance for members of these ceremonial societies. Another ritual finally releases the spirit.

Though ghosts are not feared quite as much among the Iroquois of New York State and Canada, these people do believe in them and make efforts to allay them. In case of a violent death, they dispatch a priest for prayers at the site of the murder. After four nights they sing for the release of the spirit and to aid its trip to the other world. After ten days they reinforce this supplication through song and dance. In the winter women chant and circle in the *ohgiwe* for their ancestors, with drum accompaniment. The assembly concludes with a feast and dances.

Chinese and Japanese Buddhists celebrate the Feast of Lanterns as memorials to their ancestors. Japanese villagers, especially in Asage, circle counter-clockwise in the *Bon Odori*, during mid-July or in August, in connection with harvest celebrations. Men and women sing as they gesture or clap their hands; sometimes they also have a musical accompaniment.

In some instances there may be a fusion of the concept of death and resurrection. Boys' puberty rites may enact the symbolic death of the initiates and their rebirth to a new status. Funeral rites of antiquity often included the hope of resurrection. The high kicks of Egyptian female mourners symbolized new life. The Egyptian Osiris rituals and the Greek spring festival for Dionysus mimed the death and final resurrection of the deity. Babylonians and Romans had similar customs. In the Middle Ages, funeral dances symbolized resurrection by a kiss between male and female performers, with the anticipation of new life. The Hungarian *Gyas Tanc* perpetuates this concept.

Relics in modern children's games of many countries form yet another manifestation. English and US children preserve the actions and song words of ancient funeral rites, as in *Old Roger is Dead, Jenny Jones,* and *Green Gravel.* In their Hallowe'en masks and pranks small children perpetuate All Soul's ceremonies for the return of the spirits and propitiatory food offerings.

Impersonations of death are also found in modern art dances. Two German choreographers visualized death as an ugly thing: In *Totenmahl* or *Feast for the Dead* (1929), Mary Wigman masked her group in white, cadaverous faces, as homage to the dead of World War I. In his *Green Table* (1933), Kurt Jooss (1901–79) envisaged the figure of death in wartime as a skeleton resembling the great reaper of the Middle Ages. A few years later, in 1937, José Limón (1908–72), created his *Danza de la Muerte,* and Andrée Howard (1910–68) produced *Death and the Maiden* to Schubert's music for the English Ballet Rambert. These modern spectacles echo the anxieties of folk laments.

FURTHER READING: F. Eichenberg. Dance of Death. *(New York, NY: Abbeville Press, 1983); L. P. Kurtz.* The Dance of Death and the Macabre Spirit in European Literature. *(New York, NY: 1934).*

Death

If man has always felt that the mystery of life must be explained, he seems to have had an equally urgent need to account for the humiliating outrage of death. It is almost as if life, despite its trials, was too good to be true and death, despite its apparent peace, too ghastly to be true. In stories from all over the world, death is an intruder: he was not there at the beginning but made an early entrance. Very frequently he arrives as the result of a mistake, of a message wrongly delivered. Sometimes he is a punishment, visited upon mankind for disobedience, ingratitude, or sheer stupidity. In many myths, death comes by agreement, as the outcome of a debate between divinities (one of whom may be malevolent) or among the first men and women themselves.

These three types of myth about the origin of death—the error, the penalty, and the decision—are found among many different and widely scattered peoples and it is also quite common for the various features to be combined in a single story. There is a constant recurrence of the idea that death was, in the first days, meant to be temporary and that human beings, but for a tragic and original mischance, would have repeatedly renewed their lives like the moon or like lesser beings, such as snakes and crabs, which (it was thought) took on a new lease of life when they sloughed their skins or shed their shells. This concept of lost renewal occurs in all the three main types of myth.

The Message that Went Astray

The myth of the mistake, of the message that went wrong, is especially common in Africa. In many versions, the chameleon is sent by God to tell the first men that they are to have the gift of immortality; but he dawdles on his way and is overtaken by the lizard, the swifter messenger of death. The Gallas of East Africa tell how God sent a bird with the message that men were to renew their lives by changing their skins.

Samuel Daniell's 1805 painting shows the Khoikhoi preparing to move. The Khoikhoi people believe that the moon sent an insect to tell them of death.

The bird came across a snake feeding on some meat; he was hungry and promised the snake he would tell him 'God's news' if he gave him a share. The serpent finally agreed and the bird told him that men would grow old and die but that all he had to do was cast off his skin to be young again. In his anger, God punished the bird for his treachery and greed by giving it a painful disease, which makes it sit on treetops and bleat sorrowfully, whence it is called *holowaka* or 'the sheep of God.'

In a myth of the Khoikhoi of southern Africa, the moon sent an insect to tell men that they, like herself, 'would die and dying live.' The insect, going slowly on his way, was met by a hare who asked him his business. The hare said he was quicker and was willing to take the message. The insect agreed but the hare (whether through malice or stupidity is not clear) garbled the message and told men that, unlike the moon, when they died it was the end of them. The moon was angry with the hare and struck him with a stick, splitting his lip. Some say the hare, in the struggle, scratched the moon's face with his claws, which is why her surface is pitted. Others declare it was not the hare's fault. He delivered the message correctly at first but the people refused to believe him, shouted at him, and so confused him that he finally told them the opposite of what he should.

The myth of the wrongly transmitted message is also found in southeast Asia and Oceania but there most of the death-origin stories seem to centre on the motif of skin-changing. In parts of Polynesia it is said that at the beginning, all changed their skins when they grew old and renewed their youth. One day, however, a child cried when he could not recognize his 'new' mother; she was so sorry for him that she put her old skin back on again and later died, as did all other people thereafter. There is a curiously similar African story of a couple who sent their children to fetch water in a basket while they were changing their skins. The children tired of their hopeless task and came back to the hut. The father chased them away but they crept stealthily back and saw their mother half in and half out of her new skin. Whereupon she died and brought death into the world.

God made man to be immortal and kept a close watch on Death who was always trying to pick quarrels with men and provoke them to a fight that he knew he would win.

The Arawaks of Guyana have a story according to which the benevolent creator visited the earth to see how the first men were faring but they were ungrateful and attacked him. So he took away their 'immortality' and gave it to the lizards, snakes, and beetles.

In the Orinoco basin it is believed that God intended that men should be immortal by changing their skins but an old woman laughed at such a seemingly ludicrous idea. God was offended and sentenced mankind to mortality.

The Great Punisher

The concept of death as penalty or punishment, often for the foolish action of a woman, is found in many parts of the world, besides the story of Adam and Eve in the book of Genesis. The aborigines of New South Wales tell how in the beginning God forbade the people to go near a certain hollow tree in which bees had made their nest. The men obeyed but the women wanted the honey. Finally, one of the women hit the tree with an axe and out flew death in the form of a bat that now claims all living things by touching it with its wings.

In Baganda legend, Kintu, the first man is permitted, after many trials and tests, to marry one of the daughters of heaven. God sends the pair to live on Earth and gives them gifts, including a hen. He tells them to hurry lest they meet Death (the bride's brother) and not to come back if they have forgotten anything. The woman forgets the hen's feed and goes back for it, at which God, in his displeasure, grants Death's request to accompany them. Death keeps claiming the children as they are born but is prevented from taking them. Kintu appeals to God who relents and sends another of his sons (called 'Digger') to take Death back to heaven. God ordains silence during the pursuit as Digger chases Death who has hidden in the ground; but the children's cries break the spell and Death is allowed to remain on Earth and strike down living things.

The Algonquin tribes of North America say that immortality was granted to men by the Great Hare, himself the source of vital energy. The gift was in a little package that their first ancestor was forbidden to open. But his wife, the Pandora of the New World, could not restrain her curiosity and peeped inside. As she did so immortality flew away, never to return.

There is a very odd African story, told by people living on the shores of Lake Kivu, which shows God trying to save men from death but giving up in exasperation rather than inflicting a punishment. God made man to be immortal and kept a close watch on Death who was always trying to pick quarrels with men and provoke them to a fight that he knew he would win. One day God was away and Death killed an old woman. She was buried but after a few days her grave began

***Studies of Death* illustrated cover shows Death as bats flying out of the trees. Image taken from *Studies of Death*, originally published/produced in D. Nutt: London, 1894.**

to heave as if she were coming back to life. Her daughter-in-law poured boiling water on the grave and beat it with a pestle, saying 'Die: what is dead should stay dead.' The grave was then quiet and the old woman was really dead. God returned and seeing that the old woman was not there asked what had happened. When he was told, he said he would hunt Death down. Death fled in terror and met another old woman to whom he said, 'Hide me and I shall reward you.' She let him hide under her skirt and he entered her body. God caught them up and decided that, since she was so old, it would be best to kill her and tear out Death and kill him. However, Death slipped through his fingers and this time persuaded a young girl to hide him in her belly. God despaired: if human beings kept on thwarting his efforts to save them he might as well give it up as a bad job. So he let Death do as he pleased.

Upotos of the Congo say that the immortality meant for men was granted to the moon. This happened because in the first days God commanded the inhabitants of the earth and the moon to attend on him. The moon-men came straightaway but the earth-men delayed. In his wrath, God rewarded the moon with ever-renewed life and visited the earth with death. In the Admiralty Islands it is said that the first man, pursued by an evil spirit, was hidden by a tree within itself. The tree asked for two white pigs as a reward but the man brought one white pig and a black one smeared with chalk. The tree said it would help no more, so the spirits catch men and kill them. In the Celebes there is a belief that the sky, at first, was very close to the earth and God used to lower gifts to the first people on a rope's end. He let down a stone that they refused, and then a banana that they accepted. God therefore decreed that mankind would not be like the stone, immortal, but perishable like the banana.

Fatal Debate

One of the most imaginative myths of the origin of death is that of the Wintun of the Pacific coast of North America. It is said that Olelbis, being about to create men, sent two buzzards, brothers, to build a stone stairway between earth and heaven, at the top of which there were to be two springs, one for purification and the other for drinking—the 'fountain of youth.' As they laboured, Sedit the coyote, the mischievous, and clownish creator, came and tempted them. Is all their hard work, he asks, really worth it? Will men and women want to go on ascending and descending the stairway, endlessly repeating their lives? 'Joy at birth,' he says, 'and grief for the dead are better, for these mean love.' The brothers are persuaded and destroy what they have built. But the younger says that Sedit too must take his own advice and die. In frenzied terror, Sedit makes himself wings of sunflower petals and tries to fly to heaven; but his wings wither and he falls. Olelbis says his own words have condemned him and hereafter all men will die.

The poignancy of this story is reflected in one told by the Eskimos of Greenland. At the beginning, they

say, there was no death and no sun. One old woman declared she would be happy without light if there were no death. However, another said that if it were not possible to have the one without the other, it would be better to have both, for life without light was unbearable.

This brings us to the third type of death-origin myth—mortality as the result of a debate, a theme that has appeared in some of the stories already mentioned. The tenderness of the last two tales seems to be peculiarly North American: it recurs in a Blackfoot myth of the discussion between the first old man and the first old woman. The man wanted immortality but the woman said there would then be too many people, and, besides, if people died they would be able to feel sorry for one another. They agreed to leave the matter to a sign: they would throw a piece of buffalo bone into the water—if it floated they would opt for immortality, if it sank, for death. The woman, who had magical powers, changed the fragment into a stone and hence we all die.

In Oceania the debate is, it appears, always between two supernatural beings, one of whom proposes life (often by skin-change) and the other death; the second always prevails, since he who has the last word wins. Sometimes one deity is openly malevolent. In the Banks Islands the story is told that Qat, the good god, made wooden images and vivified them by drumming and dancing before them. However, he was succeeded by Marawa, the evil and jealous god, who buried his images and killed them.

Opposite page:
Lords of the Cremation Grounds dance to protect the cremation grounds from demonic enemies that would harm the Doctrine of Buddhism, Kingdom of Bhutan

The Larder of Death

Certain tales are remarkable in that they do not fall into any of these groups. The Aranda aborigines of Australia say that at the beginning first women and then men emerged from the rocks. The leading man was envied and hated by the others because he was nearest to the women, so they pointed a magic bone at him. He fell into a coma, 'died,' and was buried. He was not really dead, and his head and neck rose out of the ground; then came Urbura, the evil and enchanted magpie, who stabbed the man in the throat and commanded him to stay dead. The other men and women were turned into lamenting birds. But for Urbura all would have been well.

Save me from the claws of him who takes for himself what he sees: may the glowing breath of his mouth not take me away.

Perhaps the strangest story of all comes from the Ewe-speakers of West Africa. Yiyi the spider (another example of the cunning and greedy demiurge found in many mythologies) cadged meat from Death during a famine. Death had plenty of meat because he had made a great clearing in the forest and set traps in it. In return for continual supplies, Yiyi gave Death his daughter in marriage. Death told his wife not to go through the clearing when she went to fetch water but one rainy day she did and was caught in a trap. Her husband chopped her up for the larder. When Yiyi discovered what had happened he attacked Death with a knife and ran away in terror to the village with Death in pursuit. Death had never been to the village before, and as he lay in wait for Yiyi he amused himself by shooting at the women as they went down to the river for water. He then realized that here was game enough and he had no need to trouble setting traps for animals.

C. DE HOGHTON

Personification of Death

One of the earliest attempts to depict the horror of death has been found at Catal Huyiik, a Neolithic settlement in Anatolia dating from the seventh millennium BC. It takes the form of representations of black birds of vulturelike appearance menacing headless human corpses. The mythologies of ancient Egypt and Mesopotamia provide our earliest written evidence of the personification of death. In the legend of Osiris, this divine hero, who became a type of 'Everyman' in the mortuary ritual, was killed by the evil god Seth, who came to be regarded as the personification of evil; in art Seth is depicted as an animal with sharp pointed ears or horns, a long muzzle or snout, and a tail splayed at the end. He is never actually portrayed as the death god, however, nor is such a baleful being ever shown as such in Egyptian art. Yet, as the following Coffin Text of the Middle Kingdom (c. 2160–1580 BC) vividly shows, the Egyptians personified death realistically: 'Save me from the claws of him who takes for himself what he sees: may the glowing breath of his mouth not take me away.' It is possible that, during the Graeco-Roman period in Egypt, the god Anubis, long associated with the Osirian mortuary ritual, became the *psy-chopompos* (guide of the dead) or the death god.

The Angel of Death

In Mesopotamia, the Babylonians named the death god Uggae; but he does not figure notably in their mythology under this name. However, death was personified in a horrific manner. Thus in the famous

Epic of Gilgamesh, Enkidu, the unfortunate friend of Gilgamesh, dreams of his coming death as seizure by an awful being:

. . . he transformed me,
That mine arms were covered with feathers like a bird.
He looks at me (and) leads me to the house of darkness, to the dwelling of Irkalla;
To the house from which he who enters never goes forth.

An Assyrian text of about 650 BC actually describes the dreaded enemy in an account of the underworld, and pictures a grim figure with the hands of a man and the feet of serpents. There was, however, much fluidity of conception in personifying death; for another Assyrian text gives directions 'For making exchange for a man wanted by the Goddess of Death.' Indeed, Mesopotamian demonology provided a variety of grisly monsters associated with the underworld.

In ancient Hebrew literature, although the origin of death is attributed to the sin of Adam in Genesis (chapter 3.19), God is regarded as ultimately responsible for the individual's death. However, Hebrew thought, which tended to separate its god, Yahweh, from direct contact with human affairs, produced the idea of the 'angel of Yahweh' as the agent of death. In later Jewish folklore the angel of death is named 'Sammael,' meaning 'the drug of God,' since it was believed that his sword was tipped with gall: the howling of dogs announced his presence in a town.

In Iranian mythology death was closely associated with time, so that Zurvan, the deification of time, was regarded as the god of death. Thus an ancient Persian text states: 'For Zurvan there is no remedy. From death there is no escape.' The Persians conceived of two forms of Zurvan: one of them, 'Time of the Long Dominion,' was the form of time associated with death, since it brings old age, decay, and death. There is evidence that the idea of this form of Zurvan, with whom Ahriman, the personification of evil, was identified, was incorporated into Mithraism, and found expression in its temple statues of a lion-headed monster, adorned with symbols of time.

In the Vedic literature of India a god of the dead is known as Yama. According to the *Rig-Veda*, he was the son of Vivasvant and 'the first of mortals to die and enter that other world.' In later writings Yama becomes the judge of the dead, and in that role he appears in Tibetan, Chinese, and Japanese Buddhism. In Chinese belief, under the name of Yen-lo wang, he presides over the fifth hell. As Emma-O, in Japanese art, he is depicted seated at his tribunal, a fearsome figure in the robes of a Chinese judge. Hinduism, however, has other personifications of death. Mara, or Mrtyu is death personified. The concept has an important role also in

Remaining seated Buddhist statue venerated in rich orange gives the Terrace of the Leper King its name

Buddhist mythology, but rather as the personification of evil, being *papman*, 'the evil one.' The Hindu god Shiva, who is conceived as having an ambivalent nature, has on one side of his being Bhairava, 'the terrible destroyer,' who haunts cemeteries, and appears wearing serpents about his head, and a necklace of skulls. An even stranger conception is the personification of Shiva's destructive energy in the form of the goddess Kali or Durga—Kali means 'time.' Kali is of horrific appearance: her colour is black, she wears a chaplet of severed heads, and her many hands hold symbols of her nature—the exterminating sword, scissors to cut short the thread of life, and the lotus of eternal generation, for existence as an unceasing cycle of birth and death.

The Last Enemy

Greek mythology personified death in two forms. The more ancient conception is the more grim. Homer refers to the *ker thanatoio* (the fate of death), which was probably imagined as a winged harpy that snatched away its victims. The more sophisticated image of Thanatos (Death) was that of a winged youth, of heroic form, armed with a sword, such as he is shown on a column, now in the British Museum, that once adorned the temple of Artemis at Ephesus. Thanatos was portrayed in performances of Euripides' *Alcestis*, described as black-robed, winged, and armed with a sword.

In Christianity death has also been personified, although theologically it is regarded as the penalty of sin. St. Paul proclaims that 'the last enemy that shall be destroyed is death' (I Corinthians, chapter 15). In the Revelation of St. John (chapter 6), death is depicted as riding on one of the baleful horses. In the myth of Christ's descent into Hades, death is sometimes identified with Satan, and in depictions of the event Death often appears as a skeletal figure prostrate beneath the triumphant Christ.

In medieval art, Death is invariably represented as an animated skeleton, armed with a dart with which he strikes the deathblow. An interesting development of the idea appears in Holbein's version of the *Dance of Death*, for the skeletal figure of Death is shown with an hour-glass, thus symbolizing his association with time. Another striking example of this association is seen in Dürer's (1471–1528) engraving *The Knight, Death, and the Devil.* From this association emerged the Renaissance figure of Father Time, whose scythe, derived from the sickle of the god Saturn, symbolizes the mortal stroke that severs human lives.

S. G. F. BRANDON

FURTHER READING: S. G. F. Brandon. History, Time and Deity. *(Manchester, UK: Manchester University Press, 1965); P. Aries, translated by Patricia Ranum.* Western Attitudes toward Death. *(Baltimore, MD: Johns Hopkins University Press, 1974); John Hick.* Death and Eternal Life. *(New York, NY: Harper & Row, 1976).*

Divine Principles

During the late 1940s and early '50s A young Korean electrical engineer named Sun M. Moon, received a series of what he took to be messages from God that acknowledged him as none other than the returned Christ. Through his divine encounters, he came to believe that a new body of knowledge, *The Divine Principles*, was being revealed to him. This doctrine unveiled the laws by which God governs man, explained the causes of mankind's problems and God's purposes in human history, and also disclosed the manner in which the perfected and eternal kingdom of God would soon be established on Earth.

By the late 1950s Sun M. Moon had assembled several hundred followers in and around Seoul, Korea. To these believers he announced that the next few years would be the 'Last Days' of the 'world as we know it,' a period of 'cosmic tribulation and judgment.' The world was soon to undergo a dramatic, supernaturally caused transformation, through which his faithful followers would become rulers of a restored, eternal, and perfect Garden of Eden. Although this imminent transformation was to be effected by 'descending spirit forces,' God's Chosen People were obliged to play a role. They were to assemble a large number of converts in order to constitute a 'foundation of the new world.' This foundation was to be the elite that would govern the theocracy of the 'New Age.' And since the restoration of man to God's grace was to involve not just Korea, but the entire world, the foundation had to include persons from a variety of nations.

Throughout the 1960s Moon sent missionaries abroad—especially to Japan and the United States—to perform this work. Over the years, the movement gained thousands of converts, claiming membership in some sixteen countries. The impact of the cult, popularly called the Moonies, was considerable.

To these believers he announced that the next few years would be the 'Last Days' of the 'world as we know it,' a period of 'cosmic tribulation and judgment.'

Spartan Simplicity

Two of the most striking features of the Divine Principles movement are the intensity of the members' efforts to win converts, and the degree to which they sacrifice themselves to 'God's newly revealed plan.' If the movement remains a rather minor one, in terms of sheer size, it is not because of any lack of effort on the part of its members. The way of life defined as exemplary by Divine Principles believers is one of spartan simplicity and a virtually total commitment to winning converts. Ideally, the believer is expected to surrender all his material wealth to the movement, retaining only enough to enable him to survive while he carries on his missionary activities. While the members often work at conventional jobs, they keep for themselves only enough funds for the bare necessities of life and for the expenses of individual proselytizing. All the rest of their wages goes into a collective fund, to be spent on the more expensive missionary endeavors, such as printing books and leaflets, and renting communal houses and lecture halls. If a convert's spouse, parent, or other relative refuses to convert, it is felt best to sever the relationship altogether rather than risk possible interference with the primary task of witnessing. Occupational career commitments must be dropped unless they increase one's access to potential new and influential converts, for the imminent advent of a perfect world renders all conventional careers meaningless.

Periodically, missionary campaigns are held lasting forty days, during which thousands of people are sent through the countryside to win new converts. In preparation for, and during, these campaigns the believers fast and deny themselves even their few normal comforts. A diet of bread and water is defined as proper during such periods. During the campaigns some missionaries live by collecting and selling waste articles. The most devoted missionaries may even become permanent itinerants, especially in South Korea. One such missionary has related:

> *'My husband and I have been pioneering in different provinces, and to do this we had to send our four children into orphanages. I climb to a mount every day and gather brush and wood to make bundles of fuel to carry down to a village and sell. With the money I buy a few pounds of oats for my living. Supporting myself in this way, I proclaim the truth day after day and month after month.'*

The movement believes in extremely active supernatural forces, whose continual presence and acts are constantly manifest in everyday events.

Suffering, and enduring that suffering, for the glory of God and the restored world on Earth is a central theme of everyday life among the believers. Indeed, one *must* experience the suffering of living humbly and of missionizing intensely in the face of rejection, if one is fully to win favour with God or, more immediately, with Moon and fellow believers. On ceremonial occasions, Moon provided special prizes and accords special recognition to those whom he judges to have 'suffered most and for a long time and made a notable achievement' in winning converts.

Battle Between God and Satan

A significant part of the movement's appeal lies in the character of what is promised them in return for their sacrifice and endurance.

Beginning with their rule over the restored and reformed Earth within a few (unspecified number of) years, believers are assured of being virtual demigods for all eternity. Those who convert early, before the truth of the Divine Principles becomes self-evident, and who thus help to bring about the inevitable, will occupy the most favoured positions in the divine theocracy. It was originally stipulated by Sun M. Moon that when the millennium comes, the mass of those who are still unconverted will come before them for judgment. Those who did most to obstruct the movement will be assigned the lowest places in the new world. In the context of such massive and eternal reward, any present suffering and hardship is viewed by believers as quite minor. Now, of course, this time has been altered, though there is still the belief that judgment will come.

A particularly valued place is promised to Koreans. Not only is Moon the successor to Jesus and the 'Lord of the Second Advent,' but Korea is the New Israel and will 'serve as the priest nation for the rest of the world,' and as 'God's Chosen People' the Koreans will be favoured in the new order. Seoul will be the world capital and Korean will be the language spoken by all mankind.

The Divine Principles conception of reality also has an appeal of a more immediate and everyday character. The movement believes in extremely active supernatural forces, whose continual presence and acts are constantly manifest in everyday events. This world of supernatural forces is populated by spirit persons—humans who have died, and eternal figures such as God, Satan, and the angels, who are themselves divided into two warring camps.

God's forces are in constant battle with Satan's forces, contending for control of man in the material world. Since the Fall of Man in Eden, Satan has more or less dominated or controlled man, although the forces of God have continually attempted to throw off this domination.

Now that God has chosen Moon as the second Christ and has revealed his divine plan, this age-old struggle is entering its final and decisive phase. In this last stage, God's forces will win a permanent victory over those of Satan. The fact that these forces are locked in a fight to the finish is constantly manifest in everyday events. All events in the material world are caused by the actions of spirit persons in one or the other of the two camps. Persons in the spirit world cause events in the material world for a purpose related to this cosmic battle. Satan's spirits hinder and God's spirits help those in the material world who help God (in the form of the Divine Principles movement). Satan's spirits help and God's spirits hinder those who help Satan (which means all who oppose the Divine Principles movement).

This conception provides believers with a simple and powerful scheme for interpreting the 'meaning' of everyday events: anything that hinders or hurts a believer, the movement or those aligned with it, is an attack by Satan's spirits: anything that helps a believer, the movement or those aligned with it, is an act of helping or leading by God's spirits. Through constant application of this scheme in everyday life, members come to have an immediate and close sense of unseen forces operating on the physical order (for example, the weather) and intervening in world affairs, in relations among nations, in the latest national disaster, and in their own daily lives. Missed or caught buses, cars breaking down or running smoothly, poor and good health, missed and kept appointments, chance and arranged meetings, lost and found property—everything and anything—belongs to a world of spirit causality.

Opposition from Parents

As might be expected, the beliefs, dedication, and missionizing intensity of Divine Principles followers have indeed generated opposition. In South Korea during the 1950s, the movement experienced an especially difficult time. It was a favourite for 'expose' magazines, an object of condemnation by more conventional religions and an object of some concern to the government. Apart from the disapproval generated by the heterodox character of their beliefs, various kinds of irregularities (sometimes sexual) were alleged to occur within the movement and it was viewed as having a strong tendency to break up families. It should be noted, however, that matters of this sort have frequently been of concern to conventional citizens when faced with intensely committed 'end of the world' religions.

Perhaps as a result of its continual growth, the Divine Principles movement has more recently experienced less condemnation in South Korea. Syncretic religions, combining different religious beliefs,have a sizeable following in that country, making them a political fact of life. Recent regimes have apparently thought it wiser to attempt to gain the cooperation of such groups in fostering social reform rather than to suppress them.

Movements like the Divine Principles have an important function in developing countries. They can transform a passive belief in the natural and inevitable character of whatever exists into a faith that things can be changed—by God, man, or both. Though political leaders are apt to put little stock in supernatural forces as catalysts of change, they agree with the fundamental belief that things can be changed, and are disposed to support this belief almost irrespective of the larger creed in which it is embedded.

Moon presides over a blessing ceremony in 1982.

In preindustrial, developing countries such religions as the Divine Principles can be viewed as cauldrons in which are forged people amenable to the modern mentality.

Outside South Korea the movement began to 'take hold' only in the early '60s. While only tenuously established in most countries in which it claims membership, it experienced relatively strong growth in Japan. And, partially paralleling the early difficulties in South Korea, the missionizing intensity and devotion of its members generated opposition among the Japanese. In the main, this opposition crystallized around the fears of parents whose offspring joined the movement. In 1967 a group of deserted parents formed a national organization dedicated to getting their youth to return home and to resume their high school or college studies. Pointing to the Divine Principles' missionary intensity and glorification of suffering, the parents charged that their children have been 'brainwashed,' 'misled,' and 'made virtual prisoners' of the movement. The parents also charged, as a consequence of the movement's fasting practices, many of their children suffer from malnutrition. The group held demonstrations outside the Divine Principles' Tokyo headquarters demanding the return of their children.

It is in the United States that the Moonies aroused the most bitter controversy outside Asia. As parents became aware of what was happening to their children, they made efforts to rescue them from the organization, and had them 'deprogrammed.'

A Change in Leadership

People who convert to the Divine Principles seem uniformly to be persons who, prior to and at the time of their conversion, are experiencing a sense of meaninglessness both in their own lives and in the larger world. The Divine Principles' view of reality has a strong capacity to overcome this and to give a sense of direction.

According to the Unification Church, Sun M Moon ascended to a high plain on September 3, 2012. After his death, his wife and youngest son, Hyung Jin Moon became the heads of the church.

Like other millenarian religions, the Divine Principles has, over the years, become increasingly equivocal on the topic of exactly when the new world order will be established. In the same way that the early Christians had progressively to attenuate their millenarian expectations as they gained power and respectability, the Divine Principles movement may be entering the early stages of transformation into merely another established religion.

JOHN LOFLAND

Drummer of Tedworth

Poltergeist, probably the earliest well-attested one in England: at Tedworth, Wiltshire, in 1662, an itinerant drummer was arrested by a magistrate, who confiscated his drum; about a month later the magistrate's family heard drumming noises on the roof and pieces of furniture began to move about of their own accord.

Dying God

Several religious myths of the ancient Near East have in common certain features that link them despite important individual variations. Historians of religion since James Frazer (1854–1941) have labeled these common features as the myth of the 'dying god.' In *The Golden Bough* (1890) Frazer complicated the discussion for later researchers by mixing up the analysis of this ancient pattern of myth with his theory of the divine king, who was believed to be the source of vitality for his people and who was ritually killed for the prosperity of his successors. Frazer's theories on this last subject have suffered severe criticism and are not now thought capable of being sustained. However, in the volumes entitled *Adonis, Attis, Osiris,* Frazer collected a mass of valuable material that can be detached from the abandoned theories within which he there presented it. The essence of the matter may be briefly summarized as follows.

The lovely spring is sadly brief, and rapidly the rich vegetation disappears as it is scorched under the cruel sun.

In ancient Egypt, Mesopotamia, and Syria, legends relate how a god is killed, often by a wild boar or by an enemy whose symbol is a boar. The corpse is deposited in a river, or he is drowned. Through his death the vitality of Nature is lost. His loss is mourned by a goddess who goes out in search of his body. The finding of the corpse is a liberating act for the vegetation, and with this liberation the god returns to life once more. The myth is attached to an annual ritual for the recovery of the vegetation after the heat of summer.

In the Near East, the contrast of weather and seasons is extremely perceptible and violent in effect. The lovely spring is sadly brief, and

The Death of Adonis **(1709) by Giuseppe Mazzuoli (c. 1644–1725)**

rapidly the rich vegetation disappears as it is scorched under the cruel sun. For long months of dry, dusty, burning heat, water comes not from the sky but only from Mother Earth's resources below in wells and rivers. Under the impact of the fierce sun the vitality of Nature, man and beast dwindles to a minimum.

Primitive men watched this annual process with some anxiety. Modern scholars have often supposed that the recurrence of the seasons must have given complete confidence that the cycle would come round again. The ancient evidence shows that this rationalist supposition is false. The seasonal cycle was not an infallible natural law, and the entire prosperity of society depended on a good harvest. A bad year was awkward, a succession of bad years calamitous. Each year the menacing desert threatened destruction. Miraculously, the seed buried in the soil at seed-time sprang up to new life in the harvest but primitive men could not take this for granted.

Weeping for Tammuz

This fundamental experience of man in relation to basic necessities of his physical existence was expressed in many of the ancient Near Eastern myths. One of the oldest attested myths is that of the Sumerian shepherd god Tammuz. In Roman times Tammuz became identified with the Phoenician Adon ('lord'), whom the Greeks appropriated as Adonis. Originally Tammuz and Adonis were independent. The ritual of Tammuz took place at a festival in July when the vegetation had already gone, and consisted of passionate lamentations. The prophet Ezekiel describes with pain and displeasure a vision in which he saw Israelite women at Jerusalem who had so far compromised their loyalty to Yahweh that they were weeping for Tammuz. Mourning for the god's death was certainly the principal feature of the rite. Sumerian hymns tell how Tammuz was drowned and how the mother goddess Inanna (or Ishtar) descended to the underworld to bring him back from his imprisonment there.

The purpose of the lamentations is not certain. It may have been an expression of sympathy for the tragedy that had befallen Tammuz. Or it may have been an attempt to avert wrath by disclaiming responsibility for the catastrophe.

The ceremonial mourning at a time when the seeds were sown was universally known, and can be seen to have influenced the proverbial saying of the Hebrew psalmist, 'They that sow in tears shall reap in joy.' However, the Hebrews did not believe that there was any annual loss and recovery of vitality in Yahweh, and did not lament his demise in the hot summer.

The Mesopotamian rites for Tammuz were for the crops and flocks. The worshippers did not suppose that if they identified themselves with the god through participating in the mourning incantations, they could gain any personal survival of death or privilege hereafter. Like the ancient Hebrews, they expected no immortality other than that of their posterity.

It is a paradox of the history of Adonis that the cult is Semitic and yet that virtually all the extant sources for the study of the cult are not Semitic but Greek. In Greek myth, Adonis, young son of the Cypriot king Cinyras, died from a wild boar when he was on a hunting expedition. The boar was proverbial for its ravages in growing crops. In the *Iliad* (book 11) Homer gives a vivid description of the disastrous damage done by a wild boar. So the animal was an appropriate killer for a vegetation god. Adonis, however, represents not the harvest so much as the spring grasses and flowers destroyed by the summer heat. It was natural that in later times Adonis stood for the tragedy of noble youth cut off in its prime.

As with Tammuz, the rite for Adonis was one of lamentation, in which the women played the leading part. At Byblos in the second century AD there were impressive ceremonies at Aphrodite's shrine, with an open-air procession and hymns that concluded with a joyful looking forward to Adonis's return to life. Unfortunately no document records, either explicitly or implicitly, the interval between the day on which Adonis was ritually mourned and the day on which his future revival was celebrated. The cheerful ending to the festival was in any event an expression of hope for the future crops rather than of

The statue of Osiris, together with his wife Isis and their son Horus, from the State Hermitage Museum, St. Petersburg, Russia

presumptive confidence in Adonis's present achievement of renewed life. The lamentation for his death was always the principal characteristic of the July festival, and several texts that describe or mention the rites conclude with the funerary mourning without going on to describe the return to life which the lamentations were intended to encourage.

Osiris, God of the Dead

Some of the best known passages in the Old Testament express the moving reflection that man's short and transitory life is like the grass that withers and the flower that fades. Once there is a religious context in which there is expectation or hope of surviving death (as there was not in early Mesopotamia), it is no great step to suggest that man's personal destiny may well have some correspondence with the seasonal cycle of spring, the dying of summer heat, and the renewal of life in the golden harvest. If the vegetation revives, may not man do the same?

This step was explicit in the worship of Osiris in ancient Egypt. The well known Book of the Dead, with its immense collection of formulae and passwords that the soul needs to learn now in order to negotiate its passage hereafter, is a sufficient reminder of the obsessive interest of the Egyptians in their proper destiny after death. Osiris was first and foremost the god of the dead, with a special relationship to Pharaoh. At the same time, Osiris had functions and powers closely akin to those of the Mesopotamian god Tammuz. He was the wheat growing up to harvest, and above all the Nile itself, on whose annual flood in the summer months the prosperity and welfare of the country wholly depended (until the Aswan dam was built in 1902). Crops were sown on the mud flats that the receding Nile left as it subsided each October, and this fall in the level of the river was Osiris's death. Yet each June the power of Osiris revived in the waters coming down from the Ethiopian highlands, but which in ancient belief welled up from a subterranean water system bubbling to the surface at the first cataract.

Old Egyptian religion had three focal interests above all others—life after death, the monarchy, and the Nile as the source of agricultural prosperity. All three aspects found expression in the sacred myth of Osiris and his wife Isis. From the marriage of Isis and Osiris, earth and water respectively, sprang the life-giving wheat. But the myth related how Osiris was killed by his wicked brother Seth, who cut up Osiris's body and threw the pieces in the Nile. The death of Osiris was annually commemorated on the seventeenth day of the Egyptian month Athyr (November 13). But Isis, together with her son Horus, who was to be his father's avenger, went in a ship in search of the pieces to put them together again. On the night of Athyr 19 (November 15) the mourning worshippers of Cairo used to go down to the Nile to join Isis in her search. At the climax the cry went up, 'We have found him, let us rejoice together.' Ceremonies connected with the Nile flood are prominent in Egyptian religion throughout its history.

Side by side with his life-giving role in relation to the Nile and the fertility of the crops, Osiris was also of the first importance as king of the underworld that was his permanent home. He did not return from it to revisit the upper world. From his kingdom in the nether regions he caused the annual flood of the Nile and daily sent up the sun on its course. But his 'resurrection' was not a resumption of divine life on Earth, for he did not leave his infernal throne.

The influence of this Egyptian cult of Isis and Osiris became considerable in the hellenistic age of the Ptolemies and in the age of the Roman Empire. In a drastically reinterpreted form the veneration of Isis as a kindly universal mother spread throughout the Roman empire. A festival of Isis on July 19 marked the official celebration of the rising of the Nile waters and of Horus's revenge upon the wicked Seth. This was still being observed in the city of Rome in the fourth century AD. In Egypt the Church came to recognize the need for a liturgical commemoration at this time and put a feast of St. Joseph on July 20, making the Christian dragon-slayer, Michael the archangel, the new patron of the Nile flood.

At the winter solstice, on December 25, the Egyptians celebrated the birth of the son of Isis, Harpocrates, and led the sacred cow of Isis seven times round the temple of the sun. Twelve days later on the night of January 5–6, in the late Roman period, there was a festival at Isis's temple in Alexandria to celebrate the birth of her child Aion, the god of eternity. On this night the Egyptians used to fetch water from the Nile, believing that it would be invested with healing properties or even (so some claimed) be turned into wine.

After the fourth century this festival of Isis in January became important to the Christian Church in Egypt for whom Christ, not Horus or Aion, was the true sun and light of the world. The earliest evidence for the Christian observance of the feast of the Epiphany on January 6 comes from Egypt, and by the second half of the fourth century Christians throughout the Greek East were celebrating this day as Christ's Nativity, his veneration by the Magi, his baptism, his wine-miracle at Cana, and his feeding of the multitude. The greatly overloaded character of the feast becomes explicable if the original motive behind the institution of the celebration was to provide a rival attraction to the rites of Isis. John Chrysostom (c. 390 AD) relates how at the great baptismal ceremonies of the Epiphany, simple Christians used to collect some of the water from the consecrated springs and preserve it for its medicinal properties.

In view of this evident influence of the festival of Isis on popular Christian customs associated with the Epiphany, it is remarkable that Isis's feast on December 25 had no influence on Egyptian Christianity. Only Western Christians observed December 25 as the Nativity of the true sun during the first half of the fourth century, and this festival was first accepted into the Egyptian Church's calendar under Western influence in the fifth century.

Attis and Cybele

The religion of the great mother of the gods had its principal centre in Anatolia. In the hills of Phrygia and Lydia she was worshipped under the names of Cybele or Agdistis, with a great sanctuary at Pessinus, not far from Ankara. At Comana in Cappadocia there was the temple of another great mother goddess of Anatolia, Ma or Bellona, whom Cybele attracted to herself as part of her attendant train. The religion of these fierce Anatolian deities generated fervent and frantic emotion. Monotonous dirges were sung to the accompaniment of drums and cymbals. Repetitive rhythms induced wild excitement among the priests and worshippers who frenziedly scourged themselves and cut their bodies with knives (much like the priests of Baal encountered by the prophet Elijah), sometimes even castrating themselves in their ecstatic condition.

Cybele had a young male consort, Attis. The myth recounted that Attis met his death either by being killed when out hunting a wild boar, or after being put by Cybele into a state of Bacchic frenzy in which he castrated himself under a pine tree. Violets were

Statue from the Roman Empire showing Attis performing a dance of the Cybele cult

born of Attis's blood as the first flowers of spring. Attis's death was commemorated at a spring festival of mourning and fasting during March, culminating in ecstatic dances on the wild Day of Blood on March 22 and on March 25, the Day of Joy (*Hilaria*). In the fourth century AD this became the feast of his recall to life by his mother and consort Cybele. The ceremonies were preceded by an all-night vigil with lights. The day following, March 26, was kept for much needed rest, and on March 27 there was a ceremony of washing Cybele's statue in warm water with a procession at which obscene songs were sung to the accompaniment of indecent gestures, the purpose of which was probably to ward off evil spirits.

Much of the surviving evidence for the cult of Attis and Cybele comes from the late Roman period, at which date the interpretations of the rites, and perhaps some of the rites themselves, had undergone development and modification under external influences. By the fourth century AD the climax of the rite was coming to lie not merely in the lamentations and frenzied acts of self-mutilation but also in the self-identification of the initiate with Attis in the dying and rising process. Here he was assured of salvation both now and hereafter, and in the most solemn act of initiation he went down into a dark pit while the blood of a bull poured over him from above. In virtue of this the initiate was 'reborn forever,' *renatus in aeternum*, as a later fourth century inscription records. Before the fourth century, so far as the evidence goes, the intention in the sacrifice of a bull in honour of Cybele was the benefit of some great cause such as the emperor. In the late Roman period it was rather a private purification for the salvation of the individual soul. The original meaning of the vegetation rite for the welfare of society became secondary to the individual's personal quest, and the rites of Attis and Cybele, like those of Isis, were practiced with special tenacity by the wealthy pagan families that required a religion capable of being a viable alternative to Christianity.

Fresco with Dionysus from Rome, Italy, (first century)

In the fifth century AD Augustine of Hippo met a priest of Cybele who assured him that the religion of Attis and the religion of Christ were one and the same. Augustine did not believe him. The story exemplifies the extent to which late Roman paganism sought to oppose Christianity by taking over some of its more characteristic themes and claiming that the meaning of their myths was identical. Nevertheless the rites of Attis and Cybele never wholly lost their significance as a rite of spring for the crops. The representations of Attis in figurines show him as a shepherd with a flute and pine tree, in one example with a scourge of knuckle-bones, or dying by his pine tree, or dancing in frantic ecstasy. The resurrection theme, however, is never clearly expressed; and the mother goddess Cybele is never portrayed as a Pieta, mourning for her dead son. One custom that survived centuries was that of planting violets on a grave. It may have derived from the cult but this is not certain.

The Dangerous God

Dionysus was a deity of Thracian origin whose cult penetrated Greece in Mycenean times. The character of the Dionysian cult provoked opposition, not least from civic authorities in Greece, who were appalled when their womenfolk went off to dance by night upon the mountains, behaved as if they were drunk and in hysterical ecstasy tore up and ate the raw flesh of an animal. The cities tamed the Dionysiac orgies by giving them official status and by controlling their organization. At Athens the cult was domesticated and rationalized by being given the ritual form of tragedy and comedy. In Rome also there was consternation when Greek missionaries from southern Italy first brought the exciting nocturnal revels. Dionysus was identified with Bacchus, the god of wine, and turned into a jovial Falstafflike figure rather than the dangerous god of ungoverned animal vitality.

Dionysus's myth had various forms. Poems written in the name of Orpheus, the legendary Thracian seer, magician, and poet, relate that as an infant Dionysus was torn to pieces and eaten by the Titans. Zeus struck the Titans with his thunderbolt and out of their smouldering ashes fashioned man who thus remains a mixture of high divinity and low aggressions. Or, it was said, Demeter (Ceres) put the pieces together so that Dionysus was reborn. These and other variations of the myth reflect the different settings in which it was interpreted. Some, including Plato (who provides perhaps the earliest evidence for the existence of the myth), took the story as a theological allegory about human nature. Others saw it as a vegetation myth in association with Demeter and her mysteries at Eleusis near Athens.

A depiction of the Last Supper from sixteenth century by Juan de Juanes (1475–1579). Held in Museo del Prado, Madrid, Spain

Dionysus made a late entry into the myths associated with Eleusis. Originally, as in the Homeric *Hymn to Demeter*, the Eleusinian story simply told how Demeter's daughter Persephone was carried down to the underworld and then returned again to her mourning mother for half of each year. Additions were made as time went on. Rites, which perhaps were once for the propitiation of spirits of the underworld, incorporated agrarian features. Demeter was the wheat mother, venerated by workers on the land in Hesiod's time. It was natural that she should welcome Dionysus to Eleusis, at least as an occasional visitor, on account of his association with the vintage. Dionysus and Demeter were identified with Osiris and Isis by Herodotus. The Eleusinian mysteries therefore absorbed influence from agrarian types of cult, and were also associated with individual hopes of a privileged life in Hades for those admitted to initiation. But the death and return pattern of Persephone's myth was not important in relation to these personal hopes.

The ancient myths of the 'dying god' of spring and harvest grew closer together as they influenced one another, until in the late Roman Empire they were all understood as allegories telling the same basic story—the myth of an eternal cosmic return. The myths themselves incorporated elements from one another, and there was also some ritual borrowing. However, the earlier in time the history of each cult is traced, the more individual and dissimilar they come to appear. The crux of the matter is that the meaning of the rites and myths may differ profoundly according to the social and cultural context.

The Dying God and Christianity

The final and perhaps most fascinating question in an inquiry into the ancient myths of the dying god is whether these ancient symbols had either direct or indirect influence upon Christianity. For Christianity has a story of death and resurrection at the centre of the New Testament, a ritual meal of bread and wine, and a spring festival. In its later history it also came to portray the suffering mother and her divine child. The external resemblances are striking. But what of the setting and meaning?

The first Christians were Jews. That is to say that Christianity originated within a community that utterly rejected the vegetation cults of the ancient world and would not compromise with them. Ezekiel's condemnation of the women weeping for Tammuz is typical of the Hebrew standpoint taken as a whole. The Judeo-Christian tradition could never accept the notion of a god who suffered periodic loss of power and needed to be revived by propitiatory rites. If the Passover was once the spring sacrifice of seminomad shepherds, as most Old Testament scholars think (though this has been contested) nevertheless the Israelites never shared the view of their Canaanite neighbours that the deity's powers required annual revival.

***Noli Me Tangere* (Touch Me Not) at the Palais des Beaux-Arts de Lille, France, shows Jesus Christ meeting Mary Magdalene (c.1548–1553). Painted by the Dutch artist Lambert Sustris or Alberto de Olanda (1515/1520–1584) in Venice during the Mannerist Italian period.**

Recent investigation of the background of the New Testament, reinforced by the Dead Sea Scrolls, has seen emergent Christianity as being set almost wholly within a Jewish matrix. The present writer believes that this tendency in recent study has succumbed to the exaggerations that often result from the impact of new material, but could not dispute the broad truth of the position. The first Christians took for granted the traditional Hebraic understanding of the deity as transcendent and as existing independently of themselves and of the world. Such belief stands in the strongest possible contrast to the theology of the vegetation cults for which the god was wholly immanent in the seasonal processes of the physical world.

The Christians simply took over from the Jews the feasts of Passover and Pentecost: why they did not also take the autumn festival of Tabernacles is a puzzle for the solution of which only very tenuous scraps of evidence survive. The origins of Easter as an annual festival lie simply in the continuing observance of the Passover meal among the Christian communities. Nothing could have been more natural. In this traditional form the rite was practiced by the Christians before it acquired its full weight of interpretation as the unique annual festival of the resurrection of Christ. In New Testament times, as can be seen from Paul's first letter to the Corinthians, the resurrection was being celebrated each week on the first day of 'Lord's Day,' *dominica* as the Latin Christians soon called it. It was not difficult to hold a special commemoration once a year on the Lord's day that fell nearest to the Jewish Passover. Late in the second century AD after some difficult controversy, the annual Easter festival was transferred from the original date, which always coincided with Passover, to the following Sunday—that is, to the Sunday after the first full moon after the spring equinox.

The myths of Attis, Adonis, and Osiris were intended to explain the rites of the cult by referring to 'events' of immemorial antiquity; and by the first century BC they were generally understood as allegorical myths with a cosmological or psychological meaning. The Christians startled the contemporary world by declaring as sober record that their master who lived recently, and died under Pilate the governor, had risen again and was now living. It is evident from Paul's dry catalogue in 1 Corinthians, chapter 15, that they would not have existed as a community if they had not believed themselves to be reporting a fact.

If, however, the ancient legends of the vegetation gods cannot explain how Christianity began, it may nevertheless be possible to see signs of influence on later developments in the Church's history. It has already been suggested above that in relation to Christmas and Epiphany the historian is able to discern fairly clear evidence of either indirect or even direct influence. The Church found it necessary to provide counter-attractions on the traditional dates of great pagan festivals like December 25, January 1, and June 24, when the Midsummer festival became the nativity of John the Baptist. Early Christians had no qualms whatever about putting harvest and vintage scenes or the seasonal cycle on their sarcophagi or their mosaic floors. Yet here again the context of these symbols was significantly modified. The seasonal cycle, if taken as being no more than a poetic illustration and analogy, would naturally suggest the eternal round of transmigration or reincarnation. This the Christians utterly rejected as inconsistent with the unique value and meaning of this life.

The difference brings out a point that emerges with clarity from this comparative survey, namely that it is a mistake to assume that beneath the various forms within which religion finds expression there must be some essential similarity. There is not a universal myth of the 'dying god' that is adopted at a certain stage of human evolution and which appears in different societies and cultures dressed up in clothing of various colours. At least, if we begin from such assumptions, it is certain that we shall miss much of the truth about these ancient religions.

H. CHADWICK

FURTHER READING: J. G. Frazer. The Golden Bough. *(London, UK: St. Martin's Press, 1980); H. Frankfort.* Kingship and the Gods. *(Chicago, IL: University of Chicago Press, 1978); E. O. James.* The Cult of the Mother Goddess. *(Santa Barbara, CA: Praeger, 1959). A. D. Nock.* Early Gentile Christianity and its Hellenistic Background. *(New York, NY: Harper & Row, 1964).*

Dystopian Literature

The nightmare scenarios conjured up by the authors of dystopian literature are, by their very definition, the antithesis of *Utopia*, the perfect world of Thomas More's (1478–1535) island community and the subject of his 1516 classic work. Dystopian literature encompasses cautionary tales, is critical of existing political systems and social conditions, and apocalyptic in its narrative and conclusions. It is also the subject of some of the world's best science fiction—a reading list that can be at once gripping and terrifying.

Oldest of all dystopian tales is the *Epic of Gilgamesh*, written in

The science fiction film *I am Legend* is based on a dystopian book by the same title

Mesopotamia between 2000 and 1500 BC. In recounting the relationship between the king, Gilgamesh, and Enkidu, the man created by the gods—but who is doomed to be sentenced to death by them—the book draws the conclusion that death is final, inevitable, and, literally, in the lap of the gods.

Themes and Variations

Human vulnerability in the face of destructive forces beyond our control, whether natural or manmade, is a central theme in dystopian writing, and it is these forces that define its chief genres. These are also apocalyptic tales created to hone human sensibility to the realities of an uncertain future:

War: Much dystopian literature was written following the bombing of Hiroshima and Nagasaki in August 1945. Among the most notable are Neville Shute's *On the Beach* (1957), in which people in Melbourne, Australia, await their deaths as nuclear radiation gradually engulfs them following nuclear war in the northern hemisphere; and Alexander Key's *The Incredible Tide* (1970) set following a third world war in which ultra-magnetic weapons have destroyed and submerged Earth's land masses. By contrast, in *Last Light* (2007) and *Afterlight* (2010) Alex Scarrow tells the tale of a doomed British civilization deprived of oil after war in the Middle East wipes out most of the world's oil supplies.

State takeover: The classic tale is George Orwell's *Nineteen Eighty-Four* (1949); in a superstate controlled by Big Brother, citizens are deprived of individuality and punished for such misdemeanors as 'thought crimes.' In Ray Bradbury's *Fahrenheit 451* (1953) books are not only outlawed but burned so as to suppress the dissemination of information and quell anti-government dissent.

Economic disaster: In his predictions of the future rise in populations the nineteenth century cleric and scholar Thomas Malthus forecast that in time the earth's resources would become so depleted that the human race would be overwhelmed by famine and disease. Although the detailed statistical conclusions of his *An Essay on the Principle of Population*, first published in 1798, have since been disproved, Malthus's warnings of the dangers of overpopulation remain relevant. In this century, James Wesley Rawles's *Survivors: A Novel of the Coming Collapse* (2011) envisages the struggles of survivors following global economic catastrophe, which he names 'The Crunch.'

Plants and animals mutate and the surviving humans regress mentally; death and disaster follow.

Pandemic: The earliest modern book of this genre is Mary Shelley's *The Last Man* (1826), a tale of people struggling to stay alive in a plague-infected world. Published in 2003, Margaret Atwood's *Oryx and Crake* relates the tale of a world populated by a group of genetically altered beings, explaining in flashbacks how humans were devastated by a manufactured virus. In *I Am Legend* (1954) Richard Matheson visualizes a world in which just one man, the virologist Robert Neville, survives a pandemic that exerts its effects via vampirism, charting his story as he struggles against the vampire hoards that attack his beleaguered home, and his attempts to discover the scientific cause of the disastrous disease.

Environmental disaster: With her best-selling *Silent Spring* (1962), a fictional account of a world in which pesticides destroy swathes of wildlife, and particularly bird populations, Rachel Carson alerted the world to the possibilities of environmental disaster. Equally unsettling are Kurt Vonnegut's *Cat's Cradle* (1963) depicting an Earth engulfed by a new kind of ice able to solidify at room temperature, and J. G. Ballard's *Drowned World* (1962) in which an increase in solar radiation causes a rise in sea level and worldwide flooding. Plants and animals mutate and the surviving humans regress mentally; death and disaster follow.

Modern technology: The potential for world domination of robots, to the detriment—and finally the extinction—of humans, was envisaged by the Czech playwright Karel Capek in his *R.U.R.* (*Rossum's Universal Robots*), first performed in 1925. Since then, technology, and our increasing reliance on it, has provided ample scope for apocalyptic visions including S. M. Stirling's *Dies the Fire* (2004) in which a catastrophic alteration in the laws of physics lead to the failure of electricity. As a result, people have to revert to medieval principles, and magic, in order to survive.

Alien invasion: Attacks on Earth from alien civilizations are a popular theme. A classic of the genre is *The Killing Star* (1995) by Charles R. Pellegrino and George Zebrowski, which concludes with the last man and woman on Earth being captured as zoo specimens ahead of their demise. In Al Sarrantonio's *Moonbane* (1989) meteors collide with the earth, releasing beings that develop into werewolves, which then go on the attack to devastating effect.

RUTH BINNEY

FURTHER READING: M. Keith Booker. The Dystopian Impulse in

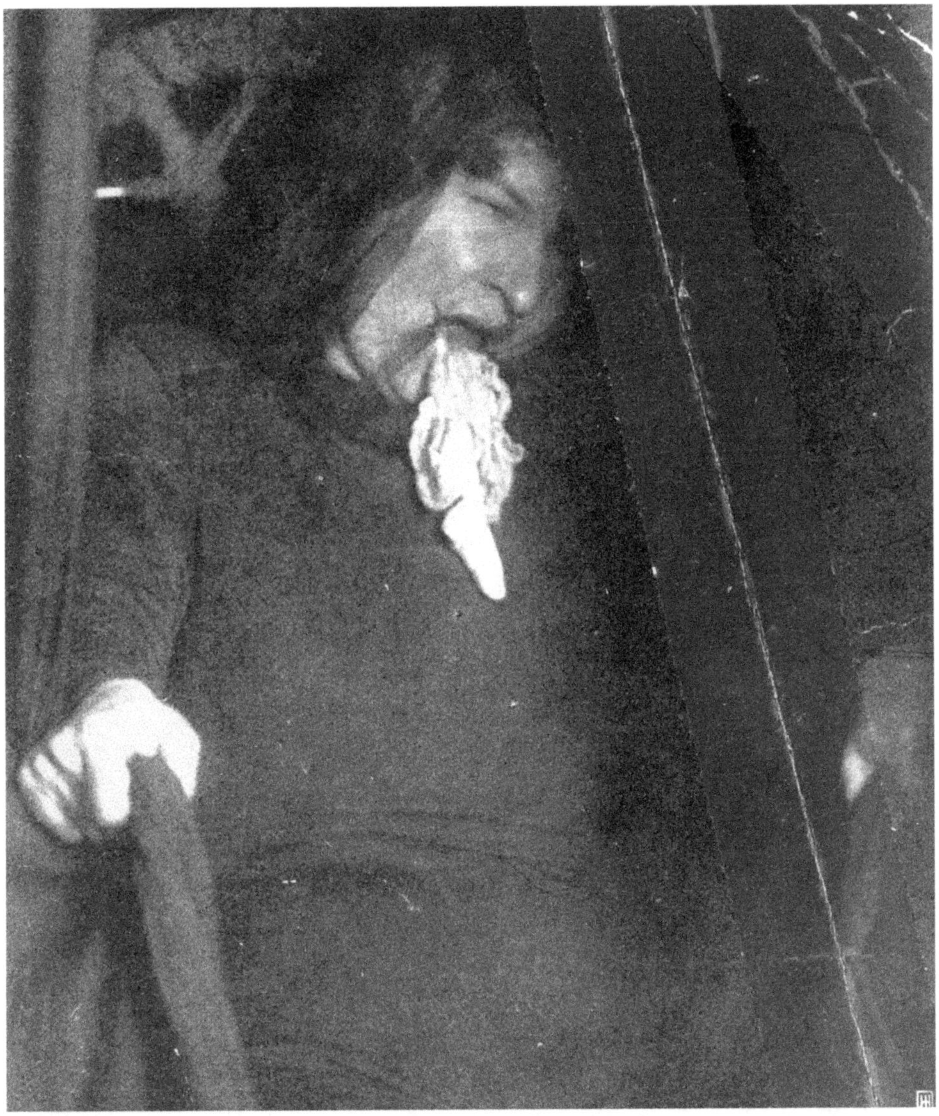

Ectoplasm, emerges from the mouth of medium Marthe Beraud during a seance (c. 1910)

Modern Literature. *(Westport, CT: Greenwood Press, 1994); M. Keith Booker.* Dystopian Literature: A Theory and Research Guide. *(Westport, CT: Greenwood Press, 1994).*

Ectoplasm

It is ironic that a word coined to describe the outer membrane of a single-celled animal such as an amoeba (as distinct from the inner cellular material, the endoplasm) should within a few years have been seized upon by observers of material phenomena at spiritualist seances, to such an extent that its original meaning should be almost forgotten. 'Ectoplasm' (also known as 'teleplastic materializations' and 'ideoplastic pseudopods') is the term used to describe a viscous-seeming substance that appeared to emanate from certain 'physical' mediums in the earlier years of the twentieth century, and which sometimes took on facial features, or even the form of a human body.

In the adoption of the word, there may have been some perceived connection with the 'ectenic force,' a postulated 'mesmeric' physical force emanating from a medium, and responsible for such phenomena as table-turning and the movement of objects without visible contact. The possible existence of such a force was first proposed by the psychic researcher Count Agénor Étienne de Gasparin (1810–71), and the term was coined by his colleague Thury.

It was, no doubt, the desire for more dramatic manifestations than table-rapping and the movement of mundane objects such as tambourines and trumpets, coupled with the need to provide a more readily recognizable form than the mere voices of departed spirits in seances, that led to the appearance of ectoplasm. The use of photography (admittedly under somewhat restricted conditions) was permitted in certain seances by the 1920s, and photographs revealed ectoplasm as a white doughy stream that issued from the mouth, nose and even the genitals of female mediums. The French investigator Professor Charles Richet 1850–1935) described it as 'a kind of liquid or pasty jelly . . . which organizes itself by degrees, acquiring the shape of a face or a limb. Under very good conditions of visibility, I have seen this paste spread on my knees . . .'

Richet was describing ectoplasm produced by the medium Marthe Beraud (b. 1886), usually known as Eva C, who was extensively investigated by Professor von Schrenck-Notzing (1862–1929). She 'materialized' ectoplasm from many different parts of her body, including her breast, thumbs, and ears, and photographs show this to be of an almost solid consistency, in which facial features are sometimes deeply sculpted. He wrote:

> *'We have no occasion to doubt that even paper like substances can be materialized (by the medium), as can substances of the nature of gauze veiling and cotton, including the morphological structure of the weft, fold sewn in, etc. Just as traces have been left of the pure, organic-teleplastic substance, so may similar fragments of the materialized products, textile, or cellular, have been left behind.'*

Despite Schrenck-Notzing's standing as a scientifically trained observer, there seems little doubt that he here reveals the true nature of ectoplasm. Whatever specimens of this 'organic-teleplastic substance' could be obtained—usually by violent seizure, to the evident distress of the medium—were found to be of white cheesecloth or a similar gauzy material, sometimes impregnated with grease, on which traces of bodily secretions could be detected. Another medium, known as Laslo, eventually admitted that he had drawn faces on gauze rolled in goose fat, which he had squeezed into a small ball and secreted in Schrenck-Notzing's pocket before being searched, subsequently retrieving it for production during the seance.

The brothers Willi (1903–71) and Rudi Schneider (1908–57), who were investigated in the 1930s and shown to be regular tricksters, also produced 'ectoplasm' of a similar nature, which was shown to be fraudulent by Professor Przibram (1878–1973) of the University of Vienna.

But despite these widely-reported cases, belief in the existence of ectoplasm survived well into the twentieth century. A series of articles in the New York *World Telegram* of 1937 included a description of an 'ectoplasm box . . . by means of which a smoky shape, roughly resembling a hooded man, floats upward'; manufactured by a small company in Chicago, it cost fifteen dollars.

End of the World

The ragged fanatic, solemnly carrying his placard announcing that 'The End of the World is at Hand,' is an object of ridicule. But the image of the mushroom cloud was an ever-present reality to every sensitive person during the Cold War. Between the two—a very real possibility of an end to the world as we know it and the attempt to pinpoint the end and express it in mythological terms—there is much more than an accidental connection. Humans have seldom been able to believe wholeheartedly in the permanence of the established order, though they have often poured scorn on the prophet who has dared to remind them of their doubts. It was so in the early centuries of the Christian era: 'Scoffers will come in the last days with scoffing, following their own passions and saying, "Where is the promise of his coming?"

A man is preparing for the end of the world in Devon, England

For ever since the fathers fell asleep, all things have continued as they were from the beginning of creation,' (2 Peter, chapter 3.3) and it is so today. The difference now is that the end of the world, if there is to be an end, is seen as coming about through, in some sense, natural causes. In the past, it was held that it would come about through supernatural causes and it was accordingly expressed in mythological terms.

The writer of 2 Peter answered the 'scoffers' by pointing out as a 'fact' that the earth had been created by God out of a watery chaos (as related in Genesis, chapter 1.1), that through this same water 'the world that then existed was deluged with water and perished' (Genesis, chapters 6–8), and that by the word of God, 'the heavens and Earth that now exist have been stored up for fire, being kept until the day of judgment and destruction of ungodly men,' (2 Peter 3.7). Here we have a mythological pattern, repeated in many parts of the world, of creation, destruction, and re-creation, and it is in this perspective that practically all end of the world myths must be seen. We may speculate interminably as to the origins of such patterns as these, without ever reaching more than a probable theory. However, it seems likely that in primitive man's experience the succession of day and night, summer and winter, rain and drought, heat and cold; the rising and setting of the sun; the phases of the moon; the wanderings of some, at least, of the stars—all contributed to a sense of insecurity with regard to man's tenure of the face of the earth.

There is no lack of evidence to show that primitive man conceived of the cosmic process not as something stable, but as a great and continuous battle between the forces of creation and destruction, order and chaos. The world had been brought into being by supernatural forces out of chaos; and unless these forces were supported—by prayer, sacrifice, and other ritual acts—then the world would inevitably return once more to that same chaos. The cosmic order was, however, maintained by the gods (particularly the High Gods of the sky), and should they so choose, it could be brought to an end. The annual festivals of agricultural peoples, with which cycles of myth are intimately associated, were meant to ensure the continued existence of the earth, particularly the seasonal renewal of its fertility and its life. But in the background was always the fear that at some time, to be appointed by the gods, a return to chaos would take place. Natural phenomena—hurricanes, floods, volcanic eruptions, and earthquakes—suggested the means: man's ritual and moral shortcomings suggested the motive.

Common to a surprisingly large number of races was the conviction that all this had, in fact, happened before. The gods had destroyed the world on certain occasions when conditions had become so bad as to be unbearable from the gods' own point of view. But why should they ever become so bad? No simple answer is possible, except that the ancients were evidently under no illusions regarding the perfectibility of mankind.

Even this pessimistic outlook, which placed man's Golden Age in a distant past, and saw his evolution as a development into greater iniquity, was not the whole of the story.

In ancient Babylon, for instance, where man's position in the cosmos paralleled that of the slave in the city-state, it was up to the gods to decide when the end should come. They had decided before: Sumerian and Babylonian—Assyrian mythology had recorded the legend of the great Deluge, and of the great Ark in which Ziusudra (Utnapishtim) had been saved (compare the Old Testament story of Noah), but had given no cogent moral reasons why this should have been so. Nor were their end of the world myths any the less arbitrary. In Seneca's words: 'Berosus (author of *A History of Babylon*) says that everything takes place according to the course of the planets, and he maintains this so confidently that he determines the times for the conflagration of the world and for the flood. He asserts that the world will burn when all the planets which now move in different courses come together in the Crab, so that they all stand together in a straight line in the same sign, and that the future flood will take place when the same conjunction occurs in Capricorn.' The astrological aspect is probably to be explained in terms of identification between the stars and the gods themselves, who were ultimately responsible for past and future catastrophes.

The link between past and future is to be seen in a slightly different form in the mythology of the Aztecs of Central America who believed in a series of world ages, each of which had so far ended in a cosmic catastrophe—famine, fire, hurricane, and flood respectively. This present age was expected to end on the completion of a fifty-two-year cycle and every fifty-two years preparations were made: all fires were extinguished and priests and people ascended a sacred mountain, waiting for the rise of the Pleiades. Only when

The gods had destroyed the world on certain occasions when conditions had become so bad as to be unbearable from the gods' own point of view.

Earthenware statue of Rudra, a major Hindu god seen as the Supreme God

this happened could the people be sure of safety for another fifty-two years.

Many Native Americans tell of a similar past catastrophe, though theirs is a less sophisticated conception. Usually the disaster is said to have been the sun or moon falling onto the earth, or destruction by fire or by snow and ice. And in most cases the horrors are sent by an angry god or culture hero—and later a few survivors, with supernatural aid, repopulate the earth. Algonquin tribes in North America have a few end-of-the-world tales, envisaging it either as a great fire or a final and all-inclusive battle.

Hindu and Buddhist belief generally looked on the history of the world as consisting in a series of four ages, or *Yugas*, each of enormous length. These have the names *Krita Yuga, Treta Yuga, Dvapara Yuga,* and *Kali Yuga*, marked by successive declines in morals, righteousness, and piety. By the end of the final age, Kali Yuga, of a Day of Brahma (a thousandfold cycle), Brahmins will have come to neglect their devotions; popular piety will be dead; fire, drought, and famine will ravage the earth. Then there will be a century of death, after which the god Vishnu assumes the form of Rudra, the destroyer, and dries up all the moisture on or beneath the earth. There follows a universal conflagration, in which the last vestiges of human occupation disappear from the face of the earth. At last the underworld, Earth and heavens disappear also in the vast whirlpool of flame; nothing remains save the eternal and uncreated Brahman. But this is a beginning, as well as an end: the cycle is begun again, and a new series of ages ensues, marked by the same stages, the same decline into sin and lawlessness (*adharma*), and earmarked for the same ultimate fate.

Prelude to New Life

Turning to an entirely different tradition, one of the best known and yet in some ways least understood myths concerning the end of the world is that which is found in the medieval Icelandic sources, and which has to some extent passed into the European consciousness through Wagner's (1813–1883) opera *Gdtterdammerung* (*The Twilight of the Gods*). The earliest version of this myth ends the first poem in the Poetic (or Verse) Edda, the *Vdluspd* (twelfth century). This is no saga, nor a logically constructed prediction of the 'last times,' but rather a poetic apocalypse, perhaps reflecting some of the tension between old and new faiths during the years when Christianity was winning its way into the minds of the Northern peoples. Once more, the end of all things is set in the framework of cosmogony: the beginning and the end are equally important and there are hints of a previous catastrophe, similar to those we have already seen.

The end is heralded by a cock-crow, and has been preceded by the 'Timbul-winter—' three winters of unprecedented severity. The catastrophe begins to unfold with the death of the blind brother of the slain Balder and the fettering of the evil Loki, and the refrain begins: Garm (the hound of death) howls by the hole of the underworld; the fetter breaks; the wolf runs free. There follows a description of the terrors of the Kingdom of the Dead, and of the moral dissolution of mankind, another consistent element in such myths. Then the cosmic tree Yggdrasill shudders, the hound Garm howls once more, the snake wound round the world begins to stir, and the gods, good and evil alike, begin to assemble for the final battle.

Odin is killed by the Fenris wolf but

is avenged, briefly, by his son; Thor is killed by the Midgard snake. The sun becomes dark, the earth sinks into the sea, the stars fall from heaven, and fire consumes both Yggdrasill and Valhalla, the home of the slain heroes. All is waste and void.

Then the miracle happens: the earth reappears, purified and fresh, ruled by the sons of the gods; Balder and his brother return, and a high and noble temple-hall shines brighter than the sun. The underworld remains, though eternally cut off from the world of light. Chaos has once more been transcended, as in the moment of the first creation; mankind is once more established on the face of the earth—though a new Earth freed from the fetters of the past. It has often been thought that the motif of new creation is not part of the original mythological tradition; and yet, allowing that the myth as we have it is post-Christian, can we not see here the fusing of Indo-European and Judaeo-Christian traditions within the framework of high poetry?

A far different Indo-European view of the end of the world, and yet one which has marked affinities with Hindu beliefs, is found in ancient Greece. The Greek writer Hesiod, in his *Works and Days*, speaks of the five ages of Gold, Silver, Bronze, Heroes, and Iron, in which there is a gradual descent from joy and innocence to guile, misery, and corruption. An elaborate theory of cyclical world history was put forward by Heraclitus (c. 500 BC) and later developed by Plato (427–347 BC); possibly this theory owes much to Babylonian influence, particularly in respect of the idea of the *magnus annus*, or great year, the period during which eight independently revolving planetary spheres return to their point of departure. In Plato's version, a total revolution in one direction is followed by a revolution in the opposite direction; thus the world as it is known is succeeded by an age of 'history in reverse.'

Also from Heraclitus came the notion of a cosmic fire, the *ekpurosis*, into which the world is periodically dissolved, and from which it is born anew. To be sure, the elements from which the world is made are indestructible, and can never be more than temporarily disturbed, returning after the conflagration to the same relationship to one another. But each cycle is none the less distinct, though hardly distinctive: indeed, one corollary of a theory of this kind was that history repeats itself exactly, down to the smallest detail. Every age is subject to the same forces of disintegration and

***Valhalla and the Midgard Serpent* (1680). Icelandic School, held at the Arni Magnusson Institute, Reykjavik, Iceland**

degeneration and each will dissolve in time, only to be recreated. This theory was developed in its most elaborate detail by the Stoic popular preachers of the second century BC and earlier, and passed over into Christianity through the Church Fathers, some of whom even undertook to attempt to prove the doctrine of ekpurosis from the Book of Genesis.

However, the cyclical theories of the Greek philosophers accorded ill with the Judaic tradition out of which Christianity developed, and these were ultimately attempts to reconcile the irreconcilable, so vast were the differences between them.

The Ways of God with Man

Turning now to this Judaeo-Christian stream of tradition, the developed Christian view of the end of the world differs in certain important respects from these other mythologies particularly in that it incorporates no trace of a cyclical view of time. It rests on the Old Testament view that in God's good time a new and better world will emerge out of this present order, thus vindicating God's final sovereignty over creation.

In later Judaism the Old Testament view was to give rise to elaborate time schemes, in which the lengths of this present age and the age of the Messiah to come—both preceding the ultimate vindication of the sole and absolute authority of God—were calculated with much precision and not a little imagination. The sequence was: first the present age, characterized by increasing moral turpitude (by now a familiar element); secondly, heralded by great tribulations, the messianic age here on Earth, in which righteousness and peace are established throughout creation; and finally, the accomplishment by God of the ultimate act of new creation.

On the practical level, the problem in late Judaism was to reconcile the wisdom, power, and justice of God with the actual misfortunes of Israel in the first century AD. An elaborate justification of the ways of God with man is contained in two Esdras (Apocrypha); beginning with man, with Adam, it then continues with the question 'When have the inhabitants of the earth not sinned in thy sight?' and its answer: 'Thou mayest indeed find individuals who have kept thy commandments, but nations thou wilt not find' (3.35), and ending with the vision: '. . . faithfulness shall flourish, and corruption shall be overcome, and the truth, which has been so long without fruit, shall be revealed' (6.27). The point here is, however, not that the world is going to come to an end, but that past and future alike are in the hands of God, and that the consummation is the responsibility of the Lord of history, just as was creation. The process is planned, and not haphazard.

. . . past and future alike are in the hands of God, and that the consummation is the responsibility of the Lord of history, just as was creation.

It is against this background that Christian ideas concerning the end of the world must be viewed. The framework of the absolute sovereignty of God is identical. So, too, is the pattern of the three ages: this present age; the age to come inaugurated by the emergence of Jesus as Messiah—'in these last days he has spoken to us by a Son' (Hebrews, chapter 1.2)—and the age to come consummated by the second appearance of Jesus Christ in power and glory.

In this present age men are helpless, being under the sway of angels, principalities and powers in enmity to God. The coming of Christ heralds the gradual breaking of the power of these evil spirits. Characteristic of this new age are certain 'powers' such as the conquest of sin, suffering, and disease.

The consummation of the new age so far as the vast majority of mankind is concerned—those who have either not heard or not heeded the Gospel—will come 'like a thief in the night,' (Thessalonians, chapter 5.2); in this passage Paul echoes Jesus' words, 'the Son of man is coming at an hour you do not expect,' (Luke, chapter 12.40). But although the actual end may be unexpected, there will have been ample signs heralding its advent: wars and rumours of wars, nation rising against nation and kingdom against kingdom, Earthquakes, and famines. The subsequent crisis will be cosmic: '. . . after that tribulation, the sun will be darkened, and the moon will not give its light, and the stars will be falling down from heaven, and the powers in the heavens will be shaken. And then they will see the Son of Man coming in clouds with great power and glory;' 'heaven and Earth will pass away . . .' (Mark, chapter 13).

***The Revelation of St. John*: *The Four Riders of the Apocalypse* by Albrecht Dürer (1471–1528)**

Alpha and Omega

There seems little doubt that the idea of the immediate end of the world passed into the consciousness of the Christian Church direct from the teaching of Jesus himself. It is prominent in Paul and certain of the later books of the New Testament: '. . . the day of the Lord will come like a thief, and then the heavens will pass away with a loud noise, and the elements will be dissolved with fire, and the earth and the works that are upon it will be burned up,' (2 Peter, chapter 3.10); and, of course, in the book of Revelation.

The book of Revelation adds little of substance, however, to the shorter and more cryptic accounts found in other New Testament books, although its imagery is considerably more elaborate. One central symbol is that of the scroll sealed with seven seals; on the opening of the sixth seal there is an Earthquake, the sun becomes 'black as sackcloth,' the stars fall, and the people run in terror; the seventh seal produces silence in heaven for a half-hour, then seven angels send seven torments, the 'seven bowls of the wrath of the Lord.' Nevertheless, these and similar convulsive symptoms are not really the point of the narrative, which is to proclaim the passing away of the old order and the coming of the new: 'Then I saw a new heaven and a new Earth; for the first heaven and the first Earth had passed away,' (Revelation, chapter 21.1). Of no less importance is the agency—the direct action of God—by which this radical renewal is accomplished: 'And he who sat upon the throne said, 'Behold, I make all things new . . . I am the Alpha and the Omega, the beginning and the end.' (Revelation, chapter 21.5–6).

Broadly speaking, the Christian Church, while continuing to believe in a vague way in the final summing up of all things in Christ, has long refused to concern itself with the details of the end of the world. There have been exceptions, of course: recurrent periods of biblical orthodoxy have given rise to more or less extravagant claims that the end is in sight. One example of the new mythology that such concerns have brought in their wake is found in the writings of Thomas Burnet (1635–1715), who reflected in his *Sacred Theory of the Earth* that the destructive fires would be kindled at Rome, the seat of the Antichrist, and would be aided and abetted by all the sources of fire in the world. Since the soil of Britain contains so much coal, he concluded, it would be preferable to be elsewhere when that day dawns.

ERIC J. SHARPE

Jim Jones, leader of the Peoples Temple, receives a Martin Luther King Jr. award in 1977

FURTHER READING: J. Ballie. The Belief in Progress. *(New York, NY: Scribner, 1951); M. Barkun.* Disaster and the Millennium. *(New Haven, CT: Yale University Press, 1974); R. H. Hiers.* Jesus and the Future. *(Louisville, KY: John Knox, 1981); S. G. F. Brandon.* The Judgment of the Dead. *(New York, NY: Scribner, 1969).*

End of the World Cults

'The end of the world is nigh' is the guiding mantra of end of the world or doomsday cults—groups who believe in impeding catastrophe and destruction and, in the most notorious some cases, attempt to bring it about. End of the world cults often include some forms of millenarianism, the belief that some great event, such as a 'second coming' will lead to the complete change of everything in society.

The term 'doomsday cult' was coined in 1966 by the US sociologist John Lofland (b. 1936), following his study of a group of members of the Unification Church of the United States in California, and the work of social psychologists Leon Festinger (1919–89), with Henry Riecken (1917–2012), and Stanley Schachter, (1922–97), who in 1956 published their seminal book *When Prophecy Fails: A Social and Psychological Study of a Modern Group That Predicted the Destruction of the World.* The work is an indepth analysis of the UFO cult called the Seekers led by the Chicago housewife Dorothy Martin, whose members had quit their jobs, colleges —and even their spouses—to await rescue from Earth by a flying saucer before the world was drowned by a massive flood on December 21, 1954, and predicted by Martin in a message received as 'automatic writing' from the fictional planet Clarion.

Although the event failed to take place, the group remained united in their belief, as a result of which *When Prophecy Fails* set out some key principles vital to the understanding of doomsday cult behaviour. These include deep conviction in a belief, a total commitment to it, and the support of like-minded individuals. Further study of doomsday cults have identified additional factors vital to their operation and success.

A leader: A cult will survive only with a charismatic leader, epitomized by the Reverend James Warren Jones (1931–78) who in 1978 ordered hundreds of members of The People's Temple in Jonestown, Guyana to drink poisoned punch, and by David Koresh (1959–93), self-styled prophet and final leader of the Branch Davidian cult destroyed by the intervention of US troops in a siege at Waco, Texas, in 1993.

Recruitment: To become cult members, candidates are vigorously recruited. Often those targeted are reticent, vulnerable, idealistic, or suffering from a mental impairment of some kind.

Indoctrination: Once members are 'signed up' then the process of indoctrination begins. One way of making this work is to isolate members from the rest of society, enhancing the belief that those outside the cult are at best misguided or at worst dangerous. So controlled is the community that the leader will ensure that there is no time for members to pause for independent thought or analysis of what they are doing.

Staying within the system: To survive within a doomsday cult, every member must stay in good favour with the leader and at the same time renounce attachment to their family and friends from before their 'conversion.' Studies have confirmed that people remain within cults because only by staying can they be saved.

The chance to leave: To leave is to condemn themselves to eternal damnation, or imminent death. The most destructive cults make leaving virtually impossible but others do allow a chink in the door from which escape can be affected.

RUTH BINNEY

FURTHER READING: Margaret Thaler Singer. Cults in Our Midst. *(Hoboken, NJ: Jossey-Bass, 1996); D. G. Bromley and J. G. Melton.* Cults, Religion & Violence. *(Cambridge, UK: Cambridge University Press, 2002); Leon Festinger, Henry Riechken, and Stanley Schachter.* When Prophecy Fails. *(New York, NY: Harper-Torchbooks, 1956).*

Environmental Apocalypse

From the flood survived by Noah in his ark to the Biblical warnings of the prophets such as Jeremiah, who reported the Christian God's predic-

James Lovelock (b. 1919), scientist and author of the *Gaia hypothesis*

tion that he would 'make them eat bitter food and drink poisoned water,' environmental apocalypse was viewed by the ancients as punishment for ill doing. In similar vein Jesus, ahead of his trial and execution warned that, as recorded in St. Luke's Gospel, 'at the time of retribution. . . Portents will appear in sun and moon and stars. On Earth nations will stand helpless, not knowing which way to turn from the roar and surge of the sea.'

Scientific thinking in the twenty-first century is more rational but by no means always less gloomy. 'If they understood astrophysics,' says Britain's Astronomer Royal Lord Martin Rees (b. 1942), aliens watching our planet 'could confidently predict that the biosphere would face doom in a few billion years when the sun flares up and dies. But could they have predicted' he continues, 'an unprecedented spike less than halfway through the earth's life—these human-induced alterations occupying, overall, less than a millionth of the elapsed lifetime and seemingly occurring with runaway speed?'

The Burning Question

In Rees's question lies the crux of the global warming debate, which comes for 'believers' with apocalyptic warnings for the future of our planet. The warming of the earth, as a result of the greenhouse effect of increased carbon dioxide levels in the atmosphere were correctly predicted in 1896 by the Swedish chemist Svante Arrhenius (1859–1927), although this was by no means a cause for alarm at this time. Nearly a century later, in 1973, James Lovelock's Gaia hypothesis, named for the Greek goddess of the earth, postulated that the totality of the earth's environment is self regulatory to an extent that is able to maintain a stable environment conducive to life without human interference.

By 2006, however, even Lovelock had come the conclusion that the changes we have set in motion make Gaia unsustainable and that by the middle of the twenty-second century the earth will be uninhabitable for humans and other life forms, due to the rise in level of the oceans and the massive increase in area of deserts. Ahead of this era of mass destruction of life, he argues, the scenario the modern environmental apocalypse scenario includes a huge surge in population, exacerbated by increased life expectancy, and with it the consumption—to the point of extinction—of the world's supply of fossil fuels. With a warmer atmosphere will come melting of the polar ice caps and a rise in the level of the oceans that will sink islands and destroy cities from New York to Tokyo and from Sydney to London.

Just as meteoroid impacts caused widespread loss of life—and probably the extinction of the dinosaurs—millions of years ago, the same could happen again.

A Sudden End?

Or the end could come with a single blow, and possibly in a similar way to that as predicted in the Book of Revelation: 'A great star shot from the sky, flaming like a torch, and fell on a third of the rivers and springs; the name of the star was Wormwood. A third of the water turned to wormwood, and great numbers of people died . . . ' Just as meteoroid impacts probably caused widespread loss of life—and probably the extinction of the dinosaurs—millions of years ago, the same could happen again.

Even more catastrophically the earth could collide with an asteroid (a small planet or planetoid), most likely one from the three groups nearest the earth, named the Apollos, Amors, and Atens. Meanwhile, NASA telescopes continue to sweep the skies, and plans to create asteroid deflecting rockets have yet to be realized. Testifying before a panel of the US Senate in March 2013, Dr. Ed Lu (b. 1963), a former NASA astronaut warned that time is not necessarily on our side, warning that only 'with ten, twenty, or thirty years notice' is it 'fairly easy to deflect an asteroid.'

RUTH BINNEY

FURTHER READING: J. E. Lovelock. The Vanishing Face of Gaia. *(New York, NY: Basic Books, 2009); Isabel Hilton.* The Reality of Global Warming. *(New York, NY: World Policy Institute, 2008); Rachel Carson.* Silent Spring. *(Boston, MA: Houghton Mifflin, 1962).*

Eschatology

The doctrine of last things, involving speculation about the ultimate destiny of man and the world, and the nature of death, judgment, heaven, and hell: Hindus believe that the individual soul is absorbed into the Divine Being after a series of reincarnations: according to Christian apocalyptic writings the end of the world will be marked by the return of Christ to overthrow the Antichrist and to preside at the Last Judgment.

Eyeless in the Next World

The eye (*akshi*) is regarded as a receptive, neutral organ, except when intent is added to seeing. It is said to be the last organ to come into activity, since the child within the womb employs all its organs except the eyes, which it opens only after birth. On this analogy sculptors used to give the final touch to an image after the rest of the work was completed, in a ritual operation called nayononmīlana (*nayana-unmīlana*, 'eye-unclosing'), the chiseling of the eye image. It was preceded by a period of meditation and prayer, and followed by the rite of 'enlivening' the idol.

Similarly it is believed that on death the deceased are quite blind, and grope about eyeless in the next world. The eye is essentially the organ of the earthly body and can only be transferred to the dead by special ceremonies, one of which is the *diakshu-dana*, 'eye-bestowal,' performed by a certain class of professional painters.

The deliberate beholding (*darśana*) of an auspicious person or thing brings blessing, since the sight of the beneficent object infuses the beholder with its own virtue. Hence the visit of devotees to their spiritual leaders, of subjects to their rulers, of pilgrims to shrines, to obtain a darśan or viewing.

BENJAMIN WALKER
Hindu World

Glass Mountain

In European legends and folktales, a mountain of glass inhabited by supernatural beings at the end of the world, on the borders of the otherworld; probably originally the home of the dead, and possibly thought to be made of amber.

***The Apocalyptic Woman* (c. 1530–1532) painted by the Dutch artist Matthias Gerung (1500–1570) shows the Great Beast of the Apocalypse.**

The Great Beast

'And I saw a beast rising out of the sea, with ten horns and seven heads, with ten diadems upon its horns and a blasphemous name upon its heads.' This creature is the Great Beast of the Apocalypse, whose identity is concealed behind hints, symbols, and a numerological puzzle.

In chapter 11 of the book of Revelation an angel announces that the kingdom of the world has become the kingdom of God. This proclamation is immediately followed by the titanic rebellion of the powers of evil and the coming of Antichrist. Satan appears as the great red dragon, there is war in heaven, and the dragon is hurled down to earth and his angels with him. A voice in heaven prophesies: 'Woe to you, O Earth and sea, for the devil has come down to you in great wrath, because he knows that his time is short.'

In chapter 13 this 'woe' takes the form of the beast that rose from the sea. It was like a leopard, with the feet of a bear and the mouth of a lion. 'And to it the dragon gave his power and his throne and great authority.' One of its heads 'seemed to have a mortal wound, but its mortal wound was healed.' The whole earth followed the beast with wonder and worshipped it, saying, 'Who is like the beast, and who can fight against it?' The beast held sway for three-and-a-half years, during which it made war on the saints and conquered them, it had power over every tribe and people, every tongue and nation, and everyone on Earth worshipped it except only those whose names were written before the foundation of the world in the book of life of the crucified Christ.

'Then I saw another beast which rose out of the earth.' This was the first beast's lieutenant, which worked great signs and wonders, and which ordered the people to make an image of the first beast and worship it. It caused everyone to be marked on the right hand or the forehead with the mark of the first beast, which was its name or its number. 'This calls for wisdom: let him who has understanding reckon the number of the beast, for it is a human number, its number is 666.'

The Antichrist

The early Christians believed in a coming struggle between God and a great opponent, an evil counterpart of Christ, who would claim to be God, work delusive miracles in parody of Christ, and deceive people into worshipping him. Some commentators on the book of Revelation identified the second beast, the one that rose from the earth, as Antichrist because it worked signs and wonders. But it is more likely that for the author of Revelation the Great Beast 666 was Antichrist though he does not use the term Antichrist itself.

The second beast is called 'the false prophet,' a reference to the 'false Christs and false prophets' of whom Jesus spoke, who will show signs and wonders to lead the elect astray (Mark, chapter 13). Its ancestry goes back further, to Deuteronomy (chapter 13), where the people are warned against a prophet and dreamer of dreams who will show a sign or a wonder and try to persuade them to worship false gods. The passage in Mark suggests that, as the second beast is the false prophet, it is likely that the first beast is the false Christ.

The first beast unites the characteristics of the four beasts seen in a vision in the book of Daniel (chapter 7), which stand for four empires that in turn oppressed the Jews—Babylon,

A coloured version of the *Whore of Babylon* illustration from Martin Luther's 1534 translation of the Bible.

Media, Persia, and the Greek Empire of Alexander the Great. The three-and-a-half years of the beast's rule also come from Daniel (chapter 12), the 'time, two times and half a time' after which the power of the persecutor will come to an end, the persecutor being Antiochus Epiphanes, the first human model for the figure of the Antichrist.

The beast comes up from the sea, which in Revelation is the home of the forces that oppose God. This harks back to Mesopotamian, Canaanite, and Jewish myths in which to create the ordered universe, or keep it in being, it is necessary for the monster of the deep, the chief of the powers of chaos, to be defeated. When Revelation comes to the creation of the new heaven and the new Earth, we are told that 'the sea was no more.'

The Whore of Babylon

It is generally accepted that if the Great Beast is Antichrist in the spiritual sphere, on Earth it is Rome, the empire that now oppressed Jews and Christians. The worship it insists on is the cult of the deified emperors, and the false prophet probably stands for the local authorities responsible for the imperial cult. The fact that the Great Beast comes from the sea (from abroad) and the false prophet from the earth (from at home) may reflect this. In chapter 17, the whore of Babylon (the city of Rome) is seen riding on a scarlet beast, which is probably identical with the Great Beast. The seven heads of this beast stand for hills (the seven hills of Rome) and also for seven kings (Roman emperors).

The head that was mortally wounded but healed looks like an allusion to the persistent rumours that Nero, the persecutor of Christians, who committed suicide in AD 68, was not really dead but would return with an army to reconquer Rome. The image of the beast recalls Caligula's orders, issued in AD 30 but never carried out, that his statue should be placed in the Holy of Holies at Jerusalem, an intended sacrilege that horrified the Jews.

In chapters 19 and 20 the beast and the kings of the earth with their armies do battle with the forces of God, led by the rider on a white horse, the Word of God. They are decisively defeated and then slaughtered. The beast and the false prophet are thrown alive into 'the lake of fire that burns with brimstone,' where they will be 'tormented day and night forever and ever.' The Devil himself is shut away in the bottomless pit for 1,000 years.

Number of the Beast

The number riddle that has produced so many solutions, some of them singularly eccentric, is an example of gematria. Evidently the Great Beast's name or title will add to 666 if its letters are turned into numbers. The most obvious candidate for the honour is Nero, but Revelation was written in Greek and his name in Greek, Neron, adds to 1,005. However, if his Greek title Neron Kaisar is turned into Hebrew letters, the total is 666. The identification with Nero also has the advantage of explaining the Western tradition that the number was really 616, for if the Latin Nero Caesar is turned into Hebrew letters, it adds to 616.

Austin Farrer (1904–68) pointed out the interesting connection between 666 and the number of Jesus, which is 888. Eight is the number of rebirth and resurrection, and 888 shows that Jesus rose from the dead on the third day, which was a Sunday, the eighth day from the beginning of Passion week. The Friday on which Jesus was crucified, and on which the powers of darkness apparently triumphed, was the sixth day from the beginning of that week. So if 888 is the number of Jesus, it is fitting that 666 should be the number of Antichrist. In addition, 8 and 666 are connected because 8+7+6+5+4+3+2+1 = 36 and if the same process of serial addition is applied to 36, the total is 666.

FURTHER READING: G. B. Caird. The Revelation of St. John the Divine. *(London, UK: Black, 1966); Austin Farrer.* The Revelation of St. John the Divine. *(Oxford, UK: Clarendon Press, 1964).*

Harrowing of Hell

The harrying or despoiling of the land of the dead by a hero who enters the underworld, defeats Death, and returns alive; the most famous example is Christ, who harrowed hell in the time between the Crucifixion and the Resurrection: in Greek mythology Hercules, Theseus, Orpheus, and others visited the underworld and returned: King Arthur was said to have successfully raided the otherworld.

Headless Spirits

The importance of the head in the constitution of the body is obvious, and from the earliest times a unique significance has been accorded to it in myth and ritual magic. Conversely, headlessness has been regarded as a baleful state of being and has inspired some strange and eerie conceptions.

In the later Paleolithic era, at Mineteda in eastern Spain, headless human figures were engraved on rocks. They are depicted in upright posture and apparently in movement, and have been interpreted as representations of spirits. Possibly the horror of a decapitated body prompted the fear that the decapitated dead would be especially baleful and vindictive toward the living.

A different significance seems to attach to the depictions of headless

Depiction of the Arthurian legend of Sir Gawain and the Green Knight (c. 1375–1400)

persons in the remarkable mural paintings found recently at Catal Hiiyuk in Anatolia. At the Neolithic settlement on this site, which dates back to the seventh millennium BC, the ruins of a shrine dedicated to a goddess were excavated. From various objects found there, it is evident that this goddess was connected with both fertility and death. Among the frescoes that adorned the shrine were pictures of great black birds, of horrific appearance, menacing decapitated bodies. These depictions have generally been interpreted as representing vultures preying on human corpses. But there are reasons for doubting this interpretation. In the first place, such a subject would seem to have no relevance, and also to be inappropriate, to the cult of a mother goddess. Then there is the problem of the headlessness of the corpses—if indeed they are corpses; for they appear very animated in their postures. Since both human and vulture skulls were found specially deposited in the sanctuary, it would seem that the headless bodies have some hidden meaning beyond our knowing.

In ancient Egypt the famous mortuary god Osiris could be conceived of as 'the headless one' for, according to his legend, his murderer, Seth, mutilated his body. His severed head was subsequently recovered and buried at Abydos, which became the chief cult-centre of Osiris. However, in ancient Egyptian iconography, Osiris is never depicted as headless (except in bas-relief at Philae where his headless corpse is the subject of a magical ceremony). The whole purpose of the Osirian mortuary ritual was, on the contrary, to ensure the complete reconstitution and eternal preservation of the body of the deceased, with emphasis upon the security of the head.

However, in Greek magical papyri of Egyptian origin, Osiris became 'the strong Headless One,' the 'Creator of heaven and Earth, day and night, light and darkness,' 'the lightener and thunderer,' 'the God who holds the eternal fire' (meaning the sun). He is also referred to as the 'good Osiris, who no one has seen with eyes.' This mysterious being, called in the Greek text *Akephalos* ('Headless'), is imagined as having a head and face at his feet, and a mouth burning with fire. In two magical papyri of the period (now at Oslo and Berlin respectively), fantastic representations are given of headless monsters, showing some distorted remembrance of Egyptian symbols. There may also be some connection in this strange and horrific imagery with the fact that the first decan god of the constellation Capricorn, in the Egyptian star-map, was shown as headless. (The decans are divisions of the zodiac signs.) This decan god was associated also with the incidence of fever. The association is particularly interesting, since there is other evidence connecting headless spirits with disease and its cure.

Another class of headless spirits were the ghosts of those who died by decapitation, and were in consequence restless and haunted the living.

A similar belief existed in connection with those who had been hanged or crucified. The folklore of many northern peoples contain instances of such belief, of which the well-known idea of the decapitated ghost, holding its head under its arm is a romanticized version. It is interesting to note also that the Nordic god Wotan, in one of his manifestations, was the 'headless rider on the white horse.'

The medieval English Romance of *Sir Gawain and the Green Knight* that is related to the Arthurian cycle of legends, contains a remarkable episode of the beheading of a being who continues to live on headless. It seems likely that the 'beheading game' in *Sir Gawain and the Green Knight* preserves some reminiscence of ancient Celtic religion in which decapitation and a cult of severed heads were practiced.

Headless deities and heroes are also known in India. In the Hindu *Markandeya Purana*, the goddess Devi assumed the form of Chhinnamastaka (the 'Headless'), in order to destroy the demon Nisumbha. In the Punjab, at Bahraich, where his headless body was buried, Ghazi Salar is venerated as a headless champion of Islam. The headless trunk of Lakkhe Shah Darwesh is fabled to have fought its way to Ambala, to curse the wells there with brackishness. At Panipat, the Binsira was a 'headless saint' of the Hindus.

Medieval Christian art graphically contributed to the imagery of the headless dead. The legends of many saints told of their martyrdom by beheading; in consequence they were sometimes depicted headless and holding their heads as, for example, St. Nicasius is represented in the sculptures of the Cathedral of Rheims in France.

S. G. F. BRANDON

A painting by Cretan artist Georgios Klontzas at the end of the sixteenth century of the Second Coming—a detail showing the punishment of the wicked in hell

Heaven

The final home of the righteous after death: the joy of the Christian heaven consists in being eternally close to God; in Valhalla, the paradise of the Norsemen, warriors engaged in tournaments during the day and feasted at night: the Egyptian dead were thought to live in eternal happiness with the sun god or to be ritually assimilated to the god Osiris: the Mohammedan paradise contained the beautiful black-eyed houris to serve the pleasures of the faithful.

Hell

'Oh, you knotty, rugged, proud piece of flesh! You stony, rocky, flinty hard-heart, what wilt thou do when thou art roaring amongst the damned?' Bellowed by a hellfire preacher of the seventeenth century, the question frightened a ten-year-old boy named John Rogers half out of his wits, and he went to sleep every night with his hands in an anxiously prayerful attitude in case the demons came to fetch him. Ola Elizabeth Winslow (1885–1977) quotes the story of John Bunyan (1628–88), who as a boy was so haunted by nightmares of hell that he wished he was a devil himself, on the principle that it would be better to be a torturer than one of the tortured. Another famous preacher of the day, Vavasor Powell (1617–70), traced his conversion to a bout of toothache that caused him to wonder, if the temporary pain of toothache was so hard to bear, what would the eternal agony of hell be like?

At this period the established doctrine of hell was beginning to be challenged, though rarely in public because those who disbelieved in it considered the threat of hell the supreme deterrent to atheism, immorality, and crime. However, hell kept its hold on most Christians, though with steadily weakening force in succeeding generations, into this century. In 1916 James Joyce published, in *A Portrait of the Artist as a Young Man*, one of the most powerful descriptions of the horrors of hell ever written, based on what he had been taught at a Roman Catholic school in Ireland. And on the Protestant front, fundamentalist hell-fire preaching is by no means extinct.

Hell retained its long grip on the Christian mind because its existence is stated in the New Testament, because of its supposed value as a deterrent, and because of the common human observation that in this life the wicked flourish while the good suffer, with the consequent demand for reward and punishments to right the balance in the life to come. In descriptions of hell, much ingenuity was frequently devoted to making the punishment fit the crime.

In addition, though to explain belief in hell solely in terms of sado-masochism is to oversimplify, there is no mistaking the lip-licking avidity with which its torments were relished. For hundreds of years the 'dooms,' horribly imaginative pictures of the tortures to come, were carved and painted on the walls of churches to warn unbelievers and sinners. The *Apocalypse of Peter* of the early second century, which ranked second in popularity among Christians only to the beauties and terrors of the Book of Revelation itself, described the 'place of punishment:'

> *'And some were there hanging by their tongues; and these were they that blasphemed the way of righteousness, and under them was laid fire flaming and tormenting them . . . And there were also others, women hanged by their hair above that mire which boiled up; and these were they that adorned themselves for adultery . . . And in another place were gravel-stones sharper than swords or any spit, heated with fire, and men and women clad in filthy rags rolled upon them in torment. And these were they that were rich and trusted in their riches . . . Beside them shall be girls clad in darkness for a garment, and they shall be sore chastised and their flesh shall be torn in pieces. These are they that kept not their virginity until they were given in marriage . . .'*

The medieval picture of hell, a gigantic concentration camp of appalling fiery heat far underground, with its entrances through volcanoes such as Etna (or through the gaping mouth of Leviathan, the terrible dragon of the Old Testament) hit on something very close to geological truth, as Jacquetta Hawkes (1910–96) has pointed out (in *A Land*) for beneath the earth's surface the rock substance is molten with heat. 'Only a score of miles below the surface on which we walk the crust is molten . . . we do in fact maintain our fragile lives on a wafer balanced between a hellish morass and unlimited space.' It also hit on a psychological truth, for accounts of hell closely resemble some visionary experiences, and some states of mind induced by drugs or by mental illness.

> *. . . generally the Egyptians thought that those who were weighed and found wanting after death would be eternally annihilated.*

Prehistoric burials suggest that the earliest human beings were believers in some sort of existence after death; and the custom of burying the remains in the earth suggests the belief that the dead lived on underground. Depictions of headless figures, if they represent the spirits of people who had been beheaded in life, may contain the glimmerings of the idea that what happened to a man while he was alive would affect him after he was dead. The headless figures attacked by huge black vultures at Catal Hiiyuk may even, at a guess, represent the wicked being punished after death.

Land of No Return

The earliest people who definitely believed in a judgement after death, with reward and punishments, were the Egyptians but they concentrated on the reward and said little of the punishments. There is one reference to the wicked being tortured in pits of fire but generally the Egyptians thought that those who were weighed and found wanting after death would be eternally annihilated.

In Mesopotamian literature there is no punishment after death, and no reward either. All the dead, good and bad, rich and poor, go to the 'land of no return,' the house of darkness that was like a gigantic communal grave, surrounded by walls and barred by gates, where the ghosts flew about like spectral birds and gnawed on clay and dust.

Homer's underworld is also not a hell but a place of dreary darkness to which nearly all, the dead go. This was the house of Hades, the god of death, whose name means 'the unseen' and who ruled what the *Iliad* calls 'the hateful Chambers of Decay that fill the gods themselves with horror.' Some vengeful lines of Sappho emphasize the hopeless condition of the dead:

> *When you are dead you will lie in*
> *your grave, forgotten forever,*
> *Because you despise the flowers of the*
> *Muse; in Hades—as here—*
> *Dimly your shadow will flit with*
> *the rest, unnoticed, obscure.*

The Greeks feared death so intensely that they did not name it, saying that someone who died had 'departed.' In the *Odyssey* the ghost of Achilles says that he would sooner be alive as the servant of a landless peasant than be king of all the dead.

The Stench of Hell

They lie in exterior darkness. For remember, the fire of hell gives forth no light. At the command of God, the fire of the Babylonian furnace lost its heat but not its light, so, at the command of God, the fire of hell, while retaining the intensity of its heat, burns eternally in darkness. It is a never ending storm of darkness, dark flames and dark smoke of burning brimstone, amid which the bodies are heaped one upon another without even a glimpse of air. Of all the plagues with which the land of the Pharaohs was smitten, one plague alone, that of darkness, was called horrible. What name, then, shall we give to the darkness of hell which is to last not for three days alone but for all eternity?

The horror of this strait and dark prison is increased by its awful stench. All the filth of the world, all the offal and scum of the world, we are told, shall run there as to a vast reeking sewer when the terrible conflagration of the last day has purged the world. The brimstone, too, which burns there in such prodigious quantity fills all hell with its intolerable stench; and the bodies of the damned themselves exhale such a pestilential odour that, as Saint Bona venture says, one of them alone would suffice to infect the whole world. The very air of this world, that pure element, becomes foul and unbreathable when it has been long enclosed. Consider then what must be the foulness of the air of hell. Imagine some foul and putrid corpse that has lain rotting and decomposing in the grave, a jellylike mass of liquid corruption. Imagine such a corpse a prey to flames, devoured by the fire of burning brimstone, and giving off dense choking fumes of nauseous loathsome decomposition. And then imagine this sickening stench, multiplied a millionfold, and a millionfold again from the millions upon millions of fetid carcasses massed together in the reeking darkness, a huge and rotting human fungus. Imagine all this, and you will have some idea of the horror of the stench of hell.

James Joyce
A Portrait of the Artist as a Young Man

Hades became a name for the underworld itself, and later a name for the Christian hell. It was either far in the West, where the sun died in the evening, or deep underground with the entrances at many places on the earth's surface. These entrances may be the legacy of an earlier belief that the dead stayed in the places where they were buried. The Styx, a stream in Arcadia, which disappeared underground, became the principal river of the underworld, across which the dead had to be ferried by Charon. What later became the most famous entrance of all ('easy is the descent to Avernus') was at the lake of Avernus, not far from Naples in Italy, which Virgil (70–19 BC) described in the *Aeneid*. 'There was a deep and rugged cave, stupendous and yawning wide, protected by a lake of black water and the glooming forest . . . poisonous the breath which streamed up from those black jaws and rose to the vault of sky.'

An intense love of, and concentration on, this life naturally tends to reduce the next world to a faint shadow-play. Although the Homeric picture of the dead remained extremely influential, there were other views. Some of the more important dead lived on their tombs, where they were venerated and consulted by mortals. Belief in different treatment for different people in the next world was stimulated by the mystery religions that promised a blessed afterlife to those who were initiated.

Illustration of Dante's *Divine Comedy* showing the inscription over Hell-Gate

Punishment in the underworld appears even in Homer. In the *Iliad* the Furies 'make men pay for perjury in the world below' and the deposed god Cronus and his allies are imprisoned in 'the bottomless pit' of Tartarus, 'where the deepest of all caverns yawns below the world, where the Iron Gates are, and the Brazen Theshold, as far below Hades as the earth is under heaven.' In the Odyssey (book 11) a fortunate few go to a happy afterlife in Elysium and a few who have personally insulted Zeus are tormented in Tartarus.

In Plato's time (fourth century BC) there were stories about punishment after death. A character in the *Republic* mentions them and says that when a man grows old he cannot help uneasily wondering whether the stories are true. In the last book of the *Republic* the 'myth of Er' describes how the dead are judged and how the unjust are sent down under the earth. For every wrong they have done they will suffer tenfold and after a journey of 1,000 years under the earth they will be purged. Er saw tyrants and other peculiarly evil men at the mouth of a cavern. When any of them who had not been sufficiently purged tried to emerge from it, the mouth 'gave a roar' and 'wild men of fiery aspect seized them, flayed them with scourges and took them away to plunge them into Tartarus.'

The descent of Aeneas to the underworld influenced the medieval picture

World War I propaganda depicting Gehenna from the American School entitled, *Times are hard your Majesty—you leave us nothing to do*

of hell, and especially Dante's *Inferno* that was so graphic that simple-minded people assumed that the poet had really visited hell. In the *Aeneid* (book 6) Aeneas sees the great battlements of Tartarus and the burning Phlegethon. The entrance is guarded by a Fury and from inside comes the sound of savage flogging, the clanking of iron chains, and a terrible lamentation.

The Valley of Fire

The picture of life after death as a powerless obscurity in darkness, found in the literature of Homeric Greece, Mesopotamia, and early Palestine, conflicts with the archeological evidence from the same areas that the dead were buried with grave goods, implying an active life in the otherworld. Evidently the literature does not adequately reflect the full range of beliefs, and in Palestine it seems clear that the adherents of Yahweh as the one supreme god deliberately discouraged belief in an active life after death, to prevent people from trafficking with any other supernatural beings.

In the older passages in the Old Testament, all the dead, good, and bad alike, go to Sheol where they live in dust and darkness (like the Mesopotamian dead) and where they know nothing, so that it is no use trying to consult them. Sheol is a great pit or a walled city, 'the land of forgetfulness,' 'the land of silence.' Maggots are the bed beneath you there and worms are your covering. No god rules in Sheol and the dead are forgotten by Yahweh. However, as the story of the witch of Endor (I Samuel, chapter 28) shows, they were not entirely forgotten by men, and some tried to enlist their help.

Jewish hatred of foreign oppressors, with the desire to see them punished in the next world if not in this, was partly responsible for a change of attitude. So was the old problem of the unfairness of life, expressed in the book of Job (chapter 21): 'One dies in full prosperity, being wholly at ease and secure, his body full of fat and the marrow of his bones moist. Another dies in bitterness of soul, never having tasted of good. They lie down alike in the dust, and the worms cover them.'

Considerations of this kind led to a growing belief that the lot of all men after death was not the same. In the second century BC the Jewish leader Judas Maccabaeus made an offering of money at Jerusalem on behalf of some of his dead soldiers, on whose bodies have been found objects consecrated to idols. This was 'a reconciliation for the dead that they might be delivered from sin' and implies the belief that they would otherwise suffer in the afterworld (2 Maccabees, chapter 12). The book of Daniel predicts the 'many of those who sleep in the dust of the earth shall awake, some to everlasting life, and some to shame and everlasting contempt.'

There is no mention of physical torture here, but there is in another work of the same period, 1 *Enoch*, which includes a vision of 'a place chaotic and horrible' with 'seven stars of the heaven bound together in it, like great mountains and burning with fire.' It was here that the angels who lusted after human women would be punished, an early trace of the belief that the fallen angels, or demons, live in hell. Then Enoch sees Sheol itself, a mountain in the West with hollow compartments in it where the souls of the dead are to wait for the day of judgement. One is for the righteous and one is for the sinners, who wait there 'in great pain' (chapters 17–22). In a later passage there is 'a deep valley with burning fire. And they brought the kings and the mighty, and began to cast them into the deep valley' (chapter 54).

This valley of fire was Gehenna where, it came to be believed, the wicked would writhe tormented in the flames. Some of the Jewish rabbis said that the punishment there would not last more than twelve months. Some said that the righteous would go straight to paradise, the wicked to eternal pain in Gehenna, and the in-between would suffer for a year in Gehenna and then be annihilated. Gehenna has three entrances, one in the wilderness, one in the sea, and one in Jerusalem. It was next door to paradise, with the implication that part of the misery of the condemned was to see the bliss they had lost, an idea that passed into Christian theology.

The development of a Jewish hell may have been influenced by Persian Zoroastrianism in which the 'followers of the lie' are punished after death. Hell is in the far north, deep down beneath the earth, dark, and stinking, the home of demons and lies, a place of filth, pain, and misery. There the damned soul must remain until Ahriman himself is destroyed, by which time it will have come to understand reality and the wickedness of Ahriman, and will be ready for its release.

A holy man named Artay Viraf saw hell in a vision induced by hashish. It was like the inside of a grave. He experienced 'cold and an icy wind, dryness and stench,' and he saw a narrow and fearful pit, thick with darkness. Noxious beasts tore and worried at the damned. This hell had also the horror of the grave's solitariness, for each soul thought 'I am alone.'

Fire and Brimstone

From Gehenna the Christian hell developed. Jesus said that when the Son of Man comes in glory, he will separate the good from the wicked like sheep from goats. The goats will be driven away 'into eternal punishment' in the fire prepared for the Devil and his angels (Matthew, chapter 25).

The association of fire with hell, sometimes taken as a symbol of purging, seems to have originated in the idea of burning up rubbish. Gehenna took its name from the valley of Hinnom where the rubbish of Jerusalem was burned. There is the same notion in Malachi (chapter 4.1): 'all evildoers will be stubble; the day that comes shall burn them up.' Again in Matthew (chapter 13) Jesus tells a parable about the burning of weeds and explains it with: 'The Son of Man will send his angels, and they will gather out of his kingdom all causes of sin and all evildoers, and throw them into the furnace of fire; there men will weep and gnash their teeth.'

Many of St. Paul's references to the fate of the wicked suggest that they will be annihilated, though in Romans (chapter 2) dealing with 'the day of wrath,' he says that for every human being who does evil 'there will be

Painting from the late fourteenth to mid fifteenth century entitled *Descent into Hell with Deesis and Selected Saints*

tribulation and distress.' In the book of Revelation (chapter 21) 'the lake that burns with fire and brimstone, which is the second death' is the final destination of the cowardly, the faithless, the polluted, murderers, fornicators, sorcerers, idolaters, and all liars. The brimstone is sulphur ('burning stone') and the reference is to Isaiah (chapter 30.33): 'For a burning place has long been prepared . . . the breath of the Lord, like a stream of brimstone, kindles it.'

Only one passage in the New Testament (Matthew, chapter 25.46) says that the punishment in hell will last for all eternity and in the third century the great theologian Origen (c. AD 185—254) suggested that the torment in hell would not last forever, that the wicked and even the Devil himself would eventually be redeemed and evil totally annihilated, and that the 'fire' of hell might not be a real fire but the pangs of guilty conscience. Even he was worried that by questioning the eternity of punishment he might weaken the chief deterrent to immorality, but in fact his views were rejected by the majority of Christians and condemned as heretical by the church.

Seventeenth-century painting depicting seven levels of Jain hell and various tortures suffered in them. Picture taken from cloth painting from Jain temple in Gujarat.

The Harrowing of Hell

In the medieval hell the damned suffered 'the pain of loss' the agony of being cut off from God, and 'the pain of sense' the physical tortures inflicted by demons. Most of the dead did not go to hell, or to heaven, but to purgatory where they were purified of sin and could be helped by the prayers of the faithful on Earth, but in most descriptions of purgatory the agonies are almost as frightful as those of hell itself. Many modern Christians have returned to the outlook of Origen, seeing hell as a place where the guilty are purged of evil and unbelief, but not by physical torture. Others reject hell entirely, believing that God's infinite mercy will extend to everyone, or alternatively, that the irredeemable are not tormented and tortured but are simply annihilated.

Christ was crucified on the first Good Friday and, as the Apostles' Creed says, 'descended into hell.' He rose from the dead on Easter Sunday and the story grew up that in the interval he had 'harrowed' or despoiled hell by conquering Death and releasing his captives. The souls of the dead were in the darkness of the underworld when at midnight there appeared a great light, like the light of the sun, and a voice like thunder demanded, 'Lift up your gates, ye princes, and be lifted up, ye everlasting gates, and the King of Glory shall come in.' Death skulking in his lair asked: 'Who is this King of Glory?' and was answered, 'The Lord strong and mighty in battle' (Psalm 24). The gates and bars were broken down, the dead were loosed from their chains, the King of Glory entered in the form of a man and all the dark places of Hades were filled with light. Christ trampled on Death and seized Satan, ordering him to be tied hand and foot. He raised up Adam and the patriarchs and prophets, the righteous men of old, from Abraham to John the Baptist, and led them to paradise.

Outside Christianity there are many stories of descents to the underworld, including those of Odysseus, Aeneas, and the hero of the *Kaleuala*. In some of the stories the hero harrows hell by stealing one of its treasures, which may carry immortality with it (as Arthur stole the otherworld cauldron), by releasing a victim from Death or by alleviating the pains of the tormented. The Greek hero Theseus went to the underworld but was held fast there until he was released by Hercules, who also fetched away Cerberus, the many-headed dog who guarded the gate of Hades. This Labour of Hercules may really have been a quest for immortality and a conquest of death. According to the *Iliad*, Hercules shot Hades with an arrow at the gate of the underworld and left him in agony. Xenophon's (430–354 BC) *Persian Expedition* says that the Greeks anchored near the Acherusian peninsula on the south coast of the Black Sea, 'where Heracles is said to have descended into the lower world to fetch Cerberus, and where they still show evidence of his descent for a quarter of a mile down into the earth.'

There is a Sumerian myth that the goddess Inanna went to the underworld to bring back her lover Dumuzi (Tammuz). She turned into a corpse but was revived by the messengers of the god Enki, and came back to Earth. It is likely that in the original tale she succeeded in rescuing Dumuzi. In Hindu mythology the god Krishna went to the kingdom of dead and obtained the release of a favourite pupil. In Buddhism a Bodhisattva often enters a hell and releases the sufferers there from pain. The Chinese Buddhist goddess Kwan Yin visited a hell and it was turned into a paradise.

King of the Dead

The word 'hell' itself comes from an Anglo-Saxon root meaning 'to cover' or 'to conceal' with an obvious application to a grave. The Scandinavian goddess Hel ruled those who died of old age or disease (those who fell in battle went to a happy afterlife in Valhalla). She was fierce and pitiless and her underworld of Nifelheim was freezing cold, like the lowest circle of hell in Dante's *Inferno*.

The Islamic picture of hell resembles the Jewish and Christian ones, by which it was influenced. In India the idea of punishment of the wicked after death is very old but in both Buddhism and Hinduism the numerous hells are not places of eternal torture but stages in the chain of birth, death, and rebirth that the self must undergo unless it can escape from the cycle altogether. At each death the self goes to a paradise or a hell corresponding to the way it has behaved in each life.

The Tibetan Book of the Dead says that after death each person goes before Yama, the King of the Dead, who holds up to him a mirror in which his deeds are reflected. 'The mirror in which Yama seems to read your past is your own memory, and also his judgement is your own. It is you yourself who pronounce your own judgement, which in its turn determines your next rebirth.' The terrible god and the frightening monsters that are seen are 'an illusion.' However, popular belief in India, China, and Japan imagines tortures and torturers as real, as vindictive and as ingenious as any in the Western traditions. The history of hell is a descent into the infernal pit of the human mind.

RICHARD CAVENDISH

Immortality

The burial customs of early man cannot be cited in proof of his belief in human survival of death and continuance into endless life. The fact that many of the skeletons found at Mount Carmel and other prehistoric sites had the legs tucked up behind the pelvis could be taken to mean that the living were afraid that the dead might 'walk' and were seeking to immobilize them. It could just as well mean that they thought of death as a return to the womb from which life came and that they were preparing the dead body accordingly, in the posture of an unborn child; or it might mean that they thought that the dead body had to be bundled up small so as to gain access to a new world, to which the sun retired each day through a tiny hole in the Western sky. Finally, given the limitations of primitive tools, the real reason might be that the living did not want to have to make a very large hole to serve as a grave. Not until written records became available along with burials is it possible to infer anything about the beliefs of the people concerned.

> *. . . that many of the skeletons found . . . had the legs tucked up behind the pelvis could be taken to mean that the living were afraid that the dead might 'walk' and were seeking to immobilize them . . .*

The great value of Herodotus, that observant Greek historian of the fifth century BC, is that he went about taking notes in the manner of the modern anthropologist. His reports of the burial customs of the Scythians in south Russia agree remarkably with what has been found there in modern times; royal *kurgan* graves have yielded up skeletons of horses (as many as fifty at a time), cup-bearers, attendants, and concubines, just as Herodotus describes. These practices, which ensured that the dead prince would be provided with a retinue, point to a belief in immortality of a sort, even though it might have been a selective immortality that was to be enjoyed by princes only.

Mesopotamian literature tells of the descent of the goddess Ishtar (or Inanna) to the underworld through its seven gates; there she is sprinkled with the water of life and then ascends through the seven gates to rejoin the world of men. The *Epic of Gilgamesh* includes an episode where the hero brings up a wonderful plant from the sea bed, the virtue of which is to restore life and youth. Where such tales were told, the belief in survival cannot have been weak.

An Egyptian papyrus dated as early as 2000 BC contains a sophisticated dialogue between a man and his own soul. At the end his soul advises: 'Desire to reach the West (the abode of the dead) when thy body goes into the earth, that I may alight after thou hast grown weary.' The papyrus describes 'those who are yonder.' They are shown as 'men of knowledge; they punish sinners and stand in the barque of the sun, giving choice gifts to the temples.' This is a remarkable description, far removed from what Hebrew thought had achieved by the same epoch.

The sojourn of the Jews in Egypt did not affect their beliefs about the fate of the dead. Jacob grieved for his lost son, Joseph, saying: 'I shall go down to Sheol to my son, mourning' (Genesis, chapter 37.35). Sheol was the darkling abode of the dead, where personal survival was at a very low ebb. Those in Sheol could not praise God but were condemned to a state of weakness and dullness. Saul might visit the witch of Endor and call up the spirit of Samuel from Sheol, but the rest of the dead had to bear an existence that was a pale shadow of life upon Earth.

Escape from Sheol

Gradually, toward the end of the Hebrew Scriptures, there appears the idea of a general rising from the dead, an escape from Sheol to a life that is once more enriched with bodily sensation. The just, in the words of the Wisdom of Solomon (in the Apocrypha), are to receive the kingdom of glory and the diadem of beauty from the hand of God. They will confront their persecutors, who will then become objects of

Temple of Kom Ombo showing the ankh, a symbol of afterlife. Kom Ombo is an unusual double temple built during the Ptolemaic dynasty in the Egyptian town of Kom Ombo.

ignominy suffering remorse. A similar picture is given by the prophet Daniel.

The Greek philosophers, according to their habit, looked at the problem in rational fashion. A distinction between body and soul, and the destiny of each, was current in Greece in the time of Herodotus, for the war memorial to the Athenians killed at the siege of Potidaea (in Macedonia) speaks of their bodies committed to the ground and their souls flying upward. Over a generation later, Plato (in the dialogue *Phaedo*) draws a portrait of Socrates discoursing on immortality during the last hours that his disciples were allowed to spend with him in the condemned cell. The setting of the dialogue implies that it was in the main a true report of what was said. The argument runs from the existence of eternal objects of knowledge that are not liable to change (such as the idea of beauty) to the eternity of the knowing subject. The whole Greek theory of knowledge rested on the proposition that like is known by like. Plato was at pains to show Socrates refuting the Pythagorean idea that the human soul was a harmony, for a harmony could be dissolved. Since death and life are contraries, the onset of death forces the soul either to withdraw or be annihilated; it cannot be annihilated, and so it withdraws from the function of animating the body.

Existence Before Birth

In an earlier dialogue, the *Gorgias*, Socrates is shown by Plato propounding a purified version of the Greek myth that there was a judgment after death and that souls passed either to the Islands of the Blest or else to prison and torture. In the *Meno* he presents the case for the pre-existence of the soul, based on the phenomena of memory and of the spontaneous understanding of mathematical problems by the young; this can be made to look like a memory of what was understood in a previous phase of existence. With this conclusion Plato formulated what has proved to be one of the great puzzles about immortality: if it is good for the future, why not for the past also? If the soul is to exist in the future, may it not also have existed in the past?

Plato never quite made up his mind about the individuality of the human soul. If it was strictly of the same nature as the eternal objects of knowledge (from which its existence was deduced) it ought to be looked on as a universal idea. Aristotle accepted this conclusion; for him there was a world-intellect that performed in each man the higher functions of understanding and that withdrew from man at death. In life a man should 'play the immortal as far as he can,' but there would be no future for him when he had done.

Transmigration of a human soul from one body to another lent it a bogus universality, and it was to this solution that Plato himself inclined. The charm of his work won for Plato many Christian admirers. In 380, Gregory, the Bishop of Nyssa, wrote a dialogue *On the Soul and the Resurrection* after the death of his brother, Basil, and his sister, Macrina; it is a close imitation of the *Phaedo* in style but its argument reaches beyond Plato.

Christian thinkers from the second century onward speak of themselves as a third race, neither Jew nor Greek, and thus one may look for some attempt by them to combine the Jewish idea of a risen and restored body in the hereafter with the Greek idea of immortality for the soul alone. It is not surprising that some of the early Christian thinkers found it difficult to combine Jewish ideas from the

Mosaic depicting School of Athens, from Pompei, Italy

Old Testament with the Greek philosophy they had learned as young men. Thus in the writings of Theophilus of Antioch in the second century AD, one finds a notion that God did not make man mortal or immortal by nature, but indifferent; if he lived a good life, he would be immortal but otherwise he would be condemned to mortality. St. Paul had left no doubt about his own beliefs; he spoke of the resurrection of the body for the just and unjust alike, as he acknowledged to the Roman governor Felix (Acts, chapter 24.15). The Athenians to whom St. Paul was preaching, seem to have thought that he was advocating the worship of two gods, Jesus and Resurrection, so much had he to say about the latter (Acts, chapter 17).

Purpose of the Soul

Athenagoras, a Christian Platonist of the late second century, wrote a lengthy treatise on the resurrection of the body, since it was this feature in Christian teaching that most scandalized the Greeks. Why say that the body would be reconstituted, when Plato and so many others had argued that immortality came through getting rid of the body? The Christians claimed that their ideas about the future life had come to them from Christ but the human mind could grasp them, when once they were set out, and could find reasons to make them plausible. It was these reasons that Athenagoras undertook to give. He dropped the threefold view of human nature, which divided it into body, soul, and spirit, though Plato, the Stoics, and the Jews all accepted it; instead, Athenagoras used a twofold division—body and soul—and this afterward became generally accepted. His main argument for immortality was based on the purpose of the creation of the soul. God did not make the soul idly, nor yet for any need of his own, nor again for the service of any other creature, since no creature with reason and judgment has been created for any other's sake. The only purpose that will answer is that man was created for society with God who is eternal.

The theologian Origen (c. AD 185—254) was so taken with this argument that he developed from it the conclusion that, since society with God was the goal for man, there would be a general amnesty for all men at the end of the world, whatever their sins might have been. The Church rejected this on the evidence of the New Testament but also on the rational ground that human free will, if once it becomes immobilized in enmity to God, is enough to exclude a man from society with God forever. The other line of thought developed by Origen was a renewal of the Platonic theory of the preexistence of the human soul. He held that the fact of some men being born with active minds and others with minds wholly obtuse and incapable of instruction pointed to their having existed in another world, where some had sinned and drawn upon themselves a punishment in the next round of life. Other Christian Platonists, such as Gregory of Nyssa (c. 335–c. 395), brushed aside the transmigration theory: a soul at death was left incomplete, but this did not mean that it must seek another body and another life. It would be completed by the resurrection.

The British philosopher McTaggart . . . held a firm conviction of human immortality that was based upon the unique and timeless quality of love.

Immortality before and after life on Earth was still a difficulty for St. Jerome (AD 340–420), who in a famous letter sets out the possibilities of the case. He rejected the idea of the emanation of the soul from God, and envisaged three alternatives: all human souls could have been created at one time and then kept in reserve until wanted for life in the world; or they could be created each time there was a human conception; or else they might be passed on from the parents. Jerome adhered to the second alternative.

Love Eternal

St. Thomas Aquinas (c. 1225–74), theologian and philosopher, held that the eternal truths that the human mind can contemplate must be anchored in a supreme truth, and that this is the goal desired by the human mind as it contemplates. He also held strongly that it was good and natural for the soul to be in a body; if all souls had been created at one time, then most of them would have suffered violence and been under restraint until they received their bodies, and of this there was no sign. In 1513 the fifth Lateran Council defined that it was heretical to say that the soul was mortal, but it did not elaborate the grounds for immortality. Luther accepted this definition.

Gradually in modern times interest in proving immortality has centered upon the value of the person and of that most personal of relationships, love. The unique quality of love lends more force than ever to the traditional argument that man is meant for society with God, once it can be entertained that love of God is a possibility. The British philosopher McTaggart (1866–1925), who was professedly an atheist, held a firm conviction of human immortality that was based upon the timeless quality of love.

One of McTaggart's difficulties

about immortality was that 'even the best men, when they die, are not in such a condition of intellectual and moral perfection as would fit them to enter heaven immediately.' As if in answer to this, Karl Rahner (1904–84) has recently been advocating the idea that death is not simply a passive condition of being snuffed out but a personal deed, a final affirmation of what one's life has been, since death must be considered to affect both body and soul. A certain amount of experimental evidence has been gathered from those who have come very close to death through some accident and then been restored to life; the trend of this evidence is to support the idea that at the moment when death was nearest they passed in review the events of their whole life. Thomas de Quincey (1785–1859) noticed this fact, a kinswoman of his having reported that she had seen the whole of her life arrayed before her when she had fallen into a river, not successively but simultaneously, 'and she had a faculty developed as suddenly for comprehending the whole and every part.'

The Attainment of 'Being'

Investigation into the phenomena of telepathy and other branches of psychical research in the present century have greatly increased the interest in the problems of immortality. The French philosopher Gabriel Marcel (1889–1973), in the Myers Memorial lecture of 1955, recounts that it was these factors that quickened his own interest. He elaborated a distinction between 'being' and 'having:' fears and desires belong to the realm of 'having,' while a loving collaboration with the liberty of another helps both to attain 'being.' Thus a basis is provided for justifying the unique and timeless quality of love. Thought transference without any physical link, where it can be verified, offers the prospect of an activity of the human mind that does not depend upon the body. The phenomena of Spiritualism are of more doubtful quality, for whatever their causation they do require a physical basis.

The value of the human person may thus be seen as the main prop of all arguments for immortality. Stunted or split personalities, or other psychologi-

The Weighing of the Heart from the Book of the Dead of Ani. At left, Ani and his wife Tutu enter the assemblage of gods. At centre, Anubis weighs Ani's heart against the feather of Maat, observed by the goddesses Renenutet and Meshkenet, the god Shay, and Ani's own ba.

cal wreckage, make no difference to the argument, which takes 'person' in the metaphysical sense of an intelligent being who is an end in himself. When Aristotle said that slaves were animated tools, cogs in the social machine, he was repudiating the notion of person as he had repudiated immortality.

J. H. CREHAN

FURTHER READING:

J. Burnet. The Socratic Doctrine of the Soul. *(Oxford, UK: Oxford University Press, 1916); F. Copleston.* History of Philosophy. *(London, UK: Burns & Oates, 1944–66); E. O. James.* Prehistoric Religion. *(London, UK: Thames & Hudson, 1957); G. Marcel.* The Mystery of Being. *(Washington D.C.: Regnery-Gateway, 1960); C. Morgan.* Liberties of the Mind. *(New York, NY: Century, 1979); E. F. Sutcliffe.* The Old Testament and the Future Life. *(London, UK: Burns & Oates, 1946); G. N. M. Tyrrell.* The Personality of Man. *(London, UK: Penguin, 1946).*

Judgment of the Dead

That the fate of the dead is decided at a post-mortem judgment is an idea that is very ancient and widespread. It naturally involves belief that the dead survive death, that they remember their past lives and are conscious that they are now dead, and that they can experience the pain of punishment and the joy of reward. Where death is regarded as the virtual extinction of personality, as it was for example in Mesopotamian and Homeric religion, there is no basis for belief in a post-mortem judgment—the shades of the dead, good, and bad, are doomed to virtual nonexistence.

The earliest known evidence of belief that the dead would be judged for their conduct in this life occurs in Egyptian records dating c. 2400 BC. The belief was obviously already well established by that date, and its origins doubtless lie back in a more remote past. In the Pyramid Texts inscribed on the interior walls of pyramids at Sakkara near Memphis, two different conceptions of this judgment were apparently current. One is of an unsophisticated kind, and it was probably inspired by contemporary juridical practice. It finds expression in a series of anticipatory declarations of innocence made by the deceased in respect of various crimes. The idea behind these declarations seems to be that in the next life complaints might be brought against the dead as they were brought against the living in this world. As, in the primitive courts of Egypt, the accused would vehemently reject the charges and protest his innocence, so it was apparently thought well to anticipate such charges in the afterlife by prior solemn declarations of guiltlessness. In these passages, however, no reference is made to a judge of the dead.

The other conception was of a much more involved kind. In one Text it is said of the dead pharaoh: 'He desires that he may be justified (*maa kheru*) through that which he has done.' The words *maa kheru* meant literally 'true of voice,' and they acquired a specific significance through the legend of Osiris. The ancient Egyptians believed that the case of the divine hero Osiris, after his resurrection from death, had been brought before a tribunal of the gods of Heliopolis. Osiris was there adjudged *maa kheru*, 'justified,' and his murderer Seth was condemned. Since the dead king, in the Pyramid Texts, was ritually identified with Osiris in order to participate in his resurrection, this identification also caused him to acquire Osiris's title in the state after death of *maa kheru*. The Pyramid Texts thus reveal the origin of an idea that later came to dominate the Egyptian conception of the judgment of the dead.

Warning from the Tomb

Certain tomb inscriptions of about the same period, or slightly later, reveal an important development in this idea of a posthumous judgment. At that time the royal government of Egypt was weakening, with much resultant social disorder. Tombs were being either robbed of their funerary equipment or taken over by others for their own mortuary use. To the law-abiding, such happenings were most terrible, for they threatened their hopes of a blissful afterlife. Some Egyptians sought to meet the danger by threatening inscriptions on their tombs. Thus Herkhuf, an Aswan noble, warns any would-be robber: 'As for any man who shall enter into this tomb as his mortuary possession, I will seize him like a wild fowl; he shall be judged for it by the Great God.'

The 'Great God' whom Herkhuf here invokes was doubtless the sun god Re, who was regarded as the upholder of *maat*, the principle of cosmic order. In other words, Herkhuf not only claims that, though dead, he was able to attack any who might rob his tomb; he confidently asserts that Re himself would punish so vile a crime. However, the thought of the divine judgment that would fall on the robber apparently led Herkhuf to think about his own situation. For he goes on in

As for any man who shall enter into this tomb as his mortuary possession, I will seize him like a wild fowl; he shall be judged for it by the Great God.

A vignette from the Book of the Dead of Ani. Ani's mummy is carried in the funeral procession

his inscription to declare: 'I was one saying good things and repeating what was loved. Never did I say aught evil, to a powerful one against any people, for I desired that it might be well with me in the Great God's presence.'

In other words, this ancient Egyptian not only threatened any would-be violator of his tomb with divine judgment; he was mindful that he had himself to undergo such judgment.

No hint is given in this earliest evidence of how the judgment after death was imagined. Some kind of tribunal was evidently envisaged. Herkhuf seems to imply that Re was the judge, but he makes no reference to the way in which the verdict was reached. A clearer picture emerges from the next document that mentions the post-mortem judgment. It is known as the Instruction for King Meri-ka-re, and dates from c. 2100 BC. The dead are depicted as being tried by a panel of judges with Thoth, the god of wisdom, acting as prosecutor. Their deeds are set before them in two heaps, presumably of the good and the bad. This imagery, however, did not establish itself and the Coffin Texts of the Middle Kingdom period (c. 2160–1580 BC) reveal a fluidity of concept about the judgment.

During this period, however, a new idea emerged that was to dominate the later conception of the judgment. References occur in the Coffin Texts to weighing on balances as the mode of assessment. How this weighing was done is obscure: in one passage the balance is actually personified as 'this god of mysterious form, whose two eyebrows are the two arms of the balance, who casts his lasso over the wicked (to hale them to) his block, who annihilates the souls, in that day when evil is assessed, in the presence of the Master of all.'

The motive that inspired the idea that the dead would be assessed by weighing is an interesting subject for speculation. On the available evidence, it would seem that the ancient Egyptians sought for an image that would express the absolute impartiality of the judgment after death. Doubtless their experience of legal chicanery caused them to avoid the imagery of Earthly tribunals. The earlier idea of assessing the dead by the witness of their good and evil deeds set out in heaps had invoked the practice of the market place; but, though a vivid image, it was evidently found inadequate. The process of weighing must obviously have been deemed a better conception, and by the New Kingdom (c. 1580–1090 BC) it was developed into one of the most impressive scenes in the religious iconography of the ancient world.

Weighed Against the Truth

The best representation of the scene, beautifully drawn and coloured, is in the Papyrus of Ani. The scene depicts the dead scribe Ani and his wife watching the weighing of Ani's heart in the Hall of the Two Truths. The balance occupies the centre of the scene. In one scale-pan the hieroglyph symbol of the heart is represented, and in the other the feather symbol of *Maat*, truth. The heart of Ani is being weighed against truth. In ancient Egyptian psychology the heart was regarded an independent censor or witness within each person and in most copies of the Book of the Dead the heart is implored not to witness against the deceased at this l moment.

The fateful balance is attended by the jackal-headed mortuary god Anubis, who adjusts its plummet, while the text above him exhorts him to be exact. To the right of the balance stands Thoth, the ibis-headed god of wisdom, who records the verdict of the weighing on his scribe's tablet. The adjacent text gives the report which Thoth makes to the divine assessors seated above. Ani is acquitted: 'His soul (*ba*) has stood in witness thereof. His case is exact on the Great Balance. No crime has been found in what he has done.' In turn, the divine tribunal is represented as replying to Thoth: 'Confirmed is that which comes forth from your mouth. Just (*maa*) and righteous is Osiris (namely) the scribe Ani. He is justified . . . Entrance into the presence of Osiris shall be granted to him.'

The scene ominously indicates the fate that awaited the guilty. Behind

Thoth is depicted the fantastic monster Am-mut, the 'eater of the dead.'

This judgment scene is followed by another representing the god Horus leading the justified Ani into the presence of Osiris, who sits enthroned and attended by the goddesses Isis and Nephthys. Subsequent vignettes in the Papyrus show Ani and his wife enjoying the delights of the otherworld, over which Osiris ruled. In most other depictions of the judgment scene Osiris is represented as presiding in person over the transaction.

The presentation of the judgment in the Book of the Dead is complicated by chapter 125, which is entitled: 'Words spoken when one enters the Hall of the Two Truths. To separate N from his sins, and to see the face of all the gods.' Then follow two lists of what are often called 'negative confessions,' but which are more correctly designated 'declarations of innocence.' The first, and shorter, is addressed to Osiris; the second to forty-two other deities. The sins, of which the deceased declares that he is innocent, range widely, and include moral offenses, such as murder and unnatural sexual relations, and ritual offenses like hindering the procession of a god. The conception of the judgment implied in this chapter is quite different from that presented by the weighing of the heart. The discrepancy is probably to be explained by the conservatism of the Egyptian mind. For these 'declarations of innocence' doubtless derive from the primitive asseverations of guiltlessness from specific sins that appear in the Pyramid Texts. Never willing to discard ancient traditions, the Egyptians retained this one even when the idea of the weighing of the heart had become the dominant theme of the judgment. They apparently reconciled the differing conceptions by representing the 'Declarations' as being made first by the deceased on arrival at the Hall of the Two Truths. The subsequent weighing of his heart against the symbol of truth proved whether his protestation of innocence could be accepted as truly justified.

This Egyptian conception of the judgment after death is unique in the ancient world. It remained an effective belief in Egypt until the Christian era; it is only in Christianity that the idea achieved a like importance and such dramatic presentation.

Until the second century BC Hebrew religion did not provide the necessary basis for belief in a judgment after death. According to its view of human nature, man was a psycho-physical organism which death irreparably shattered. The shade that survived this dissolution descended to Sheol, conceived as a deep pit far below the foundations of the world, where all the shades of the dead dwelt in dust and gloom, with no distinction between the just and the unjust. However, about the time of the

***The Last Judgment*—an icon of first half of the seventeenth century. Painted by Michelangelo, Sistine Chapel, Vatican City, Rome, Italy**

Maccabaean Wars, a change took place. Belief in a resurrection of the dead suddenly made its appearance, together with the idea of a judgment of the dead. The earliest evidence is the following brief statement in the book of Daniel (chapter 12.2): 'And many of those who sleep in the dust of the earth shall awake . . . some to everlasting life, and some to shame and everlasting contempt.' The statement is admittedly obscure, particularly in its limitation of resurrection to an undefined 'many.' However, this first problematic evidence of the belief is soon supported in Jewish literature by an abundance of references to, and descriptions of, a future judgment of the dead. In turn, the conception of Sheol changes from the place where all the dead dwell, undifferentiated by their moral character, to a place of punishment for the wicked.

The Jewish conception of the judgment of the dead was essentially conditioned by the strong nationalist factor in Judaism. It had long been believed that there would be a 'Day of Yahweh' when the god of Israel would signally punish the oppressors of his people. In later Jewish apocalyptic literature, owing to the deterioration of Israel's political position, this belief was gradually changed into an intense conviction that Yahweh would soon intervene dramatically in the existing world situation. The Day of Yahweh was, in consequence, transformed into a Last Judgment, coincident with the catastrophic end of the world. The following passage from the apocalyptic writing known as II (IV) *Esdras* (chapter 6) vividly presents this Last Judgment at which the god of Israel would pronounce the doom of the Gentile Nations, who had afflicted his people:

'And the earth shall restore those that are asleep in her, and so shall the dust those that dwell in silence, and the secret places shall deliver those souls that are committed unto them. And the Most High shall be revealed on the seat of judgment, and compassion shall pass away, and longsuffering shall be withdrawn: but judgment only shall remain. . . And the pit of torment shall appear, and over against it shall be the place of rest: and the furnace of hell shall be shewed, and over against it the paradise of delight. And then shall the Most High say to the nations that are raised from the dead, see and understand whom ye have denied, or whom ye have not served, or whose commandment ye have despised. Look on this side and that: here is delight and rest, and there fire and torments. Thus shall he speak unto them in the day of judgment.'

In Jewish apocalyptic belief the Last Judgment was primarily an 'Assize of Nations,' at which the Gentiles would be punished for their oppression of Israel. It was to be preceded by a general resurrection of the dead, and accompanied by cosmic cataclysm. In some versions of the belief the Messiah, instead of God (Yahweh), would be the judge. This idea of a Last Judgment was taken over by Christianity, and profoundly influenced its doctrine concerning the 'last things.'

Punishment in Hades

Neither the Greek nor the Roman religion offered hope of a significant afterlife, and therefore no ground existed for belief in a post-mortem judgment. The description of the dead given in Homer's *Odyssey* (book 11) set the pattern for what might be called the classical view of human destiny. At death the *psyche*, a wraithlike image of the living person, descended to the gloomy realm of Hades. There it joined the other dead, who dwelt there bereft of consciousness. The logic of this situation negated belief in a judgment after death.

The idea of Hades as a place of retribution, thus implying a judgment, gradually developed, chiefly through the influence of Orphism and Neo-Pythagoreanism. The fate of the dead turned on whether they had been initiated or not into the Mystery cults concerned. However, the post-mortem judgment gradually came to be thought of as a moral test. A vivid description of Hades as a place of

Judgment in Black and White

O nobly born (so-and-so), listen. That thou art suffering so cometh from thine own karma; it is not due to anyone else's; it is by thine own *karma*. Accordingly, pray earnestly to the Precious Trinity; that will protect thee. If thou neither prayest nor knowest how to meditate upon the Great Symbol nor upon any tutelary deity, the Good Genius who was born simultaneously with thee, will come now and count out thy good deeds (with) white pebbles, and the Evil Genius who was born simultaneously with thee, will come and count out thy evil deeds (with) black pebbles. Thereupon, thou wilt be greatly frightened, awed, and terrified, and wilt tremble; and thou wilt attempt to tell lies, saying 'I have not committed any evil deed.' Then the Lord of Death will say, 'I will consult the Mirror of *Karma*.'

So saying, he will look in the Mirror, wherein every good and evil act is vividly reflected. Lying will be of no avail.

The (one of the Executive Furies of) the Lord of Death will place round thy neck a rope and drag thee along; he will cut off thy head, extract thy heart, pull out thy intestines, lick up thy brain, drink thy blood, eat thy flesh, and gnaw thy bones; but thou wilt be incapable of dying. Although thy body be hacked to pieces, it will revive again. The repeated hacking will Cause intense pain and torture. Even at the time that the pebbles are being counted out, be not frightened, nor terrified; tell no lies; and fear not the Lord of Death.

Thy body being a mental body is incapable of dying even though beheaded and quartered. In reality thy body is of the nature of voidness; thou needest not be afraid. The Lords of Death are thine own hallucinations. Thy desire-body is a body of propensities, and void.

W. Y. Evans-Wentz, ed.
The Tibetan Book of the Dead

retributive punishment for sins is given by Virgil (70–19 BC) in the *Aeneid* (book 6). In the underworld, his hero Aeneas comes to a parting of ways: one leads to Elysium; the other to Dis, a great fortresslike place, encircled by a flaming river. Here Rhadamanthys 'holds his iron sway; he chastises, and hears the tale of guilt, exacting confessions of crimes, whenever in the world above any man rejoicing in vain deceit, has put off atonement for sin until death's late hour.' Awful demons, with writhing snakes, torment these sinners. This horrific depiction greatly influenced Dante (1265–1321) as his *Inferno* shows, and it is reflected in many medieval descriptions of hell.

Bridge of the Separator

The teaching of Zarathustra, the ancient Iranian prophet (c. 628–51 BC) faced every man with the fateful decision of aligning himself on the side either of the principle of Good or of Evil, which struggled unceasingly for mastery of the universe. In the *Gathas*, in which Zarathustra's teaching is preserved, there are enigmatic references to the consequences in the afterlife of each person's decision. Mention is made of retributive punishment by molten metal; but more notable is his reference to the *Cinvato paratu* or 'Bridge of the Separator.' The crossing of this bridge appears to constitute a post-mortem ordeal for the dead—the wicked would fall from it to some awful doom below. In the later literature of Zoroastrianism the crossing of this fateful bridge is elaborated into a definite act of judgment. A deity named 'just Rashnu' weighs the deeds of the dead with the strictest precision. Those adjudged just pass with ease across the bridge to eternal bliss, while the wicked, unmasked by Rashnu, are seized by the demon Vizarsh. This judgment apparently took place shortly after the death of the individual; but Zoroastrian doctrine also included a final judgment. In the classic description of it in the *Bundahisn*, at the ultimate rehabilitation, the dead would be resurrected and all mankind assembled for judgment. They become aware of their good and evil deeds, and the good go to heaven and the wicked are cast into hell. How this ultimate judgment was related to the immediate judgment after death is not clear; a similar problem exists in Christian doctrine.

The Last Trump

Christianity originated in Judaea as a Jewish messianic movement. Its outlook was thus conditioned by current apocalyptic belief. Jesus was identified with the Messiah and, after his crucifixion, it was believed that he would soon return with supernatural power to complete his messianic task. This belief finds dramatic expression in the gospel of Matthew (chapter 25.31—33), where he presides at the Last Judgment: 'When the Son of man shall come in his glory, and all the angels with him, then shall he sit on the throne of his glory: and before him shall be gathered all the nations, and he will separate them one from another as a shepherd separates the sheep from the goats, and he will place the sheep at his right hand, but the goats at the left.' Although the passage at this point suddenly changes from envisaging an Assize of Nations, according to Jewish apocalyptic, into a

Scene depicting *The Last Judgement* by the Italian Renaissance master Michelangelo

Painting depicting the prophet Mohammed sitting between other prophets in the ancient temple of Kubbat al-Sakhra, Jerusalem

trial of individual persons, the judgment is the traditional Last Judgment at the end of the world. The most graphic presentation of this Judgment in the New Testament is given in the Revelation of John (chapter 20.11—13); it conforms to the traditional apocalyptic pattern by including the resurrection of the dead: 'Then I saw a great white throne and him who sat upon it; from his presence earth and sky fled away, and no place was found for them. And I saw the dead, great and small, standing before the throne, and books were opened. Also another book was opened, which is the book of life. And the dead were judged by what was written in the books, by what they had done. And the sea gave up the dead in it, Death and Hades gave up the dead in them, and all were judged by what they had done.'

The first Christians believed that the return of Christ and the Last Judgment would happen within their own lifetime. But the nonfulfillment of this expectation gradually caused a change of outlook. Although belief in an apocalyptic Last Judgment was never abandoned, subsequent generations of Christians had to adapt their faith to the fact that they would doubtless die before Christ returned. The question inevitably arose, therefore, of the situation of the dead until the Last Judgment determined their eternal fate. A solution was found in the idea of a judgment immediately after death, which was implied by Christ's parable of Dives and Lazarus (Luke, chapter 16). Hence emerged the concept of two post-mortem judgments in Christianity: an immediate or particular judgment and a final judgment. And with it developed the doctrine of purgatory. It was taught that immediately after death the soul would be judged and sent to purgatory, unless its sins were such that it was already damned beyond redemption. In purgatory expiation was made for past sins, in the hope of ultimate acquittal at the Last Judgment, when the purified soul would be admitted to the beatific vision.

A distinction was drawn between the torments of purgatory and those of hell. In purgatory the souls of the dead were disembodied; hence their sufferings were not physical as they would be in hell, where the damned suffered in their resurrected bodies. Further, the souls in purgatory suffered in the hope of ultimate deliverance; but the pains of hell were eternal. However, despite these theological distinctions, it would appear from medieval art and literature that the torments of purgatory were imagined just as realistically as those of hell.

The prospect of immediate judgment and purgatory did not lessen concern about the judgment to come. From about the twelfth century the representation of the Last Judgment became a major theme of Christian art in both the Eastern and Western Church. These medieval depictions are generally composed of three registers of scenes. At the top Christ appears as the awful Judge; he shows the wounds of Crucifixion, and attendant angels bear the symbols of his Passion. On either side the Virgin Mary and St. John kneel, supplicating the stern

Christ to spare sinful humanity. In the bottom register, the dead rise from their graves at the sound of the Last Trump. It is in the central register, however, that the crucial drama is enacted. Generally, the Archangel Michael is represented weighing the souls of men, and repelling the attempts of the Devil to interfere with the verdict. This *psychostasia* or weighing of souls was derived from ancient Egypt, by way of Coptic Christianity; its adoption into the medieval Doom constitutes a fascinating instance of the transference of ideas.

In the Doom (the name by which representations of the Last Judgment are known in England, where they often appear on the chancel arch of a church), the weighing of souls divided the two groups of the redeemed and the damned; the division was intended to denote its decisive nature. The redeemed are usually represented as being carried by angels to Abraham's bosom (Luke, chapter 16.22). Abraham is depicted as seated, with a crowd of diminutive souls looking complacently out from the bosom of his robe. The damned, on the other side, are herded by demons, horrible and relentless, toward the mouth of hell or cast into the cauldron of hell. The medieval Doom vividly testifies to the importance of the idea of the Last Judgment in medieval Christianity. Although the depiction of it virtually ceased after the Reformation, the idea continued to haunt Christians and it was a basic theme of Christian teaching until the nineteenth century.

In Islam the final judgment was a foremost topic of Mohammed's teaching, and reflects Judaeo-Christian concepts. However, each individual has to pass a judgment after death.

***The Ascent of the Blessed* by Hieronymus Bosch (c. 1450–1516)**

***The Blessed Ranieri Frees the Poor from a Florentine Jail* by Stefano Giovanni (c. 1392–1450)**

After burial, a Muslim is asked three questions: *Who was your Lord? What is your religion? Who is this man who was sent among you?* If they answer the questions correctly, two angels appear and carry the soul up to heaven. However, if the questions are not answered correctly, the grave will tighten on the corpse and crush its ribs.

The idea of a post-mortem judgment occurs also in popular Buddhism, where it has been adapted to the idea of the transmigration of the soul and the doctrine of *karma*.

S. G. F. BRANDON

FURTHER READING: S. G. F. Brandon. The Judgment of the Dead. *(London, UK: Weidenfeld & Nicolson, 1967); S. G. F. Brandon. 'The Weighing of the Soul,' in* Myths and Symbols: Studies in honour of Mircea Eliade. *(Chicago, IL: Chicago University Press, 1969).*

Near-Death Experience

The question of man's survival of bodily death was one of the first areas investigated by psychical researchers.

Soon, however, it became apparent that no conclusions could be reached through even the most thorough study of mediums and seance room activity, due to the prevalence of fraud and the unpredictability of the phenomena. Ironically, however, it seems that the most persuasive evidence for an afterlife has come, not from the work of parapsychologists but from medical practice—in the near-death experience (NDE).

In recent years improved clinical resuscitation techniques have resulted in many people being, almost literally, 'dragged back from the brink of the grave,' and it is this that has presented researchers with a wealth of provocative detail about what happens to human consciousness when the body is, however briefly, clinically dead. In the United States, Drs. Raymond Moody (b. 1944), Michael Sabom (b. 1945), and Elisabeth Kubler-Ross (1926–2004) have accumulated the evidence of hundreds of cases, most of which appear to share strikingly common features.

Dark Tunnel and Cities of Light

People who have been restored to life have reported a range of experiences of a similar nature. These fall, in general, into the following categories, in the following order:

Calmness. A sense of beginning to draw away from the activity all around. At this point the individual may be in an ambulance or receiving frantic resuscitation ministrations, but the inner peace increases.

Buzzing sound. Not all report this feature, but often it is accompanied by a slight tingling sensation, and it seems to herald the moment of leaving the body.

Out-of-body-experience (OOBE). Individuals discover, often in great surprise, that they are separated from their body and floating above it, while continuing to observe clearly what is taking place beneath. They are frequently so emotionally detached that they are amused by the scurrying figures who are trying to bring life back to the body. They may also experience the sensation of traveling invisibly around the area, eavesdropping on conversations—and it is this that often provides verifiable evidence for at least this part of the NDE at a later time.

Dark tunnel. Many individuals find themselves being propelled along a dark tunnel at enormous speed toward a brilliant light. Most do not report any negative emotions; many find the experience highly uplifting and in cases ecstatic.

Bewildered spirits. A relatively infrequent aspect in which the individual appears to encounter those who have not 'moved on' to higher realms, but remain tied to Earthly pursuits. Suicides are often numbered among these.

The Being of Light. Often without recognizable identity—although specifically Jesus and the Virgin Mary have been sometimes described—the Being radiates love and compassion as he greets the dying individual at the end of the Black Tunnel, then acts as guide for the rest of the 'journey.'

The Garden. The traveler is shown round a beautiful garden, with many-hued streams, and flowers, and brilliant sunlight. There may be indescribable music, sometimes referred to as 'the music of the spheres.'

The Life Review. The individual is shown something resembling a swift 'film show' of his or her life, and in it often sees how many opportunities have been missed to better both the self and others, in a spiritual sense.

The Vision of Knowledge. Individuals are given a glimpse of another realm of reality in which all knowledge seems to coexist beyond time and space. They may feel that they have brought back some of this knowledge on returning to life, and claim to have developed a 'sixth sense' as a result of this experience.

Meeting others (this may happen at any point after reaching the end of the Black Tunnel). Deceased relatives and friends are met, among them some whom the individual had not realized were dead (subsequent investigation will often prove this to be true). They are welcoming, but sometimes explain that it is not the right time for the individual to stay with them, and that he or she must return.

Cities of Light. A rare experience: cities that appear to be made of crystal or glass, suffused with a golden light.

Rescue or reprieve. Occasionally some spiritual agency announces that the individual must return because of a specific task left undone, or a person to be looked after, such as a child or a spouse.

The return. Frequently described in terms of great disappointment, as the individual is told that he or she must return to life. Sometimes he or she begs to be allowed to stay, but the Being of Light is adamant.

The aftermath. The person returned to life after these experiences often makes striking changes to his or her way of life: most who live to tell the tale come to the realization that material things are of lesser importance, and they often take up some good cause—although, as the afterlife has been seen to be nondenominational, they rarely return to a specific religious faith. After the experience, the individual no longer fears death, although continuing to maintain a natural dislike of the process of dying.

The Medical Response

Reports of these near-death experiences are often met with incredulity and dismissal, especially among nurses and doctors, who tend to relegate it to the category of 'dreams' or drug-induced wishful thinking. They are not alone in this —several psychologists and clinicians have also sought to explain the NDE in terms of 'the brain's last fling.' The sense of floating and the Black Tunnel, for example, are cited as being the results of chemical changes in the brain and optic nerves as they 'shut down' shortly before death. British sceptic Dr. Susan Blackmore (b. 1951 has said: 'the whole NDE scenario appears to be a reflex response to help the dying person over the death experience.'

This, however, poses an interesting question: if death is oblivion, then what is the person being helped *over* to? The NDE can hardly be the 'brain's last fling,' since the person returns to life physiologically sound and, as there is no survival value in providing the dying with hallucinatory comfort, Darwinistic principles do not apply.

Neither can the NDE be seen merely as dreamlike images of wish fulfillment, for the experience shows remarkable consistency over hundreds of cases, despite wide differences in the cultural backgrounds of the people involved. Belief in Jesus, Buddha, or Vishnu seems to make little overall difference to the content or quality of the NDE, and even atheists who have always believed that death was the end have also found themselves confronting an apparent contradiction of their beliefs.

Sceptics Persuaded

One of the most exhaustive studies of this phenomenon was undertaken over a five-year period in the 1980s by Dr. Michael Sabom. He began as a sceptic, having read Dr. Raymond Moody's *Life after Life*, of which he later wrote: 'I felt that these experiences were either fabrications . . . or embellishments . . . Five years and 116 interviews later, I am convinced that my original suspicions were wrong.'

He took all the sceptical and medical explanations—such as lack of oxygen to the brain, temporal lobe seizures, the effect of endorphins, and so on—and dismissed them one by one. He also examined those who reported NDE for their awareness of events around them when they were 'dead,' with remarkable results. He asked twenty-five cardiac patients who had reported an NDE to describe the resuscitation techniques that had been used on them—and he asked the same number of a control group what would be done to them if they suffered a cardiac arrest. Nearly all of the control group made a major error in their descriptions, but the resuscitated patients made no such mistakes. He took this as clear evidence that the patients were not making educated guesses about the techniques that had been used to bring them back to life.

Another cardiologist, Maurice Rawlings (1922–2010), has added to the literature by opening up the subject of 'negative NDES—'hellish experiences. The experience of a very small percentage—but the number is in itself highly controversial—of all NDES has been said to contain such horror that individuals are desperate to return to life.

One such case was that of a twenty-three-year-old British woman known as Gail. In 1986 she lost her job, broke up with her boyfriend, and felt that life had nothing more to offer. She took a large number of sleeping pills that she washed down with half a bottle of gin. A neighbour found her unconscious and soon she was being rushed into hospital by ambulance, the paramedics frantically trying to revive her. She was later to recall:

> *'I felt hotter and hotter and there was a sort of gritty feeling behind my eyelids. I thought I was going to burst and began to panic, although I knew I couldn't move at all. There was a horrible sense that something awful*

I felt hotter and hotter and there was a sort of gritty feeling behind my eyelids. I thought I was going to burst and began to panic, although I knew I couldn't move at all.

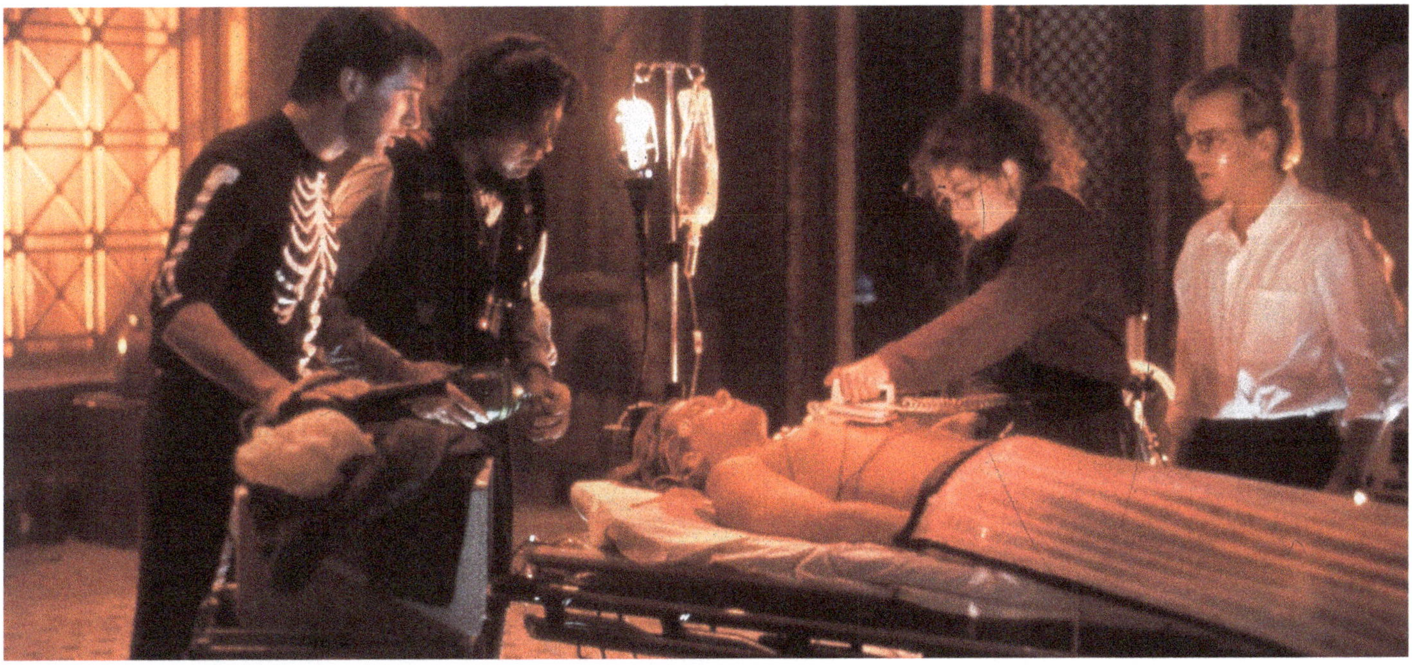

Still from the film *Flatliners* (1990) with William Baldwin, Oliver Platt, Keifer Sutherland, Julia Roberts, and Kevin Bacon

was going to happen. It seemed to me that I opened my eyes and saw I was in a huge glowing cavern deep under the earth somewhere . . . the ground was like coal. I could only shuffle about. . . somewhere there was a huge booming sound like machinery and for some reason it filled me with the worst dread I have ever experienced. Then through some pillars of this coal I could just make out a tall figure of infinite kindness, Jesus maybe . . . he looked over at me, smiled, and went away . . . I started screaming and sobbing for him to come and take me with him . . . it was the worst feeling of all, utter desolation . . . then suddenly I gave a huge jump and realized I was having my face slapped. I was back, alive, and I sobbed with joy.'

Some researchers have suggested that these negative NDEs are simply the results of drug overdoses, either self-administered or accidentally given in hospital. Others try to draw a moral, saying that all suicides suffer from negative NDEs, although it is also known that suicides do report blissful experiences.

The Eye of Innocence

Of all known NDEs, the most persuasive are those of tiny children, who could not have read any literature, whether religious or medical, and therefore could not have known what to expect. One such was Durdana Khan, who temporarily died, aged two and a half, in 1968 in Pakistan.

Attended by her father, Dr. A. G. Khan, the child became very ill from a virus infection, and eventually slipped into coma. Unable to find any signs of life, Dr. Khan began to try all possible ways to revive her, all the time saying out loud: 'Come back, my child, come back!' After fifteen minutes Durdana rallied, and soon began to recover. It was during her convalescence that her mother asked her: 'Where have you been when you went away from Mummy?'

'To the stars,' said the little girl immediately, and described how she went into a beautiful garden, met 'your mummy's mummy' and other relatives, and how she talked to God, who she has always only described as being 'blue.' God told her that her father was calling and that she must go back—and I woke up.' Later, she saw photographs of her dead relatives for the first time and recognized them as people she had met 'in the stars.'

Durdana's experience had an interesting sequel. In the late 1970s, when the Khans had moved to London, she was invited on to a BBC Television programme to tell the story of her experiences and show the pictures she had painted from memory of the garden she had visited. One viewer, a Mrs. Goldsmith of north London, was amazed. 'My God!' she cried. 'I've been to that place.'

Coincidentally, Mrs. Goldsmith was a patient of Dr. Khan, so a meeting with Durdana was easily set up. At first Durdana thought that the old lady meant that she, too, had been to a similar place, but soon realized that it was literally the same garden, which Mrs. Goldsmith had 'visited' when she had briefly died during her incarceration in a Nazi concentration camp. In fact, she had seen more of it than Durdana had, and went on to describe what it was like round the next corner . . .

The NDE has been the subject of several Hollywood films, such as *Flatliners*, where the experience was deliberately induced by medical students hoping to push back the frontiers of human knowledge, and has featured in books, such as *Twilight* by Peter James (b. 1948), besides receiving a great deal of attention in magazines, on television, and other media. Most people have now heard of NDEs and a great many have come to believe that there is an afterlife because of them. If this relieves people of the age-old terror of death then surely it is to be welcomed, but so far there is no evidence that knowledge of the phenomenon of the NDE has any marked effect upon the way one lives one's life. It seems that one has to experience it for one self for that to happen.

Necromancy

The blackest of all the black arts is undoubtedly necromancy (from Greek words meaning 'dead' and 'divination'), the ancient method of communication with the dead. Necromancy, a word corrupted by medieval Latin writers into *nigromantia*, can be divided into two main branches: divination by means of ghosts, and divination from corpses, both of which represent related forms of forbidden knowledge. The second method led to the disinterment of corpses and rifling of graves for the grisly charms which magicians and witches considered necessary for the effective performance of the magical arts.

It is not possible to understand the mysteries of necromancy without some knowledge of an attitude toward the souls of the dead that prevailed until comparatively modern times. It was taken for granted that under normal circumstances the dead did not return as ghosts, and that if they did so it must have been for some special reason. It follows that if a living person desired to establish communication with the dead on his own terms—in other words, to summon the spirits from their last resting places in defiance of their wishes—it would be necessary to institute the most elaborate precautions that magic could provide as insurance against becoming the victims of their righteous anger.

The motives of those who sought communication with the dead were largely of a mercenary character. Because of the prevailing assumption that the dead, unrestricted by human limitations, were all-knowing and all-seeing, they were usually consulted by magicians or their clients wanting to know the whereabouts of buried treasure. These enquiries were generally restricted to the twelve months following death that folklore had decreed to be the statutory period during which the shade lingered in the vicinity of its grave.

To evoke the dead the magician needed to obtain the help of powerful spirits, both for his own protection and to compel the corpse or ghost to submit to his will.

The subordination of the will of the dead to the whims of the living demanded a specialized technique known only to the most highly-skilled magicians. The annals of sorcery in the British Isles include innumerable references to 'nigramauncers,' as they were called, 'who by figures and markings upon the dead body of beast or man operate to get knowledge.' In 1371 a wizard of Southwark in London was caught in possession of 'the head and face of a dead man,' and these tokens of necromancy, with his book of magic, were consigned to the flames.

Evidence suggests that there was some confusion between the spirit of the dead, or ghost, and the elemental spirit or familiar that was one of the lesser demons. It was perhaps for this reason that the Statute of 1542 against witchcraft covered the situation with a blanket condemnation of those 'divers and sundry persons (who) unlawfully have devised and practiced invocations and conjurations of spirits pretending by such means to get knowledge for their own lucre in what places treasure of gold or silver should or might be found.'

In actual practice the punishment administered by the courts was comparatively light. In 1598 a Cunning Man named Robert Browning was merely placed in the pillory after being found guilty of fraudulently persuading the 'King's subjects' that by conjuration of 'evil spirits they might discover hidden hoards of gold and silver and regain lost goods.'

To evoke the dead the magician needed to obtain the help of powerful spirits, both for his own protection and to compel the corpse or ghost to submit to his will. A spell from ancient Greece calls upon the powers of the mighty Kore, Persephone, Ereshkigal, Adonis, Hermes, and Thoth, to bind the dead. According to a ritual described by Seneca, the Roman dramatist, the summoning of the dead involved not only a burned sacrifice but a blood-drenched altar.

Powerful Circles

In European necromancy, the methods employed for the raising of the dead, whether in body or spirit, demanded rigid compliance with the accepted laws of magic. The site for the operation had to be chosen with care, the most favourable being some

Opposite page:
Necromancer's cloth mask from Tibet (1850–1900)

Edward Kelley (b.1555) and his partner John Dee (1527–1608) raising a ghost

lonely crossroads, a vault, a ruin, an unfrequented forest, or a blasted heath. Once a time had been decided upon for the seance, a series of concentric circles of power would be drawn on the ground within which were inscribed crosses and other symbols, together with holy names of God. The circle would be blessed and consecrated, with the magician and his assistant standing at its centre, protected by the holy names from all danger. Then, wand in hand, the magician summoned the dead to rise.

Eliphas Levi (1810–75) and other magicians have suggested the need for some attempt at identification between the living and the dead, as, for example, the presence of a portrait, and a portion of bread that the ghost would be invited to consume. In his evocation, the magician summoned the dead by name and, if he were successful, he would then have to face the frightening ordeal of a phantom screaming and gibbering with rage at having been compelled against its will to return to the realms of the living. Sometimes the dead were known to appear in the shapes of furious beasts raging about the circle and threatening to tear the sorcerer to pieces. When the dead finally decided to submit to the magician's will they would often become transformed into one or more naked men who would then be willing to answer the questions put to them.

After the seance it was necessary to dismiss the dead, who usually vanished amid clouds of sulfur. Under no circumstances was the magician to leave the protection of the magic circle before this, and even so he might not leave until he had performed certain prescribed rituals. He also had to remove all flowers from the place and after burning them, to bury the ashes deeply in the earth.

The whole operation was fraught with terrible dangers, for the slightest departure from the rites could involve the destruction of the operator and even inflict injuries upon his soul. In the seventeenth century, a popular Egyptian fortune teller named Chiancungi, who quitted the magic circle too hurriedly, was crushed to death by an enraged ghost.

Summoned from the Tomb

Churchyard necromancy, a specialized branch of the art, required a rather different technique. As the hour of midnight struck, the magician, having undertaken the preliminary rites, would intone in a sepulchral voice: 'The dead rise and come to me,' and then he advanced into the churchyard scattering graveyard earth about him. In summoning the dead from the tomb he cried: '*Ego sum te peto et videre queo.*' To dismiss the dead he commanded: 'Return to the Kingdom of the Chosen.'

There is an old print depicting Dr. John Dee's assistant, Edward Kelley, standing in a churchyard, holding a magic wand and reading from a book of spells, while his assistant illuminates the macabre midnight scene with a flaming torch. In the light can be seen a newly-resurrected corpse rigid in its shroud. The two sorcerers have taken the precaution of placing themselves at the centre of a magic circle inscribed with the names of certain protective angels, 'Raphael, Rael, Miraton, Tarmiel, and Rex.'

The use of corpses as ingredients of charms and philtres was closely associated with necromancy, and is one of the best known techniques of witchcraft. Death by violence, or any premature termination of life, enhanced the magical value of human flesh, since it could then be assumed to contain some element of unconsumed vitality within it. The old Norse wizards were said to know spells that could compel even a corpse on a gallows to speak. As Paolus Grillandus, a judge in witch trials at Rome in the early sixteenth century, wrote: 'Some take a small piece of buried corpse, especially the corpse of anyone who has been hanged or otherwise suffered a shameful death . . . the nails or teeth . . . the hair, ears or eyes . . . sinews, bones, or flesh.' The demand for similar ghoulish remains, particularly the flesh of unbaptized babies, was responsible for many graves being rifled. Among the best-known cases involving human flesh in magic was that of the Irish witch, Alice Kyteler (1280–later than 1325), who was accused of using the hair of a corpse and the skull of a thief in one of her formulas. A moss that grew on the skull of a hanged man was always in considerable demand.

The attitude of the Church toward all forms of communication with the dead was, in the past at least, one of unremitting hostility. Such practices are prohibited in the Bible and this condemnation is emphasized in the story of Saul who consulted the dead Samuel through the agency of the Witch of Endor (1 Samuel, chapter 28). In the third century, Tertullian, the theologian, condemned those magicians who defiled the graves of the dead and counterfeited oracles, but witch-fearing clerics of the sixteenth and seventeenth centuries went further and refused to admit the possibility of a ghost being anything other than a demon in disguise. In his *Discourse of the Damned Art of Witchcraft* William Perkins (1558–1602) observed: 'The Devil being sought unto by witches appears to them in the likeness of a dead body.' John Cotta (1575–1650) ventured further still in his *Trial of Witchcraft* (1616) by declaring clairvoyance to be no more than one of the forms of diabolic possession. It is not surprising then that Shakespeare's Hamlet, when confronted with the ghost of his father, should have asked: 'Be thou a spirit of health or goblin damned? Bring with thee airs from heaven or blasts from hell?'

The complete separation of the concept of the ghost from that of the demon did not take place until much later, not until the problem of witchcraft had largely disappeared from the theological concern. The confusion between ghost and devil is apparent in an account of a seance conducted by Parson Rudall in Cornwall, England, in 1665, when the clergyman, having drawn the customary magic circle into which he conjured the ghost, demanded a sign from the shade 'that it was a true spirit and not a false fiend.'

It was some years after this, at the close of the seventeenth century, that ancient necromancy began gradually to develop into modern spiritism. There is no record of prosecution for necromancy in the whole of the seventeenth century, and with the

Scenes of divination, including haruspication, pyromancy, and necromancy (engraving), Hans Burgkmair (c. 1473–1531)

decline in the practice of utilizing the bodies of the dead for magical purposes greater emphasis was put upon what was later known as mediumship. For example, Joseph Glanvill (1636–80) who has been called the Father of Psychical Research, with Dr. Francis van Helmont, Dr. Henry More, and Robert Boyle, conducted seances at Ragley Castle, Warwickshire at which early mediums demonstrated the art of communication with the world of spirits.

Later still the curious incident of the Cock Lane ghost, even if it served no other purpose, did at least indicate the growth of the belief that the dead and living could communicate by means of a series of knocks. This ghost, which haunted a London house in Cock Lane, Smithfields, was that of a woman who had lived there with her dead sister's husband. Her hauntings provoked two people to hold a seance to discover the reason for her return.

True and False Spirits

The whole question of raising the dead, even when it ceased to concern the guardians of the public conscience, was too deeply rooted in folk culture to be legislated out of existence. Nevertheless the revised Witchcraft Act of 1735, in imposing imprisonment and pillory for all pretence at communication with spirits, must have successfully suppressed most aspiring witches and necromancers, for after that date there is no evidence of any prosecution under this Act until the present century, when several fraudulent mediums were charged with counterfeiting spirit manifestations. In 1944 two women, Jane Yorke and Helen Duncan, both Spiritualists, were brought before the courts under the terms of this Act, although the latter maintained that her spirits were good ones and not evil. As the result of these prosecutions and the subsequent struggle of the English Spiritualists to remove from their activities any suggestion of necromancy, in 1951 Parliament replaced the old Witchcraft Act with the Fraudulent Mediums Act.

To declare that necromancy of the old type is quite dead would perhaps be premature. Innumerable churchyard desecrations still take place, some of which involve the actual disturbance of the corpse. The most famous case of this character in recent times was the exhumation of a woman's skeleton at Clophill in Bedfordshire England in 1963 and its subsequent use in the rites of black magic. Even more macabre was the disinterment of a man's body in a North London cemetery in the autumn of 1968, when the corpse was discovered pierced with a wooden stake close to a huge circle of flowers taken from nearby graves.

Among the most cherished anecdotes of the more sophisticated type of magician is the amazing nineteenth century seance conducted by Eliphas Levi (1810–75) the French occultist who attempted to raise the shade of the pagan magician Apollonius of Tyana in London in 1854. The room in which the seance was conducted contained mirrors, a pentagram and, for the protection of the wizard, a magic circle of magnetized iron. The materialization of a shrouded spectre, 'lean, melancholy and beardless,' robbed the magician, temporarily at least, of his powers of speech.

Current occult theory indicates that the departing soul, in ascending to a higher plane, leaves behind it a secondary human body, known as the astral corpse, which contains some vestiges of life and which, because of its intense desire to live again, can sometimes be lured back to the physical world by the power of magic. It has even been suggested that the astral corpse has the power to absorb life from human beings rather in the manner of a psychic vampire. Some occultists are of the opinion that the medium, in calling upon the spirits of the dead, in reality summons not the ghost but the astral corpse, and if this is so it could perhaps be said that necromancy has never truly died.

ERIC MAPLE

FURTHER READING: R. Cavendish. The Black Arts. *(London, UK: Routledge, 1967).*

An atomic bomb explosion

Classic ouija board used to communicate with spirits shows the top board, which was usually on castors so it could slide about

Nuclear Holocaust

The date of August 6, 1945, defined a new era for planet Earth. Once the world had awoken to the devastating consequences of the nuclear attack on Hiroshima, and its successor three days later on Nagasaki, then the concept of a nuclear holocaust had secured a place in the collective conscience. Today, the cataclysm of nuclear war is still regarded as a prime threat to Earth and its inhabitants.

The holocaust scenario is envisaged as having two seasons. First comes the nuclear winter, when smoke and soot sent into the atmosphere by fires blot out sunlight. In a prolonged period of darkness and freezing temperatures, plant and animal life would perish on a vast scale. Any survivors—including humans—would be subject to genetic damage threatening the viability of future generations.

Then would come an equally damaging nuclear summer. As bombs exploded, scientists conjecture, the nitrogen oxides and carbon dioxide they produce would result in destruction of the earth's protective ozone 'blanket,' allowing damaging amounts of ultraviolet light to penetrate from the sun to the earth's surface, and triggering runaway climate change so swift that it life would become unsustainable. Even if this end point were not reached, any surviving life forms would remain subject to gene mutation severe enough to minimize the possibility of successful reproduction and threaten the mass extinction of plants, animals and even microbes.

The last creatures to survive on Earth would certainly not be human, but might possibly be insects such as cockroaches. In experiments in which cockroaches were blasted with 1,000 rads (radon units) of cobalt 60, enough to kill a human in 10 minutes, followed by exposures to 10,000 and 100,000 rads, as many as 10 percent of the last group, with the maximum exposure, not only lived but were healthy enough to give rise to a new generation.

RUTH BINNEY

FURTHER READING: Neville Shute. On the Beach. *(Portsmouth, NH: Heinemann, 1957).*

Ouija Boards

The name ouija derives from the French and German words for '*yes,*' *oui* and *ja*. A ouija board is a flat, polished sheet of wood, about 18 inches by 12, which has the

Medium using a ouija board and glass to communicate with spirits in the 1950s

alphabet written in a wide half moon along its longer side. On top of this board is placed a much smaller one, heart-shaped and mounted on tiny castors that enable it to slide about. If one or more persons place their fingertips lightly on the smaller board, in many cases it will slide, without being consciously pushed, so that the apex of the heart points from letter to letter, making words or even sentences that are not expected by the performers. Sometimes, though not often, information comes to them that is not at the time known to their conscious minds, though it may have been known to one or more of them in the past and then forgotten. Very occasionally it seems not to have been known to any of them at all.

One variant of the ouija board is called a planchette. In this case a pencil is attached to the apex of the heart-shaped pointer and a blank sheet of paper is placed on the larger board. Again, this sometimes but not always results in the pencil moving about without being consciously pushed, and what it writes may range from aimless marks to whole sentences and even long stories. As a rule, however, its productions do not make much sense. A second variant of a ouija board may be made by cutting out the letters of the alphabet and setting them in a circle on a polished table. If a wine glass or smooth-rimmed tumbler is then placed upside down within the circle, and the fingers of one or more persons lightly rested upon it (preferably one finger, per hand, per person) it will sometimes slide from letter to letter forming words in the same manner as the heart-shaped pointer. Why such devices can be made to function by some people and not by others is not known. It may be a matter of the psychological attitude of the performers, or—a wild speculation—the cause might even be an electrical one.

Shortcut to the Surface

Table tilting—or tipping, or turning, as it is sometimes called—works on the same general principle as a ouija board although it is slower and more laborious. If one or more persons place their fingers on a table, preferably a small circular one on a three-footed pedestal, on some occasions, which cannot be predicted in advance, it will tip up and tap a foot without being consciously pushed by any of the performers. As a rule Spiritualists make use of a code by which it can answer questions—one tap for 'yes,' two for 'uncertain,' and three for 'no.' Or letters of the alphabet may be recited and responded to by taps—and so on. Such activities are still popular in Spiritualistic circles, and they were extremely so, even among the sophisticated, in the nineteenth century. Queen Victoria and Prince Albert are on record as having once tilted a table. In those days the entities that purported to communicate through the board or table were widely assumed to be what they claimed to be, discarnate spirits, but nowadays modern psychology has produced a rival source nearer at hand—the subconscious of one or more of the performers.

It is now for the most part accepted that much mental and emotional activity in the human psyche takes place beyond the threshold of consciousness. Glimpses of it can be seen in dreams and its results may also come to the surface unexpectedly, 'out of the blue,' and can range from idealistic and creative ideas at one end to apparently motiveless destructive impulses at the other. It seems, in fact, as if those hidden areas contain all kinds of material, some of it 'higher' in quality than the conscious self, some of it 'lower.' Psychoanalysis has also emphasized that memories of distressing events can be repressed into those areas because they are too painful to be faced by the conscious self, and that goes too for desires that do not fit into the pattern of life ordained by that self. A natural conclusion from this is that the highway from subconscious to conscious may sometimes be blocked, that there may be some sort of psychological censorship. The symbolic nature of many dreams hints at such censorship.

There are certain procedures that seem to open up what may be called shortcuts from subconscious to conscious, and by means of these censored material is sometimes able to get through. Such procedures have been given the blanket name of automatisms, since what they produce has not been consciously willed or even known in advance, and they often seem to involve some degree of dissociation, however slight. One form of automatism is trance medium ship; another is automatic writing and even automatic speech uttered in a less than trance state—for occasionally an individual will make statements or, say, preach a sermon, without the motivation coming from his conscious self, but still without that self being entirely in abeyance. Ouija board conversations, planchette writing, and table-tipping are usually practiced by several persons at a time and may then be called collective automatisms; these have the advantage that each participant can assume that the motive force comes from, or through, one of the others and that he himself is free from responsibility for what is said. In this context it is of interest that in most traditional attempts to provide information acquired through ESP even the individual sensitive uses some kind of procedure that implies that the information is being mediated to him through some outside source such, for instance, as a medium's control, a possessing god, a crystal, tea-leaves, hands, bones, a pendulum, a divining rod, or automatically written messages that claim to come from a discarnate entity. To believe in any such procedure may be of genuine help to the performer for several reasons: it frees him from responsibility for what is said—he is only the transmitter; it reduces the analytical conscious mind to a passive role, hence its activity is less likely to blur faint intimations that may well up from beyond the threshold; and it may also tend to encourage slight dissociation which appears to facilitate the emergence of subconscious material.

Automatic Poetry

Incidents of oija board usage could easily be dismissed as accidental coincidences, were it not for the existence of others similar but so much more complicated that to ascribe the many resemblances in them to chance is very difficult. Take the following case investigated by the Society for Psychical Research. A group of six Spiritualists used to meet regularly at Flushing in Holland with the idea of getting into communication with the dead. On the evening of July 23, 1922, they began by table tilting but had no success. Then they turned to a device similar in principle to a ouija board in which a moveable pointer was held over the alphabet. This time things went better: they spelled out that an Englishman was communicating and that he was prepared to write them a song. (Four of them knew no English; the other two had once learned it but had not kept it up.) A poem was then spelled out (see C in panel) as from the Englishman who was, presumably, in view of the following facts, a subconscious dramatization resulting from their Spiritualist beliefs.

Opposite the house where the meetings took place lived a fifteen-year-old boy, who, scenting a mystery, very much wanted to attend the gatherings, but was not allowed to. On that July evening he watched the visitors go into the house for the meeting and ardently longed to join them. Then, disconsolately, having nothing to do, he got out an old school book that contained an English poem (see A) he had once had to learn, and drowsed over it during the course of the meeting across the road. The next day one of the participants at the meeting heard what he had been doing during the meeting and asked him to type out the poem from memory (see B).

However intriguing, suggestive, and complicated such material may be, so far nearly all of it is anecdotal; hence the sceptic can always dismiss each instance of it separately as due to fraud;

Automatic Poetry

A

Original Poem—Evening Song

The sun has set
And now anew
With fallen dew
The grass is wet.
Each little bird
Has sunk to rest
Within its nest
No song is heard

B

Boy's Version—Evening Song

The sun has set,
and now a new
With fallen dew
The grass is wet
And little burd
is sing to rest
Within his nest
No song is heard

C

Automatists' Version

THE SUN HAS SET
AND NOW A new
WITH FALL END EW
THE GRASS IS WET
FIrSt parT
each little bird
Has sunk storest
with ts netstn
O Sng is hear

it must, he insists, be produced in controlled conditions to order. This is a tough challenge for neither investigator nor performer has any idea of the psychological processes involved since these are entirely unconscious—how unconscious is neatly demonstrated in some ingenious experiments carried out by the eminent French psychologist, Professor Charles Richet (1850–1935), in the early days of psychical research. Another psychologist, Dr. Alan Gauld (1932), has recently summarized them as follows in *The Founders of Psychical Research* (1968):

'The set-up was complex. At a small table sat two persons, A and B, with the alphabet laid out in front of them. A passed a pointer continually over the alphabet. B noted down the letter over which the pointer was each time he heard a bell ring. The bell was rung automatically whenever another table in the room, at which sat three other persons, C, D, and E, was tilted. C, D, and E had their hands on the table in ordinary 'table-tilting' fashion; they were so seated that they could not see the activities of A and B. A sixth person, F (usually Richet), sat apart from both groups, concentrating on a name (obtained randomly from a reference book). The letters spelled out in many cases closely followed the letters of the name on which F was concentrating. It was easy to show that the coincidences between them greatly exceeded chance. Yet C, D, and E did not know what they were spelling out, and A and B, who did know it, did not know the target.

Such scattered hints of unconscious inter-linkage between the living are not uncommon, but for the most part scientists are inclined to look on them with a jaundiced eye. This is natural enough, for to them the process implied is a heresy; it does not fit into the pattern of the physical world as they envisage it. Worse, many of the people who provide the material containing such hints want to believe that their material comes from the dead, and to orthodox materialist science that is a primitive superstition. There is a further reason for regret, that the questions of survival and of unconscious interlink age between the living are so often entangled: at present there seems no way to prove—or disprove—survival, which therefore becomes a remote problem, whereas experimental research into ESP suggests that the interlink age hinted at by ouija board and similar activities may one day be recognized as a constantly occurring natural phenomenon.

ROSALIND HEYWOOD

***Adam and Eve in Paradise (The Fall)* by the German painter Lucas Cranach (1472–1553)**

Paradise

Happiness was associated with enclosures rather than open spaces in the ancient Middle East, for deserts and hills, the wind and the sun, were generally too harsh to man. When he thought of a pleasant place, he thought of an oasis or garden, where he could relax in the shade with ample water and fruit. Given the resources, he might create such a place for himself.

The word 'paradise' is of Old Persian origin. It means an enclosure, and especially a royal park or hunting ground, a piece of land made more agreeable than its surroundings by cultivation. The Greek translators of the Old Testament, about the middle of the third century BC, employed the word once or twice in that sense, for example in Ecclesiastes, chapter 2.5: 'I made myself gardens and parks, and I planted in them all kinds of fruit trees.' But their most momentous use of it was in referring to the garden of Eden, the divinely appointed home of Adam.

This appears in Genesis, chapter 2. After creating the world, God plants the garden 'in Eden, in the east.' He places Adam in it and creates the first woman, Eve. The name 'Eden' may be Babylonian. Among the luscious vegetation, God's garden contains the Tree of Life, and the Tree of the Knowledge of Good and Evil. A river flows through it and splits up into four streams.

Life in this Earthly paradise is instinctively innocent, with the Lord as a close companion. It is no lazy idyll: Adam must till and keep the garden, with Eve's aid. God forbids them to eat of the Tree of Knowledge. When they disobey, they are expelled. The reason given (Genesis, chapter 3) is that if they stayed, they might eat the fruit of the Tree of Life also, and live forever. This would have been permissible before; now it is not. Henceforth men must drudge to live. Women must be subject to male dominance and bear children in pain. Meanwhile the garden exists but an armed angel at the gate keeps out fallen humanity.

St. Brendan and a Siren, from the German translation of _Navigatio Sancti Brendani Abbatis_, German School (c. 1476)

While the Judaeo-Christian Fall of Man is in some ways unique, the garden has partial parallels in non-Hebrew mythologies. Two motifs, in particular, connect other 'paradises' with this one. First, Genesis gives the Hebrew version of a widespread idea—the idea of a definite place, an 'otherwhere' or even an 'otherworld,' which is part of the universe we know, yet different in quality from the part we live in: a good place, blessed, and happy.

Second, Genesis directs attention to the many legends of a lost Golden Age. Long ago, human beings were carefree and guiltless. They were immortal, or at any rate felt no reason to fear death. They lived without sickness in a kindly climate, and never had to work hard. Gods dwelt familiarly among them. For whatever reason, the Golden Age is no more. The gods have withdrawn. Death and disease and wickedness have poisoned life.

However, in some mythologies the

two themes converge; the paradisal good place not only exists, but it is also a fragment of the golden world that remains inviolate. If we could reach it we could still find there the delights and divine companionship of the Golden Age.

In classical myth, the Golden Age was the epoch when the Titan Cronus, or Saturn, was supreme god. After his son Zeus ousted him, the world declined. Cronus went on reigning in exile, in the regions of sunset. There, for the Greeks, was the 'good place,' out over the Atlantic behind a barrier of water. There lay the Isles of the Blest where, in Hesiod's words, 'the bounteous Earth beareth honey-sweet fruit fresh thrice a year.' There lay the plain of Elysium 'at the world's end' where, according to Homer, 'living is made easiest for mankind, no snow falls, no strong winds blow, and there is never any rain.'

Celtic myth looked in the same direction. The Isle of Avalon was a warm Western Elysium, sometimes described in language borrowed from classical literature. Irish seafaring romances, such as *The Voyage of Bran* tell of an enchanted archipelago beyond the horizon, including an Island of the Blest which is larger in extent than Erin itself, a place 'without grief, without sorrow, without death.'

Medieval Irish legend drew the pagan and Christian paradises together. The usual Christian belief was that the earthly paradise of Genesis was in a remote part of Asia. Some Irish Christians, however, located it in one of their own legendary lands beyond the Atlantic, and gave it a Celtic atmosphere. The greatest of all their voyage-romances tells how St. Brendan sailed in quest of it, and finally arrived on its borders. The author of *St. Brendan's Voyage* probably knew that the world is round, and he may have harmonized his fancies with orthodoxy by imagining that Brendan reached Asia by sailing west.

Paradise and Heaven

Adam's lost abode remains, humanly speaking, empty. Other paradises are variously peopled. The Golden Age dream of freedom from the curse of death is recurrent. The citizens of paradise are, as a rule, immortals. In the Babylonian epic of *Gilgamesh*, the hero, grief-stricken at human evanescence, goes to an island-otherworld expressly for the secret of immortality. He meets Utnapishtim, the chief survivor of the flood, who is indeed exempt from death. But Gilgamesh achieves nothing by his visit.

In more familiar mythologies, such places as Elysium are likely to be the homes of gods, demigods, or fairy-folk, all undying. When human beings do enter, we hear (in the oldest stories) of only a chosen few transported there while alive, and endowed with immortality as a special gift. Homer names Menelaus, husband of Helen of Troy. A better known instance is King Arthur who is said to have gone to Avalon after his last battle, and to be still living there.

Classical Greece carried the idea a step further. Pindar describes the Isles of the Blest as inhabited by a select few of the noble dead, with Cronus as their king. Here the Blest have actually died; the Golden Age motif, though still present in the person of Cronus, has receded somewhat; the Elysian realm is becoming a sort of heaven.

Even when conduct is a passport, and the good place has to be earned, entry may depend on having performed a ritual, or undergone an initiation.

Within the mainstream of Greek religion, this idea remained tentative. But farther afield, similar beliefs are asserted with more conviction. Sometimes the good place, the 'otherwhere,' has little or no explicit Golden Age aura and is more essentially a home of the dead. Where admission is a reward of virtue we approach the concept of heaven in its full Judaeo-Christian meaning: the eternal, blissful abode of all those among the dead whose lives have earned such a reward and of no others; the final beatitude; the ultimate goal.

The approach, however, is by degrees. At the more naive mythical levels, the good place may be simply the place of the dead in general. Everybody goes there, to an improved version of Earthly life. The spirit realm of the Tumbuka, in Malawi, is an underworld where the departed are always young and never hungry or sad. Such beliefs occur also in New Guinea and New Caledonia. Some Native Americans, the Ojibways and Choctaws for example, have kindred hopes about the region of sunset, or a happy hunting-ground in some secret country. These places are paradises and the homes of the dead, but scarcely heavens, because they are not selective. The goodness of the good place is not a reward.

When selectivity does come in, it may still not take an ethical form. Admission may depend upon social rank. In the Leeward Islands in the Caribbean, aristocratic spirits go to 'sweet-scented Rohutu' and commoners go to 'foul-scented Rohutu.' In Peru, the mansions of the sun were reserved for the Incas and their nobles. Even when conduct is a passport, and the good place has to be earned, entry may depend on having performed a ritual, or undergone an initiation.

The motif of achieving the good place for one's afterlife through merit appears crudely in the Norse Valhalla, which was reached by martial prowess. Celestial dwellings for the dead are nearly always selective; the wicked and ignoble seldom go upward. In Egypt during the third millennium BC, the pharaohs hoped to join the sun god and attend him on his journeys through space. While this is another instance of privilege through rank, texts show that the god's attitude to a deceased ruler depended partly on his virtues. Later, when similar hopes were extended to lesser men, this idea of judgement became more prominent.

In the Vedic religion of India the monarch of the dead was called Yama, and he reigned in the outer sky, a realm of light, over all the worthy departed. Their life was an enhancement of Earthly life with music, sexual fulfillment, and many more pleasures with no pain or care.

Hinduism allots regions above the clouds to Indra, Shiva, and other deities. Each is a place of beauty and sensual joy, to be gained by a combination of correct ritual and correct morality. Buddhism inherited such schemes from Hinduism. In its advanced Mahayana form it has a graded series of paradises in a vague, nonastronomical sky. Ecstasies become more spiritual as Earth is left farther below. The ascent is by way of virtue and holy meditation.

Baoen Sutra Paradise was discovered at the Mogao Caves near Dun Huang, China, in the '1000 Buddha cave.' Shakyamuni is seated in the centre of the image. The left and right sides show scenes of Prince Siddhartha as described in the Baoen Sutra.

Salvation in the Sky

It is important to grasp that these quasi-heavens of Hinduism and Buddhism still belong to a mythological order of ideas. They are not ultimate, nor are they central to the philosophy of either religion. The goal of the highest quest is not personal happiness, but total release from the bondage of personality—Nirvana. The celestial realms, therefore, are consolation prizes. They appeal to those whose minds are not ready to transcend personal desire and descriptions of them are poetic, not doctrinal. They are also temporary. The soul may dwell in them for aeons, but if it goes there at all, it has not completed its pilgrimage and must eventually leave. The sole exception is in a popular form of Chinese and Japanese Buddhism, the Pure Land sect.

In the Mediterranean world the good place acquires dogmatic status as the final reward of all mankind's spiritual strivings, with salvation consisting in its attainment, damnation in

its loss. Heaven in this full sense is associated with Hebrew monotheism and ethical seriousness; with Hellenic firmness of outline and appetite for truth.

As long as Greece had no positive doctrine of immortality, and dismissed the dead as shades, Elysium could survive as a fantasy without raising major issues. But from the sixth century BC onward, the mystics of the Orphic cult were asserting such a doctrine and, for those who accepted it, the island-paradise would no longer serve. An abode for the blest on the familiar Earth was out of keeping with Orphic ideas, which proclaimed salvation as a release from Earthly bondage.

A more exotic home was offered to the right-living initiate. The Orphics adopted the word Elysium and altered its meaning, speaking of 'Elysian Fields' in an underworld of strange brightness, a happy resting place for pure spirits. But besides this—in Orphism apparently and in later Mystery cults undoubtedly—there was also a disposition to look upward. Gradually the good place was transferred to the sky, as in Asia.

The 'heavens' that the teachers of mystical doctrines drew into their systems were at first simply the upper regions. The prevailing astronomy made them concentric spheres, the spheres of the sun, moon, planets, and fixed stars, rotating around the earth. Now, by becoming involved with notions about the soul's ascent, 'heaven' acquired a paradisal and even more-than-paradisal sense as well as an astronomical one. The Mysteries (with Egyptian influence from the cult of Osiris) and the gnostic schools of the early Christian era envisaged purified souls as rising. Instructed in the right passwords, the adept eluded the planetary demons of middle space. He soared (by grace of his chosen savior, such as Mithras) to a superior heaven outside the visible system. Here he lived blissfully with the gods and fellow-initiates, forever.

Heaven on Earth

In the contemporary Hebrew world of ideas, two trends had emerged. When most of the Old Testament was composed, Israel's religion had no clear notion of personal immortality. Its only paradise was the lost garden. Heaven, as elsewhere, meant the sky, with the added concept of a preeminent heaven beyond, where God sat enthroned among his angels.

For the first Christians, the resurrection of Christ was proof of the coming resurrection of all the dead . . . the Last Judgement would allot them their destinies according to their deserts.

Judaism, as it grew after the exile in Babylon, slowly adopted a more cheerful outlook. Probably under Zoroastrian influence, it spoke of a future resurrection of the dead, a last judgement, a world to come. No unanimity on these matters was reached, nor has it ever been. Rabbinic tradition, however, has usually resisted world-spurning metaphysical speculations. It has its own place, Gan Eden, where the righteous will dwell after the resurrection. Gan Eden is, in effect, Adam's paradise restored. Its citizens will go there as living people, not shades.

In the time of Jesus, such hopes were bound up with apocalyptic and Messianic dreams. The Lord's Anointed would appear, life would be transfigured, the dead would be raised, the earthly Kingdom of God would bring paradise regained . . . for the righteous. Jesus employed apocalyptic language himself, but to convey a message of spiritual revolution: the kingdom, he declared, is 'within you.' This teaching opened the way to a fusion of Hebrew and Hellenic motifs.

For the first Christians, the resurrection of Christ was proof of the coming resurrection of all the dead. When that happened the Last Judgement would allot them their destinies according to their deserts. The book of Revelation looks ahead not only to the Judgement, but to a material New Jerusalem for the resurrected saints. This, like Jewish Gan Eden, will be the second paradise; Christ is the second Adam.

When the resurrection and judgement did not come quickly, a question arose as to what was happening to the dead meanwhile. Christ himself had promised the penitent thief, one of the two criminals who were put to death with him, an immediate paradise (Luke, chapter 23), which must therefore be in existence. In the Christian apocalypse there is already a heaven apart from Earth. It is, as ever, the celestial dwelling place of God. The New Jerusalem, when it comes, will come 'down out of heaven.' Until then the souls of the blessed have their heavenly places near God, where, a perfect society, they await final reunion with their bodies.

Christianity compiled its heaven from both Hebraic and Hellenic sources. From Judaism it adopted the region of the sky where God and his angels dwelt. From Greece the Christians took the celestial machinery, the spheres outside one another, the spiritual journeyings. The idea of seven heavens, with the seventh as proverbially the most exalted, is also Greek.

The Place Where God Is

While it carried the concept of heaven to its loftiest heights, Christianity

Opposite Page:
***Ascent of the Prophet Muhammad to Heaven* by Mirak, Aqa (c.1520–1576)**

never resolved certain queries. If the souls of the saved went to heaven at once, what would be the point of the future Last Judgement? It could only confirm a destiny already fixed. St. Augustine maintained that, until the end of the world, spiritual life in heaven was an interim state, a foretaste, an answer that may have owed a debt to a tradition inherited via Judaism from Zoroastrianism.

Nor have Christians agreed about the qualifications for entry. Even baptism is not universally insisted upon, despite the words of Jesus that 'unless one is born of water and the Spirit, he cannot enter the kingdom of God,' (John, chapter 3.5). Luther dismissed salvation by works in favour of salvation by faith. Calvin taught salvation by arbitrary divine choice. Islam, in its own version of the Judaeo-Christian scheme, distinguished seven heavens and various hells, temporary or permanent; and it made everything depend on faith. Every Muslim, however wicked, would get to a paradise of some kind; no infidel would.

James M. Herrmann's family in its poltergeist-ridden home, Long Island, United States

What happens in heaven? The paradises of mythology offer ardent, fairly civilized sensual delights, but Islam is the only major religion that does so. The Koran promises the faithful a reward suited to male Arab tastes. Their home will be a sort of splendid oasis with gardens, rivers, and trees. Men will wear silken robes and lie on couches, with unlimited fruit and wine, and virtually unlimited harems.

More recently, however, Muslim thinkers have joined Jews and Christians in a more abstract opinion. heaven is the place where God is; so the final happiness is the beatific vision of God, the source of all good, and therefore completely satisfying.

There is no logical flaw in this conception of a Supreme Good from which the soul would never willingly turn away. However, in practice it is hard to imagine a convincing heaven, because any perfection that we can specifically think of would pall. The philosopher Schopenhauer (1788–1860) observed that imaginative authors are more successful with hells than with heavens, because their own lives furnish materials for the former, but not the latter.

GEOFFREY ASHE

Poltergeists

The word poltergeist was originally a German folklore term compounded from *polter* (a noise or racket) and *geist* (a spirit or sprite), indicating a Nature spirit of like status to elf or goblin or 'things that go bump in the night.' Subsequently the term acquired a wider sense. Phenomena ascribed to poltergeists included a remarkable variety of alleged happenings: movements of domestic objects, flinging of mud, teleportation, and the production of noises such as raps, bangs, or scratchings, and sounds imitating the human voice whistling, singing, or talking. Despite the fantastic nature of the phenomena, investigators during the late nineteenth century, such as Frederic Myers (1843–1901), Frank Podmore (1856–1910), Andrew Lang (1844–1912), and the criminologist Cesare Lombroso (1835–1909), thought them worthy of unbiased study. But in order not to prejudge the issue they used the term poltergeist in an adjectival sense, to describe the type of happenings reported, which were said to constitute a 'poltergeist disturbance.' This descriptive approach leaves open the question as to whether poltergeists exist as 'spirits' or discarnate entities, so that to begin with we are concerned only with poltergeist phenomena, real or alleged.

Not an Evil Spirit

Early writers on poltergeist outbreaks naturally offered many theories as to why they happened. The poltergeist was usually described vaguely as an evil spirit, without necessarily implying that it was one of Satan's own imps. Giraldus Cambrensis (1147–1223) refers to cases where mud was flung, holes cut in garments, and a 'spirit' conversed with men in an aggressive and derisory fashion. His curiosity was aroused by the fact that rites of exorcism were ineffective. He concluded that sacraments are effective against true demons but not against merely mischievous ones. During the Reformation period, for theological reasons, writers preferred either the demonic interpretation or explanation in terms of natural causes, ranging from death-watch beetles to the pranks of children or the trickery of adults.

Modern Spiritualism gained its first impetus in 1848 from an outbreak of rapping noises in the home of John Fox at Hydesville, in New York State. Subsequently Spiritualists tend to interpret poltergeist outbreaks as attempts at communication by the spirits of the dead.

In view of the fantastic happenings alleged in poltergeist cases and their speculative interpretations, there is naturally also a strong tendency to regard them as merely tall stories, or due to badly observed natural causes or trickery. Frank Podmore, who inclined to the view that poltergeist phenomena were the result of tricks by mischievous or maladjusted persons, laid down important criteria for assessing the evidential value of testimony in alleged poltergeist cases. Written statements from literate and intelligent observers providing circumstantial and mutually corroborative detail should be obtained as soon as possible after the occurrences. Nowadays the investigator likes also, if possible, to have video and tape-recordings, bearing in mind that such things can be faked and remembering that the reliability of a mechanical record is not, in the final analysis, greatly superior to that of the person who offers it in evidence. While mechanical records can be very informative, in the end the investigator has to depend on the integrity of the witnesses. It is a typical and very puzzling feature of poltergeist outbreaks that they do not continue indefinitely. They may last only a few days or weeks. It is difficult therefore to get conclusive evidence; by the time an outbreak becomes known outside the immediate vicinity, it is likely to be over or on the decline. When the investigator arrives on the scene things may be quiet again and he has to depend on the testimony of others. Very often the witnesses are persons of intelligence and integrity but the investigator may hesitate to accept what they say at its face value if they are members of the disturbed household, because he may feel that they are inclined to 'back one another up' or are trying to shield a member of the family whom they suspect of trickery.

It is a typical and very puzzling feature of poltergeist outbreaks that they do not continue indefinitely. They may last only a few days or weeks.

Events at Tidworth

The investigator does not always arrive too late. Since the seventeenth century there have been eye-witness accounts by men of education, and independent of the family affected by the disturbance. In 1668 the Rev. Joseph Glanvill (1636–1680), a scholar and philosopher of some distinction, published his own experiences of the 'drummer of Tidworth.'

Glanvill went upstairs and found 'two modest little girls in bed between seven and eleven years old.' A strange scratching sound seemed to come from behind the bolster. Glanvill exonerated the girls, whose hands were outside the bedclothes and, he says, 'made all the search that possible I could to find if there was any trick, contrivance or common cause of it, like did my friend but we could discover nothing . . . ' Later, says Glanvill, 'I chanced to see as it had been something (what I thought was a rat or mouse) moving in a linen bag, that hung up against another bed . . . I stepped and caught it by the upper end with one hand, with which I held it, and drew it through the other, but found nothing at all in it. There was nobody near to shake the bag, or if there had, no one could make such a motion . . . as if a living creature had moved in it.'

Glanvill's narrative seems eminently sensible and matter of fact. It was written in an era when superstition was still rife but, interestingly enough, reports of poltergeist cases were no more numerous than they are today. Out of 470 witchcraft trials in England only about five involved poltergeist activity; and since Glanvill's time only one or two poltergeist cases have been reported annually in Britain. This suggests strongly that assertions of poltergeist activity are independent of the current climate of opinion. Outbreaks sufficiently dramatic or prolonged to become widely known are clearly rare, and both the rarity and the short duration of poltergeist disturbances are hindrances to scientific investigation. Nonetheless there is an appreciable number of cases where it is very difficult to find a good reason for setting aside the testimony of eye-witnesses.

If there are genuine poltergeist cases in which these strange movements of objects occur, it raises challenging problems. At the least we have proof that there are physical forces at present unknown to science. Even if these forces should prove to be operated by 'spirits,' or 'elementals,' nonetheless they are physical forces as defined by the engineer, because to lift a mass of only an ounce requires a force of one ounce weight. The 'poltergeist force,' if not generated 'super-naturally,' may have a purely physiological origin. On the other hand, psychological factors may play a part in the genesis of this mysterious force.

The Phenomenon at First Hand

Any modern case with good witnesses is very exciting as it can cast some light on the mode by which the poltergeist force comes into play. It was the writer's privilege in 1961 to visit the scene of a poltergeist happening and obtain from no less than five first-class eye-witnesses written testimony based on their diary notes made only a few days before. The possibility of 'mass-hallucination' was ruled out, one of the witnesses having made a tape-recording of some of the poltergeist noises. As in so many poltergeist cases the phenomena were associated with a particular person.

The centre of the disturbance was a pretty little girl of eleven years of age, named Virginia. In the autumn of 1960 she was staying with her elder brother and his wife in Sauchie, a suburb of the town of Alloa on the river Forth in Scotland. Virginia was loved and cared for by her relatives, endowed with physical and mental health. At the time school tests showed her intelligence to be above average.

He also noticed a linen chest raise itself slightly from the floor with an uneasy rocking motion, travel with a jerky movement through a distance of about 18 inches . . . and then go back to its starting point.

When Virginia went to bed on Tuesaday, November 22, 1960, a sound like a ball bouncing, sounded in her bedroom. When she came downstairs to complain, the sound followed her, sounding in the wall of the stairway, and then in the wall of the livingroom. As with all the subsequent manifestations, it ceased entirely when Virginia eventually fell asleep. At teatime next day she was sitting in an armchair next to a sideboard. Her relatives saw the sideboard move out five inches from the wall and then return to its place. No one had touched it throughout.

Witnesses who were brought into the case in their professional capacities, and on whom special reliance may be placed, include the Rev. T. W. Lund, Dr. W.H. Nisbet, and Dr. William Logan, Mrs. Sheila Logan (Dr Logan's wife, also a qualified physician), and Miss Margaret Stewart, Virginia's class teacher. Their statements are detailed and where they overlap, are mutually corroborative. None of these witnesses was at all connected with the family or knew them other than slightly.

On November 23, when Virginia was in bed but still awake, the Rev. Lund (who was called in about midnight) found that violent knocking sounds were coming from the bed-head in circumstances that proved that it was not being struck by Virginia or by anyone else. He gripped the bed-head and felt it vibrating as it sounded. He also noticed a linen chest raise itself slightly from the floor with an uneasy rocking motion, travel with a jerky movement through a distance of about 18 inches along the floor and then go back to its starting point. Putting his hand on it, Rev. Lund found the chest to be vibrating.

Attending Virginia's bedside on the following evening, Dr. Nisbet heard knocking and a 'sawing noise.' He saw a peculiar rippling or puckering motion pass in a wave over the surface of the pillow. Later that night Rev. Lund saw the pillow swing horizontally to a large angle from its proper position. Virginia's head was on one end of it but he saw no way by which she herself could cause this movement, by twisting her head or otherwise.

Virginia was kept at home for several days. When she returned to school, during a period of silent reading, Miss Stewart saw Virginia trying to hold down the lid of her desk, which was forcing itself upward. It rose three times. The teacher was able to see that Virginia was not pushing it up with her knees. A little later on, the boy sitting behind Virginia left his desk to fetch a book. Miss Steward saw this empty desk rise bodily into the air. The motion was quite slow and the desk rose only an inch or so off the floor before settling down gently a little out of its original position. The teacher, who had not yet heard of the events at Virginia's home, could not believe her eyes, but went straight to the spot and saw that no strings or mechanism were in operation.

Phenomena continued in Virginia's bedroom that night. Dr. Nisbet heard spells of knocking even when Virginia was lying motionless and uncovered by bedding. He saw the linen chest move distances of about a foot. There were swingings of the pillow and ripples along the bedcover.

On Saturday night Dr. Logan saw the puckerings of the coverlet and a rotary pillow movement. Sunday was peaceful, but activity recommenced at school on Monday morning. While Virginia was standing a little aside from Miss Stewart's desk with her hands clasped behind her back, a blackboard pointer lying on the desk started to vibrate, worked itself to the edge and fell off. Meanwhile, the desk vibrated and slewed itself round.

That evening, in the hope that a change of air might be salutary, Virginia was sent to stay with an aunt at the neighbouring town of Dollar. When Dr. Nisbet visited, he heard knockings, audible from outside the front door. On the following Tuesday, Dr. and Mrs. Logan searched diligently for the source of noises ranging from gentle tappings to violent raps. Unsuccessful in finding any normal cause for the sounds, they found that at one stage the noises seemed to be emanating from a point in mid-air near Virginia's bed.

Virginia returned to Sauchie on November 30, when all stayed quiet. But the next evening was an active one. Rigging up lights and cine-camera, Dr. Nisbet and Dr. Logan tried to record on film some of the ripplings of the bedspread. This proved difficult as the movements were of short duration. However a tape-recorder was kept running and collected sounds ranging from barely perceptible taps to agitated knocks emanating from a variety of apparent points of origin in the walls, floor, and at times in mid-air. A persistent harsh, rasping noise often occurred simultaneously with the knockings. Meanwhile a service of intercession (not an exorcism), consisting of prayers and reading, was being held in the house, in the hope that it might do some good. As it happened, thereafter the poltergeist phenomena became muted and infrequent, dying out altogether in a few weeks.

A Diagnostic Case

This account may seem unbelievable. But there is no ground for setting aside any of the testimony, which has been recorded in much greater detail elsewhere. Poltergeist phenomena are a fact, and a very interesting one, although one that is not easy to assimilate to existing scientific knowledge. The Sauchie case illustrates the sporadic, unpredictable yet repetitive occurrence of the poltergeist phenomena. The repetition is very typical of many other published cases. As the testimony is both detailed and reliable the case happens to be a wonderfully 'diagnostic' one. It was clear that the happenings were connected only with Virginia and had nothing to do with the place where she might be. The Sauchie case is a particularly clear-cut example of a type of outbreak in which there is a complete correlation between the occurrence of poltergeist phenomena and a particular person whom we can describe as the 'poltergeist focus.' This correlation has far-reaching logical implications. For instance, it rules out the possibility that the events are random breakdowns in the laws of Nature, or the result of random fluctuations of atoms, and so on.

When we ask if the phenomena are supernatural, we encounter the usual difficulties attaching to the term. Few people nowadays believe that poltergeists are imps called up by witches to harass their enemies. But what of the supreme Adversary himself? Many Roman Catholic devout, including the Cure of Ars, seem to have suffered persecutions similar to poltergeist doings, and some Catholic writers have regarded these assaults as diabolical miracles. The people who, in secular poltergeist cases, function temporarily as poltergeist foci tend to be decent and respectable, but they can hardly be said to be so religious or devout as to invite the attention of his infernal Majesty.

In problems of natural as opposed to supernatural causation, assistance may be gained from a helpful principle first enunciated by Hippocrates (c. 460–380 BC), which may be called the principle of correlation. Writing of epilepsy, a supposedly miraculous disease induced entirely at the will of the gods, he noted that it did not strike at random but was correlated with a certain type of person.

What kind of people are more likely to be the centre of a poltergeist upheaval? The present writer listed twenty-seven cases in which the testimony seemed reasonably reliable and the events appeared to be associated with a particular individual. The poltergeist focus was female in seventeen cases and male in the remaining ten. In seventy-nine cases of varying evidential levels, there were fifty-three females to twenty-six males. Thus there is a sex-effect in phenomena, but males are far from enjoying immunity.

There seems also to be a strong age-factor involved. In the twenty-seven cases, most were aged between ten and twenty years (though there were some notable exceptions). Of the foci in Gauld and Cornell's *Poltergeists*, 152 were under twenty, and forty-two were twenty or older. It seems therefore that poltergeist outbreaks do not occur randomly, but are correlated with juvenility and femininity, suggesting some obscure natural cause.

The Naturalistic Theory

Even if we acknowledge the presence of obscure natural causes as factors, we are still left with a serious logical choice to make, because the spiritualistic type of explanation cannot be set aside without scientific reasons for so doing. The spiritualist explanation assumes that the poltergeist focus is really a 'medium,' a link or intermediary enabling a disembodied spirit to manifest its presence. On this view two elements are required for poltergeist phenomena; a spirit and a living medium. The spiritualist explanation leaves many questions open. For instance, does the spirit itself move the objects, or merely endow the medium with the capacity to act at a distance (the faculty sometimes called psychokinesis)? An alternative explanation assumes that the poltergeist focus is herself capable of psychokinesis—usually without conscious intent or awareness of the fact. On this view there is no 'spirit' involved other than that of the living focus.

It would, of course, be improper to prefer the naturalistic explanation if, in the type of poltergeist case under discussion, there were definite indications of attempted communication from another world or from beyond the grave. However, in only a small proportion of cases is it alleged that the noises appear to take the form of coded raps. Even in these cases, such communications as are inferred do not seem to be readily identifiable with such as we might expect from spirits of the dead, or even with coherent personalities. Apparitions are rare in poltergeist cases. There are some moderately well-evidenced cases, though only a few, in which the poltergeist

Illustration depicting what appears to be poltergeist when very heavy blocks of bricks are strewn about by unknown source.

(it is said) has carried on long conversations in human speech. Since speech is merely a form of sound these allegations are not necessarily preposterous, even though we cannot as yet place much reliance on them being true. However, such talking poltergeists as have been reported bring no important messages from other worlds. They are usually cheeky, flippant, fanciful, and scatter-brained, and appear to have no stock of notions in any way different from those of the historical period in which they are manifested. This supports the concept of the poltergeist as a functioning of an unconscious part of a living human mind rather than as a messenger from the dead.

It needs to be stressed that the evidence against the spiritualist hypothesis is of a purely negative kind. Nor do I wish to insist that deceased persons never communicate; a question which remains open. However, I think that the naturalistic explanation is to be preferred for poltergeist cases of the type under consideration, where the happenings centre on a poltergeist focus. On this theory the poltergeist individual herself activates physical forces of obscure origin. Because of their selective mode of application, these forces are not attributable to electricity, magnetism, or gravitation, but are of a new kind. Also the forces show no especial affinity with those supposed to be productive of physical phenomena at mediumistic séances. Ectoplasm is conspicuously absent in poltergeist cases. Poltergeist phenomena rarely require darkness and are almost invariably observed in full light. In the few poltergeist cases where anything resembling a trance is reported, the phenomena do not seem to happen during the trance but at other times.

On the naturalistic theory, should poltergeist studies be regarded as falling in the field of psychical research—as opposed to physics and physiology? Is there anything psychic about them? The answer is, yes. Poltergeist phenomena never centre on animals: no poltergeist cats and dogs are known. In addition, no phenomena occur when the poltergeist individual is in normal sleep. Thus the higher brain centres are in some way involved, and the problem can be seen as psychobiological as well as physico-physiological. This suggests that it is profitable to look for psychological factors in causation.

Pubertal Changes

Sometimes emphasis has been placed on purely biological factors. Thus the juvenility of poltergeist individuals encouraged the distinguished parapsychologist Hereward Carrington (1880–1958), writing in 1930, to associate the phenomenon with puberty: 'An energy seems to be radiated from the body . . . when the sexual energies are blossoming into maturity . . . It would almost seem as if these energies instead of taking the normal course . . . find this curious means of externalization.' Now I perceive in this remark the germ of a correct theory but it will not do as it stands. Admittedly it is a curious fact that many poltergeist foci do enjoy good physical health and their intelligence is at least average. However, the amount of energy used in poltergeist manifestations is trivial in relation to the normal physical activities of youth. Also Carrington's theory can hardly apply to cases of adult poltergeist individuals. Despite the fact that many poltergeist foci are in the age range ten to twenty, it is by no means clear that the poltergeist disturbances coincide at all precisely with pubertal changes. However, there may be something to be said for a modified form of Carrington's theory, in which we think not of physiological energy but of emotional tension, which can occur both before and after puberty.

> *Esther Cox, the heroine of the sensational poltergeist haunting . . . was said to swell visibly, signifying the occurrence of . . . aerophagy, in which air is sucked involuntarily into the stomach.*

Although poltergeist individuals are in the main healthy, a few of them have suffered from curious fits. A careful examination of the case histories shows that these fits are not epileptic but something different—hysterical attacks.

One of the most interesting examples was that of 'Karin N.' who lived in a house in the middle of a forest in southern Sweden—for the very good reason that in 1897 she had married Mr. N., an inspector of forests. In 1905 Karin, then aged 27, was investigated by Dr. Hjalmar Wijk and Dr. Paul Bjerre. Karin was basically healthy and of strong physical constitution, but the marriage was childless, and from 1898 Karin exhibited various neurotic symptoms. These took the form of fainting fits, which sometimes occurred several times a day. A fit would be preceded by a violent and unconquerable feeling of anxiety that ceased when the fit commenced. During the fit Karin's arms, and sometimes her whole body, would tremble. She would then lie in a paroxysm of tears and laughter with partially veiled consciousness, incapable of voluntary speech or motion. From May 1904, the villa that Karin and her husband occupied was agitated by mysterious knockings, occurring (as is typical of many poltergeist cases) in the evenings when Karin was in bed but not asleep. Karin's illness was correctly diagnosed as hysteria, a condition in which the patient is truly ill but totally ignorant of the real cause of his or her illness, which is psychological and locked away in the unconscious inner part of the mind.

Hysterical 'Absences'

Karin is not, by far, the sole instance of a poltergeist focus with a hysterical illness. Hysterical fits, faints, and comas were characteristic of Floralina in India in 1897, of Mary Langdon at Youghal near Cork in 1661, and of Germaine Maire at Nancy, France, in 1910, who suffered from transitory losses of full consciousness which could well have been hysterical 'absences.' Esther Cox, the heroine of the sensational poltergeist haunting at Amherst, Nova Scotia, in 1878, was said to swell visibly, signifying the occurrence of hysterical meteorism, or aerophagy, in which air is sucked involuntarily into the stomach.

About 1867, a servant-girl in Boston named Mary Carrick was pursued by raps on the walls of any room where she was working and quite heavy objects would move in her presence. Knockings occurred by her bedside while she slept—in apparent exception to the rule that a waking state is necessary. She would cry out and stir agitatedly in her sleep, which was also not normal on these occasions. In fact Mary was a somnambulist. She would rise in the night and do housework while sleep-walking.

In about 1840, Mary Jobson of Sunderland had pains in the head, abdominal swelling, convulsive fits, and insensitivity in regions of the skin. Then she became blind, deaf, and dumb. Poltergeist phenomena ensued: throwings of water and violent knockings. The illness was not mortal, and she had a sudden recovery, which amply confirms a diagnosis of hysteria. Angelique Cottin, investigated by the French Academy of Science in 1846, had some symptoms also reconcilable with hysteria. Her left arm was at a raised temperature; it trembled, and was easily put into a muscular spasm.

It would be wrong to suggest that all poltergeist foci are or have been hysterical. Indeed the majority show no sign of this or any other psychological ailment. But the proportion of markedly hysterical persons is certainly high among poltergeist foci as compared with a random sample of the general population. This suggests rather forcibly that poltergeist happenings, like hysteria, are psychologically triggered. We must suppose also that the psychological mechanism which precipitates a poltergeist outbreak involves some of the same factors as are encountered in the production of a hysterical illness.

Hysteria and dissociative reactions constitute only one group of a class of ailments known as neuroses. Neuroses have no organic cause; they are psychological illnesses, and a neurotic has no derangement of his mind or reason. One kind of neurosis is the anxiety attack, spells of 'free-floating' dread such as Karin had before her fits. Betsy Bell of Tennessee, the centre of elaborate poltergeist events in 1817, seems not to have been hysterical but to have suffered from the 'hyper-ventilation syndrome,' in which the victim faints from temporary oxygen-poisoning. It was following these fainting fits that the Bell poltergeist activity would begin each evening. It is tempting to suppose that in some way the poltergeist phenomena relieved Betsy's anxiety. In Karin's case her anxiety was relieved by her hysterical fits. As we say: the anxiety was 'converted' into the hysterical symptoms. We can therefore hazard the guess that for Karin there were two forms of relief of anxiety—conversion into hysterical symptoms, and poltergeist activity. In each case the process would be an unconscious one.

The Offensive Perriwig

An account of the Daemon of Spraiton in the County of Devon, Anno. 1682.

One time the young man's head was thrust into a very strait place, betwixt a Beds head, and a Wall, and forced by the strength of diver's men to be removed thence, and that not without being much hurt, and bruised, so that much blood appeared about it: upon this, it was advised he should be bleeded, to prevent any ill accident that might come of the bruise; after bleeding, the ligature, or binder of his Arm was removed from thence, and conveyed about his middle, where it was strained with such violence, that the girding had almost stopp'd his breath, and kill'd him, and being cut asunder, it made a *strange and dismal noise*, so that the standers by were affrighted at it. At divers other times he hath been in danger to be strangled with Cravats, and Handkerchiefs, that he hath worn about his Neck, which have been drawn so close, that with the sudden violence he hath near been choaked, and hardly escaped death.

The Spectre hath shewed great offence at the Perriwigs which the young man used to wear, for they are often torn from his head after a very strange manner, one, that he esteemed above the rest, he put in a small box, and that box he placed in another, which he set against the wall of his Chamber, placing a Joint-stool, with other weight, a top of it; but in short time the boxes were broken in sunder, and the Perriwig rended into many small parts and tatters:

Another time, lying in his Masters Chamber, with his Perriwig on his Head, to secure it from danger, within a little time it was torn from him, and reduced into very small fragments. At another time one of his Shoe-strings was observed (without the assistance of any hand) to come of its own accord out of his shoe, and fling itself to the other side of the Room; the other was crawling after it, but a Maid espying that, with her hand drew it out, and it strangely *clasp'd*, and *curl'd* about her hand like a living Eel . . .

Are poltergeist phenomena therefore manifestations of a conversion neurosis? Is anxiety converted into noises and flinging of objects? This temptingly simple theory is not quite adequate. Unless relieved suddenly by one of the 'miracle' cures so typical of this field, hysterical conversion symptoms tend to be durable.

Looked at from this point of view, the mystery of poltergeist activity is not so much why it starts as why it usually stops. We could liken it to a mild infection, such as chickenpox, from which the victim usually recovers in a week or two. It runs its course like a fever. And fever is not so much the disease itself as the body's effort at cure. Pursuing this analogy, we might guess that poltergeist phenomena start and eventually terminate because they are not a disease but the cure.

'Blowing Off Steam'

In 1895 Sigmund Freud (1856–1939) and Josef Breuer (1842–1925) published a series of papers entitled 'Studies on Hysteria' in which they sought for a scientific theory of how hysteria comes about. Much of what they said is directly applicable to the poltergeist problem.

In all human beings there is a natural tendency to keep the emotional tension (or 'excitation' as Freud called it) down to a moderate level. A surplus of excitement is disturbing and the individual therefore has a variety of means for dissipating it. Sometimes this can be achieved in a direct way. Love or anger can he subdued by erotic activity or by taking revenge. Life is not always so simple, but fortunately there is another mechanism that is usually effective. This is the wearing away or erosion of the excitation, which takes place by a process of intellectual activity, 'cooling off' by thinking around the situation or 'talking it over,' even if only with oneself.

In addition, Freud and Breuer drew attention to a third normal mechanism, 'working-off,' for disposing of the charge of emotional tension. This mode of reducing tension employs physical activity and tends to occur in an automatic and instinctive fashion. When fearful or enraged or in mental or physical pain, we are apt to tense our muscles, pace the floor, utter lamentations or curses, or indulge in sobs and tears. These activities are often quite pointless as regards improving the objective situation, but popular wisdom acknowledges their role in reducing tension by such proverbial phrases as 'blowing off steam' or 'crying oneself out.'

***Of predestynacion*, illustration from Alexander Barclay's English translation of *The Ship of Fools*, from an edition published in 1874 (engraving)**

The physical activity, or 'working-out,' is itself a substitute for direct fulfillment. According to Freud and Breuer, when Bismarck (1815–98), the German chancellor, had to suppress angry feelings in the king's presence he would resolve the tension created by smashing a vase upon the floor. A similar delayed or surrogate reaction is sometimes observed in small but generally well-behaved children who occasionally astonish their elders by sudden and isolated acts of vandalism accompanied by no outward sign of temper or irritation.

This brings us close to the psychological meaning of poltergeist activity. I believe that it is a 'working-off' of emotional tension. There is some reason to believe that it happens by an unconscious process, because the poltergeist focus usually seems to have no conscious control over the happenings and only the dimmest awareness that she or he is responsible for them. This suggests that the phenomena occur in those most liable to psychological repression; which squares with the fact that many actual hysterics are represented among poltergeist foci. More elaborate features may be superimposed on the process and the form of the manifestation (like the symptoms of hysteria and other neuroses) may be capable of having a symbolic content reflecting the specific emotional issues involved. This theory, while explaining several of the curious features of poltergeist phenomena, of course sheds no light on the physical nature of the poltergeist force, and little light on the mysterious age factor.

A. R. G. OWEN

FURTHER READING: C. Wilson. Poltergeist! *(London, UK: New English Library, 1981); Loyd Auerbach.* ESP, Hauntings and Poltergeists: A Parapsychologist's Handbook. *(New York, NY: Warner Books, 1986).*

RICHARD BOVET

Predestination

Various doctrines have been elaborated within the Christian Church that seek to explain the manner in which God, it is supposed, calls some individuals to eternal life and condemns others to everlasting punishment. Theories of predestination encounter acute difficulties in reconciling man's freedom of will with the complete knowledge of the future that theologians ascribe to God, and which imperils our notion of time. Few laymen now have much interest in the minutiae of theology but the problem of free will is still a tantalizing one.

Problems of destiny, determinism, and free will came under discussion in the ancient Greek and Roman world long before the Christian era. The ideas of both determinism and providence derive from the orderliness of natural phenomena, such as the succession of the seasons, which suggest that physical and biological events progress according to invariable laws. Implicit in the notion of determinism is the idea of causality that is firmly rooted in the human mind as a result of very elementary experiences. A child pushes an object and it moves. The operator of any machine, however humble, is completely familiar with the concept of causality. However, it can be recognized only if the nature of things does not change capriciously. The laws of Nature must be invariable. It was by recognition of natural law that the philosophers were led to a monotheistic form of theism. The uniformity and lawfulness of Nature must, they thought, result from a single mind. This intelligence was often identified with Zeus, traditionally the chief of the gods, but just as often considered as a mere abstract kind of being.

Views differed as to the relations between the deity and the world. Aristotle (384–322 BC) thought of the universe after its creation as running more or less under its own steam according to natural causality. A minority of thinkers including Epicurus (341–270 BC) postulated an entirely self-sufficient uncreated universe lasting for all eternity and running on purely mechanical lines, a remarkable anticipation of modern scientific materialism. Such a scheme (except that it included an element of randomness or chance) represented a determinism of a mechanical kind without any additional determinism imposed by an overriding providence.

A mosaic from the lid of a tomb of a child. The tomb was found in Tabarka, Tunisia.

The teaching of the Stoics started with Zeno (336–264 BC). Their doctrines developed into a kind of materialistic pantheism. (Pantheistic theologies are those that regard the deity as permeating the world to a degree that makes it hard to distinguish between God and the world.) According to the Stoics the soul consists of a fine material. So also does the Soul of the World (God) who, or which, suffuses all other matter. Everything therefore happens in a purely mechanical way but also in accordance with the will of the World Soul that is the ultimate cause of all motion and change. The Stoics taught acceptance of the Will's decrees, and this is why the adjective stoical is used nowadays to describe fortitude and resignation. In Stoicism the ideas of mechanical determinism and overriding providence were curiously fused together. According to the Stoics everything was predetermined by the immanent or indwelling World Soul, and they gave credence to the arts of augury, divination, and astrology.

In fact the ancient thinkers, while recognizing a considerable degree of determinism (either mechanical or providential) in the world, were uncertain as to whether all physical happenings are strictly determined and they puzzled over the meaning of free will. Epicurus claimed that atoms have a random motion that is completely uncaused. Similarly, operations of the will in man are uncaused, so that human choice is totally free. Carneades (c. 214–c. 129 BC), one of the Sceptics (philosophers who tended to probe into all assumptions and question all statements), argued that the wayward course of both the atom and the human soul was not uncaused, but resulted from their own inner natures. He admitted that the inner cause of action might well be unknowable, so that human actions were unpredictable. Carneades was perhaps the first thinker to make a clear distinction between determinism and predictability.

In Judaic tradition God created the angels, giving them freedom to obey or disobey him. Satan, Prince of the Angels, disobeyed, together with a considerable following of other ranks. Adam, though created in a state of sinless virtue, yielded to Satan's persuasion and also disobeyed, and having fallen into sin forfeited his immortality. According to St. Paul and all the early Christians the sinfulness of Adam was 'inherited' by all his descendants.

According to this concept, all men owed a debt or penalty to God and were therefore subject either to eternal death (a forfeiting of immortality) or, in the more traditional view, to everlasting punishment. However Christ's sacrifice of himself upon the cross was, so Paul believed, a complete and adequate discharge of the debt.

Some of the Pauline epistles can be read as if implying that it was God's will that everyone should be saved: '. . . God our Saviour, who desires all men to be saved' (1 Timothy, chapter 2.3). However, other passages imply that, as was almost universally believed in the Church, the salvation of individuals was conditional on factors additional to the Incarnation and Crucifixion. For example, '. . . for those who are factious and do not obey the truth . . . there will be wrath and fury' (Romans, chapter 2.8). In fact Paul tells his readers they will be saved if they have in their hearts the faith that God raised Jesus from the dead.

Christians have always averred that the individual's faith in Christ is essential for salvation. Naturally there has been controversy as to what is meant by 'faith.' Clearly it ought to go deeper than superficial intellectual assent. According to Paul, in order to have saving faith the grace of God, that is, the power to have real faith which is bestowed on the believer as God's free gift, is necessary. The word 'grace' derives from Latin *gratia*—a gift. All the work of salvation is therefore God's and not man's. God paid the penalty of sacrifice, and also bestows the grace

***St. Augustine of Hippo* (354–430) created by the Spanish painter El Greco (1541–1614)**

necessary for the faith that saves. In the epistles Paul was not writing a theological treatise and so does not set out a fully elaborated doctrine of predestination. But there are several texts that can be, and were, interpreted as meaning that God chooses those whom he will save. For instance, Paul says that 'For those whom he foreknew he also predestined to be conformed to the image of his Son . . . and those whom he predestined he also called . . .' (Romans, chapter 8.29–30). Clearly, whether or not Paul intended it, a fully predestinarían doctrine can be extracted from this: at the beginning of the world God knew all men that would be born, and decreed in advance who would be saved.

The doctrine of predestination remained in the somewhat nebulous Pauline form until the Pelagian controversy of the fifth century. Pelagius (360–420), whose name means 'man of the sea,' came from Britain. Like many provincial visitors to Rome before and since, he was scandalized by the decadent life of the city. The licentious Romans blandly pleaded human frailty as an extenuating circumstance. Pelagius was therefore prompted to stress the positive qualities in human nature, and maintained that, if need be, a man's salvation could be achieved by his own efforts unassisted by grace. He did not, of course, deny that if grace were given it would aid the process of salvation. Pelagianism, as the resulting doctrines were called, affirmed the freedom of the will, maintaining that it is at any time free to choose good or evil. This is also true at the moment of birth. Having no innate bias to evil, we lack original sin. According to Pelagianism, no individual was predestined to be saved or lost.

St. Augustine (354–430) of Hippo, near Carthage in North Africa, one of the greatest of the Fathers of the Church, was provoked by Pelagianism into formulating a theory of predestination that was to have lasting influence. He maintained that man was free to do good or ill, to seek for God or reject him. Therefore men might differ in their natural merit. But a man was not saved by his natural merit, which was ineffective for salvation unless assisted by grace dispensed by the Holy Spirit. Merit assisted, or instilled, by grace was supernatural merit and only supernatural merits were able to save. The giving or withholding of grace, resulting in salvation or damnation, was God's free choice. Lest it seem that God might be unfair to the damned, Augustine was concerned to stress the totally undeserving condition of fallen man. Because of original sin we deserved eternal punishment; but God in his mercy raised some to blessedness by grace gratuitously given. The graceless therefore should not complain of injustice.

God's foresight differs from man's. He does not predict events as a super-computer might if fed with all possible information about the present and the past.

The Ineffable Vision

So far so good; God chooses those whom he will make his own. But why is it predestination? According to Augustine, because of God's perfect foreknowledge of all events. Christians traditionally set no limits to God's powers. His omniscience means that he has a complete knowledge of the future. God's foresight differs from man's. He does not predict events as a super-computer might if fed with all possible information about the present and the past. God, according to Augustine and later theologians, knows everything *directly*, whether past, present, or future, because his existence is outside of time. His knowledge consists of 'one eternal, immutable and ineffable vision.' According to Augustine, God foresees even the free acts of men and knows in advance how their free choices will turn out. He also foresees at the Creation all that he will himself bring to pass, including the dispensation of grace. Augustine was therefore able to say, 'Predestination is nothing else than the foreknowledge and fore-ordaining of those gratuitous gifts by which God makes certain the salvation of those who are saved.'

The status of free will remains somewhat ambiguous in St. Augustine's system. The Roman statesman and philosopher Boethius (480–525) wrote that if from eternity God foreknows the wills of men, there can be no free will. Augustine clearly implied that God predestines the blessed to salvation, but left in obscurity the question whether God can be said to fore-ordain the graceless sinner to perdition. The question was particularly acute in respect of infants dying unbaptized. Baptism was generally considered adequate to confer saving grace and blessedness on children who died shortly after receiving the sacrament: but the unbaptized were in an unmitigated state of original sin. According to one solution, their fate was settled by God through his foreknowledge of whether, if they had lived, they would have received (from him) supernatural merit through grace. According to a milder solution unbaptized infants go to limbo, a region adjacent to hell and inhabited by virtuous pagans who had died before Christ's coming.

It was easy to move from Augustine's teaching to the doctrine of Predestinarianism. In the fifth century, Lucidus, a Gallic priest, taught that

Portrait of John Calvin in a stained-glass window in the Evangelical Church in Hockenheim, Germany

Christ did not die for the nonelect who had been created expressly to go to hell. Similarly, in the ninth century in France, the monk Gottschalk of Orbais was condemned for saying the same, and maintaining that original sin had cancelled free will. The resulting controversy had to be settled by a synod of bishops in 860, which decided that God desires the salvation of all men. Despite original sin, the will is free and is aided by grace. The damnation of the lost results from their abuse of free will. St. Bonaventure (1221–74) supported this formulation and held that while God offers saving grace to all, men are wholly free to reject it.

St. Thomas Aquinas (1226–74) revived a formula originally developed by the Greek theologian St. John of Damascus (676–754). A man is free to accept or reject the gratuitous gift of grace which God offers to all. God *antecedently* wills to save him, but in the very instant of the Creation foresees how he will respond and, in the light of this prevision, God *consequently* wills his salvation or reprobation. Of course the antecedent and consequent wills of God are not separated in time, and this solution will seem to many to be mere sophistry and logic-chopping. The Roman Catholic Church has never spoken authoritatively on the doctrine of predestination as a whole. Catholic theologians tend to favour a theory similar to that of St. Thomas Aquinas, involving God's antecedent and consequent will.

Predestinarianism really came into its own among the Protestant reformers. Martin Luther was concerned to stress faith and grace as being superior to good works, and maintained that God absolutely predestines his elect to glory without regard to their human merits. Free will went out when original sin came in, and all human acts are subject to the overriding providence of God. It was Ulrich Zwingli (1484–1531), the Swiss reformer,

***Dante and the Divine Comedy* painted in 1465 by Domenico di Michelino (1417–91) shows the seven story mountain. Fresco in the nave of the Duomo of Florence, Italy.**

who went to the extent of declaring that God fore-ordained some men to perdition in order that his justice be made manifest, though it is John Calvin (1509–64) who is usually associated with this doctrine.

Few modern Christian sects put much stress on predestination or related doctrines. Salvation is primarily the gift of God through grace. The ways to making oneself receptive of grace are the sacraments, prayer, moral effort, and striving to love God and one's neighbour. None can be sure of salvation but all may hope.

A. R. G. OWEN

FURTHER READING: L. Boettner. The Reformed Doctrine of Predestination. *(Grand Rapids, MI: Eetdmans Publishing Co., 1932); John Calvin.* Concerning the Eternal Predestination of God. *(Cambridge, UK: James Clarke, 1961 reprint); M. J. Farrelly.* Predestination, Grace and Free Will. *(London, UK: Burns & Oates, 1963).*

Purgatory

That the sanctions for unjust and immoral conduct that can be imposed in this life are inadequate might occur to any thinking man. What form the penalties of another life might take would be a matter for guesswork, but that there should be some penalty seems reasonable to many who believe in the immortality of the soul and who accept purgatory as a condition or place of spiritual cleansing for the dead. That there should be a restoration of the human soul to a lost integrity, where that is possible, also seems reasonable. In the *Aeneid* Virgil (70–19 BC) pictured a threefold purgation of souls that were too Earthy, the elements of fire, water, and air being called upon to do the work; some were seared with fire, others hung out as on a clothesline to suffer the action of the air, and a third sort churned in a vast whirlpool. Virgil was governed by the Stoic idea that this process lasted for 1,000 years and that then the life of the world began anew.

The Pythagoreans, with whose views Virgil was not unfamiliar, held that the soul at death passed through the air, then through the waters above the air, and finally through the atmosphere warmed by the sun, until it was deposited in the Isles of the Blest. This passage through air, water, and solar radiation was looked upon as the purgation of the soul. Once in the Isles of the Blest it might be left for a time and then escorted to a still higher Elysium, or it might be sent down to join another body on Earth. The Isles of the Blest were located in the moon and disembarkation there was considered to be endangered by certain 'customs officers' who might rob the soul of its assets. Ritual acts performed while on Earth might be a guarantee that the soul would escape harm from these searchers.

Toward the end of Old Testament times, Jewish belief was centered on prayer and sacrifice for the dead in such cases where hope for the remission of their sins might be entertained. The famous incident of Judas Maccabeus set the pattern; after a victory he had found that some of his dead warriors had pagan amulets under their tunics. They had died nobly for the liberty of their Jewish faith, but they had also offended God by superstition or else by greed. Judas directed that sacrifice should be offered for them at Jerusalem that they might be set free from their sins (2 Maccabees, chapter 12). The book of Enoch (chapter 22.12) holds out a prospect that sinners who are themselves sinned against will not stay forever in Gehenna with those sinners who have no such asset.

The coming of Christianity meant that the two books of Maccabees were taken over as part of the scriptures of the Church and the incident there reported was valued as precedent. Prayer for the dead (as distinct from prayer to those who had died by martyrdom) was a Christian practice from the beginning. The mention of 'the house of Onesiphorus' (2 Timothy, chapter 1) in a context where the past good works of its head are commemorated, implies that this Onesiphorus was already dead and is being commended to mercy. Inscriptions of the second century ask the passer-by to intercede for the soul of the dead person who is named.

Inscriptions of the second century ask the passer-by to intercede for the soul of the dead person who is named.

St. Paul himself once indicated that he held the same belief. In 1 Corinthians (chapter 3) he speaks of the varying work of evangelists; some are good builders, others run up a shack with anything that is to hand. When a fire sweeps through the town, the good building of stone will stand, but the shack will burn, and its occupant may only just manage to get out, 'being saved as it were through the fire.' The careful evangelist is rewarded; the careless one is saved, but only just. This is an allegory of heaven and purgatory, though not a direct formal pronouncement of belief. The saying in the gospel of St. Luke (chapter 59) about the officer of the law putting in ward the evil-doer and keeping him there till he pay the last farthing was likewise taken as an indirect way of describing the fate after death of the soul whose sin was not irremediable.

Depiction of purgatory on the Holy Cross altar in Maria Saal Church, Austria

The Keys of Pardon

While urging prayer for the dead, the Church was also teaching that there were certain capital sins that, if they were not forgiven in this world, could never be pardoned. Thus the category of what came to be called venial sins (those which could be pardoned) was established, and the conclusion was reached that it was these that the

Circle of Envy

My master said: 'This circle castigates
The sin of envy . . .'
I do not think that there exists on earth
Even at the present day, a man so hard
That he would not be moved by what
  I saw.
For when I had drawn near enough
  to them
So that their actions were made clear
  to me,
I grieved so, that the tears sprang from
  my eyes.
Their clothing seemed to be of coarsest
  haircloth;
One leaned upon the shoulder of another,
And all of them were leaning on the bank.
Thus do the blind who beg their
  daily bread
Take station in the churches of
  indulgence . . .
And as the sun doth not avail the blind,
So to those spirits whom I have described,
The light of heaven hath here denied its
  blessing:
For through their eyelids runs an iron wire,
Sewing them shut — as it is often done
To a wild falconet, to keep him quiet.
It seemed to me that I was doing wrong
To stare at others, while unseen
  myself. . .

Dante Purgatorio
(trans. L. G. White)

living by their prayers could cause to be remitted for their dead friends. Not without a purpose did the Church at Rome substitute a feast of the *Cathedra* of St. Peter for the pagan festival of the *cara cognatio* on February 22. On that day pagan Roman families celebrated the memory of their departed relatives by setting out food for their spirits. Christians were reminded by the Petrine feast that the keys of pardon had been assumed by St. Peter when he was set to guard the gates of heaven.

Infiltrations of pagan practice troubled the Christian Church from time to time, and a Gallican Church council at Tours in 567 had to forbid the practice of putting out food for the spirits of the dead on this feast. Origen included in his writings the figures of the evil 'customs officials' who wait on the boundary of the world to despoil the dead of their hard-won merits. Origen also pictured Christ as standing like another John the Baptist by the side of a river of fire, baptizing in fire those who came forward to cross the river. In a Christian poem by Commodian (c. AD 250) the myth is introduced of the lost tribes of Israel living in tranquillity across the river of Persia, with toil and death but with no disease and no sin, awaiting the end of the world.

One notable difference between Christian practice and other religions was that monarchs and other famous men sought to be buried within Christian churches, so that they might benefit after death from their being remembered by the priests praying at the altars. The Emperor Constantine set this fashion in 337, soon after the building of the first great basilicas; and the tombs in Westminster Abbey, London, are originally due to the same motive. The prayers in the liturgy, as witnessed by the oldest of the Sacramentaries, correspond with this idea, asking for 'purgation after death' for the departed faithful. The nature of this purgation was much debated.

The institution of a system of public penance by the Church was more exactly carried out in the West, with its juridical background of Roman law, than in the East. The Western belief that a penitent who was admitted to Communion on his deathbed could work off the remainder of his public penance in purgatory was not so clearly understood in the East. At the Council of Florence (1439) the Greeks accepted the lawfulness of praying for the dead. After discussion they also agreed on a formulation of the expiatory character of purgatory for penitents who had not carried out their full penance. Soon after this the Western mystic St. Catherine of Genoa (1447–1510) gave a new direction to theological thought by her account of her mystic experiences. She claimed that those in purgatory rejoiced at their growing awareness of the removal of all obstacles to their future union with God. Having passed beyond their period of free will they could no longer sin, and so could not grudge the happiness of those who departed from purgatory before themselves; neither could they gloat over the thought of leaving before others.

The *Purgatorio* of Dante is a seven-story mountain where the expiation goes on of what was due to the seven capital sins that a man may have repented of before death. Dante uses purgatory to read a lesson to those still alive who incline to the capital vices, very much as Chaucer's Wife of Bath said of her dead husband: 'On Earth, I was his Purgatory.' St. Patrick's Purgatory, the Irish penitential sanctuary on Lough Derg, became famous before Dante's time and indeed influenced him. The short and sharp penance done there was held to mitigate enormously what might await the sinner in the next life. The other great work of literature inspired by purgatory, Cardinal Newman's 'Dream of Gerontius,' has through Elgar's music brought the idea of purgatory once more into the awareness of the English-speaking world from which it had so largely faded at the Reformation. The medieval painting of a weighing of souls, still to be seen in the church at Catherington in Hampshire, may owe its form to the classical picture of Hermes weighing Achilles against Memnon, but here the hand of the Virgin Mary has adjusted the arm of the balance to the advantage of the soul that is being weighed against his sins. There is a mildness about Christianity that paganism did not dare to envisage.

J. H. CREHAN

FURTHER READING: Franz Cumont. Afterlife in Roman Paganism.

(New Haven, CT: Yale University Press, 1922); Shane Leslie. St. Patrick's Purgatory. *(London, UK: Burns & Oates, 1932); J. Le Goff.* The Birth of Purgatory. *(Chicago, IL: University of Chicago Press, 1984); F. X. Shouppe.* Purgatory. *(Rockford, IL: TAN Books, 1973).*

Raudive Voices

The possibility that communication with the dead might be made by some form of radio was first put forward by Thomas Edison (1847–1931) in an interview he gave to *Scientific American* in 1920. Nearly another forty years were to pass, however, before the Swedish artist Friedrich Jürgenson (1903–87) reported what appeared to be the first demonstration.

Jürgenson had taken a tape recorder into remote Swedish countryside to record birdsong and, on playing back the tape later, he heard, as well as the birdsong, faint voices that he identified as those of dead relatives and friends addressing him. A book that Jürgenson wrote subsequently attracted the attention of the eminent parapsychologist Dr. Hans Bender (1907–91), and also that of Dr. Konstantin Raudive (1906–74), former professor of psychology at Uppsala University. Both men carried out strictly controlled experiments, and were convinced that factory-clean tapes, run through a tape-recorder in a silent environment, could record the sound of human voices speaking intelligible words.

Raudive's book on his work attracted the attention of a British publisher, who subsequently brought out an English-language edition, under the title of *Breakthrough* (1971). Before publication, he set up a sophisticated series of experiments. Since it might be argued that the voices came from everyday radio broadcasts picked up by induction, some of the recordings were carried out inside a Faraday cage, providing a complete screen to all radio-frequency emissions. The experiments were supervised by electronics experts and recording engineers.

More than 200 voices are reported to have been heard on the tapes, some so clearly that they were intelligible to everyone present. The publisher's chairman was sure that he heard the voice of an old friend, the late pianist Artur Schnabel (1882–1951), and Dr. Raudive was addressed by his childhood nickname.

Various hypotheses have been advanced to account for these 'Raudive voices.' The most attractive is that they are imprinted on the tape by some kind of involuntary psychokinesis on the part of the recipient; this would account for the voices speaking only in languages with which he is familiar.

> *The living water which the earth hath for its dwellers is stagnant water for me . . . I no longer know where I am, now that I have arrived in this valley [of the dead].*

Refrigerium

A latin word meaning 'refreshment,' *refrigerium* was adopted by early Latin-speaking Christians to describe the hoped-for bliss that would reward the faithful after death. The term implies a concept of the afterlife in which refreshing coolness was regarded as a most desirable thing. As used in Christian texts, a reference is often implied to the parable of Dives and Lazarus, the rich man and the beggar (Luke, chapter 16). For after death the rich man implores Abraham to send Lazarus 'to dip the end of his finger in water and cool my tongue, for I am in anguish in this flame.' Dives seeks this refreshment because he is in a fiery hell—a fate that he deserved for his former way of life. But the idea of the dead in need of cool water is far older than Christianity.

As far back as the Pyramid Texts (c. 2400 BC), the dead pharaohs were assured that libations of water would be made for them. In subsequent Egyptian tomb-paintings, and in the vignettes of the Book of the Dead, the deceased is frequently depicted receiving draughts of water, often from a goddess. And in the Hellenistic period inscriptions abound with formulas such as 'May Osiris give thee cool water.' But the most significant of all is doubtless this inscription, about 46 BC, in which a dead woman addresses her husband from the tomb: 'The living water which the earth hath for its dwellers is stagnant water for me . . . I no longer know where I am, now that I have arrived in this valley [of the dead]. Would that I had water to drink from a running stream and one to say to me, "Remove not thy pitcher from the stream!" O that my face were turned toward the north wind on the river bank that the coolness thereof might quiet the anguish of my heart!'

This belief that the dead crave for fresh water and cool breezes also found expression in Mesopotamia. In the *Epic of Gilgamesh* it is said of the dead that 'dust is their food and clay their sustenance,' and they long for offerings of water to be made to them by their surviving relatives. The evidence of tombs often reveals the provision made to convey liquid offering to the dead: for example, in the Canaanite city of Ugarit (now Ras Shamra) many graves were equipped with pipes leading down from ground level.

That the dead should be regarded

as parched and in need of cool water is an idea that naturally occurred in the dry hot lands of the Near East. The image of a celestial stream or fountain of refreshing, life-giving water, which appears in many of the ancient religions of this area, found dramatic expression in the culminating vision of John in the book of Revelation (chapter 22): 'Then he showed me the river of the water of life, bright as crystal, flowing from the throne of God and of the Lamb . . . The Spirit and the Bride say, "Come" . . . And let him who is thirsty come, let him who desires take the water of life without price.'

The words *refrigerare* and *refrigerium* abound in early Christian funerary inscriptions and liturgical formulas, expressing the intuitions of a faith that had its roots in the hot Mediterranean lands. This southern aspiration for an eternal state of refreshing coolness contrasts notably with the view of the northern barbarians, who imagined Valhalla as a hall, brightly lighted, and closed against cold and damp, where dead heroes warmed themselves by drinking the intoxicating liquor that flowed from the goat Heidrun.

Statue of Strabo (64/63 BC–c. AD 24) in Amasia, Turkey, along the Iris River

Revenant

One who returns from the dead, a ghost, from the French *revenir*, 'to return;' ghosts of the departed appear to the living for many reasons: sometimes because they are the victims of murder and seek vengeance on those who have harmed them: often because they have died a premature or violent death; although there are kindly ghosts, others, return solely for evil purposes.

Sin Eater

The function of the person known as a 'sin eater' was to act as a human scapegoat for the sins of someone who had just died. By eating bread and drinking either milk, beer, or wine that had been placed on the body of the corpse, the sin eater took upon himself the sins of the departed, absorbing them into his own body. He was paid a small amount of money for saving a soul from hell in this way.

Sin eaters were first recorded by the antiquary John Aubrey (1626–97) in the seventeenth century, in his book *Remaines of Gentilisme and Judaisme:* 'In the County of Hereford was an old custom at funerals to hire poor people who have to take upon them all the sinnes of the parting deceased . . . The manner was that when the corpse was brought out of the house and laid in the biere, a loaf of bread was brought out and delivered to the sinne-eater over the corpse was also a mazar bowl of maple full of beer (which he was to drink up) and sixpence in money in consideration whereof he took upon him (*ipso facto*) all the sinnes of the defunct and freed him or her from walking after they were dead.' In North Wales, according to Aubrey, milk was used instead of beer.

A later writer, Bagford (1650/51–1716), referring to information obtained from Aubrey, described the sin eaters of Shropshire: 'Within the memory of our fathers . . . when a person died there was a notice given to an old sire (for so they called him) who presently repaired to the place where the deceased lay and stood before the door of the house when some of the family came out and furnished him with a cricket (stool) . . . Then they gave him a goat which he put in his pocket; a crust of bread which he ate, and a full bowl of ale which he drank off at a draught . . . (after which) he pronounced the ease and rest of the soul departed for which he would pawn his own soul.'

In the late seventeenth century sixpence or a groat (four pence) were worth very much more than they are today but even allowing for this, it seems a ridiculously small fee for the redemption of a human soul.

The concept of a scapegoat, who takes upon himself other peoples' sins, is based upon the primitive idea that the qualities of a human being or animal, whether good or evil, can be transmitted to another by some supernatural agency. Some primitive peoples ate the flesh of the newly-dead in order to acquire their strength. In ancient Europe human blood (which was identified with the soul) was frequently drunk in order that the living might share in the strength or valor of the dead. The Greek geographer Strabo writes that in the British Isles it was the custom for sons to eat the flesh of their dead parents in order to prevent their ghosts from returning to haunt them. It is probable that the bread consumed by the sin eater represented the body of the deceased and the wine, beer, or milk symbolized the blood.

Rites developed by human beings for the purpose of keeping the soul at rest seem to have been based on the principle that unless obligations to the dead were fulfilled, the soul was bound to suffer. For this reason it was imperative to remove the burden of sin from the person who had died.

As long as the doctrine of hellfire was preached, the sin eater could always find work. In *Sighs From Hell, or the Groans of a Damned Soul*, published in 1658, John Bunyan (1628–88) compared the agonies of the dying with those of the unsaved dead who were transferred from the discomforts of 'a long sickness to a longer hell—from the griping of death to the everlasting torments of hell.'

Although later references to sin eaters are scarce, they probably survived in remote places in the British Isles until well into the eighteenth century. They were occasionally seen in the lowlands of Scotland at this time; in this area it was essential that the sin eater was a stranger to the dead person, and that he did not consume the food and drink 'with a grudge in his heart.' There is reason to believe that vestiges of the custom continued to influence funeral rites in Welsh border districts for a considerable period; for instance, a poor man might be given a present of money at the graveside. In Derbyshire, England, in the nineteenth century a glass of wine from a box resting at the foot of the coffin would be offered to mourners, the intention behind the ceremony being the sacramental 'killing' of the sins of the deceased.

It seems that in East Anglia an unsuspecting tramp or beggar who happened to apply for charity at the door of a household where an unburied body awaited interment, would sometimes be tricked into taking the sins of the dead person upon himself. A piece of bread that had been passed over the corpse would be given to the vagrant who would eat it in good faith, unaware of the meaning of this innocent act. The last relic of this ancient superstition is possibly the reluctance of tramps to beg where there is a dead body in the house.

A piece of bread that had been passed over the corpse would be given to the vagrant who would eat it in good faith, unaware of the meaning of this innocent act.

Specter

From Latin *spectrum*, 'vision,' a ghost or apparition, especially one which is frightening: the Specter of the Brocken is a huge shadow, often accompanied by rings of coloured light, cast by an observer on top of a hill on the upper surfaces of clouds that are below him.

Spiritualism

The modern spiritualist movement arose in the United States in 1848 as a result of the publicity given to the events that occurred in the home of the Fox family in Hydesville, New York State. The Fox family moved into the house in December 1847, and for the next three months they were disturbed by strange noises that frequently kept them awake at night. The family consisted of John Fox, his wife, and two young daughters, Margaretta and Kate. On Friday March 31, 1848, the family retired to bed early. Mrs. Fox described the events of that night:

> *'It was very early when we went to bed on this night—hardly dark. I had been so broken of rest I was almost sick—I had just lain down when it commenced as usual—the children, who slept in the other bed in the room, heard the rapping, and tried to make similar sounds by snapping their fingers.*
>
> *My youngest child, Cathie, said:*

A lithograph of the Fox sisters

'Mr. Splitfoot, do as I do,' clapping her hands. The sound instantly followed her with the same number of raps. When she stopped the sound ceased for a short time.

Then Margaretta said, in sport: 'Now do just as I do. Count one, two, three, four, striking one hand against the other at the same time—' and the raps came as before. She was afraid to repeat them.

I then thought I could put a test that no one in the place could answer. I asked the 'noise' to rap my different children's ages successively.

Instantly, each one of my children's ages was given correctly, pausing between them sufficiently long enough to individualize them until the seventh —at which a longer pause was made, and then three more emphatic raps were given, corresponding to the age of the little one that died, which was my youngest child.

I then asked: 'Is this a human being that answers my questions correctly?' There was no rap.

I asked: 'Is it a spirit? If it is, make two raps.'

Two sounds were given as soon as the request was made.'

In this way Mrs. Fox and her daughters believed they had discovered a means of communication with a spirit who claimed to have been murdered in the house. Sir Arthur Conan Doyle (1859–1930) in his *History of Spiritualism* (1926) says that excavations on the site disclosed human remains.

The Fox family were plagued not only by spirit noises, but also by sensation seekers, so Mrs. Fox and the girls went to live with her married daughter in Rochester. Their psychic abilities continued, and around them developed the first Spiritualist circle. In 1849 the girls gave a public demonstration in Rochester and followed this with demonstrations in other towns in the eastern states. Their activities created sensation. Their popularity was not affected by pronouncements made by three professors from the University of Buffalo, following an investigation in 1851, that the raps were produced by movements of the knee joints, or by the subsequent alleged confession by Kate that they were produced by cracking her toes.

'Spirit rapping' became a craze in the United States, and in the early stages Spiritualism was as much a popular scientific movement as a religious movement. People who had attended a mediumistic demonstration, or had read about such events, held seances in their homes. They were often motivated by curiosity and the spirit of scientific enquiry. They met to test the claims of Spiritualists, they continued to meet if they felt that such claims were being confirmed by their experiences within the circle, and it was on the basis of such successful groups that permanent organizations, societies, and churches began to develop.

The National Union

The Spiritualist movement was introduced to Britain in 1852 when Mrs. Hayden, a US medium, gave demonstrations. She was followed by other mediums and, as in the United States, a short-lived craze swept the country. The early days in Britain were similar to those in the United States: the movement of that period consisting of 'home circles' of friends and followers who gathered round a medium.

The visits of D. D. Home (1833–86) to Britain in the 1850s and 60s created considerable interest. There were only two known professional mediums in London as late as 1867, though there were many private mediums in that period, including the infant prodigy of mediumship, Master Willie Turketine.

During the 1860s, Spiritualist societies began to appear, as the more successful circles developed organizations. These first appeared in London and in Yorkshire, which formed the two centres from which Spiritualism spread. Outside London the movement in the second half of the nineteenth century was most successful in Yorkshire and Lancashire and the mining areas of the northeast. The first national organization, the British Association of Progressive Spiritualists, was formed in 1865. They were attacked by the more conventional Spiritualists for being 'anti-Christian' and their organization collapsed in 1868.

A photograph of two women, possibly taken by William Hope (1863–1933). A woman's face appears above the heads of the women, surrounded in an ethereal-looking 'mist.'

At this time many Spiritualists feared the development of organizations that they held would destroy the freedom and spontaneity that were essential to the movement, and would lead to the growth of bureaucracy and oligarchy. A writer of the period expressed these feelings by pointing out that the movement would one day become 'controlled by the lower stratum of minds—minds that live and work almost solely for the interests of organizations.'

In spite of misgivings of this sort a further attempt to establish a national organization in 1873 led to the rise of the British National Association of Spiritualists. It consisted mainly of Spiritualists from the London area and was gradually forced to recognize its failure to acquire national status. In 1883 it was reconstituted as the London Spiritualist Alliance.

In the 1870s and 80s local Spiritualist societies in many areas began to associate with each other for mutual benefit and to form district organizations. The first of these, the Lancashire Association, was formed in 1875, and by 1912, there were fifteen of these associations. The first effective national organization was formed in 1890; the Spiritualists' National Federation was a federation of local churches that made rapid progress, mainly in the north, and by 1896 had fifty-eight societies affiliated to it. In order that the movement could obtain legal status, the Federation was reconstituted as the Spiritualists' National Union Ltd (S.N.U) in 1902.

In Britain the Spiritualist movement grew most rapidly in the period between the two world wars, a period in which there was no lack of able mediums, including Rudi Schneider (1908–57) and Mrs. Leonard (1882–1968), and the movement was also greatly assisted by the work of three able proponents, none of whom seems to have had any psychic gift themselves. Sir Oliver Lodge (1851–1940) was an eminent scientist whose account of communications with his son, who had been killed in World War I, was published under the title of *Raymond* in 1916. Sir Arthur Conan Doyle, then at the height of his fame as the creator of Sherlock Holmes, was converted in 1917 and until his death, worked ceaselessly to promote Spiritualism. Hannen Swaffer (1879–1962) set out to investigate Spiritualism for *The People*, of which he was the editor. In the course of his investigations, he believed that he had received evidence of the survival of his old chief—Lord Northcliffe. He organized a public meeting at the Queens Hall in January 1925 to announce his conversion. Swaffer became an active protagonist and it was through the medium in Swaffer's private circle that the messages of the guide named Silver Birch were communicated.

Science or Religion

Although the Spiritualist movement seems to have arisen out of a semi-scientific curiosity about the nature of 'psychic phenomena,' religious aspects began to appear at a very early date. The idea of communication with spirits is readily associated with religious concepts, and since many early Spiritualists were searching for a system of belief to replace Christianity they quickly seized on the 'messages' that were given by spirits through the mediums, for although these were often evidence intended to prove survival, many spirits could not resist the temptation to preach their philosophy. Spiritualist meetings also began to develop rituals that included music, hymn singing, prayer, and Bible reading. Such rituals are claimed to create an atmosphere conducive to the appearance of phenomena and to the prevention of the disruption of the seance by evil spirits. By the 1870s many societies were adopting the title of churches.

Non-Christian Spiritualists frequently held that Spiritualism was a new religion that would ultimately replace Christianity, while others saw it as the basis of all religion. The Christian Churches as a whole attacked Spiritualism, arguing that communication with the dead was forbidden by the authority of the Bible, and that the communicators were evil entities dispatched by the Devil to mislead men. The Roman Catholic Church has maintained this attitude, as have such sects as the Jehovah's Witnesses and the Pentecostal movement, but the 'Free Churches' and the Anglicans have moved toward a more tolerant position, reflected in the

Spirit unmasked. Top: Forming circle. Center: Medium's assistant being placed behind curtain (left). Spirit manifestations (right). Bottom: A very substantial 'spirit' apprehended.

THE GRAPHIC

AN ILLUSTRATED WEEKLY NEWSPAPER

No 532.—Vol. XXI. Regd at General Post Office as a Newspaper | SATURDAY, FEBRUARY 7, 1880 | Price Sixpence Or by Post Sixpence Halfpenny

THE CAPTURE OF A SPIRIT

SKETCHES AT A RECENT SPIRITUALISTIC SÉANCE IN GREAT RUSSELL STREET FROM NOTES SUPPLIED BY SIR G. SITWELL AND MR. VON BUCH establishment of the Churches' Fellowship for Psychical Study in 1953. Christian Spiritualists have always argued that they were attempting to restore to the Church those practices that were commonly accepted by the early Christians.

Spiritualists were subjected not only to verbal attack by the Churches, the Press, and rationalists, but also to legal prosecution up to 1951, when the Fraudulent Mediums Act was passed. As late as 1945 a Spiritualist church at Redhill had been forced to close as a result of threats of prosecution, and in the previous year the medium Helen Duncan (1897–1956) had been sentenced to imprisonment for nine months. Under earlier acts, the professional practice of mediumship (even if admitted to be genuine) could be construed as illegal, but the new act made it necessary for the prosecution to prove that fraud had been committed, thus implicitly accepting that genuine mediumship was a possibility.

One of the main sources of conflict within the movement has centered around the acceptance of Christian teachings. While accepting a broadly religious basis, the S.N.U has consistently refused to adopt specifically Christian doctrine. After the failure in 1928 of Conan Doyle's attempt to convert the S.N.U. to Christianity and of a number of attempts to organize Christian Spiritualists, the medium Winifred Moyes established the Greater World Christian Spiritualist League in 1931. The League was an immediate success and by 1935 it had 580 affiliated churches.

In the United States, Spiritualist associations include the National Spiritualist Alliance of the United States, founded in 1913, with its headquarters in Lake Pleasant, Massachusetts, and the International General Assembly of Spiritualists, in Norfolk, Virginia, which dates from 1936. On the whole, however, the movement consists of small, independent churches and groups, held together by the personality of an individual minister or medium. Services are similar to those in Protestant churches. Women have always had a strong position in the leadership.

The Seven Principles

Spiritualism is a movement and not an organization. It consists of international and national associations and of many independent local societies and of numerous home circles and individuals who are unattached to any formal organization. You do not have to join any organization to be a Spiritualist. There is no agreement on a Spiritualist creed of beliefs, beyond the two broad beliefs already mentioned.

Spiritualist beliefs are the result of messages received from the spirits through a medium, and the teachings of the spirits display wide differences. Spiritualists explain that spirits are human beings who have survived death; transition to the afterlife does not immediately make a man wise, he takes with him the ideas he had in life, and continues to hold to these beliefs at least during his stay in the lower planes of the afterlife. Spirits who have moved upward after death, to increasingly high planes of existence, find it more difficult to communicate through mediums, so that communications usually come from the recently dead and those who have made little progress in the afterlife. It is not surprising therefore to find a wide diversity of belief held by Spiritualists

In Europe and Latin America, most Spiritualists believe in reincarnation, while in England and America few Spiritualists do. Some Spiritualists are agnostic, since there appears to be no greater proof of the existence of God in the lowest levels of the spirit world than on Earth.

There is no Spiritualist creed or bible. The most widely accepted book is *Spirit Teachings*, a series of communications from the spirit world transmitted through the automatic writing mediumship of Rev. W. Stainton Moses (1839–92).

The Mediumship of W. S. Moses

Mr. Moses himself, in his published writings, was wont to attach considerable importance to the evidence for the doctrines of Spiritualism afforded by the communications, ostensibly from the spirits of deceased persons, received through his mediumship. Of communicators who thus claimed to furnish definite proof of their identity, Mr. Myers, who has collected the evidence under this head in a convenient form, reckons thirty-eight in all. Of these thirty-eight persons some had been known in life to Moses himself or to other members of the circle; some, such as Bishop Wilberforce, Swedenborg, or President Garfield, were historical personages; yet others were individuals of no special eminence, and without any point of contact with Mr. Moses or his circle.

In one important particular the evidence of identity in these cases is superior to that generally furnished through so-called clairvoyant mediums. In marked contrast to the vague generalities that commonly pass for tests, Mr. Moses' spirits were prodigal of names, dates, and other concrete facts that lend themselves to ready verification. Here is an example: 'On February 28th, 1874, a spirit came by raps and gave the name 'Rosamira.' She said that she died at Torquay on January 10th 1874, and that she had lived at Kilburn. She stated that her husband's name was 'Lancaster;' and added later that his Christian name was 'Ben.' As a matter of fact the whole of these particulars, given at the seance at the end of February, are to be found in the notice of the death in the *Daily Telegraph* of January 5 preceding.

The case is typical. Mr. Moses' spirits habitually furnished accurate obituaries, or gave such other particulars of their lives as could be gathered from the daily papers, from published biographies, or from the *Annual Register* and other works of reference.

F. Podmore
Modern Spiritualism

A widely accepted credal statement is to be found in the Seven Principles subscribed to by all members of the S.N.U., which were derived from a spirit communication received through Emma Hardinge-Britten (1823–99). The principles are: the fatherhood of God; the brotherhood of man; the communion of spirits and the ministry of angels; the continuous existence of the human soul; personal responsibility; compensation and retribution hereafter for all the good and evil deeds done on Earth; eternal progress open to every human soul.

The S.N.U. has about 460 affiliated churches with some 15,000 members and represents the non-Christian element in Spiritualism. The Greater World Christian Spiritualist League, with more than 200 churches represents the specifically Christian influence in the Spiritualist movement. There are also many churches not affiliated to either organization offering a variety of beliefs and practices.

While it is difficult to generalize about Spiritualist beliefs, most Spiritualists in Britain and the United States would probably accept the following beliefs. Man is an immortal being composed of two elements, a body and a soul or spirit, and on death, the spirit leaves the body and enters a phase of existence in a 'spiritual plane.' The universe consists of seven such planes of existence, of which the material (earth) is the lowest. After death most souls awake into the second plane, known to many as the Summerland, a level of existence in which life is not unlike that on Earth except for the absence of pain and suffering. In this plane, as on Earth, each soul has the opportunity for spiritual development that opens up the possibility of ascent to high planes.

Every individual has the opportunity of rising through the ascending order of spiritual levels until he reaches the seventh heaven, in which he will finally be united with God and all the great souls who have preceded him. Great souls such as Jesus are said to have risen directly to the seventh heaven, but just as goodness leads to spiritual advancement, so evil leads to decline; men are not punished, they punish themselves by opting for a course of action that prevents their spiritual development.

Evil men find themselves after death in a condition of limbo in which they perceive themselves as alone and lost in a fog, but this situation is not irretrievable. Through remorse and repentance they may find their way back to the light. Some Spiritualist societies organize 'rescue circles' with the aim of contacting and aiding such lost souls.

Those who are over-attached to Earthly things may find themselves unable after death to leave the material world. Such 'Earthbound' spirits may be perceived by those who have psychic abilities as ghosts, but these may also free themselves from their attachments and develop spiritually.

Many Spiritualists also believe that animals have souls and are active in antivivisection and other animal welfare movements. Some believe that the spiritual universe is not only inhabited by human spirits but also by many spirits who have never been incarnated as humans, ranging from poltergeists and Earth elementals, such as fairies, to cosmic powers of good and evil, angels, and demons.

From the early days Spiritualism has involved phenomena in which material objects have been moved by what many have claimed to be supernatural forces.

Spirit and Matter

Spiritualists' beliefs are derived from communication with the spirit world and such communication may take any one of a number of forms. The spirits may speak directly through the medium who is in trance, or the medium may use his own voice to convey the message. In the case of automatic writing the medium's hand is controlled by the 'spirit,' and the ouija board is a device that facilitates this form of communication. Other methods are the raps (used by the Fox sisters) and slate writing, a popular Victorian technique, both of which methods were open to fraud. Clairvoyance and clairaudience in which the medium sees, hears, or senses information that he attempts to transmit to the sitter are the most common forms of mediumship.

From the early days Spiritualism has involved phenomena in which material objects have been moved by what many have claimed to be supernatural forces. As early as 1849 there is the record of a table being levitated six inches. The first instance of the levitation of a human being, a Mr. Gordon, was reported in the journal *Spirit World* in February 1851. Materialization of a spirit and the 'apport' or mysterious appearance of a physical object were also early forms of manifestations. At some seances coloured lights appeared, which floated round the room, and at others musical instruments were mysteriously played.

Spirit photography was first practiced by William Mumler, a Boston photographer, in 1862, but his work was soon exposed as fraudulent.

Opposite page:
A table levitating during a seance in 1898 with Eusapia Palladino (1854–1918)

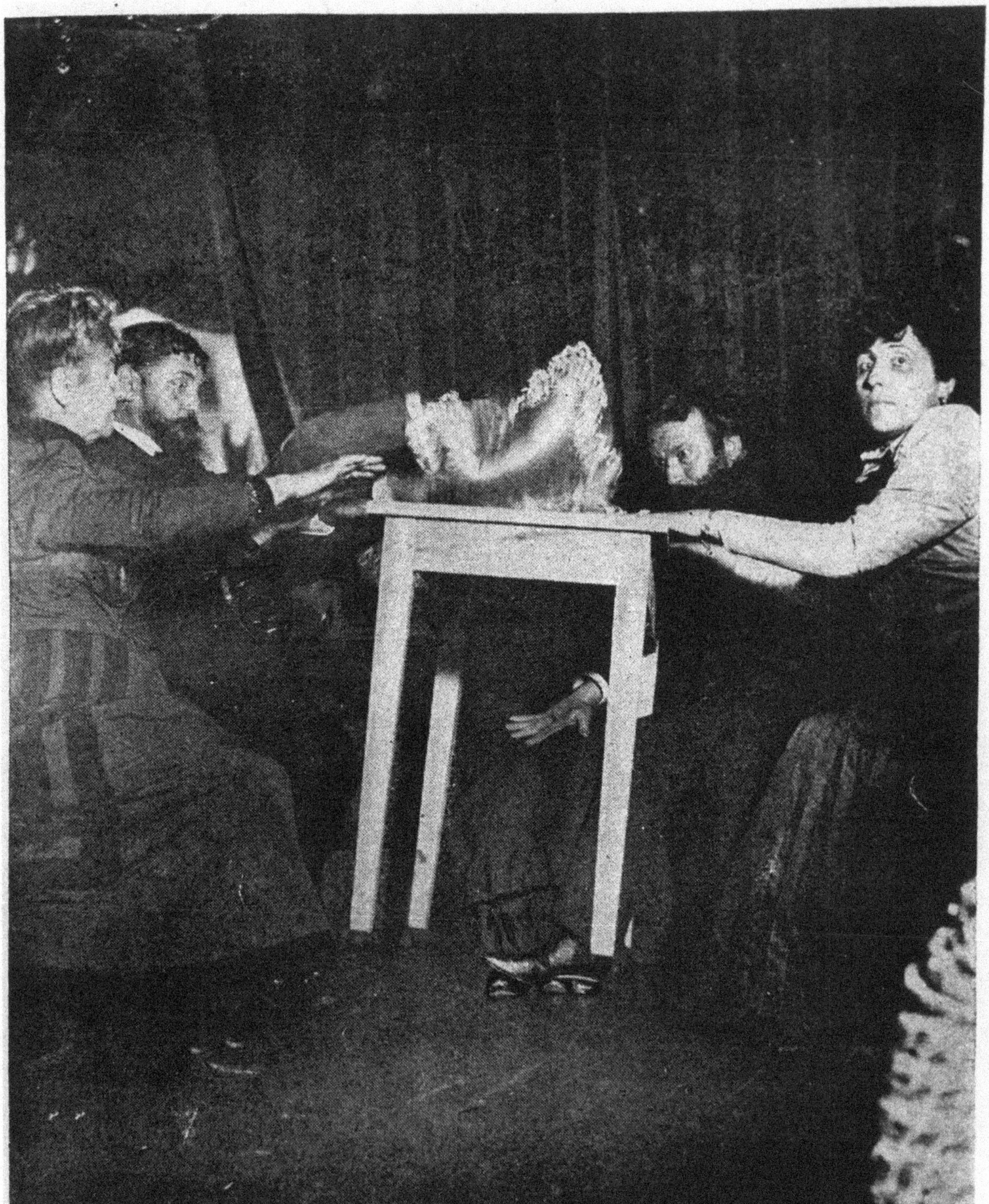

SOULÈVEMENT COMPLET D'UNE TABLE

Photographie prise dans le salon de M. FLAMMARION, le 12 Novembre 1898. (Le premier pied, à gauche, est à 18 centimètres au-dessus du parquet, le second à 13, celui de droite, au fond, à 8, et celui de droite en avant, à 14). Un assistant cache, à l'aide d'un coussin, les yeux du médium contre la lumière subite du magnésium. Ce médium (EUSAPIA) est mis dans l'impossibilité absolue de faire aucun mouvement suspect.

Frederick Hudson was the first spirit photographer in Britain, but he was exposed by the well-known Spiritualist writer W. H. Harrison in *The Spiritualist* in 1872. The most famous spirit photographer was William Hope (died 1933) who worked with the Crewe circle: his work was also exposed, but he found a faithful champion in Sir Arthur Conan Doyle.

There appears to have been a decline in physical mediumship since World War II, which cynics have attributed to the greater ease of detecting fraud by modern scientific methods. From the first, Spiritualists practiced 'spirit healing,' and this has become an important part of their work.

The key role in the Spiritualist movement is played by the medium, through which the 'spirit world' communicates with the material world. In theory all people are potential mediums, but it is clear that while some

Bust of Allan Kardec, installed on his grave in Père Lachaise Cemetery, Paris, France

people are endowed with psychic abilities that may appear spontaneously, others require years of training before they can make use of their abilities. Many of the most gifted mediums report that they had spontaneous psychic experiences when they were children. The claims of Spiritualists have frequently been investigated by critics. During the nineteenth century in particular, psychic phenomena were subjected to rigorous study by a series of eminent scientists. Some were convinced that not all Spiritualist manifestations could be explained by theories of fraud or illusion, but in spite of a considerable body of accumulated evidence, most scientists have remained unconvinced by the Spiritualist interpretation.

A Latter-Day Druid

Britain and the United States were the main centres of Spiritualism down to World War II, but the movement's most spectacular growth since the middle of the last century has occurred in Brazil. The key figure in this development was a Frenchman, Hypolyte Leon Denizard Rivail (1804–69). Born at Lyons, he studied under the Swiss educationist Johann Heinrich Pestalozzi (1746–1827). Failing to set up a school on Pestalozzi lines in France, he practiced as a doctor, wrote numerous books on science and mathematics, joined the French Society of Magnetists and became interested in Mesmerism.

In the 1850s Rivail took up Spiritism with enthusiasm, founded, and led the Parisian Society for Spiritist Studies, ran a monthly magazine, *La Revue Spirite*, and wrote a string of books exploring his new field, including *The Book of Spirits* (1857) and *The Book of Mediums* (1861). Both of these are said to have been dictated from the spirit world to a medium through automatic writing, in part by the spirit of the departed Franz Mesmer. Rivail now adopted the pseudonym Allan Kardec, which combined names he believed had been his in previous lives—as revealed to him by Spiritualist mediums—in one of which he had been a Druid in ancient Gaul.

Kardec believed that spiritual progress is gained only through a succession of reincarnations and was convinced that the spirits had entrusted him with a mission to humanity. Much impressed by automatic writing, he poured cold water on many of the phenomena of physical mediumship that were all the rage at the time—spirit voices, ectoplasm, and the rest—and his skepticism helped to delay the development of serious psychical research in France.

Kardec has remained almost unknown to Spiritualists in North America and Britain but disciples planted his ideas in Brazil. Translated into Portuguese, they found fertile soil there and the Brazilian Spiritist Federation was founded in Rio de Janeiro in 1874. Though Kardec had prided himself on his scientific attitude to the phenomena of mediumship, in Brazil his teachings were clothed in religious garments and blended readily with both the established Roman Catholic Christianity of the country and the Voodou-style communities that had originated among Brazil's African slaves. By 1950, though it was officially calculated that 'Spiritists' numbered only two percent of the population, the movement was growing at phenomenal speed, in its own right and as a vigorous ingredient of the Afro-Christian Umbanda religion.

The Sociology of Spiritualism

If psychic phenomena are a universal feature of human life, why did the modern Spiritualist movement arise in the United States and Britain in the nineteenth century? Sociologists attempt to explain the rise (or decline) of social movements in terms of the conditions affecting the lives of the members of a society, in terms of the processes going on within the society and of the changes in the structure of that society.

Spiritualism certainly offers man a new view of the universe and man's place in it and is particularly concerned with the place of psychic experiences in human life.

Modern Spiritualism is one of a particular type of religious movements known to sociologists as cults. Such movements are characterized by two general features; they are outside the major religious tradition of the society in which they originate (as already mentioned, Spiritualism owes more to non-Christian than to Christian sources), and they are attempts to solve the problems of individuals, particularly those problems that arise out of man's aim to understand the world in which he lives, to give meaning to his life, and to experiences of a psychic or mystical nature. Spiritualism certainly offers man a new view of the universe and man's place in it and is particularly concerned with the place of psychic experiences in human life.

Cults seem to arise in the greatest profusion, and to gain the most adherents, when a society is disorganized by rapid changes. In such circumstances the old religious traditions are challenged and men find the old views of life no longer satisfying. US society in the middle of the nineteenth century was going through a period of rapid change as the result of the influx of immigrants, mainly from Europe, as well as the early effects of the industrial revolution. In Britain the industrial revolution was changing the traditional way of life; in particular this was the period of rapid urban expansion, and Spiritualism was from the first predominantly an urban religion.

The rationalism of the eighteenth century intellectual was beginning to spread more widely through society and men began to demand proof of religious claims. While not claiming to offer proof of the existence of God, Spiritualism did claim to provide proof of the survival of the soul .

Many of the early Spiritualists were agnostics or atheists, men who had ceased to find Christianity credible but who nevertheless sought a philosophy of life that went beyond scientific materialism, while yet remaining consistent with science. Spiritualism was at first closely connected with psychical research, though the two movements gradually drifted apart. In common with many modern cults, it started as an attempt to study phenomena that were not seriously studied by orthodox science, and indeed which did not 'fit' the established scientific theories of the time. In each case the movements developed into religions, because they offered solutions that were not only intellectually but emotionally satisfactory to certain key problems in the lives of individuals. The nineteenth century was obsessed with death but many people were losing faith in the Christian explanation, as a result of the growth of belief in science. Death was a major source of tension in the lives of such persons, who were not satisfied with faith but needed proof of the survival of the soul after death. Spiritualism was attractive because it offered evidence of survival.

It was during World War I and in the following years that the movement experienced its greatest growth, thus reflecting the tension created by the high death rate. In the second half of the twentieth century death has ceased to be an obsession and many people are more concerned with a search for the meaning of life; this has meant on the one hand that the Spiritualist movement has ceased to grow, and on the other that within the movement there is less concern with proofs of survival and a greater interest in the philosophy of Spiritualism.

G. K. NELSON

FURTHER READING: R. Brandon. The Spiritualists. *(Amherst, NY: Prometheus Books, 1984); S. Brown.* The Heyday of Spiritualism. *(New York, NY: Hawthorn, 1971); William S. Moses.* Spirit Teachings. *(New York, NY: Arno, 1976); G. K. Nelson.* Spiritualism and Society. *(Berlin: Schocken, 1969).*

Table Turning

Or table tilting, a method of communicating with 'spirits;' the table tilts up and raps on the floor with its foot in response to questions, without being consciously pushed by the experimenters, who rest their fingers on it.

Wraith

The double or apparition of someone who is alive; its appearance is generally taken as an omen of the person's imminent death, or as a sign that he is in serious danger or trouble.

Zombie Apocalypse

On the day that the zombies take over the world, we can expect the characters who hold the power to resemble those whose stories have been documented down the decades. Among the most powerful of these was 'Black Cat' Mama Couteaux, a terrifying figure who wore around her neck and waist a necklace and belt adorned with more than 1,000 dried tongues of the dead, trophies acquired through her ability not only to create zombies but also to control them. Emerging from the swamps of Louisiana in the spring of 1835, Mama Couteaux entered New Orleans with her zombie army. It was here that she encountered serious opposition from other perpetrators of evil and their 'living dead' creations. War ensued, but after more than a month, Mama Couteaux's zombie army was defeated, victory going to the Voodoo kings and queens of

New Orleans, among them Dr. John Montenet, who ground up plants and animals to ensure the success of his zombification techniques.

The movies provide zombie scenarios by the hundred, none more chilling than George A. Romero's 1968 classic *Night of the Living Dead* (the first of a series of six) in which Ben, Barbra, and their five companions are trapped in a remote farmhouse and attacked by zombies arisen from the graveyard where Barbra's father is buried. Across the eastern United States, a plague of zombies is reported to have risen up and to be consuming the flesh of the living. At the house, violent deaths are followed by reincarnations, with zombies systematically eating the flesh of the living. As the movie ends, Ben awakes to see the zombies being shot by sheriff's department deputies, but is mistakenly taken for a zombie and killed before being deposited on a funeral pyre with the other corpses.

Voodou History

The notion zombies, the 'living dead' with gruesome and deadly powers and propensity to devour their victims, has its origins in the Vodun or Voodou religion and can be reliably traced to the Yoruba people who lived in the parts of Africa now called Benin, Nigeria, and Togo. Many inhabitants of these lands were enslaved and taken to the islands of Hispaniola, including Haiti, where Voodou not only remains a central tenet of religion but also where cases of zombification are annually reported by the hundred. So seriously is the zombie threat regarded that the country's penal code still states that zombification is a category of murder, even if death does not ensue. New Orleans and other locations in the American South are also centres of Voodou.

A zombie crowd from the film *Resident Evil: Apocalypse* (2004)

FOLLOW THE
RED ASPHALT ROAD
Zombie Apocalypse The Musical
JASON LYBECK

The Making of Zombie Forms

Zombies appear in two major forms —either a body without a soul or a soul without a body and are alleged to be created by sorcerers using an 'animating principle' or *gwo-bon anj*. When a person becomes zombified their *ti-bon anj*, equivalent to their soul or consciousness, is removed from the victim and stored in an earthenware jar known as a zombie astral or head-pot. In 1982 the Canadian ethnobotanist Wade Davis (b. 1953) traveled to Haiti to study the Voodou practices, specifically the toxic white powder or *coupe poudre* used in zombification. When placed on the skin, irritants in the power cause small wounds through which the toxins enter, producing a coma or a state in which they appear to have no self will. The victims are then buried alive, 'returning' to life a few days later as zombies after being deliberately disinterred. Another way of making a zombie is to exchange the soul of a person, whilst they are still alive, for that of a lizard, chicken, or some other small creature.

Davis concluded, and recorded in his books *The Serpent and the Rainbow* (1985) and *Passage of Darkness: the Ethnobiology of the Haitian Zombie* (1988) that the main ingredient of *coupe poudre* is tetrodotoxin, a natural substance produced by pufferfish (a Japanese delicacy), although toxins from cane toads (*Bufo marinus*) and the hyla tree frog (*Osteopilus dominicensis*) were also used, as were the plant *Datura stramonium* known to contain the drug atropine. Also central to Davis's theories is that to eat someone or *manger moun*, involves a community request for punishment of someone who has violated standards or codes, usually related to land disputes. Other students of zombies believe that such as the Scottish psychiatrist R. D. Laing (1927–89) have made great play of the role of mental illness, compulsion, and cultural expectations in the process of zombification.

Opposite page:
Front cover for the Zombie Apocalypse musical *Follow the Red Asphalt Road*

And Today?

In our age of genetic engineering, the zombie apocalypse might indeed come from a creature mutated deliberately, or accidentally by nuclear radiation. It could be brought about by an incurable virus spread through open wounds, by infected blood, or saliva. Alternatively it could even be enforced through a type of poison produced by alien cells, either in our own bodies or ingested from other life forms. Or the rise of the zombies could be the result of radiation produced by the machines that are our own creation, nanotechnology or even alien warfare. However they are generated, the most feared consequence of releasing a zombie is the revenge it will exact, both physically and mentally, on its creator or owner.

However they are generated, the most feared consequence of releasing a zombie is the revenge it will exact, both physically and mentally, on its creator or owner.

The concept of the Zombie Apocalypse, separate from Voodou traditions, is a popular topic of many films, video games, and books. In popular culture, these 'infected' creatures are animalistic, violent, and on the hunt for humans. Generally, a human is infected as described above, and then dies, succumbing to disease, only to rise again with an insatiable bloodlust. The zombies run the gambit from terrifying to silly, fast to slow, hyperaware to incredibly dumb. However, the true power of the any zombie comes from its complete lack of pain receptors and the fact that a zombie only truly dies from damage to the brain.

The zombie is used often as an allegory for social upheaval—the connection between a zombie and its hunt for brains is essential. As a virus spreads so does an idea—and the only way to kill an idea is to attack the mind it lives in. However, this allegory goes further in most representations, as zombie apocalypses incorporate the total destruction of societal infrastructure. The power lines go down, news sources collapse, and the heroes in most tales are left to their own devices as total anarchy reigns. Hunting and gathering become key, as does becoming a skilled killer of the infected.

If the worst should happen, how should we react? In one of many such guides *The Zombie Survival Guide* by Joseph D. Tremblay and Christopher Philbrook (2010) lists everything needed, from food and water to a pair of pistols and a rifle. The latter are, the manual stresses, essential, since the only way to kill a zombie is to kill its brain. 'Something in the brain' they say, 'has taken control and given "apparent" life to a dead organism . . . [with] one primary goal, that is to eat living flesh . . . don't bother with the why. Just remember the simple equation: brain death = zombie death.'

RUTH BINNEY

FURTHER READING: Brad Steiger. Real Zombies. *(Canton, MI: Visible Ink Press, 2010); Max Brooks.* The Zombie Survival Guide. *(New York, NY: Three Rivers Press, 2003).*

Glossary

Adamant Unshakable, stubborn, sticking to one's opinions or convictions.

Adumbrate To suggest or foreshadow.

Agnostic Unshakable, stubborn, sticking to one's opinions or convictions.

Agrarian Rural, relating to fields or farming.

Astral Involving the spirit, to be on a nonphysical plane.

Baleful Threatening or harmful.

Blaspheme To speak out against or be irreverent of religion.

Cataclysm Sudden, violent change; a catastrophe.

Conflagration A particularly destructive fire, also a war.

Cosmogony The creation or origin of the universe.

Demiurge A being responsible for the creation of the universe.

Diabolic Similar to the devil, evil, unpleasant.

Epistle A letter as literary form, specifically a book from the New Testament.

Eviscerate To disembowel.

Extemporise To improvise, to do without prior planning.

Filial Relating to offspring, of a son or daughter.

Furze Gorse, from the pea family, a yellow-flowering shrub.

Hashish Cannabis.

Houris Beautiful young woman, particularly associated with Muslim afterlife.

Impetus A catalyst, something that accelerates an action.

Inconsonant Incompatible, creating disharmony.

Itinerant Moving frequently, traveling from place to place.

Macabre Involving death, frightening, gruesome, or horrid.

Martyr One who dies or is persecuted for their beliefs, often religious.

Metaphysical Things that exist but are beyond perception, supernatural.

Posthumous After death.

Propitiatory To please someone (often a diety) in order to win their favour.

Scourge Something that causes trouble or suffering.

Tabernacle A moveable dwelling such as a tent.

Table-tilting A technique of tilting a table with a Ouija board to change the outcome of the message the board gives.

Turpitude Evil or depraved behaviour.

Vestige A trace of something long gone.

Index

A
Abraham 89
Achilles 24–25, 74, 122
Adam and Eve 24, 42, 46, 78, 102, 103, 116–117
Adonis 51, 56
Aeneid (Virgil) 74–75, 87, 120
aerophagy 113
afterlife, belief in 17, 34, 73, 86
see also Book of the Dead; immortality; near-death experience; Spiritualism
alchemy 24
alien invasions 58
All Saints 38
All Souls 38, 41
Anatolia 53, 71
ancestor worship 34–39
angels 9–10, 48, 53, 64, 65, 75–76, 88–89, 103
Angel of Death 45
Angel of Peace 9
Angels of Mons 10
animal sacrifice 17, 24, 32, 36, 54
Antichrist 10–11, 65, 67, 68, 69, 70
Antiochus IV Epiphanes 11, 70
Anubis 45, 84
apocalyptic visions 47, 57, 58, 61, 62–63, 66–67, 88, 99, 137
see also dystopian literature; end of the world
Arawaks 42
Archangel Michael 9, 10, 53, 89
Aristotle 80, 83, 116
Ashanti 34, 35, 36–37, 39
Ashanti stool 37
Assyrians 46, 61
astral corpse 98
Athenagoras 81
Attis 53, 54, 56
Atwood, Margaret 58
Australian aborigines 34, 39, 42, 45
automatic art 11–15
automatic poetry 101
automatic writing 11–12, 13, 14, 15, 27–29, 101, 129, 130, 133
automatisms 101
Aztecs 61

B
Babylonia 41, 61, 63, 104
Bacchic frenzies 53
Bacchus 54
Ballard, J. G. 58
Banks Islands 45
baptism 53, 118
Bardo Thodol see Tibetan Book of the Dead
Bavaria 31
Beraud, Marthe 59
Bible 9, 11, 47, 51, 52, 56, 60–61, 64, 65, 67, 68–70, 73, 75, 76–77, 79, 86, 87, 88, 97, 103, 108, 121, 123, 124
Blake, William 13
Blavatsky, Madame 16
Bodhisattvas 78
Boethius 118
Boniface, Pope VIII 11
Book of Revelation 9, 11, 47, 65, 67, 68–69, 70, 73, 77, 88, 124
Book of the Dead 52, 82, 84–85, 123
see also Tibetan Book of the Dead
Bradbury, Ray 58
Brahman 62
Branch Davidian cult 66
Brazil 133
Breuer, Josef 114, 115
Britain 18–19, 22, 23, 24, 26, 41, 50, 94, 98, 110–111, 114, 124–125, 127–129, 130, 133, 134
Brown, Rosemary 13
Browning, Robert 23
Buddhism 16–17, 40, 46, 62, 78, 90, 105
Bunyan, John 72, 125
burial 17–24, 30–33, 73, 78, 79, 122
burning 24
see also cremation

C
Caligula, Emperor 70
Calvin, John 108, 119, 120
cannibalism 21–22, 30, 39, 125
Capek, Karel 58
capital sins 121, 122
Carneades 116
Carson, Rachel 58
Catal Huyiik 31, 45, 71, 73
Catholicism 19, 26–27, 40, 73, 111, 119, 128, 133
cave art 20
Celts 104
channeling 12
children
games 41
unbaptized 22, 118
China 17, 30, 32, 34, 35, 36, 38, 40, 46, 78, 105
Christianity 11, 18, 25, 36, 47, 53, 54, 55–57, 60–61, 64–65, 67, 68–70, 73, 76–78, 80–81, 85, 87–89, 104, 107–108, 117–121, 123, 128–129
Christmas 53, 57
churchyard desecrations 98
churchyard necromancy 96–97
clairaudience 130
clairvoyance 13, 14, 130
Cock Lane ghost 98
Coffin Texts 45, 84
coffins and caskets 18, 19
Cold War 60
Constantine, Emperor 122
Coptic Christianity 89
cosmic fire 63, 65
cremation 24–27
Cronus 104
cross-correspondences 15, 27–29

crossroads burials 22
cult of the dead 29–39
cults, features of 133–134
Cybele 53, 54

D
Dahomey 38
Dance of Death 39–41, 47
Day of Judgment *see* Judgment of the Dead
de Quincey, Thomas 82
Dead Sea Scrolls 56
death 41–47
  death-origin stories 24, 41–44
  myth of the debate 45
  myth of the mistake 41–42
  myth of the penalty 42–43, 45
  personification of 45–47, 77
  see also cult of the dead; Dance of Death; Judgment of the Dead
Dee, John 96, 97
Deluge 61, 66
Demeter 54, 55
demons 97
  see also Satan
Denmark 24
determinism 116
Devil *see* Satan
Dionysiac orgies 54
Dionysus 41, 54, 55
Dives and Lazarus parable 88, 123
divination 94, 97
Divine Comedy (Dante) 74, 120, 122
Divine Principles movement 47–50
Doom 89
  see also Judgment of the Dead
doomsday cults *see* end of the world cults
Doyle, Sir Arthur Conan 126, 128, 129, 132
'Dream of Gerontius' 122
druids 26, 133
Drummer of Tedworth 50, 109
dualism 20
dying god 50–57
dystopian literature 57–59

E
Easter 56
economic catastrophe 58
ectenic force 59
ectoplasm 59–60, 113
Eden 49, 103, 107
Edison, Thomas 123
Egypt 17, 32, 39, 41, 45, 50, 52–53, 71, 72, 73, 79, 83–85, 105, 123
Eleusinian mysteries 54, 55, 107
Elysium 104, 107, 121
embalming 18, 19
end of the world 60–65, 67, 88
  see also apocalyptic visions; Judgment of the Dead
end of the world cults 65–66
environmental apocalypse 66–67
environmental disaster 58
Epic of Gilgamesh 46, 57–58, 79, 104
Epicurus 116
Epiphany 53, 57
eschatology 67
Eskimos 43
ESP 102
exorcism 40, 109
eyeless in the next world 67–68

F
Fall of Man 49, 103
false prophets 69, 70
Father Time 47
First World War 10
food for the dead 38, 122
Fox family 125–126
France 30, 32, 33, 114
fratricide 39
free will 116, 118, 119, 122
  see also predestination
Freud, Sigmund 23, 114–115
funeral directors 18, 19
funerals 18–19, 23, 24, 35
  see also burial; cremation

G
Gaia hypothesis 67
Garrett, Eileen 14
Gehenna 76
Germany 24, 41
Ghana 21, 37
ghats 25, 26
ghosts 17, 22, 23, 35, 38, 39, 40, 71–72, 73, 94, 96, 97, 98, 124, 125, 130
Gill, Madge 13
Giraldus Cambrensis 109
glass mountain 68
global warming 67
gnosticism 107
God 9, 10, 18, 24, 42, 43, 46, 47, 48, 49, 61, 64, 65, 69, 70, 77, 116, 117, 118
Golden Age 61, 103, 104
The Golden Bough 50
Golding, William 24
grace 117, 118, 119, 120
grave goods 17, 20, 22, 23, 31–32, 33, 75
Great Beast of the Apocalypse 11, 68–70
Greece 24–25, 32, 34, 41, 47, 51, 54, 63, 73–74, 78, 80, 86–87, 104, 107, 116
Grim Reaper 30, 41
guardian angels 9

H
Hades 47, 54–55, 73, 74, 78, 86–87
  see also hell
Haiti 135, 137
Hallowe'en 38, 41
hara-kiri 39
harrowing of hell 47, 70, 77–78

headhunters 31
headless spirits 70–72, 73
heaven 72, 107, 108, 121
hell 70, 72–78, 87, 88, 89
 harrowing of hell 70, 77–78
 see also Hades
hell-fire preaching 72, 73
Heraclitus 63
heretics 24
Herodotus 32, 55, 78–79, 80
Hesiod 63, 104
Hinduism 25, 27, 34, 35, 46, 47, 62, 63, 67, 72, 78, 105
Hippocrates 111
Hitler, Adolf 11
Homer 47, 51, 73, 104
 see also Iliad; Odyssey
Horus 52, 53, 85
human sacrifice 17, 22, 32, 38–39, 79
Hungary 41
hysterical illness 13, 113, 114–115

I
Iceland 62
Iliad (Homer) 24–25, 51, 73, 78
immortality 21, 32, 41, 42, 45, 51, 78–83, 117
Incas 104
incest 39
India 25, 26, 35, 38, 46, 47, 72, 78, 105
Inferno (Dante) 74, 78, 87
Ireland 32, 40, 104, 122
Ishtar 51, 79
Isis 52–53, 55
Islam 9, 36, 78, 89–90, 108
Isle of Avalon 104
Isles of the Blest 80, 104, 121
Italy 26, 29, 40

J
Japan 24, 38, 39, 40, 46, 47, 50, 78
Jeremiah 66–67
Jesus Christ 47, 53, 56, 64, 67, 69, 70, 76, 77, 87, 88–89, 108, 117, 122, 130
 harrowing of hell 47, 70, 77–78
 Messiah 64, 87, 107
 resurrection 9, 11, 55, 56, 70, 77, 107
 Second Coming 48, 49, 64, 65, 67
John XXII, Pope 11
Jones, Jim 65, 66
Joyce, James 73, 74
Judaism 46, 51, 64, 75–76, 79–80, 85–86, 107, 108, 116–117, 121
Judas Maccabeus 75, 121
Judeo-Christianity 9, 55, 56, 63, 64, 89, 103, 104, 108
Judgment of the Dead 25, 67, 76, 83–90, 108
 Bridge of the Separator 87
 Christian beliefs 87–89
 Egyptian beliefs 83–85
 Greek beliefs 86–87
 Islamic beliefs 89–90
 Jewish beliefs 85–86
 weighing of souls 82, 84–85, 89, 122
Jung, Carl 17

K
Kali 47
Kardec, Allan 132, 133
karma 90
Kelley, Edward 96–97
Key, Alexander 58
Khoikhoi 42
Koran 108
Koresh, David 66
Krishna 78
Kyteler, Alice 97

L
Labour of Hercules 78
Last Days 47
 see also end of the world
Last Judgment *see* Judgment of the Dead
Last Supper 55
last things, doctrine of 67
Law of Manu 35
Leeward Islands 104
Leviathan 73
levitation 130, 131
limbo 118, 130
Lodge, Sir Oliver 128
love 81, 82
Lovelock, James 66, 67
Luther, Martin 108, 119

M
magic circles 29, 96, 97, 98
magicians 94, 96, 97, 98
Mahayana Buddhism 105
Malawi 104
Malthus, Thomas 58
Mama Couteaux 134–135
Manning, Matthew 13
Martin, Dorothy 66
Matheson, Richard 58
mediums 14, 59–60, 91, 98, 112, 127, 129, 130, 133
 see also Spiritualism
megalithic tombs 32, 33
memorialization of the dead 36, 37, 40
 see also cult of the dead
menhirs 33
Mesmerism 133
Mesopotamia 32, 45, 46, 50, 51, 52, 73, 79, 83, 123
Messiah 64, 87, 107
Mexico 40
millenarian cults 65
 see also Divine Principles movement
Mithraism 46, 107
Mohammed 88, 106
Moon, Sun M. 47, 48, 49, 50

Moonies *see* Divine Principles movement
Moses, W. Stainton 13
mother goddess 31, 33, 51, 53, 71
mourning 19, 51
mummification 32
music
automatic playing and composing 13
of the spheres 91

N
Native Americans 21, 38, 40, 42, 43, 45, 62, 104
nayononmīlana 68
near-death experience (NDE) 10, 82, 90–94
necromancy 94–98
Neo-Pythagoreanism 86
Nero, Emperor 70
neuroses 114
New Age 12, 47
New Caledonia 104
New Guinea 22, 104
New Jerusalem 107
Nifelheim 78
Nile flooding 52–53
Nirvana 16, 105
nuclear holocaust 58, 99
nuclear winter 99
number of the Beast 11, 69, 70

O
obituary services 23
Odyssey (Homer) 74, 78, 86
Origen 77, 81, 122
original sin 118, 119
Orphism 86, 107
Orwell, George 58
Osiris 39, 41, 45, 52–53, 55, 56, 71, 72, 83, 85, 107
ouija boards 12, 99–102, 130
out-of-body experience (OBE) 91

P
Palestine 30, 31
pandemics 58
pantheistic theologies 116
Paradise 102–108
Passover 55, 56
Pelagian controversy 118
Pellegrino, Charles R. 58
The People's Temple cult 66
Persephone 54
Peru 104
Piper, Leonora 14–15
plagues 9, 10, 58
planchettes 100, 101
Plato 54, 63, 74, 80, 81
poltergeists 50, 108–115
predestination 116–120
prehistoric burials and cremations 20–21, 24, 30–31, 73, 78
Price, William 26
providence 116
psychic art 13
psychoanalytic theory 11, 23, 100–101
psychokinesis 112, 123
puberty rites 41
Pure Land Buddhism 105
purgatory 77, 88, 120–123
Pyramid Texts 83, 85, 123
pyramids 32, 39
Pythagoreans 120–121

R
rapping 13, 125–126, 130
Raudive voices 123
Rawles, James Wesley 58
Re 83, 84
rebirth *see* reincarnation; resurrection
refrigerium 123–124
reincarnation 67, 129, 133
resurrection 53, 54
of Christ 9, 11, 55, 56, 70, 77, 107
of the body 25, 39, 41, 81, 86, 88, 107
revenants 124
see also ghosts
Rig-Veda 46
Rivail, Hypolyte 133
Romans 25, 34, 39, 41, 51, 53, 54, 55, 94, 118
Rome 65, 70
royal ancestor worship 39
Russia 32

S
St. Augustine of Hippo 54, 108, 117, 118
St. Brendan 103, 104
St. George 10
St. Jerome 81
St. Patrick's Purgatory 122
St. Paul 47, 56, 64, 65, 76–77, 81, 117, 118, 121
St. Thomas Aquinas 81, 119
salvation 54, 108, 117, 118, 119, 120
Sarrantonio, Al 58
Satan 47, 48, 49, 68, 70, 77, 78, 97, 116, 128
Scandinavia 21, 72, 78, 105
scapegoats 124–125
Scarrow, Alex 58
Sceptics 116
Scythians 17, 32, 79
seances 98, 126, 128, 129
see also Spiritualism
seasonal cycle 50–51, 52, 57, 61
Second Coming 48, 49, 64, 65, 67
Seekers 66
self-mutilation 53, 54
Shelley, Mary 58
Sheol 75, 76, 79, 85, 86
Shiva 47, 105
shrines, ancestral 36–37
Shute, Neville 58
sin eaters 124–125
Sir Gawaine and the Green Knight 71, 72

skeleton figures 39–40, 41, 47
slate writing 130
Society for Psychical Research 15, 27
Socrates 80
somnambulism 11, 114
soul
 creation of the 81
 transmigration of the 80, 81, 90
 weighing of the 82, 84–85, 89, 122
South Korea 47, 48, 49, 50
Spain 32, 33, 40, 70
speaking in tongues 11
Specter of the Brocken 125
specters 125
 see also ghosts
spirit healing 132
spirit photography 132
Spiritualism 13, 15, 59–60, 82, 98, 100, 109, 112, 125–134
state control, total 58
state funerals 18
Stirling, S. M. 58
Stoics 64, 81, 116
Strabo 124, 125
suicides 22, 25, 38–39, 91, 93
Sumerians 51, 61, 78
Swaffer, Hannen 128
Switzerland 26
syncretic religions 49
Syria 50

T
table-tilting 13, 100, 101, 102, 134
Tammuz 51, 52, 78
technological domination 58
telepathy 11, 14–15, 29
teleportation 108
Thanatos 15, 47
Theseus 78
Thompson-Gifford case 14
Tibetan Book of the Dead 15–17, 78, 86
tombs *see* burial
trances 11, 101, 113, 130
Tree of Life 103
tumuli 21
Turkey 31

U
UFO cult 66
undertakers 18, 19
Unification Church *see* Divine Principles movement
USA 19, 24, 26, 27, 38, 40, 41, 47, 50, 113–114, 125–126, 129, 130, 133–134
Uzbekistan 30

V
Valhalla 63, 72, 78, 105
vampirism 58
Vdluspd 62–63
vegetation cults 50–51, 54, 55, 57, 61
venial sins 121–122
Vishnu 62
Vonnegut, Kurt 58
Voodou 36, 135, 137

W
wakes 40
water burial 21
water, life-giving 123–124
Whore of Babylon 69, 70
winter solstice 53
Wisdom of Solomon 79
witches, witchcraft 22, 23, 24, 94, 97, 98, 110
world ages 61–62, 63
worship of the dead 35–36
 see also ancestor worship
Worth, Patience 12
Wotan 72
wraiths 134

Y
Yahweh 46, 51, 75, 86
Yazatas 9
Yoruba people 135

Z
Zarathustra 87
Zebrowski, George 58
Zend-Avesta 21
Zeno 116
Zeus 54, 104, 116
zombie apocalypse 134–137
Zoroastrianism 9, 21, 76, 87, 107, 108
Zurvan 46
Zwingli, Ulrich 119–120

Author List

Contributors to *Man, Myth, and Magic: Apocalyptic Visions: End of Life, the Afterlife, and the End of the World*

Geoffrey Ashe is the author of several titles, including *King Arthur's Avalon, From Caesar to Arthur, Land to the West, The Land and the Book; Gandhi: a Study in Revolution,* and *Camelot and the Vision of Albion.*

Ruth Binney graduated from the University of Cambridge, England, with a degree in Natural Sciences. She has authored twelve books, including the *Wise Words* series.

S. G. F. Brandon (the late) was formerly Professor of Comparative Religion, Manchester University. Brandon wrote numerous books including *Man and his Destiny in the Great Religions, Creation Legends of the Ancient Near East, History, Time and Deity, The Judgment of the Dead,* and *The Trial of Jesus of Nazareth.* Brandon also edited the *Dictionary of Comparative Religion* and was a special consultant to *Man, Myth, and Magic.*

Richard Cavendish is the editor of *Man, Myth, and Magic* and the author of *The Black Arts.*

Rev. Henry Chadwick is the Dean of Christ Church and Regius Professor of Divinity, the University of Oxford. His books include *Early Christian Thought and the Classical Tradition* and *The Early Church.*

Rev. J. H. Crehan, S. J. is a contributor to the *Dictionary of Catholic Theology* and has edited works by the late Father Thurston, including *Physical Phenomena of Mysticism.*

Glyn Daniel is Fellow of St. John's College, Cambridge, and editor of *Antiquity* and of the *Ancient Peoples and Places* series. Daniel's books include *The Idea of Prehistory, Man Discovers His Past, The Origins and Growth of Archaeology,* and *The First Civilizations.* Daniel is a member of the Editorial Board of *Man, Myth, and Magic.*

Charles De Hoghton is a former Political and Economic Planning researcher, co-author of *And Now the Future.*

E. R. Dodds (the late) was formerly Regius Professor of Greek, University of Oxford, and past President of the Society for Psychical Research. Dodds's books include *The Greeks and the Irrational* and *Pagan and Christian in an Age of Anxiety.* Dodds was a member of the Editorial Board of *Man, Myth, and Magic.*

Alan Gauld is a lecturer in Psychology, University of Nottingham. He is a member of the Council of the Society for Psychical Research and author of *The Founders of Psychical Research.*

Jack Goody is Fellow of St. John's College and Director of the African Studies Centre, University of Cambridge. He is the author of *Death, Property and the Ancestors* and *Comparative Studies in Kinship*, to name a few.

Rosalind Heywood is a vice-president of the Society for Psychical Research and the author of *The Sixth Sense* and *The Infinite Hive.* She has contributed to *Science and E.S.P.* and *Man's Concern with Death.*

Barbara Jones is a painter, designer, and writer. She is the author of *Design for Death.*

John Lofland is the assistant professor of sociology, Michigan University and the author of *Doomsday Cult and Deviance and Identity.*

Eric Maple is the author of *The Dark World of Witches, The Realm of Ghosts, The Domain of Devils, Magic, Medicine, and Quackery,* and *Superstition and the Superstitious*

G. K. Nelson is a senior lecturer in sociology at Birmingham Polytechnic and author of *Spiritualism and Society* and *Mobility and Religious Commitment* (with R. A. Clews) amongst others.

A. R. G. Owen is Fellow of Trinity College, University of Cambridge, and a Director of New Horizons Research Foundation, Toronto. Owen is the author of several titles including *Can We Explain the Poltergeist?, Hypnosis and Healing,* and *Science and the Spook.*

Eric J. Sharpe is the Senior Lecturer in Religious Studies, University of Lancaster, England, and the author of *Not to Destroy but to Fulfill.*

Benjamin Walker is the author of *Hindu World, Sex and the Supernatural, Angkor Empire,* and *Persian Pageant.* He is formerly the joint editor of *Asia.*